RC Wallace

# Ka-Batin-Guy

**a novel by**

*Robert Clifton-Wallace*

***Ka-Batin-Guy*** is a work of fiction and the characters within its pages are portrayed entirely in a dramatic sense with no intended resemblance to any known individuals. Any similarity to persons living or dead is purely coincidental.

Printed in the United States of America

This edition was printed on recycled paper at additional expense and saved the cutting of 24 trees.

ISBN: 0-963-4992-0-3 First edition

Published by Robert T. Clifton, Inc.
Lakeport, California

Cover-art by Carol Dellinger

# FORWARD

Much credit must be afforded those who record the seemingly small and unusual events having taken place in the many hamlets of our pioneering America during those early years of growing pains. Thanks to Alice Deacon for her recorded legacy of Scotts Valley, and to Henry Mauldin for his records of those early years and his recordings of that time, and of the Pomo Indians. Thanks to Nelson Hopper of the Rancheria Pomo for his gift of ideas, and to R.S. Rodman for his poem of *Clearlake* and thereby providing us with yet another glimpse into that period of yesteryear.

*Church Going* by Seth Clement Towle was first told to me by my uncle Keith when he introduced me to the poetry of Batiste. I hope in the near future to publish a collection of Batiste poems; an endeavor calculated to stir his witty revival. "Batiste lives," Uncle Keith.

A vote of thanks must also go to my wife Rena and to my son Russ, for without their support and help I might not have gotten this book to the printer and retained any balance of mentality, and the computer, that obstinate critter, might otherwise have outlived it's usefulness as a pile of junk in the street .

R.C.W.

# Prologue

There was a time long ago when earthly spirits sang of wonders that joined with the human souls, telling of the order of life and rebirth. Many such places were not uncommon in the earth's realm then. Perhaps, although isolated, some remnants still remain to this day.

The Indians called it Ka-Batin-Guy, meaning land of the big water basin; and so it later came to be translated into: *The big water basin.*

These Indians of long ago, the Pomo and their neighbors led a healthy and peaceful life for the most part. They knew astronomy and their year was much as our own, with twelve months, and in case of overlap, sometimes thirteen.

They believed the North Star to be the eye of their creator and this creator-spirit watched over them. They could tell directions by the North Star, and a shooting star was thought to be fire dropping from the sky, and this was the creators sign of joy.

Some thought that during that time between death and rebirth the good spirits dwelled within the enormous caverns of Mount Konocti of the Ka-Batin-Guy, and watched over those who did good deeds, and also had power to punish those who would abuse the creator's Ka-Batin-Guy.

Of the lunar months, they had given each a name, such as; clover, crop moon, acorn moon, and leaves fall now moon, and so on.

Most believed that the sun was the male and that the moon was his female, and they found joy in simple celebrations to honor them.

Spring was called, *Earth Went Out*; and summer was designated; *Sunlight Over*. The season of fall meant, *Anything Falling*, and winter was named, *End of Season, Rest Up*.

In addition to their lunar names each month had a meaning, such as; hard to hunt and fish, can get acorns, go to the ocean, and go gather acorns.

Even long before the first white man came, these Indians were no strangers to the equinox and the solstice. They knew the longest and the shortest days, and in addition they were aware of the cycles of the moon.

And yet they had no need for dates, because they cared little about the time they were born, and did not record the year.

These Pomo and their neighbors believed that their easy going way of life was an achievement in the overall daily cycle of maturation and one which was a part of the reincarnation chain of life and re-birth.

Each morning and day was a re-birth, and they were grateful for small favors, and each in return promised to live with an inner feeling of contentment and understanding, bearing no harm towards other living and non-living things of their world, even the rocks and water. . .

They believed the creator-spirit spoke to them in simple and profound words of wisdom, often reminding them; "My children, when you leave this place, you must leave it a better place than when you found it."

Each day the Pomo promised the creator that they would take from the earth only that which they needed for food and clothing; and that they would kill no more than was necessary, as did the wolf and the eagle.

And, they would give thanks for the crystal clear waters of the Ka-Batin-Guy which abounded with fish and bird and game. They gave thanks for the tule reeds from which they fashioned canoes, unique artistic baskets, and winter huts. Each day they vowed they would live a better life than they had the day before.

Later, when others came and told them that their ancestors had migrated from a land far to the south they rejected the idea. And still later when others tried to convince them that their ancestors had crossed the great ice bridge of the Bering Strait from another continent, they rejected that also.

To them, the Ka-Batin-Guy, land of the Big Water Basin was their place of creation. Ka-Batin-Guy, bounded by the security of the dramatic circle of mountains was their lasting paradise.

Here, since their creation, and for aeons of time they have existed. Their ancestors had told it so, passing along customs and cultural traditions which have been cherished day upon day of re-birth.

They had no need nor did they experience the idea of land ownership, or belongings, or legal rights. . .

Then the white man came, and he called their Ka-Batin-Guy the Clear Lake Basin.

The fog hung still and heavy with a damp musty smell on the opening day of duck season in that year of 1991. It was not unusual to find hunters swarming around the usual haunts waiting anxiously for the opening daybreak hour, eager to score their first shots and set the mode for the rest of the season.

This was a strange place, remote and hidden for the four waiting hunters, two in each boat about fifty yards apart, lurking among the tules. They had a temporary blind for disguise and each was wearing the latest in heavy waterproof boots, camouflage pants, hat, and jacket. Beneath the jacket each wore a vest loaded heavily with spare cartridges for easy access. In one boat a hunter, chilled and eager, fingers the grip of his Winchester pump action shotgun while his partner fidgets with his Remington automatic.

In the other boat, a hunter strokes the golden fur coat of his favorite retriever, saying; "Easy Jiggs, you'll get your chance." He raised his head to peer over the blind, "soupy damn stuff," he groans, while his partner recklessly tosses an empty beer can overboard and pops the top of another, grunting; ". . .try the duck call again." They have the latest in technology, duck calls, automatic weapons and each has set out a string of a dozen decoys.

Click-click, goes the sound of a walkie-talkie, "hey man, you guys still there? This damn fog ever lifts, we're gonna have one helluva great shoot, huh. I can feel it, nobody around but us, man. What luck we found this place."

Click-click, "Hey, let's give them another call," quack-quack-quack, ". . .you hear them damn things quacking up a storm over that way somewhere. . ."

Click-click, "There's constant chatter over on that damn island. . ."

Click. . ."Four dozen decoys will get their attention, soon's this damn fog lifts. . ." Click-click.

Click-click, "Damn ducks don't care if it's foggy or not, how they know it makes any difference—?"

Click. . ."I thought you said somebody told you they don't have fog at Clear Lake!"

Click. . ."not often, he said. I didn't say never. . ."

". . .Well it gives me the creeps, man, sitting here waiting, this soupy damn stuff stirring all around, eerie feeling, shit."

Click-click, "Yeah, and those damn ducks just sitting out there like they're laughing at us. . . must be a thousand of em."

"Well, less than ten minutes to legal shooting time, hey Jeter old boy."

"Ruff-ruff."

Click-click,"Hey, was that Jiggs? Well keep him quiet, dammit." Click.

"Quiet boy, you'll get your chance soon."

"Gimme another beer."

". . .Don't think this soup will ever break up. . . never seen it like this, cept over in the valley."

Click-click, "Hey, you guys, knock off the chatter or we'll never get a shot." Click.

Click-click, "What the hell, you think it's gonna make any difference if they hear us. Hell, last year I got a hundred and fifty of em and it didn't make any difference." Click.

Click. . ."A bit over the limit, wasn't it?"

". . .Who's gonna tell? You for Christ sake, man, wise up."

". . .Hey, you gonna eat that many?"

"That's my business, we get our limit, we go store em away, no game warden's gonna stop us, we de-tag em and use the tags again. Who's gonna tell? So many God damn ducks and geese, who's gonna count?" Click. "Hey, gimme another beer."

Click-click, "Hey, you guys hear about the guy who brought along a bitch in heat, couldn't keep the other dogs quiet, jinxed their whole God damn season after that. . ."

Click. . ."Shit, that's stupid, everybody knows you don't bring along a bitch in heat. That's just plain stupid, man."

Click-click, "Yeah, and don't shoot no shovellers on the first shot. That's a jinx too, ruins the whole day, stupid."

Click.."When they start flying in, I'm gonna shoot anything that flies, coots, pintails, mallards; I don't believe in jinxes. . ."

"Miss your first duck, and that's a jinx. . ."

"I don't miss."

Click-click, "Don't stammer again on the next call. They can tell. It warns them away."

Click. . ."This place gives me the creeps, just sitin here gettin chilled, eerie God damn feeling. . ."

Click-click, "What do you think, the ducks gonna attack like the birds in that Hitchcock movie. Wow, man, wouldn't that be something? What a shoot, man. I wish they would, blam-blam. Ha-ha, how you gonna explain being over the limit, huh?"

"That's only if the ducks don't talk. . ."

Click. . ."Yeah, you got fifty, and the limits one mallard hen, two drakes and a pintail. . ."

Click-click, "That's only if they don't attack, ha-ha, get it, Donald Duck on the attack, some comedy, man, blow his fuckin tail feathers right off. . ."

Click, "Hey you guys, knock it off out there, will you? I

think I'm gonna wade out a little ways, see what's happening."

". . .Not me man, my boots sprung a leak last year, ain't gettin my feet wet. . .That's what we got old Jiggs and Jeter for, huh Jiggs?"

Click. . . "Think I'll move here. . . The Valley's not too far and the pheasant huntin's good there. I hear the fishin's good here. . ."

Click-click, "How you gonna do all that shit, you want a new Winchester?"

Click. . ."Put my old lady to work at Kmart, while I hunt and fish, hang out. . ."

". . .I thought your old lady kicked you out. . ."

"Yeah, but that's only temporary, a little sweet talk, promise to get a job, she knows what's good. Maybe get a little job from time to time, like Taco Bell, or McDonalds, Kmart maybe, think they'd make me a manager so I can cop that new Winchester, get a little unemployment. I hear the welfare's easy here, and there's plenty of hash and other shit. Hey what's that noise? What the hell was that? You guys hear something?" Click-click, "come back," Click-click, "Come back you guys. . .Jack, you there? What the hell's happenin over there man?"

"Chuck, did you hear that?"

A sudden and eerie chill strikes the air with a gripping stillness. . .

". . .I told you this place gives me the creeps."

"Break out the oars, let's go see, don't want to start the motor, case maybe they flipped over or something. Jack, Chuck, you guys okay—?"

"Maybe they flipped their boat over, too much beer, you think?"

"Nah, Hell, I don't know. Hey you guys, we're comin over. . . don't shoot. . . ha-ha."

"I told you this place gives me the creeps, what's that? What's happening? What's that sound? Hey Chuck, Jack, what's happenin. . . no-no, gulp, no." Splash-splash. . . .

When the disturbance settles and the water swirls around in

pools, there is silence, except for the frantic barking of two dogs swimming in desperate circles, and finally their whining sounds as they swim towards the shoreline. . . then the chatter of distant quacking ducks. Moments later, the busy vigor of flapping wings returns. And then, the final ominous sounds of nature mix with a return to peaceful silence.

# ONE

They say a daughter should look like her mom. My mom was a petite blond who was very pretty with bold dark eyes. She had a figure that wouldn't quit and she was the envy of all my teen-age friends.

If I brought a boy home to meet my family, which always proved to be a problem in itself, because he was invariably intimidated by my dad, and then he would drool around my mother, asking foolish questions.

Mom's hair was long, wavy, and ever so manageable, and while I may have her dark eyes, my hair is red, kinky and at times wildly unmanageable.

When I was fifteen I could wear her clothes, and she mine. As a game, we used to exchange clothes and dress up as if we were playing roles in a play, but then I grew out of hers.

It is not that I have a bad figure, but mine in no way compares to hers. My own mouth seems to pout at times which, I think, gives me a dour serious look. My lips are too full, fat really, where hers were perfect. She had one of those sweet mouths that compelled you to watch her when she spoke, and a smile always happy with beautiful white teeth, and I have an occlusion, like two fangs. Her complexion was smooth and creamy, whereas mine became freckly at an early age.

I remember the day of my mother's death. Kathleen Margaret O'Grady-Kreeszowski was her name, but everybody had pitched in to give her the name of Molly, and that was how she was known. Simply; Molly.

My father Archie originally fashioned the name for her and always declared that it was his gift to her Irish heritage. Dad believed a lot in maintaining one's heritage. "Your roots are an important reminder of where we came from, and what we stand for, never forget it," he would say. All too often I recall that day she died, and I recorded it in my diary, my deepest emotions bared, exposed to the bone amid a torrent of tears that flowed to splotch those frantic painfully scribbled words that failed miserably to describe my loss and subsequent grief. We were close, closer than sisters, closer than twins, and the most devoted of friends.

But just now, I don't want to think of that day, of Molly's passing. Another time perhaps.

Even though it was I who looked more like a Molly than Mom, my mother would not consent to me being labeled another stereotyped; *Molly*. "She needs her own identity," she had argued, and so I; Mary Kathryn Kreeszowski was labeled Kitty by my father, and so the moniker stuck.

Then, for some inescapable reason, there are those who swear that I favor my dad. God forbid.

My father, Archibald Sidney Kreeszowski, is sheriff of Lake County, and as the name implies he is Polish. Yet, due to my mother's influence I would swear that he is more Irish than the wild mixture he often claims.

Unlike my mother or myself, Archie, as his friends affectionately call him, has almost no hair. He was an early victim of that common affliction called male pattern baldness. What little hair he still does have, a small bank of grayish white above the ears and around the back of his neck appears as a little patch of fuzzy growth which he keeps fastidiously cut and groomed. I think it must be his trademark. His head is a shiny pate, sort of flat on top. His eyes are a deep green and always mischievously alert with a suspicious gleam.

I can't ever remember my dad with hair, but my mother has brought out pictures of the past to prove it.

They grew up together and she used to tease that he had such a wild crop of hair that it would jam any sheep shears, and what was really needed was a lawn mower with which to attack it. Nothing less would do. In those days of their youth he had been a lean, mean mischievous kid, often in fights and scraps, and mostly of his own instigation.

Now, he is about five feet, nine or ten inches and weighs around two hundred and fifty jolly pounds.

On the surface my dad is the ultimate macho tough guy, only on the inside I know he is a real softy. There is absolutely no way he could pass by a panhandler without making a generous contribution.

He's a sentimental fool too, and that is why he never remarried.

He still lives in that same old two story house built around the nineteen thirties, hidden by overgrown trees and vines and bushes, with upstairs gables on all sides. My room is upstairs overlooking the lake just a few short blocks away, and the only bathroom is downstairs. Who needs another bathroom?

He lives in that same old house with the same old furniture, just as Mom had left it. Oh, he has had lady friends, and though he won't admit it, my mother's imprint is on him too deeply for him to get really involved with anyone.

Where it concerns the affairs of mom, he is a sentimental idiot, even though he goes to great lengths to hide it.

I'm twenty four now, and after a two year break to replenish revenues and renew my direction, I am back at Stanford in pursuit of my Master's degree in Clinical Psychology.

Those two years I worked as an assistant to Carolyn Kosloff, the widely accepted criminal psychologist in Southern California, was an education of a vitally different dimension.

I think my specialty will be Criminal Psychology, and for that reason dad allows my presence during many of his otherwise confidential conversations. I suspect I wore him down over the years to finally accepting me in the spirit of the professional family convention. You see his idea of a future for me was to get married and produce lots of little Irish-Polacks in the good Catholic tradition.

My dad has absolutely no ego problem, nor false vanity, and he will argue that issue with me adamantly. With so many handsome tall uniformed deputies, I know the real reason he wears cowboy boots is to appear taller among his colleagues.

He started at the bottom when the primary pre-requisite for a uniform was just how well he could handle himself in a brawl. In the interim he worked hard, studying law enforcement religiously, eventually acquiring every degree and FBI credential available.

I was still a baby when we moved to Lakeport. Well not Lakeport right away, but that was a time before my memory, so that a few years in the measure of time doesn't really count anyway.

You see, it was his fellow officers who coined the nickname of Arch, or Archie and planted it on him, and so the moniker stuck. That was back in a time before my memory also.

It was this way: my Dad can do a fair imitation of Carrol O'Connor's Archie Bunker, and my Dad, Archie had accumulated quite a repertoire of Polish jokes for auspicious occasions, and being a Pole he could get away with it. The guys would say; "Hey Arch you got any new Polack jokes?" And my dad would rip off a couple and then finish with; "Ain't yooz meatheads got nuttin better to do? Get back to work." He used to call me Little Girl, too. If the mood suited him he would tell a story from his vast reserve, most often made up for the occasion by himself, then he would call out; "Get back to work yooz meatheads," in the Archie Bunker fashion.

Invariably someone would cajole him into doing his Jackie Gleason shuffle, and he would.

He could do an exquisite Jackie Gleason imitation, including the shuffle, saying; "And awaaay we goooo."

In the case of the Archie Bunker imitation, it was all a game to play, a charade, and there the charade stopped.

To my dad, law enforcement was serious business and he

treated it as such, with total commitment and admirable objectivity. He had started at the very bottom, and now had some eighty officers and staff under his jurisdiction. It was more than a full time job, and responsibility was just the type of medicine he thrived on.

I just can't think of my dad, Archie Kreeszowski as being capable of a single bigoted thought. His imitation of Archie Bunker was just that, an impersonation, and there the similarity stopped.

At Stanford University, after my first years away from home, I used to come home regularly. It was for the three S's, I called it. That was when I finally decided what I wanted to do with my life.

I felt Dad really needed me, at least to do his cleaning and to organize the household; shirts, shorts, and socks. Later, I realized there was a fourth S; sheets. All of this he outwardly discouraged, chiding me in his best Archie Bunker idiom; "Ain't yooz got nuttin better to do, Little Girl?" Or, "What happened to dat meathead yooz was goin wit, da one wit out no brains?"

This crafty performance was always done with a serious tone of voice and meant to impress me with his spirit of independence.

But you see, responsibility was a built-in factor. It was one of those qualities I inherited in my genes along with kinky red hair and dark brown eyes, and almost no boobs and a little too much flare in my hips, from my grandmother Kreeszowski I am told.

This past summer, I had returned home only twice. I had enrolled in summer classes in order to gain extra credits toward my master's degree. One visit was for the annual Fourth of July fireworks display at Library Park, an occasion that always spelled good times with old friends and tourist crowds as well. Only, most of the old friends were either married and settled down with babies, or gone off to seek their fortunes elsewhere. At times crowds can be very lonely.

The other occasion was one of the regular concert gatherings at Library Park on Friday evening, featuring notable performing artists. I had to see and hear Spencer Brewer perform my latest favorite; *Dorian's Legacy.*

Dad usually wasn't too surprised when I showed up unannounced, besides I had just broken up with my latest heart-throb, an occasion always guaranteed to steer me homeward to that comforting nest of my childhood.

Although she was long gone there always remained something of my mom's spirit still about for me to latch onto.

For some unknown reason, I wanted to be home to record my most inner thoughts in my diary.

Alone at home where I sometimes sat at Dad's old roll-top desk of aged oak I would open my diary and scribble for hours. Other times I would settle at the matching dining room table to pour out my innermost secrets.

Dear diary: I started, then pen between my teeth, I tried to compose serious words which eluded me suddenly. Then, for longer moments I thought, ah the hell with it. He wasn't worth recording. So what, we slept together, and we played and romped and danced, and went to concerts. All seemed destined to guarantee a future life of bliss and happiness. . .then blooey. The shit flew and the spell was over. The bubble burst. So, with a vengeful fury I scribbled his name in large caps, then I struck vicious lines through it. The confounded ballpoint ran out of ink anyway.

It was the last Friday in October. I had stopped at home first, and finding no one there I headed for the usual luncheon hang outs. Lakeport is a good walking town and when I come home I park my old Camaro and I walk. When I was in high school the big thing was to drive, drive anywhere, or drive nowhere, just so others could see you driving around, cruising, saying to other people, look at me, I'm a big shot now, and I can burn rubber, and I can play loud obnoxious noises, called Rock.

I hoped to intercept Dad for lunch, and found him at his favorite spot, The Park View Cafe. It was just a few blocks from home off Main Street on Second, across from Library Park, the reason for its name.

Clam chowder was Dad's all time Friday favorite at the Park View. It was the first weekend after the opening of duck season. I remember it because Dad never used to miss opening day. That was years ago. For some reason he gave up hunting and his trusty twelve gauge shotgun rests in the glass doored gun case as silent testimony to a once vigorous and youthful past, removed only for an occasional cleaning after months of sitting there gathering dust.

It was just as I had guessed, he was busy having his usual second bowl of clam chowder, and that's when I saw Emile for the first time, next to the corner booth. Beside him sat Kimberly, and across from them Dad took up most of the seat for himself.

Kimberly Clark Lambertis and I were old friends. She often visited our home on official business and more often unofficially. She liked being with us because she said we were like family, and it seemed her visits occurred more often when she was between romantic interludes, such as my own dilemma of late.

She had advanced in status to assistant district attorney position on the county prosecutor's staff. The fact that she was eight years older than myself in no way hindered our close relationship.

With Emile sitting beside her, they made an uncommonly handsome couple, although he was more my age group than hers. For a brief moment I puzzled over their relationship. That would have seemed odd, not because Kimberly was the choosy sort, but because most of her romantic interests came from the professional sector. She was dressed exquisitely in her usual woman's business suit, and he in faded jeans and a sort of tattered sweatshirt with a wildlife scene on the front, his sandy hair windblown and somewhat unruly. Such opposites, I thought, she with her long shiny hair immaculately drawn back in a shiny gold barrette. I envied her so because she always looked as if she had just stepped off the cover of some fashion magazine, no matter what she wore, whereas I had a corruption of jeans, odd sweaters, print and plain blouses and jogging coordinates for a wardrobe. Oh, I have a few pairs of slacks and three dresses, one for church, one for rare parties, and another one for rarer dates. A lot of greens and browns, with a few lavenders thrown in for fair measure." For that brief moment I felt like a pauper, until Daddy, as if reading my mind, moved over, patted the seat and motioned for me to sit down.'I shifted in beside him, pecked him on the cheek as usual, and he as usual being a prude when it came to public displays of affection, said; "Ah cut that out now, what you want people to think, huh, I'm playing around with some young chick?"

"I don't care what people think, you know why?"

"You're gonna tell me why, I'll bet. . ."

"You got me fooled, cause you really know how to flatter a girl. . ."I kidded, then stole another peck.

He was saying something in his usual Archie voice, like okay little girl, have it your own way, and; ". . .Did yooz bring dat meathead wit yooz—?"

What he said only partially sank in because he was busy wiping the chowder bowl with the last piece of French bread, and my eyes were locked on those of the guy across from me.

Kimberly, as always looked to be in top form. She should have been a model or a television spokesperson. I never understood why she chose law as her profession. She was sure-footed and good at it though, with an uncompromising dedication. And of course, she is very intuitive.

"Hi Kitty," she said, greeting me in a smooth voice. "Long time, no see. This is Emile. Emile, meet Kitty. Kitty is Sheriff Kreeszowski's daughter. He's sort of new around here. . . But I have a feeling you two will get along just fine," she added, winking with a knowing smile.

Dad was saying something, ". . .Had your lunch yet? How about some clam chowder, or a Louie salad." He waved Louise the waitress over.

"No thanks Dad, I'm really not hungry. . ."

"You gotta eat something, good for your bones, best clam

chowder anywhere. You gotta try it."

". . .really not hungry," I tried to sound convincing, but knowing my Dad, I relented; "A side salad maybe, and a cup of decaf."

"Honey, you gonna shrink into a bag of bones." Not likely I thought, but said nothing. "You need something with substance, like beans, meat or potatoes. Something more than a little watery lettuce. . ."

Yea, I thought, like things that stick to my thighs, thanks, but no thanks.

My eyes were locked on Emile's with a warm glow, and I felt Kimberly measuring me. I hoped Dad was preoccupied. He said, "Louise, bring Kitty a bowl of clam chowder and a side salad with light Italian on the side. . .and a cup of decaf. And bring her some more French bread, too."

Louise said something like; "Hi Kitty," and left. Dad called after her, ". . .Put it on my check."

Kim said; "Oh you're paying. It must be official then."

"My treat," said my dad magnanimously. He never charged a cent to the county, and never accepted a gratuity. He was adamant on the subject of a clean record, and I pity the poor soul who might have offered him a bribe. He would never have considered cheating on his income tax, and thereby felt he had the right to expect the same regard from everyone else.

"Look Honey, I gotta go. You should have come sooner. You been home yet? Come up to the office. Tell me what you're up to, but take your time. Sorry, gotta go."

For a moment I trapped him and kissed him on the cheek. That always got a rise, like getting even for calling me Honey. I disliked the sound of Honey almost as much as Kitty. "Cut that out," he grunted, "Here in public." And I got the calculated blush. Almost, like getting even.

I watched briefly as he and Kimberly left together, their heads locked in serious confidential business, a definite sign that something of sober consequence stirred the air.

# TWO

Louise returned dutifully, setting the chowder before me, which I did not want, and the salad which I might have eaten, and the decaf which I toyed with forcibly.

God, I was lost from the first moment our eyes locked. Those deep inquisitive blue eyes and the soulful virile smile. He seemed so lean and vitally healthy, like windblown sea and fresh air, like wood chips and trees. He appeared to be about Dad's height but so lean by comparison. He was wearing a Clear Lake High School Cardinal sweatshirt and I knew he had not attended Clearlake High. I surely would have remembered. Then I recalled Kimberly saying that he was new around here.

He didn't say a word, just looked at me with something of a magnetic intensity while I studied him in silent awe. There was a captivatingly humorous glint in his eyes and he exuded a potent electricity.

There was something familiar in his smile that I only identified some time later.

His hair might have been blond or sandy. I don't know for sure to this day. It didn't matter. What mattered were the eyes and the casual way in which he considered me.

I fumbled with the decaf in an effort to appear nonchalant and unaffected. . . God, if he had asked me to undress right there, I would have, and run through the park with our own version of naked in the park. And, to his bed I would have raced that very instant without the slightest embarrassment. I was lost, and he knew it, or at least I thought he felt it.

If he reached to touch me, I would have collapsed. I couldn't tear myself away.

I hope Dad hadn't sensed my foolish helplessness. I feared Kimberly did.

Dad, the playful Archie, so intuitive in his own way, and a witness to my own captivation. I mean he can be such a prude when it comes to public displays of affection or emotion.

Dad doesn't miss a trick though. He's somewhat sly that way, and if I'm alert I can tell because his eyes narrow to intense scrutinizing slits, perceptible only to those who know him. Ned Turner might be one, and Mom could read him like a book.

As it turned out, it was B.B. who interrupted and broke my spell with one of his diatribes.

B.B. sat with his back to mine in the adjoining booth facing Maria Littletree, another deputy, and Detective Lieutenant Ned Turner.

I should have guessed something was up with all the heads together in one place at the same time, locked in sober contemplation. Only Emile seemed out of place, and detached from any underlying tension.

When I had first approached the group I had acknowledged them with the usual wink and head nod. With lunch time over, most of the patrons had suddenly disappeared leaving us almost alone and isolated in two remote corner booths. It was my Dad's usual place on Friday. He had a standing reservation.

B.B. had been telling some of his usual stories for Ned Turner and Maria's benefit.

The story, which I found not to be in the least bit entertaining was directed to my ears for purposes of my clinical collection. Everyone, it seems was somehow concerned with my education.

B.B. is a nickname for Deputy Orrin Kenny. You see, Orrin Kenny, of locker room fame got his title in this way; while in high school he sported about proudly a big wad of meat in his too tight jockey shorts. So you guessed all right. The guys, his teammates and buddies tagged upon him the sobriquet of Big

Balls.

Now Orrin Big Balls grew into a tall handsome jock of a kid with a playful manner about himself and when some of the bolder girls got hold of this spicy bit of gossip, they referred to him as B.B. in mixed company. It started as a private joke, but some of the other girls present soon guessed at the connotation and pressed B.B., actually they teased, cajoled and pestered him unmercifully about his new nickname.

In response Orrin B.B., backed by some of his smirking buddies confessed that B.B. actually meant Bad Boy.

No one was fooled, and when some of the teachers asked why B.B., the response was Bad Boy, of course.

Orrin Kenny became somewhat of a jock with the girls and for some dumb reason tried desperately to live up to his new title of Bad Boy.

On any field of play and on the courts, B.B. had found new fame and he became a terror. He grew to about six foot, six inches at last measure, and later retained his style as a mischievous handsome brute in a sheriff's uniform. His hair became darker and wavier and he was in demand among the ladies, except for myself.

As part of his pride and reputation he promptly steered a course designed to remedy my own lack of interest, and for my benefit with frequent off-color stories aimed at supporting his lusty affliction.

As a result, my resistance only served to feed his appetite for challenge and a need to add me to his scoreboard.

For some unexplained reason I always seemed to find myself trapped by B.B. and I shall attempt to relate the story somewhat as he did:

"They have this guy in custody up at Willits. His name is Manchester, Woody Manchester. He's been on this man's trail for almost twenty years now, all the way from back in New Hampshire, New England, you know. This Manchester tracked this guy for twenty years. Now that's perseverance, don't you think? Tracked this guy relentlessly for twenty years before catching up to him, north along the Canadian border, and south to Brownsville, Texas, and finally here on the west coast."

I felt like shouting; get on with it B.B., but B.B. had a way about taking his time, like making sure he had everyone's attention before going on with the story.

"The guy's name was Warren Brewster. Well the trouble started out when Warren Brewster took Woody Manchester's two little daughters for a walk in the woods for a bit of neighborly fun and games. Manchester's daughters were tender young things, twelve and fourteen years old, next door neighbors. Old Warren's a real clever guy, see, and he gets the girls to let him tie them up to trees while he dances around playin; me Indian warrior and they were his maiden captives.

"The game got out of hand when Brewster starts stripping their clothes off and he's getting excited. His libido is on the rise by this time and he's proud of his thing, shows it to them, like wantin their approval, you know what I mean."

A swollen libido, huh, I thought, shaking my head at B.B. and at the same time wondering how Emile was taking this little tale. Ned looked anxious, like he had someplace to go and Maria smiled as if totally impressed.

". . .Well, he unties the older one, name's Lillian, first and plays a little game of chase with her until he finally catches her and rapes her.

"Then he ties her back up, plays around some more till he's ready again, then unties the younger one, names Betty, and proceeds to play the same game all over again with Lillian for an audience this time. Well the game gets further out of hand because, it seems Lillian gets jealous while he's trying to rape little sister, Betty. Only Betty is not as cooperative, and when Warren wrestles her to the ground, strips her clothes and starts to rape her, she panics, bites him and kicks him in the balls, and gets loose.

"Now you can well imagine the scene with big sister tied up, jealous and pissed off while warrior Warren chases little sister around in a frenzy trying to catch her and rape her."

"Did he catch her?" I found myself asking, hoping to speed up the conclusion, suspecting the others agreed.

". . .Catches her again, slaps her around a bit, probably cause his libido is shrunk, and threatens to kill her if she ever tells anybody what happened. . ."

"How old was this Brewster?" I found myself asking.

". . .Sister Lillian and Warren Brewster stayed around for a little more game playing while sister Betty ran home and reported the whole incident to Mother Manchester."

"Brave girl," I snapped.

"Mother Manchester calls in the law and father Woody Manchester takes off after warrior Warren with his shotgun. Fortunately for young Brewster the law gets there in time and saves his ass. You see Woody Manchester is from the old school of values and he's ready to crucify Warren.

"Well, they bring young Brewster before the judge at the tender young age of a month under eighteen and the judge feels compassion for the energetic young lad. You see, young Brewster has been a busy lad and he has already raped some eight other girls under similar circumstances. Eight that is who are willing to come forth and testify. . .well to make a long story short. . ."

"Please do," I said with some urgency.

". . .Oh, I didn't know you were listening, Kitty."

I looked at Emile, then at Ned and Maria who snickered uncontrollably.

"Warren Brewster serves sixty days, not bad huh? Just enough to whet his appetite. When he gets out, he's gone cause old man Manchester wants his nuts for trophies. You see, that's why Woody Manchester tracks Brewster for twenty years until he catches up with him. His wife dies later, and Manchester is a religious man, an eye for an eye kinda stuff. And being a descendant of old pilgrim stock he doesn't take that shit. His two young daughters are ruined. Lillian takes to a life of promiscuity and loose morals and little sister Betty becomes frigid, eventually marries her childhood sweetheart in spite of the Brewster legacy, but can't consummate her marriage.

"Get this; Brewster seems to have developed a change in

style, he's rehabilitated. He works as a Canadian Border Patrol and then does the same thing in Texas and moves around in various other jobs, even works as a bounty hunter for a while, and a prison guard in a women's prison. Charmed life, huh? He must have felt Manchester breathin down his neck though.

"For a while he was here in Lake County, but it was Willits where Manchester catches up to him in a deserted place in the woods. Old Manchester strung up Warren Brewster, trussed him up Indian style, hanging from a tree, and cut off his genitals and left him to bleed to death. Manchester turned himself into the law later on, figuring by his code anyway, justice was served."

There was quiet for awhile, then B.B. asked; "Do you want to hear how Manchester stayed on his trail all those years?"

"Do we have to?" I said with a shudder.

"He tracked him by following reports on rape cases. He tracked Brewster to here in Lake County for awhile, and the D A, Martin Rosswell wants to prosecute Manchester right here in Lakeport. It seems the old man compiled quite a history on Warren Brewster; some three hundred and eighty seven rape cases over the years."

I toyed with my cold coffee and glanced at Emile. The others got to their feet, ready to leave.

B.B. said to me, "Some pay back, huh. I thought you would like to know that for the record, Kitty."

"You know something B.B.?" I said, seriously with just a touch of venom in my voice.

"What?"

"You should apply for the all time *SCHLEPP* award."

"What's that?"

"Look it up."

"Where?" he asked, grinning egotistically.

"Why, a dictionary, where else. You know what a dictionary is, don't you B.B. . . It's a *BIG BOOK*."

"Oh!"

"Come on you meatheads," urged Ned. "Let's get to work before the chief starts chewing butts all the way to Thanksgiving." He slapped B.B. on the shoulder, pushing him along.

"Don't mind him Kitty," said Maria, her voice firm with sisterly consolation. "He's just a big harmless lug who likes to tease. Good to see you home for a change. We should get together sometime."

I watched Maria as she followed behind the two men. Even in a uniform she still looked good. It was her attitude that set her apart from so many others. Even her walk smiled with gentle forgiveness. She was a full figured woman, larger than average, like those Amazons you hear about, with a tolerant kindness commonly inherent in her easy-going Pomo background. In return, the years had treated her kindly. Younger, she had been a plain girl, yet one of those who improved steadily with age and she had blossomed into a handsome female figure. While others who had started young and pretty had gotten fat and sloppy, their teeth dark from smoking and a raspy hacking voice. Maria was a model example for better living. Her teeth were sparkling white and showed even more against her smooth chocolate complexion. But it was her black intense eyes that hinted of an endless vitality. With age she had also improved her gentle caring nature. Maria was indeed a paradox for the fountain of youth.

I have heard Dad say that she could be counted on to hold her own in any scrap, and had proven it many times.

I often wondered about Maria's sexuality. Whatever her preferences, she was secretive and the epitome of discretion.

God, I hope I hold together and mature like Maria.

# THREE

The gathering place was almost like a ghost scene at twenty minutes past as Emile and I sat alone. The perfunctory tidying up and progressive preparation for the regular evening mealtime already taking shape.

I toyed with bits of my salad and hadn't touched the chowder or tepid decaf while Emile stared fixedly through the glass at something in Library Park. He seemed such a strange mystery, distantly detached and in the next instant intensely valiant, yet always impenetrably private.

I looked where he looked, Library Park, in summertime a beehive of activity, and in the autumn just a little less so on most nice days. Library Park, with its new ornate gazebo as the focal point for summer concerts, weddings and various celebrations and Friday night concerts, surrounded by new instant lawn, by now well established among varieties of towering shade trees. With boat launches at either end it had become a haven for children and brightly colored parasailers. After extensive renovation and expanded parking, Library Park had come of age. It had become a busy summer hub for playful children with dotting mothers in the playground section. Families, boating enthusiasts and fishermen alike found a whole new scenario of activities for interest, such as the annual model airplane contests, vintage seaplane fly-ins and endless bass fishing contests.

Springtime always heralded a series of sailboat regattas flirting with the winds to enchant visitors and locals alike.

It was fall now and the beehive gave way to causal strollers, and of course the ducks, always the ducks and sea gulls lolling about waiting for a handout.

I knew it would sound corny, but I had to ask; "A penny for your thoughts," I said.

His gaze came back to mine, again casting that unwitting spell. He said, "It's a beautiful park, isn't it?"

How strange I felt when he uttered such simple words that I was affected so intensely. I found my voice again, as if we had been sitting together for ages and had known each other for a long, long time. "Yes, it has changed, the city fathers you know. The best move they ever made, don't you think? But it's your thoughts I'm after. Your attention was so much farther away than the park. . . How about a nickel?"

"Ha, you could get gypped that way, I mean being so extravagant," he said, as our eyes pried deeper into the others. The spell was definitely back, then he added; "A nickel huh, a nickel should buy a nickel's worth."

"I'll settle with that for starters."

". . .And you get four pennies change. I was just looking at Quercus Island, see out there," he pointed to a place across the lake water, obscured by the shoreline and backed by towering Mount Konocti.

"Where? There? I don't see any island. It all looks like one shoreline of trees and background to me," I said. Then, "I don't see anything unusual."

"But it isn't just obscure shoreline, just looks that way, when in reality it is a whole different world, tule flats, islands and inlets and secret lagoons. There are places hidden and almost untouched, this time of year. There are places, channels among the tules where wildlife is teaming unnoticed, where the water is only one to three feet deep now. See out there where the land seems to come to a point, that's Quercus Island. It is about five to six miles from here, and there, just a mile and a half is Long

Tule Point. It resembles a long drooping finger on the map. . . It is a popular place for duck hunters."

I studied his face, his expression was a question mark, but there seemed an obvious mixture of emotional strain, and equal portions of reverence, all stirred into a wary anxiety, all hidden beneath a mask of easy going composure.

Yet he was the newcomer and I the complacent home town girl. I wondered if he had found some elusive charm I and others had overlooked by taking this unique natural beauty for granted day after day. He made it seem like a waiting adventure, a challenge, stirring one's imagination.

"Have you been out there?" I asked, rather tentatively.

"Say, are you going to eat that salad?"

I nodded, "I don't think so."

"I thought not. Grab the bread and crackers. Let's go feed the ducks and sea gulls."

In a flash I was up and after him, like a young girl trailing behind a boy she has just found a new crush on.

I bounced after him across Third Street and in minutes we were in the park. He had a bag in his hand which I had not noticed and from it he took out bits of bread, some crackers and an odd assortment of happy duck food.

The ducks and sea gulls at Library Park have long been accustomed to people who come to feed them with scraps of bread and leftovers, and they seem to expect it.

A favorite pastime among children who cannot resist their charm is to chase them about while they squawk and scramble over crumbs. To the children they are irresistible and on occasion you can see a bright eyed little girl or boy sitting on the ground while rocking and petting one, with a happy gleam in the eyes of both. On other occasions, mischievous boys will throw rocks or attempt to shoot them with sling shots, causing the birds to become spooky and distrustful for long periods of time afterwards. Fortunately, the ducks seem to possess an extra sense about those who can be trusted.

In most instances, people just toss their gift of crumbled

bread on the ground while fifty or so ducks, mostly mallards, scramble about fighting for a share of the hand-outs.

This day, the park was almost empty, except for a few mothers with their toddlers in the far playground area.

As we headed along the railing at the water's edge towards the pier, I realized we were being followed, or rather being chased by a quacking procession at our feet. Sea gulls swooped overhead with their startling calls. They too had learned to pay attention to the sight of a paper bag from whence food came, and who not to be wary of.

Emile, it was obvious, was no stranger to them. They gathered around his ankles quacking pleasantly, and he quacked back as if they were talking the same language, and the cadence in their sounds was unusual now, as if they were old friends, greeting each other.

As was the usual custom, I broke up my bread in smaller pieces and tossed it on the ground, setting off a squabbling free-for-all.

My offerings gone, Emile was much more miserly with his handouts, I noticed. He knelt down and summoned them forward in orderly fashion while they fed willingly from his fingers.

Then he ignored the ducks momentarily and started imitating a call to the sea gulls. At first they dove in a swarm but soon adjusted to a more orderly pattern in response to his screeching calls.

Just two feet above his head they hovered gracefully catching a tossed cracker, then swooping off only to line up for another pass. I soon realized they were putting on a show, a grand and glorious display of acrobatics I had never witnessed before, "I think they like you," he said. . .

"Meeee!"

"I mean they don't usually make this big of a deal over a few crackers. True, they're a bit flamboyant, so it has to be you. They like you, or maybe they have a thing about red hair—"

"Yeah, sure, you mean they would like to line their nests with it maybe."

He motioned me to his side, saying; "Here you try it." My own cracker faltered hopelessly, fluttering to the ground amid a squawking audience.

"It's easy," he prompted, ". . .Just a gentle underhanded toss and the wind will do the rest, kinda like sailing a Frisbee, see, like this. A cracker is ideal because it is flat and can follow a trajectory. They love to perform and compete. At heart they're showoffs, but you have to tempt them. It's a game they like to play, like playing catch."

"If they carry on like this for a cracker, I can imagine what they'll do for a piece of fish," I remarked.

A beautiful gray and white sea gull hovered just inches from his hand until he flipped the cracker gently, then the gull caught the offering expertly, zooming away while two others chased after it, attempting to take the cracker away.

"The chase," he said, sailing another cracker high and far out over the water. With lightning anticipation they responded, flying after it, like a football receiver streaking after a long pass, with the first one snatching it from the air, racing for a touchdown. He sailed another and this time it was like an outfielder chasing a long hit ball to the fence. So far, they were uncanny and had not missed a single catch. I gave credit too soon as he sailed the next one outward, the first gull nipped it, dropping the missile, only to see another dive after and catch his prize. He sailed another and it broke into pieces with most being caught in breathtaking dives to the water, where always there were others awaiting the scraps.

Emile continued the show while the gulls willingly demonstrated their aerial agility and swiftness, their dramatic acrobatics, somersaults and even flying upside-down.

Then he paused, smiling, his face a mask of pure delight and pride. He looked down at a handsome mottled brown and white drake perched on his shoe tugging at his pant leg.

" Well Jason," he said, apologetically, "I didn't know you were there."

"Quack-quack-quack," Jason responded.

"I am sorry. No, I didn't mean to ignore you. No, you know the gulls are not my favorites. You know I love you all. . . here quack-quack-quack," he said. "And you too Europa and Juno."

While he quacked, imitating their own language sounds, each approached in turn to feed from his hand in an orderly fashion as he called them in turn by name.

"What, no Donald duck?" I scolded.

"Donald," he quacked, "come here and meet Kitty."

"Ha-ha, you've got to be kidding. Sure, some cute show, and I'll bet you're going to claim next that it's all for my benefit." Just then a fine white drake fluttered over to land on my foot. "Donald, don't you dare poop on my shoes." I warned, half expecting him to understand me.

"Kitty wants to give you something, Donald." And to me he said, "Here Kitty, give this to Donald." Now I really had something to laugh about. But, I was not to be outdone yet; "I suppose you have names for all of them, including Donald's mischievous nephews."

"Huey, Louie, Dewey, come and meet Kitty."

"You're kidding. Surely you jest. You've been training them, and now you're just putting on an act for me. Clever, very clever. I'm astonished, really. What else can I say? I'm impressed."

He flashed a smug grin. That was for my benefit also, I thought. What a way to impresse a girl.

Then, looking down, I said, "Are you trained, Huey, Louie and Dewey?"

"Quack-quack-quack," they replied, waddling off with their heads nodding vigorously.

"I heard that," I scoffed, "but, what if they poop on your shoes?"

Jason was still sitting there as if taking it all in intelligently.

"They wouldn't," Emile said to me, and to Jason; "Would you Jason?"

I said, "I know, that quack meant he said, no." Then he popped over to perch on my foot. I shook a finger at his bill in warning; "Don't you dare poop on my shoes."

"He wants you to feed him. He likes you. Here, try this."

"You're serious about all this, aren't you?"

# FOUR

He scattered the remaining crumbs on the ground among the group, and then turned his attention to the demanding squawk of hovering sea gulls. Emptying the bag, he sailed the last crackers far out over the water, saying; "Sorry guys, all gone. Sorry for such plain fare. Better luck tomorrow."

Then returning his attention to the ducks he motioned to a gorgeous plump mallard hen and said, "This is Aphrodite. She is the Greek goddess of love." And to her, he said, "Come, love goddess." Eagerly, she waddled over to perch delicately on his left foot, cooing gentle duck sounds. He proffered to her his last bit of bread, saying; "Careful, don't bite now."

He winked at me with an impish grin, "This is her husband, of sorts, Eros. Say hi to Kitty, Eros." And to me he whispered; "Eros can become jealous when she nibbles my finger like that. She won't do it when strangers are about. Not proper in public."

Playing along, I said, "I hope it doesn't cause any troubles between them."

"No, just now she's preoccupied with the crumbs, and besides Eros has his eye on you. I think he likes you."

"Oh I see, she's only intimate in private, and he likes to flirt with human redheads."

Brushing the crumbs from his hands, he gave me a devilish grin, then walked over to toss the bags in a nearby trash can.

". . .So that was plain fare, I take it," I said, succinctly, then followed unwittingly at his heels.

"Their favorites are graham crackers and blueberry pancakes. You should see what they will do with those."

"I can imagine, I think," I said, trying desperately not to sound childish at his game.

"For a few Grahams, the gulls will put on quite a show. Fish is their favorite. For anything with a hint of fish smell or taste they will do battle, almost kill for it. When motivated, the ducks can put on an aerial display unequal in daring and carefree frivolity."

We walked quietly to the corner, past a mother with three children playing on the slides, drinking in their joyous laughter, like sounds of a happy musical.

I found myself trailing beside him, ready to slip my hand into his like some young crush laden teenager with a tingling obedience.

Two short blocks up to Main Street and we crossed Second Street in view of Courthouse Square, and the old county courthouse, now a museum. Behind it, facing Forbes Street, bounded by Second and Third Streets stands the towering structure of the contrasting modern courthouse on the hill.

We were walking south along Main Street. My house is north, in the opposite direction. The sheriff's office and jail are directly behind the new courthouse building. I wondered if Dad could be up there somewhere watching us.

One Sixty Two Main Street was the fourth in a line of older stores. Most ambitious tenants had moved to new shopping centers on the outer fringes of the city for more space and better parking, adding to the dilemma of high vacancy factors of older shops who tries to retain some of the charm by keeping their stores up with ever changing decorated paint jobs.

We paused at the door while he unlocked it, stepped aside and motioned me in first. Very gentlemanly, I thought.

I knew this store from even before the exodus. It and so

many others like it with no air conditioning struggled to retain some of that old time charm with an endless array of short span tenants. It was one of four small shops and had been a Tee-shirt store, and before that an adult paraphernalia shop, which most locals avoided like the plague. At numerous times, I seem to recall it had been a beauty shop, whose ambitious owners had moved to the corner for more space and better exposure. At one time it had been a sweet shop and at another time an accountant had occupied it. He had lasted the longest in my memory, three years, I think. He too had moved to a place with better exposure, more space and more available parking at the new shopping center.

It was an obscure place for a wood carver and inside it seemed even smaller because it had been partitioned off for a small display room in front and the larger area used for a workshop in the rear.

Stepping inside was a thrill I was in no way prepared for. There was an aura of overwhelming excitement suspended in a different world of nature and birds so real and eternal that I felt compelled to reach out and touch them, to test if they were indeed real living specimens.

Looking to the ceiling I felt myself caught in a grip of breathlessness at the sight of a gorgeous bald eagle, suspended in flight and ready to strike.

From hidden speakers music was playing the haunting song of *Ebb Tide. . .at last we're face to face, and when we kiss in an embrace, I can tell, I can feel, you are loved, you are real, really mine, like the tide, that rushes in . . .*

I don't know how long I stood there, as if stunned by the eternal glare of the suspended eagle. The realism was beyond belief, yet reality escaped me. I seemed to be floating and lost, suddenly drawn into a land of enchantment.

"Go ahead, you can touch it," he urged. "It won't bite. It's made of wood."

"But it looks so startling, almost frightening, here among all these other passive creatures. And that thing, an owl, it looks almost mesmerizing, yet so docile and almost sleeping at the same time. . ."

". . .A great horned owl."

"And this?"

"A wren perched in reeds, on a spalted maple base."

*Ebb Tide* had finished its last haunting chords, and a new melody started; *My prayer is to linger with you, till the end of my days, till my heart kneels to pray. . .*"

"This is a gadwell preening its feathers," he said, his eyes so alive with pride. There was no doubt that Emile liked what he was doing. His face showed it and his manner was that of a man completely at peace with himself while among his work.

"The eyes are so. . .so, vibrant," I said.

"They're glass," he said, simply.

"How do you do it? These are all yours I take it?" I turned to consider him closely, knowing they were all his own creations. They seemed an extension of Emile, as if they were a part of him. But I wanted to hear it from his own lips.

"They are basswood mostly," he said, decorously. "They are decoys made for show. Anyone can do it. It is mostly an acquired skill with a little talent and a lot of practice."

"I don't think you're giving yourself enough credit. It looks like talent to me. Pure raw talent. I couldn't even think of trying my hand at it."

"Here is a meadowlark. It took first of show, and so did this pair of kestrels poised for mock mating combat."

"How do you do it? I mean they're so real, so lifelike, as if they could fly right out of here. . .and, this one; a hummingbird, poised in flight to take nectar from a flower, and this?"

"A goldeneye."

"These, I know."

"A pair of common mallards."

"Oh my God, aren't these darling?"

"A mother Carolina wood duck with her ducklings."

"And these?"

"A pair of ruddy's in a pond. It looks like water, but actually it's just epoxy."

"Unbelievable. I can't find words to describe. . . and oh these are darlings. They have to be my favorites. They're mandarins aren't they?"

"Miniature mandarins, very rare, and especially precious in China. . ."

I wanted to touch them, cuddle them and hold them close. I knew then they were my favorites, but I resisted and started on to the next one. First, I rotated the brightly colored mandarin drake to the light so that my eyes caught a glimpse of the price for the pair on the tag. For an instant I felt stunned, almost dropping it. Very carefully, I returned it to its place on the shelf.

Moving to the next one I hesitated touching it, "What's this funny looking thing?" I inquired, somberly, knowing I would never own it.

". . .A red breasted merganser. Their habitat is around the polar regions. They live on fish."

"That's some wicked looking beak."

He chuckled. When I paused, resolutely refusing to touch the next one also. He said, "A white pekin, purest of the domestic lines."

"Amazing," I said in a confessing tone of voice, and hoped I hadn't sounded condescending. "It's so pure white looking, and how do you do it, I mean the feathers, and the feet?"

"I have a shop in the back. It's really not as hard as it looks. Anyone can do it if they want to."

We moved to the workshop in the back room. It was a small room, compact and cluttered with wooden parts and an assortment of various tools scattered about. There was a stool by the workbench and he switched on the light. He picked up a piece of partially shaped wood resembling a duck decoy and handed it to me for inspection. It had a unique clean smell of trees and wood dust, with finely carved lines. I studied it with the uneasy curiosity of a child ready for a new discovery. The scent seemed almost overpowering, and for some unexplainable reason, I wanted terribly to taste the wood. . .

". . .See, you shape the body and main parts out of basswood. It's the most workable of all woods. Some carvers chew on a wood chip while working, but some woods are toxic to work with. Basswood is the best because it is the most stable and lasting. It is the favored wood among carvers. The head and all other protruding feathers and parts are carved separately, and then you just stick them all together and, *voilà*, there you are. Then you have the feathers." He reached over and got another piece and handed it to me, saying; "See, this is what we call a vermiculated feather, ready for attachment."

"You make it sound so easy. I think you're just being modest."

He teased me with that tempting smile again and handed me a magnifying glass; "First, you burn in the shaft lines and the barbs, and the barbicels. Each feather has to be done individually. For the finishing, I use an India ink, but a thinned oil or acrylic will work almost as well."

"Then what?"

"Then, I sell them. Mallards are my favorites, but I specialize in all ducks."

"What about fierce looking eagles?"

"One of a kind. Every so often I have to try something different."

I thought of the price tag, and said; "And you sell these right here in Lakeport?"

"Occasionally I sell something here, but mostly people just come in to look. Most of my work I ship to galleries around the country."

"My dad has a pair of mallards. . ."

"He bought them from me. I gave him a special price."

"I should have guessed you did those. I saw them at home. Did you know about our cat, Cuddles? Well, she's part tiger-stripe and part Siamese, with very faint tiger markings and instead of orange she has light tan lines. Mostly, she is white. She sits and watches the two carved ducks for such a long time as if she's really not quite sure whether they're alive or not.

Finally, she sneaks over to them, not sure they won't fly away, and she sniffs them, both of them. She smells them all over, then waddles away shaking her head, as if in disbelief. If they had the right smell I think she would pounce on them."

"I'd like to see that," he said.

Ever since entering the shop, I had been thinking of Kimberly, and wondering which ones might be her favorites.

"Are you and Kimberly an item," I asked boldly. Too boldly really. I felt like I had babbled blatantly. How shall I ever be a psychologist if I can't watch my tongue.

"Gosh no," he blushed boyishly.

I waited, sharing his blush, realizing with my telltale hair I must have been the redder one.

". . .She comes in sometimes. Her favorites are the hummer and a pair of meadowlarks. . ."

"I thought, well, the two of you sitting there together. . .you know, you looked good together, and. . ." I looked up into his fixed gaze. The spell was definitely upon me again and he waited, and waited. I could have been kissed because he wore that roguish virile smile of a great seducer, and yet it seemed that any act of seduction would be left purely up to me.

Dammit, I thought, the spell was suddenly shattered again as the sound of customers entered the front shop are. "You have customers," I said plaintively.

"I know, but they may not stay long."

"I have to go, meet with my Dad. . .perhaps later. . ."

"Would you like to go out to Quercus Island tomorrow morning? It's about five or six miles by canoe along the shoreline. If you don't like to paddle, I'll do it. I'll make up a batch of blueberry pancakes, and take some graham crackers and some cracked corn. . ."

"For the ducks, of course. I'd like that." Actually, I had something sooner than tomorrow morning in mind, but kept my own counsel for once.

"Have you ever canoed before?"

"Oh yes, lots of times. I can make some pancakes too, and I'd like to paddle."

"Great. It's a date then, here at five o'clock in the morning. The canoe is down at Willow Point campgrounds, a friend lets me keep it there."

We said good-by, and I went outside while he attended to his prospective customers.

Then the reality hit me like a shock wave; a date at five in the morning. Seven is my absolute earliest. I may have to use toothpicks on my eye-lids, and I have never been in a canoe in my whole life. Oh well, what the hell.

# FIVE

The Lake County Courthouse building was just a short walk uphill to 255 Forbes Street. The more recent structure of dark brown brick, tall arches and high glass windows of five floors had been completed in 1968 and towered by comparison over the antiquated vine covered building in front of it. The old courthouse, built in 1871 of weathered gray stucco and provincial style remained as a museum for cultural art, Lake County History and a wide assortment of early Indian artifacts. The older preserved courthouse rested in the center of what is called appropriately, Courthouse Square, fronting on Main Street. It is surrounded by vintage trees, shrubs and well maintained lawn, and of course guarding the entrance at Main Street there are the usual ornaments of two ancient looking rusty old cannons. These two sets of structures pose a unique contrast in periods of the old and the new.

Just behind the new courthouse building and built as a later extension is the county jail and sheriff's office. This whole complex, small by any other municipal standards overlooks the center of town, the park and the lake.

My dad's corner office occupies the second floor of the jail building with a view looking down Third Street and a partial view of Clear Lake.

Dorothy said, "Hi Kitty. Good to see you. Your Dad said to send you right in."

I had known Dorothy from my high school days when Dad was first elected sheriff some eight years ago. She has an efficient and gracious businesslike manner, a pretty face, and of course an ever expanding broad bottom from sitting too much. She is devoted to her job and has never married. I have often wondered about the relationship between she and my father. Nothing obvious or on the surface you understand.

I tapped twice on the door, opened it a little and peeked in; "Hi, it's me, if I'm intruding I can come back later."

"Come on in Honey," came Dad's voice. "Just Ned and me. We've been expecting you."

It took years before I was finally accepted into that realm of male dominance concerning law enforcement. Dad had always remained so secretive and protective where it concerned my ears and mom's also. Only after years of persistent study and intimating myself among the legal affairs of our family's blue coat tradition had he considered my efforts as serious.

His office was the normal picture of efficient austerity with little adornment of anything impractical. There were the usual framed diplomas and certificates of merit and a few memorabilia photos of buddies in uniforms from his naval service days, plus the ordinary presentations by political figures. On his desk there were still the early photos of mom and me, buckteeth, fangs and all. I was a self avowed tomboy back then, trying desperately to become the boy I thought Dad always wanted.

I had the urge to rush over and plant a kiss on him, but I knew all to well he would say; "Ah, cut that stuff out, and have a seat," so I had a seat next to Ned and opposite the large dulled walnut desk. In public, I often did just that; rush and plant an unwanted kiss on his face just to embarrass him and expose his crusty manner. I took a certain pleasure in it. At home he could be a sentimental sissy, often cuddling me protectively in his arms while we watched television.

Ned seemed quietly somber while Dad leaned forward with elbows on the desk and hands clasped to his chin. I knew the signs. Something serious and portentous was in the air.

"Ned was just filling me in on some things before the weekend watch," Dad said. "Go ahead Ned."

Lieutenant Detective Ned Turner and my dad go back a long

way together. His small round cherubic face seemed at odds with his cop image. As usual, this day he wore a dark blue suit, white shirt and plain tie, all solids. Dad was just the opposite with sports coat and slacks and bold colored ties. Ned has a full head of white wavy hair, dark considerate eyes with a ruddy complexion. I always thought he looked more like a priest than a cop. He had a scratchy voice and an easy way with street conversation. He could be unwittingly disarming on cue. Yet, his best asset is that he listens, and he seldom misses a trick.

When he and Dad have had a few drinks Ned invariably flaunts his full head of hair over Dad's shiny bald pate and Dad retaliates that he, Ned Turner is the shortest man on the force. Ned claims that if one of them had grown to an even six feet, then at least one of them might have been governor by now. Jokingly ofcourse; Ned a politician—no way.

Whenever Ned feels it necessary, he will remind me that he had diapered me and if need be he could do it again. Ned Turner is also my Godfather.

He was saying; "Kitty you know that place out on Bell Hill Road, the one with hub-caps all over the place—?"

"Yeah, must be thousands of them."

". . .A quarter mile of fence covered with them, and the old house and barn too. There's this house and dilapidated old barn and some sheds and loads of oak tree, all decorated with hub-caps. Loony Lonny, people call him. His name's Lonny Lawless, but they call him Loony Lonny Lawless because he's a crotchety neurotic old guy, and he's always collecting hub-caps. He's obsessed with hub-caps. The shinier and the fancier they are the better he likes them. Always wondered what made a guy like that tick, you know, what goes on in his little brain to make him that obsessive. . ."

"Compulsive obsessive syndrome, I suppose, or something like that." Dad, chuckled, his little college girl showing off like that, with college words.

". . .Well you're the psychologist, not me, maybe you got a handle on it. Anyway, Loony Lonny has been picking up hub-caps for years, maybe all his life I suppose, or at least up till now," Ned snickered. "He might have gotten a cure now though. It got so that picking them up along the road wasn't enough; I guess cause his taste improved over the years and he took a special liking for some particularly ornate ones, and he took to stealing the real collector's items from parked or unattended vehicles along the roadside. Mostly from passer-bys stopped overnight at a rest stop. Loony Lonny's obsessive nature got the better of him one night about twenty miles south of here when he couldn't resist some big shiny ones on one of those fancy RV motor homes. But while Lonny is at work at three o'clock in the morning removing the hub-caps, the owner wakes up, hearing the racket, switches on his outside lights and charges out to catch Loony Lonny in the act; he charges out with a little nickel plated twenty two caliber revolver in his hand, and according to Lonny says something like; "This may look like just a little pea shooter, but it's loaded with bird shot and it can make one hell of a noise in addition to making a hell of a mess out of your face."

"What happened next we're still not clear on, but Loony Lonny Lawless has more holes in him than he has fingers to plug them with. . ."

"Oh my God no, and all over a few hub-caps," I said sympathetically.

". . .Anyway, this RV'er keeps on shootin, and according to Lonny he says something like; 'Uh-oh, that must be the last bird shot, the rest must be hollow points. . .tough luck, asshole. Excuse the terminology, Kitty."

"I've seen him around. Is he okay?"

"He stumbled into the hospital emergency room on his own after one of our night officers picked him up. He was bleeding like a sieve. Fortunately they were all flesh wounds. I mean this RV'er, whoever he was must have known what he was doing cause he popped every leg and arm muscle on Loony Lonny's body. Only one bird shot though. A .22 bird shot can sound like a cannon going off. But get this, the guy took Lonny's pickup keys and threw them somewhere out in the woods. Loony Lonny was crying cause he had to walk in that condition, and his biggest gripe was that he didn't even get to keep those fancy hub-caps."

"It sounds bizarre, to say the least." I shifted uneasily in my chair, uncrossing one leg and crossing the other. "And, what about the RV'er?"

"Gone. No description. No license number, cause it was dark. We got an all-points out, but. . ."

"What do you think, Kitty?" asked my dad, rearing back in his chair, hands crossed behind his head, his face a thoughtful mask. It really boosted my self-esteem when Dad asked for an opinion of mine, although I doubt he ever gave much consideration to anything I said. He was silent for a time, then he said; "Does this fit into any of your psychology profiles?"

"I'm sure it does. I'd like to think about it before giving you an opinion," I said, seriously. I think that since Dad helped finance my first four years of college he had a vested interest in the final product. However, it was not so much my immediate evaluation that he considered important but that I would gain some insight of value.

"How are things at Stanford?" asked Ned.

"As usual, on key"

"You still majoring in Criminology?"

"I smiled graciously. *Clinical Psychology*, with a specialty in *Criminology*."

Dad shifted his bulk seeking some elusive ultimate position in comfort. ". . .Bring that meathead home with you again?" The term meathead could mean affection, but he had met William Horace Lord only one time, and that had been more than sufficient for both of them. In Horace Lord's case the term meathead had become the ultimate derogative.

"That's all over with. Done. Finished." I said, with precise finality.

"Humph," he grunted, snapping back to his formal forward posture with hands gripped together on the desk.

I had a feeling they were contemplating whether to share some obscure matter with me or not.

He leaned back to his semi-reclined position, hands clasped behind his head before he finally got it out; "Did you learn anything?"

"Dad, why am I always supposed to learn something from everything? If you must know, yes I learned something. A hell of a lot. . . Satisfied?"

There it was, the squinted eyes, the grin, the all knowing smile of confidence and complacency. . . The look that got him elected for two consecutive terms, and would no doubt guarantee at least one more term. "Four years at Stanford, two years with Carolyn Kossloff, and how long with this; what's his face, and he was the pick of the litter, figure the guy's got to be a nickels worth of learning or something," he glared.

Ned butted in, "Hey, if this is gonna turn into a family row I'm leaving."

Funny how a timely word from Ned can change things. Suddenly Dad was more serious, he glanced at Ned and Ned at me and both seemed to nod agreeably.

"What is it?" I managed to say.

"Kitty, have you heard anything about the death of four duck hunters?"

"Why no. Should I have?"

"Ned was just about to fill me in on the latest. You can get in on it too, if you want?"

"I want."

Dad nodded, giving Ned the formal go-ahead.

"Well, to bring you up on it, Kitty, four duck hunters were found drowned two days ago."

"An accident? Where?"

"Maybe. . . Autopsy revealed they all drowned. There were some minor bruises, but drowning is the official cause of death. No excessive sign of trauma, like they all took a big gulp of water and swallowed their tongues, and bang, that's it."

"Drugs? Were they drunk?"

"Better start from the beginning, Ned," said my dad.

"Two pickup campers with empty boat trailers were found early that morning by Chief Wilson Johns and Joseph Littletree out at the Rancheria Reservation. The Indians call it Tule Point," Ned said thoughtfully.

"I know the place. Joe is Maria's cousin."

"Yeah, all three hundred pounds of him. Maria's the family beauty. All the rest weigh a ton or more. Well Joe was awakened that morning by two whining, howling dogs. Two golden setters, Jiggs and Jeter by their name tags. Joe drags himself out of bed and follows the dogs to find the two locked and deserted campers and realizes something isn't right. Two beauties. Sure would like to have them."

"What, the dogs or the campers?"

"Dogs. The campers were almost junk. Anyway Joe Littletree suspects something's up and he goes to get Wilson Johns who is up already, and awake because of the dogs, and together they take their runabout and go searching. With the dogs leading them, they discover two overturned boats and four bodies washed into the tules, gear all over the place and so they come call us."

"Where were the boats and the bodies?"

"About a half a mile away, little more maybe. From what we can tell, the boats must have been about forty yards apart with two hunters in each one, cause one boat and two bodies were found on one side of Long Tule Point and the other two about forty or fifty yards away. Must of been a dog in each boat. The bodies were found tangled among the tules face down, all heavily clad in hunting gear. The weapons, shotguns were recovered near the boats, none fired recently it seems. You think I got it all Arch?"

Dad nodded thoughtfully, and I said, "It was an accident and they all drowned?"

"All four of them. It sure looks that way, but the water's only one to five feet deep all around there. Christ, they could have stood up anywhere."

"How about drugs?"

"Pathology says no signs; but they had been drinking a lot of beer."

"Maybe they had a fight?"

"No marks or other indications to bear it out. But, if that were the case you would think at least one of them might still be alive to tell about it."

"Perhaps there were others."

"That's a possibility we haven't ruled out entirely, but absolutely no evidence points in that direction."

"The whole damn thing is strange as hell," said Ned with a hint of frustration in his voice. "Not a single, solid clue of any kind, yet."

I felt drawn in now, part of the system, like one of the guys, wanting to make a contribution; "Maybe it was just a coincidence, accidents do happen you know."

Dad shifted forward, thoughtful again; "This has a bad taste about it. Something just doesn't add up."

"Ned said, "We're contacting relatives, and maybe someone will turn over a clue there."

"They are not local, I take it."

"No, Bay Area."

"You don't think the Indians had anything to do with it, do you, Dad?"

"Who knows. No sign of a struggle. I know Chief Johns, and I trust his word. He knows everything that happens on the reservation, besides it was he and his people who reported it, and helped us recover the bodies and everything. Deception is not their way. They're too candid. Besides, the most they might do is inform the hunters they were trespassing on private reservation property and the sight of a few Joseph Littletrees can have a sobering effect on the bravest of souls even if they are toting shotguns. Oh, don't get me wrong, they can get riled up but they are not usually aggressive unless provoked. No, I don't think they had a hand in whatever happened. It was a foggy night and the four hunters thought they found a nice private spot. Unfortunately for them it just happened to be on the reservation. Beyond that the whole thing smells fishy."

That was a lot for my dad to say at one time and I felt extremely flattered to be in his confidence, and that he might consider me helpful in some way. "What's next?" I asked.

Ned leaned forward, "Criminal Psychology, huh . . .in those two years with that criminologist, Carolyn Kossloff, did you ever come across anything that fits this profile?"

I shook my head thoughtfully, "Not that I can recall, off hand. I can call her. We're on good terms. She approved of my returning to Stanford to work on my Master's. . ."

Dad leaned forward and said, "If you think of anything let us know, but don't go to any trouble." Then looking at me directly, he said, "Kitty, I want you to keep this under your hat. We would like to get this thing resolved without a lot of fuss, but if you have any thoughts on it, let us know. Okay?"

"Sure Dad."

"Ned, I want you to go back out there. I know forensic has been all over the place with a fine tooth comb. . ."

"Bring Wilson Johns and Joseph Littletree in?"

"Christ no, ask them to come at their convenience. Soon though. Take Maria. Don't send B.B. near the place. He's liable to mention the Bloody Island Massacre and start the Indian wars all over again."

Ned chuckled, "B.B. and Joseph Littletree, now that would be a war all by itself. . ."

"That's precisely why I don't want him out there. We don't need that kind of aggravation. Take Maria though."

I thought if there was any tension just now, sending Maria was an excellent idea, since she has a genuine way of pacifying the rowdiest of men, her own people included.

"Looks like you'll be here all afternoon," Ned said.

"I'd like to go out myself. I should, but we got those two FBI VIP's coming in on that other business and three of the supervisors trying like hell to hear themselves think, insisting on a budget update and prognosis report because of this hunter mess. Besides, if I went out there just now the media would be right on my heels. I'd like to get this thing settled down so we got less interference, maybe get something done."

"Right. Media's crawling all over the place right now, snapping pictures, asking dumb questions."

"Figures. Another good reason for me to stay away, and have Joseph and Chief Johns come in so we can sit down together, have a little private informal talk."

I sensed a pause and jumped in, "Looks like you may be late tonight," I said.

"Sorry Honey. Don't fix anything, or wait up for me. Enjoy yourself."

Like going to a movie alone or out for a hamburger, I thought.

"Anything else Ned?"

"One other thing. . ."

"You want me to leave you two in private?" I asked.

"Stick around for a few minutes, soon's Ned is done you can tell me how things are going. You got a few minutes?"

I nodded cheerfully, and he winked back.

Ned said, "Just what we need for a Friday afternoon. Old Chester Cowan's up in arms again."

"What's he done this time?"

"The usual of lately, refused to show up for Judge Wooden's jury summons. Says it's all a waste of taxpayer's time. Judges playing God, showboating petty lawyers, and criminal punks who plea bargain their way out of crimes while honest people who have better things to do have to sit around and wait. These savage animals, he claims, are making a mockery of the legal system and he refuses to be any part of it, quote, unquote. Chester's becoming a real activist for the right wing legal cause."

"What's Judge Wooden say?"

"He issued a Bench Warrant for Mister Cowan's arrest on Contempt of Court charges."

"Oh shit. Sorry Kitty. You mean Wooden actually woke up

long enough to catch it?"

"Old Chester has become a real thorn in Judge Wooden's crown these days, you know."

"Yeah. You say he issued an arrest warrant?"

Ned nodded, "FORTHWITH."

"Okay. Better send somebody out to his Scotts Valley place and have him picked up. Give him the weekend in jail to think it over. A couple nights behind bars can prove very convincing for some people. Probably not Chester though. Sometimes I think he likes to visit us here." Dad said, with a sheepish grin.

"We're short handed with this hunter thing and the weekend shift coming up. Several officers are out on vacation. Two others on sick leave. . ."

"Maybe I'll go out myself. No, on second thought I better stay here. . ."

"B.B.'s on the two p.m. to ten shift. . ."

"Good, send B.B. alone, Cowan's harmless, and B.B. has a way with the old guy. Maybe they speak a different language. Cripes sake, if he keeps his eyes open, B.B. can probably pick him up down at the park. He's there feeding the ducks almost daily."

Ned stood up and shook his pant legs loose, tugging at the crease.

Dad said, "Is that it for now?"

"Isn't that enough? If you want some more there's some minor stuff. . ."

"No, you take care of it, fill me in later. With this budget thing looks like I may be here tomorrow and part of Sunday too. Every time somebody unzips his fly the supervisors demand an update."

Ned was at the door when I said, "I'll wait up for you, Dad."

"No, don't bother with anything for me Honey. You do your own thing. Tomorrow's a wash also, but church on Sunday is a date. Okay?"

# SIX

Here I am home again for three S's plus sheets, with my first priority, a change into dry panties. Emile's spell was still upon me. I'm not sure when I first wet them. Perhaps it was when our eyes first met, or later when we sat alone. Perhaps both.

At the dining room table I sit with my diary before me. Dear Diary: I write. Just for the record, as for William Horace Lord whom Dad referred to as the *meathead*, and who I named more aptly as the *peckerhead*, or Horace the *sausage*, past interest of my once intended object of future and eternal connubial bliss. Yes, Dad I did learn something from Horace, as he preferred to be called. Actually it was his mother's preference. I have since come up with a variety of names which I am certain she would not have approved.

Be that as it may, from Horace the sausage, Horace the peckerhead, I learned about GISMO. Daddy dear, if you have not yet heard, GISMO is an acronym for: "Guaranteed Instant Spontaneous Multi Orgasms." It's not even a club, or a disease, yet. Actually, I just made it up. I think it may become a popular metaphor.

Intrinsically, Horace seemed more addicted to oral stimulation; his tongue, my stimulation, and to my spontaneous guaranteed orgasms. God, he was a hunk, what a chunk of meat. Like a limp, impotent sausage though, and I thought his impotence was all my fault. But GISMO was the great persuader.

Just how was I, the student, specializing in Clinical Psychology supposed to know he was gay, or bisexual. No, gay.

I bet you knew it all along, huh Dad? You never miss a thing, and you let me go ahead and find out for myself.

How did I find out, you might ask? It happened this way: It was a bad day to start with. A day predictably jammed with classes and tests after so much cramming and preparation. A day starting with a sore raspy throat, stuffiness and nausea, and that head-achey all over feeling, as they say in the TV commercials. Still, with watery itching eyes, sniffling and on wobbly legs, I dragged my aching body off to my first class.

Once there, my condition seemed only to worsen and I was forced to beg off with promises to make up tests later. I hauled my weary body back to my apartment seriously considering suicide. The flu bug had triumphed and I wished only for the security of my own bed. In my feeble mind and body, racked alternately with chills and fiery flashes, I wanted nothing more than my own darkened room. With that thought in mind I had struggled homeward to that place where I could be alone to suffer or die. The latter I would have gladly accepted over any other alternatives.

And, there they were, bold as hell, in my very own bed, my bed, the object of my worship, my faith, my only hope, two naked dickheads, one black and one white, in my VERY OWN BED! How could I tell you a thing like that, Father.

Well I can tell you one thing though, I was not born with this flaming red hair without reason. This day, in spite of the invader virus, my hair must have been wildly on fire, and kinkier than ever. Of course I lost my cool. I threw everything in my room at those two glaring, smirking dickheads, my carefully compiled notes, my books and anything, and everything I could think of or get my hands on. My words too, carried a most eloquent sting as well, like dickheads and dirty filthy, double-crossing peckerheads, two timing meatheads, while they sat there smugly glaring at the best I could come up with for the occasion. Considering my condition and predicament, they must have thought it was all a big joke. . . Did they really expect me to calmly crawl in between them for a party?

When the black guy scrambled for his clothes, I kicked him in his arrogant sausage, not just once, but, oh hell, who kept count anyway?

As for peckerhead Horace, who came to his lover's aid, I smashed a violent fist on his bony nose, with blood spurting everywhere. I think I broke it! With the two of them scrambling chaotically, mostly to escape my onslaught. I had not yet finished. I chased both of them into the hallway, down the stairs, and out into the street, raining blows on their heads and balls until they stumbled and finally stood naked in the street, traffic stopped, neighbors howling and jeering. Two naked queers, bleeding and pathetic, one black and one white. Two once erect sausages, now limp weenies, or more like teeny-weeny-peenies. "Damn you William Horace Lord," I said emphatically; "How come you never had a hard-on like that for me?"

And so, except for this last diary entry, that was the end of meathead Horace Lord.

In the throes of an anxiety fit I had completely forgotten my flu symptoms.

On the way home to 102 Clear Lake Avenue I had a lot to think about. If it is true that one's mind can cover enough material in ten minutes to write about for a lifetime, I believe it. In that short half mile walk north on Main Street to the corner of Main and Clear Lake Avenue my poor brain rattled around inside my skull uncontrollably, seizing on events and crises long forgotten.

My home and the days of my youth loomed ahead like an ancient sentinel as I passed Saint Mary's Catholic Church. Four towering palm trees, while so common to Southern California are a rarity here in the north. These dominate our yard, as do the decrepit trees and overgrown bushes which overpower and obscure the old two story gray house. Surrounding the whole affair is a low, dilapidated and peeling picket fence. Dad promises that some day he will trim the trees and remove the deadwood, and that we will paint the house a new cheerful color, white, or perhaps a soft yellow like sunshine, with lots of white trim. A sunshiny yellow to brighten it up is what I would like to see. I like green, but mom's favorite color was yellow.

For too many years the house on the corner, my home, has had a dark foreboding aura about it. It is one of those places that can go unnoticed if you don't know it's there.

Before my Mother's passing it was always cheerful, with lots of lights at Christmas time which were clearly visible when walking home on Main Street. The bushes were always trimmed low with lots of colorful flowers adorning the yard. Lacy curtains in lighted windows lighted the night with a warm glowing welcome. My home should have been pictured on a Hallmark Christmas card. Because of the offset in the street continuation, it stood out like a beacon of comfort from anyplace along Main Street.

Lakeport is my hometown and I liked growing up here, though I failed to realize it until I had gone off to further my education in the tradition of youthful pioneering spirit.

Upon my graduation from high school, my dad's most solemn promise was that my education was just beginning. I wonder if I shall tell that to my own children someday.

For a twenty four year old, I don't think I'm very bright. Oh, I get good grades all right, but I wonder if I really ever learn anything. Perhaps that is why I come home in times of trouble; "back to basics," so the saying goes.

Lakeport is, or was a small remote town, nestled on the shore, among the mountains of the Clear Lake Basin.

I can still walk or ride my bicycle anywhere, to the store, the park, to school, for Saturday night pizza and to the only movie theater. Always there is the scenery of the lake and the surrounding mountains with dramatic Mount Konocti looming in the distance. It is a good place for thinking while walking, getting one's motives and goals into clear focus; or I always thought so.

Sometimes when I walk, I think about the history of Lakeport. We like to call it the friendly city, where youngsters smile and speak cordially to adults and seniors. Except for the summer influx, we all know each other anyway. It was first named Forbestown, after William Forbes who settled here in 1858. In 1889 it was incorporated and just a few years later the name was changed to Lakeport, and in 1861 it was chosen as the county seat. The population in 1888 was a whopping eight hundred. Now, it is about five thousand.

The first pioneers who came to Scotts Valley were mostly itinerant trappers and hunters. That was about 1829 or 1830, and the first settlers came later.

If my memory works at all, it was the year of 1836 when General Mariana Vallejo led the first expedition of Mexican soldiers into the area from his headquarters at the Presidio in Sonoma.

In consideration for his effort General Vallejo's brother Captain Salvador Vallejo laid claim to the entire surface of the lake and all the lands surrounding it and the Grant became known as the Lup-Yomi Grant. The Spaniards treated the Indians kindly and found them to be extremely cooperative. For the first time the Indians were introduced to horses and guns.

For years it puzzled me that the lake had been named Clear Lake. As far back as I can recall the lake waters had always been a sort of brown or green with algae pockets over its surface. Of course there are some areas of clear water around uninhabited rocky shores.

When I asked Maria, she said that her ancestors told of times when it was as clear as crystal springs, and in the winter it used to freeze over so they could skate and walk on it.

But in my own lifetime I do remember when there was not a single traffic light or stop sign in the whole county. Now, it seems there are far too many.

There is no natural gas, nor is their a railroad. I hear there is plenty of natural gas, but piping among the mountainous terrain would make it prohibitively expensive considering the small comparative population.

Two out of four doesn't seem too bad, I guess. And who knows what the future holds. As for the present, I expect more traffic lights and stop signs.

At one time the whole county was the responsibility of a single sheriff, and then a sheriff and two deputies. Now my dad has eighty. Wow, how we have grown.

As for the railroad, they tried once in those early days only to be confronted by a pioneer woman named Narcissa Jones who bravely stood her ground with shotgun in hand until the surveyors were finally driven off. After that, some aggressive squatters tried to take over her land and she drove them away also. I have to wonder if they were put up to the scheme by the railroad people. Most of what I remember comes from school days, and of course there is no single hint of such a thing in the history books.

Dad was fond of limericks. He had a hundred of them and had no memory of where they came from. The one he used to recite about Mabel Jones always stuck in my mind.

It goes:

Here lie the bones of Mabel Jones
For her, life held no terrors,
Born a maid, died a maid,
No hits, no runs, no errors.

But for Narcissa Jones of Scotts Valley pioneer days, this limerick never seemed a fitting rhyme for so courageous a lady. She should have a different verse to mark her resting place. History tells us she was really no terror, but a gentle woman of good Christian stock, with an abiding sense of humor and everlasting determination, who only met terror when necessary and turned it away. She became a stalwart symbol of strength to her friends and neighbors and was an emotional support who could be counted on during trying times.

"My promise to you, Narcissa Jones is that I shall work on a more fitting epitaph to mark your memory."

And when I think of Scotts Valley I think of the Jones, the Hurts, and the Wardens, and the Scotts Valley murders. And most of all I think of Chester Cowan. The Chester Cowan of today. His ancestry goes way back and he is one of the few remaining to testify about those early pioneer days.

Dad usually refers to Chester as, "That crusty old fart." Dad should know crusty old farts if anyone does.

# SEVEN

Uh-oh, time to change those three S's from washer to dryer.

Back again.

In those good old days of my capricious youth there were a lot of stories about Chester floating about. I remember when I was sixteen and still in high school. It was Dad's first year as elected sheriff. You see, back then it was pretty common knowledge that Chester used to hunt ducks, pheasants, and anything else he chose to whenever he pleased, in or out of season. Pheasants were plentiful back then on his own property off Hendricks Canyon just a short distance off Scotts Valley Road. Ducks abounded along the lake.

He used a lever action twenty-two caliber rifle and only shot when they were in flight. Aiming at the tip of the beak, he always dropped them with the first shot, and always a head or eye hit. Chester never missed, so the rumor went.

There was also a story bouncing around; that Chester took part in a shooting demonstration once and had scored ninety nine consecutive hits in rapid fire sequence, the target being a small match or cartridge box, bouncing it about from point to point without actually hitting it. Each shot had to be timed so that the box was made to flip and jump about by the bullet striking the ground just under it, before it hit the ground. This was open sight shooting of course, and Chester could have hit the box at any time. But that would have ended the game. The only pause allowed was for reloading and tossing out a new box when necessary.

As for hunting pheasants, his strategy was the same. He shot only after flushing them and they were in flight.

Dad felt it was his personal duty to warn Chester that the use of solid bore rifles was against the law for hunting game birds.

The outcome was quite unpredictable. Chester, as it turned out was quite amiable, claiming that the use of shotguns for hunting birds was totally unsporting for the birds, and that he had decided not to hunt ducks or pheasants anymore because they were such beautiful creatures. He further told Dad that after killing the creatures he was always filled with remorse and guilt anyway.

From this simple declaration a bond of mutual respect developed, and I have always felt that was the reason Dad gave up duck hunting also.

I had heard so much about the Chester Cowan place and one Saturday when Dad was to visit there, by invitation of course, and unofficially, I pleaded and begged for him to take me along. I promised to listen and not to gawk and to clean and straighten my room, and not to stay on the telephone over five minutes. After all, I would have much to tell, for I was to be the only kid in school to have actually seen the Cowan place.

It was a strange and rewarding experience, and I kept every promise I made.

The entrance was through a long winding gravel course beneath low arched overhanging trees. I did gawk though, but only because I was captivated by the charm. It looked more like an oversized doll house sprouting to life from a small sized medieval castle. Something popping to life from out of a fairy tale book.

That was back a peice when Chester's wife Flora was still alive.

There it was tucked away, out of sight, at the end of a hidden canyon on a rising knoll, among unmolested, wooded hills surrounding it. A private place with bird-songs for music.

Now, sitting here, I still recall it as though it were yesterday, Chester dashing out to greet us with Flora waddling close at his heels. She was the grandmotherly type with silver hair in disarray, smelling of cake flour, almost toothless yet whole-some and merry.

I wiped the tears from my cheeks, recalling how I had cried when hearing two years later that she had died. Poor Chester.

Chester had to personally show me the house while Flora set out fresh milk and sugar cookies, all three floors with curved glass windows in the spire rooms and towers. Richardsonian Romanesque, he called it. The exterior was of an odd mixture of random uncut and cut stone. In the front there was an ornate balustrade porch, oval dormers at different angles, and a steeply pitched spire roof with a variety of arched windows. At one corner of the structure there was a spired tower with triple leaded glass windows while at the other corner there was a crenelated tower with its walk and look-out stretching above all other. The stories had failed miserably to do it justice. As for style though, it seemed more like a corruption of architecture than a specific design.

As for charm, it lacked nothing. Over-all the building seemed to have an imposing gothic majesty, with arched doorways inside at every room, and massive wooden beams sporting half finished Celtic carvings on them. There were several decorative stone fireplaces whose outside chimneys appeared held up by endless vines threatening to devour it.

Still, it had that gay storybook quality and flowery cheerfulness that spoke of Chester's family pride and Flora Cowan's personal touch.

Although it testified to a lifetime of effort there was no electricity nor running water. The Cowans needed none. The kitchen was a simple thing, reflecting a fundamental way of living. To the casual eye there seemed much pretense, yet these were not pretentious people. Everything held a purpose.

I was saddened to learn that rumors claimed that the place had fallen into a state of dire disrepair, taking on the eerie aura of a haunted manor.

Indeed, though I had been one of the few privileged to witness its life during that heyday, I will always remember it, even though it has come to be called that haunted place out in Scotts Valley.

Now that I have dwelled on it for awhile, I remember the pride in Chester's face as he told me how his grandfather, Ian Glamis McCowan had arrived here after traveling across the country before the turn of the century from Edinburgh, Scotland. He was not a young man then, and had worked as a stone mason and builder in the old country. In Scotts Valley he had found the place he had been searching for and had settled down immediately. In the process, he had taken a local woman for his wife from the pioneer stock of that time, and had started to build his castle. At that time the access had been from Scotts Valley Road, but after a fierce winter of storms a rock and mud slide had forced the access closure, and hence the present drive from Hendricks Road.

Chester's father's name was Keith McCowan, and later the Mc had been dropped. He said that Keith also was from a family surname of DeKeith from the Scottish/Norman clan which had fought with Robert The Bruce at the battle of Bannockburn in the year 1314.

There have been recordings that grizzly bears abounded in the Scotts Valley, and the Clear Lake Basin in those early pioneer days. The rumor goes that one morning back when Chester had just turned fourteen years old, he and his father had been awakened by the wild screaming sounds of one of his prized hogs. When father Keith, lantern in hand, went to investigate with young Chester close on his heels, they were greeted by the sight of a giant grizzly who had ripped down their fence and was in the process of chewing up one of their prize sows.

Keith wounded the grizzly forcing it to take off. That same morning as soon as light allowed, Chester and his father went hunting after the bear. Chester, who weighed no more than one hundred and ten pounds toted a double-barreled twelve gauge shotgun loaded with lead slugs.

The story goes that when they came upon the grizzly bear, the two had somehow gotten separated and when the wounded beast charged Chester, Keith found himself helpless, Chester being in his line of sight.

The bear charged Chester, and just a few feet before reaching him, reared up, giant clawed arms striking the air wildly and jaw opened wide with bared fangs. Chester stuck the muzzle in the bear's mouth and squeezed both triggers. The blast nearly tore the bear's head off, while the recoil knocked young Chester about ten feet backward, clearing him of the beast's clawing fall. Chester admits that he never has touched a shotgun since that time.

Today, Chester is only about five feet, six or seven, and weighs no more than one hundred thirty five pounds, but the bear was all of the eighteen hundred pounds it was claimed to be and I can vouch for that, because I saw the bearskin rug on the floor of the great room, stretched before the fire-place, and it did look as though the monstrous head might have been sewn back in place. However, when I asked Chester about it, Dad predictably nudged me, reminding me of my pledge while Chester smiled smugly and Flora, grinning toothlessly pushed the cookie plate to me.

The stories about the Cowan family followed that they had never worked at any job, so they must have found gold up there, at least enough to have built that mansion and not ever have had to work, other than by panning Hendricks creek, extracting it all before any reached Scotts Valley Creek.

However, no one has ever found proof that any gold or silver was ever found in the area.

When I visited there I do recall that there was a large well tended garden area, some fruit trees, a variety of domestic animals and a patch of wine grapes.

The whole place seemed to have an air of self-sufficiency about it. As for the claim that that was the last grizzly to be seen in the basin, I do believe it.

# EIGHT

The history of Scotts Valley started long before Chester's time, and even before Ian Glamis McCowan worked his way across the North Atlantic and the vast western plains in search of his own happy patch of earth.

Although the first pioneers were not settlers, they most assuredly left their mark on the land as a variety of hardy wandering men, explorers, hunters, and traders. There had been an abundance of deer, elk, and grizzly along with a full range of fur bearing animals which had lured them on. The wild vastness had then been free of feudal overlords and rights of ownership belonged to those strong enough to hold it. Nameless lakes such as Clear Lake teamed with varieties of fish and game now almost extinct.

Russian traders and trappers worked their way from Fort Ross and Bodega Bay to make brief contact with the Ka-Batin-Guy about 1830.

At that time the Spanish had found their way only as far as Sonoma and the Napa Valley.

From Oregon came the first Americans, hunters, trappers, and traders, and they too stayed only long enough to leave small memories.

In the year 1836, General Mariana Guadalupe Vallejo organized an expedition led by his brother, Captain Salvador Vallejo and Ramon Carillo. The Indians were introduced to cattle and horses for the first time and took to training as vaqueros as if born to the saddle.

In 1847 Vallejo departed after selling his herd of some eight hundred animals to two men named Stone and Kelsey.

I seems strange now, how I seem to recall all these forgotten details from my school days by just sitting and thinking about them.

Although the Indians had fared well enough with the Spaniards, Stone and Kelsey treated them cruelly and no better than slaves. They were forced to work for no pay and very little food.

I recall it now because the episodic sequence of events led to the massacre of Stone and Kelsey by a desperate and starving group of Indians from Scotts Valley after butchering a hog and eating it. When these Indians were finally overtaken and subdued at the junction of Scotts Valley and Blue Lakes Canyon they were herded back to the Kelsey Ranch where they were mistreated severely.

Order had been restored, but in 1849 the Indians could no longer tolerate the abuses and the tribe became aroused and rebelled in anger.

The story goes that an old squaw woman filled Kelsey and Stone's guns with water, and while they were having breakfast the Indians attacked.

Kelsey was the first to be caught and killed with an arrow, while Stone, running up the stairs, leaped from a window and ran up Kelsey Creek to hide among the tules, only to be discovered by another Indian who beat him to death by bashing his head in with a rock.

The reason I mention this event is because it was this very incident that ultimately led to the *Bloody Island Massacre*, mentioned by my Dad and Ned Turner.

The Indians having at last freed themselves of their tormentors moved back into the Scotts Valley and Upper Lake area and proceeded to celebrate their freedom.

How were they to know that their hard won liberty was to be so short lived? When a detachment of soldiers caught up with them, they were surprised and scattered. I always wondered how anyone could have known what must have happened. Anyway, many of them got away and collected, for safety's sake on an island at the north end of the lake, which in winter and spring was surrounded by deep water. When the soldiers fired on them their shots fell short, and the Indians gathered along the shore of the island, dancing, laughing and jeering. To the Indians the whole affair must have seemed like a game of catch-me-if-you-can. Two whale-boats with cannons were brought in over Howell Mountain on the first wagons in the Lake Basin and assembled at the lower end of the lake.

While the soldiers resumed their attack on one shore the Indians gathered to laugh at them and were attacked by the boats and cannons from the opposite end. The assault proved to be a complete surprise and when the Indians tried to escape by swimming to the mainland the soldiers slaughtered them unmercifully.

The soldiers tirade of butchery continued on to Potter Valley, Ukiah, and finally south along the Russian River to Santa Rosa, Sonoma and back to Benicia.

The island, though connected now to the mainland is still known as Bloody Island and is marked by an historic stone and plaque. A short time later the remaining Indians were summoned to the Kelsey Ranch and treated to a feast and signing of a peace treaty.

Unlike the first white men who came after the Spaniards, hunters and explorers who moved on after a short interlude, William Scott came to the valley to stay. He arrived in the valley in 1848 and although he stayed only a few short years, he was the first to live there and give the valley its name. He built a cabin on the west side of Scotts Creek at the foot of a hill.

Until 1853 no others left any trace until Thomas Jefferson Warden came, bringing with him cattle, horses, and other domestic stock.

I don't know why this issue of Scotts Valley history so dominates my thoughts right now. Perhaps it comes to mind from school days of local history, or perhaps it is the memory of

Flora and Chester Cowan that triggered the opening of that often elusive trapdoor to the sub-conscious mind, and thereby freeing tidbits of forgotten stories and information.

"Uh-oh, the dryer's done again."

"I'm back, now where was I?" Oh yes, 1853. In 1853 Tom Warden built a cabin, the third, I think, not counting those built by Vallejo, and Kelsey and Stone.

In the years that followed more people arrived, and in 1859 while attending a horse race where the Lake County Fairgrounds now stands, Jack Hurt and Tom Warden got into an argument in which Jack Hurt stabbed Warden in the throat and killed him. The Hurts, as I recall, were reputed as terrors of the valley at that time.

There were many settlers by then, such as a Frenchman by the name of Fournier. There was also Joseph Jones Hendricks who settled up in the canyon where the creek and road still bear his name.

Then there was C.G. Cord, or was it G.C. Cord, that one escapes me. I think he was a blacksmith, and his party included a man named Odom, and their wives.

John Waller was another name I remember now, along with Callahan, Stevens, Gordon and Morrison.

There was Alec Tate, son-in-law of John Waller. But if in those days when Scotts Valley grew by leaps and bounds, Lakeport grew even more.

By 1888, the two combined sported a population of seven hundred. In those days it must have seemed that Lakeport and Scotts Valley were one and the same. Space must have seemed smaller with property lines uncertain and with descriptions by leaps and bounds, or point-to-point, from a tree to a rock and along a creek with an ever changing boundary.

With prospects of gold others poured in, claim jumping and squatting on what were thought to be established lines.

Young John Waller was too easy going and when J.D. Stevens jumped a portion of his land he did nothing. But, when squatters attempted the same on Narcissa McCabe-Jones she proved not as easy a mark. She was a resolute woman of religious stock, and she ran them off with her shotgun. She was also a courageous woman, so the story goes, and always ready to help her neighbors in trouble and in sickness, with little sympathy for bullies. It was Narcissa who confronted the railroad surveyors day after day, shotgun in hand when they attempted to cross her land.

There should be a more fitting limerick in her honor. "Narcissa, I'm working on it."

As for homicides, there was that first recorded murder of J.T. Warden by Jack Hurt at the race track in 1859. In April, 1860 when Jack Hurt was in jail awaiting trial he dug a hole through the wall and escaped. In 1873 Jack Hurt was once again captured and when he stood trial the charges were dis-missed for lack of evidence and witness availability.

If my memory serves me at all, I think it was April, 1861 when a quarrel erupted between Farrell and Holman over a property line dispute, and after several confrontations, Farrell shot Holman in the head. Farrell was arrested and brought to speak before the Grand Jury. Since there were no witnesses and Farrell claimed self-defense the case was summarily dropped and he was released.

Later in 1867, I think it was, there was the killing of John Rhodes by Charles Coram. Young Coram lived alone with his mother and John Rhodes was reportedly abusive towards them, the mother in particular, until one day young Coram was prepared when Rhodes came to their cabin. The story goes, that both men drew their revolvers, and Young Coram being the quicker and more accurate shot Rhodes to death.

Then there was the case of Daniel Wedig, Dutch Dan he was called, who was killed by Indian Tom. . .that was 1870—.

I always wondered if the people in this remote settlement had been aware that a civil war of so much consequence had recently been fought some two thousand miles to the east.

Anyway, the next recorded killing was of Sheriff Kemp in May of. . .1910. I remember that one in particular because the thought struck me fearfully, and because the subject came up while Mom was still alive. Dad had tried to minimize the impact, and explained that he had studied the case thoroughly, and that Sheriff Kemp had acted foolishly by confronting the renegades alone and without declaring himself.

It had caused me considerable anxiety, and because my dad was sheriff, I had looked it up, and because occasionally differences between the law and the local Indians had a way of breaking spontaneously.

This one was different in that the times were so diverse then compared to now. I like to believe there is a measure of sanity in our law and order now, and those bloody, foolish confrontations are a thing of the past.

Anyway, the whole thing started when a small group of Indians had decided to pursue the renegade scenario, and stole some horses and saddles. A posse was formed the very next day and soon the trail was picked up. It was soon learned that the Indians had also acquired some guns and ammunition. Eventually, the trail led to a campsite where the stolen horses were tethered, and when the posse spread out, the sheriff was left alone. When the Indians returned unexpectedly, Kemp attempted to face them alone and was shot.

Later, the entire band of would-be renegades was captured, and of the two leaders; Augustine, who had fired the fatal shot was sentenced to hang and the other, an Indian named Moore was sentenced to life in prison.

I recall Dad saying, that the two Indians had returned to the reservation where they were captured, and for awhile the whole tribe had become quite hostile, and for a time it was a touch and go situation.

Hop barns in those days were the usual scene for community dances and gatherings. There were bitter rivalries and fist fights often broke into threatening quarrels, especially after imbibing too much whiskey.

In the same year. . . 1890, one of those confrontations did get out of hand with Will Stevens and Jim Farrell threatening to kill each other; when Stevens waited along the road one day and shot Jim Farrell. Men are so insensible when it comes to handling their tempers while we girls just cry and pull hair. When will they learn?

I have to wonder what, if any of this has to do with the mysterious death of those four duck hunters Dad and Ned Turner told me about.

I do recall a more recent incident at the fairgrounds one weekend of the races when a bunch of Indians in the top rows of the bleachers became rowdy. A city police officer named Bud Lassiter foolishly attempted to quiet them down alone, and was thrown bodily down the steps, putting him in the hospital with multiple fractures and bruises, summarily ending his law enforcement career.

Sheriff's deputies had to be called in for and it was my dad's level headed approach that finally settled the affair.

For the Indians, it was not a malicious act. They simply got carried away and reacted as if they were playing in a game. I wonder if in the days of their ancestors, before the introduction of alcohol if they had been more casual and reasonable about their athletic endeavors.

When I was a little girl, I had heard stories about a big Indian named Steve Raymond from the southern end of the lake who was noted for feats of strength and physical prowess, especially while touring the bars and drinking. It seems he got himself into regular quarrels and when an offended man left the bar and returned with a shotgun, Steve Raymond grabbed the weapon and bent the barrel around his own neck into a *U-shape*, then gave it back with instructions to shoot it now.

That too, just goes to show how an incident or playful situation can suddenly evolve into a serious situation if not handled carefully.

Oh God! Look at the time. It's after five o'clock. Oh well, looks like this pen is going dry too. Think I'll take a stroll in town, get a hamburger or something, maybe stop by Emile's shop.

# NINE

Dear diary: I've got it;

Here lies the bones of Narcissa Jones,
For some, pioneer life was a terror.
But, woe be to those
Who step on her toes,
She was good news
to her family and neighbors.

I hope you like it, Narcissa. As I walked the words kept playing around in my head like a jumble of syllables tumbling about, seeking a place and rhythm to settle into. It was a silly thing, but it was stimulating and exciting and fun and somewhere about Saint Mary's Catholic Church, suddenly it was there, after seeking its own order.

Puff-puff; not having anything to write it down on or with, I almost ran all the way home. To record it, seemed at the time so urgent and commanding, yet now that I see it written down on paper, the silly thing seems so dumb. I hope no one ever reads it.

The sun was already setting when I had finally left my humble abode. I had hurried along Main Street as if rushing for an important appointment, trying not to notice cars driven by teens with their mega XX boom boxes blasting their insolent noise pollution, the young male drivers staring, appraising, and seeming to shout; "Look at me! Look at me! Ain't I something?"

It is hard for me to believe I was that age once, loud and obnoxious, but boom-boxes weren't the *IN thing*, then.

At 162 Main Street I found myself staring hopefully into the window of Emile's shop. There was a single accent light focused on the pair of miniature mandarin ducks. They had a certain appearance so lively and vital, yet peaceful and serene, as all the others seemed poised and shrouded in half darkness, while the eagle hovered above silent and brooding and ready to strike. Even the great horned owl seemed awakened, lurking and threatening somehow.

In the corner, the pair of pintails had appeared to be lurching into flight, as if startled by the monster, predator eagle.

My eyes fastened on the mandarins once again, by comparison, so casual and at ease, yet at an instant's cue they too might disappear dramatically. No doubt about it, they are my favorites.

The sign in the door glass read, "Closed," but I tried the knob anyway. I had wanted to call out. Until that moment I had not realized just how much I had hoped he would be there.

After waiting a bit, I strolled casually down the block past the video store and the bar and finally crossed at the corner. Once across Main Street, I paused before the bakery window with the days left over cakes and pastries discharging their sweet scent of cinnamon and toasty spices wafting through the door. A sign in the door declared it was also closed. For that few minutes I realized I was not only hungry, I was famished.

Back along the same block, and across from Emile's, I paused before the lighted windows of the ice cream parlor. A group of children were busy, laughing and enjoying their Friday night treats.

For a time I forgot my hunger and crossed the street to stand in front of Emile's carving shop once again.

If only he could have been there, I would gladly eat anything he offered. No doubt his diet consisted of bland tasteless stuff made with unrefined flour, no sugar and all natural unprocessed foods. And, absolutely no chemicals. Fresh fruit would be his dessert, perhaps with cottage cheese or yogurt, or a salad maybe with light oil, or steamed vegetables, whole grains, seeds, nuts and berries. Everything natural. He was that type, so lean and yet vigorously healthy, not a sign of anemia. He was good looking in a clean-cut sort of way, quiet, sensual and erotic. But, Emile had deserted me, and just then I could willingly have knocked down any old lady for a donut.

Back across Main Street to the ice cream parlor I went, for a big double dip of dense creamy, high butterfat, high cholesterol stuff that clings to the thighs. Isn't it written somewhere in stone that ice cream is definitely medicinal?

For some inexplicable reason, I found myself strolling to the park, hoping I suppose, that Emile might be there feeding the ducks.

He was not.

However, I watched from a distance as two young mothers chatted mindfully over their children who played energetically among the recently installed slides and ladders, tossing sand about and having a ball. One child lost her shoe and started crying while a sibling mischievously buried it. Both of the mothers I remember from high school days. Both had been two years behind me, and now they were obviously married young mothers with families, momentarily detached while their husbands, also familiar, sat nearby on benches guzzling beer and scarfing down pizza. At home they probably hollered, "Get the kids out of here. Can't you see I'm tryin to watch football?"

I started over. I was sure they would remember me, and no doubt ask, "Kitty, how good to see you. What are you doing these days? What? You're not married? No children? Oh how sad."

Once more the mood was suddenly interrupted by none other than Orin Big Balls Kenny. He pulled up behind me in a patrol car. Maria came out of the passenger side, stretching, "Hello, Kitty," she said, with a smile on her face that said she felt pleased with herself. B.B. got out, stretched lazily, and leaned on the open door, "Wha cha doin all alone"

"Just out for a little walk," I said.

B.B. managed a couple more stretches and went back to leaning on the door, one foot crossed casually over the other, a smug cynical look on his face, police chatter spilling from the radio in the background. He said, "I got this story for ya."

"Nooo," I got out, glumly.

". . .You'll like it."

"But you're going to tell it anyway, huh?"

"This young couple decided to go on the AMTRAK train for their honeymoon, see. And, that night the husband gives his shoes to the porter to have them shined and polished."

"Polished and shined. . ."

"Huh? Yeah, but he tells the porter don't bother them that night cause they're on their honeymoon, see, just leave the shoes outside the door. He'll get them in the morning. Well, in the morning, he says, 'Honey, reach outside the door and get my shoes, will ya?' Well, she does but the train lurches, sending her stumbling into the hallway, the door slams and locks, and there she is, standin alone naked in the hall with only this pair of man's shoes in her hands. This drunk comes staggering down the hallway towards her, and she doesn't know what to do, so she's standin there like this, like a statue, holdin the man's shoes in front of her bush. . . And the drunk wobbles on by her, then he stops, and turns back to look at her. You know what he says—?"

"You're going to tell me, right. No don't. . ."

"He says, ''That's the way buddy, give her all you got.' She's standin there like this, get it, ha ha, get it?"

"Maria," I said, "How do you put up with this jerk?"

Maria just smiled generously.

"Come on Kitty, cheer up," B.B. pleaded. "Wanna hear another one?"

"No."

"Just a little one. No four letter words, promise. . . There's these two black kids layin across the railroad tracks, screwin away, see?"

"B.B., there's no railroad in Lake County."

"Somewhere else. Doesn't matter where. Anyway the train comes tootin along, and the engineer sees these two kids screwin on the tracks and he blasts away on his whistle, but they don't stop. He blows the whistle again, and they keep on screwin, and he blows the whistle and starts puttin on the brakes. . . Till the train comes up to them in a screeching halt, just inches from them, see? The man gets out, walks over to them, and waits and waits till they finish, and when they finally do he asks them; what's the matter with you? Didn't you hear me comin, blowin my whistle? . . .And you know what the black guy says?"

"Never mind."

"He says, Mister Conductor, it's like this, see; 'yuse is a comin. I's is a comin and she's a comin. . . an yuse is de ony one gots brakes. . . Brakes!' Get it? Ha-ha."

I shook my head in disgust. "B.B., you're an impossible clod. Maria, how can you stand this—?"

"Sorry, gotta go. There's our code. See ya later Kitty. Let's hit it Maria."

It was really on the way back home when the jingle about Narcissa came to life in my head. Perhaps B.B. really did have something to do with lightening the mood.

Dear diary: Orin Big Balls is really not a bad guy, I guess, but his abrasive manner grates on me like a dentist's drill on a raw nerve.

He thinks he is God's gift to women, and has tried to get in my pants in the most obscene and crudest ways. Sometimes I wish he would come right out and ask so I could put an end to it by plainly saying, NO. Forget it.

He always catches me off guard, like in an ambush, when my defenses are down, and I always over-react, and then I reproach myself. And here I'm the one who's supposed to be the psychologist.

Dad seems to think B.B. is a good cop. At times I think he is a little vague on the *good* part though.

End of diary note.

Over the years I have found my diary to be a great companion, and yet when the pen is set down, and the cover closed, I find myself unprepared for another desolate evening alone and sadly neglected. In search of some cheering up I scanned the channels for old re-runs of Barney Miller and WKRP- Cincinnati, knowing all too well that before long I will fall away into a contorted sleep.

Instead of comedy, I found one of those vintage movies; *Hold Back The Dawn*, where romantic tragedy plays on the impressionable mind in a mixture of fantasy and reality. Although I had seen it before, I found myself hanging on every word as Olivia de Haviland, the essence of the naive school marm crashes her vintage convertible and winds up on the hospital death bed. Can you ever really imagine Olivia de Haviland being taken advantage of? And yet she does the vulnerability bit so convincingly, and always captivates her man, no matter how much of a rogue he is. And imagine too, all this drama after having gotten rid of her class of spoiled brats. . .and Charles Boyer, the con-man/gigolo comes to his senses in time to save her. Ah, such honest tear-jerking romantic drama. They just don't make them that way anymore.

I was dreaming of my Charles Boyer, Emile, when Father woke me and sent me stumbling off to my bed.

# TEN

While Dad slept like an old bear, I was out early. I left a note:

Dear Daddy,
Gone canoeing with Emile. Love ya. Kitty.

I felt like a silly teenager again leaving home on her first adventure, walking along deserted Main Street toting a Kmart shopping bag filled with last night's pancakes. Simple fare for ducks who prefer graham crackers and blueberry specialties.

On my feet I wore an old pair of sneakers. As an extra protection against the morning chill I wore a peach colored Adidas jogger set, to be shed later, should the Sun God favor us with some day-time warmth. Beneath those I had on a pair of those satin lime-green running shorts, the loose flouncy kind, and for a top I wore a hot pink halter. Although the nights are usually cool and misty, day-time in the fall at Clear Lake can be surprisingly warm, like summer, and who knows when one might like to go swimming.

At 5:30 a.m. I found myself at his door, a time I can't remember being out of bed before. The sign still read CLOSED, but another hand printed note read: Gone for the day.

This time, when I tried the door, I found it unlocked, so I stepped in and called out; "Hello, I'm here." Once again I found my eyes fixed on the pair of miniature mandarins while the accent light was still focused on them. For some reason the eagle seemed less threatening. Perhaps it was the morning hour, when all creatures should be asleep, except bass fishermen, of course.

I wondered how I might begin to describe something so vividly colorful and indescribably beautiful. The warm eyes sensed my closeness and dared me to touch, and when I did pet the drake's head I was momentarily shocked when it remained unmoved. I wondered how Cuddles might react if turned loose in the shop among so much prey.

"I'll be down in a minute," came the voice from somewhere above the back shop.

Suddenly, in my spellbound state he appeared there, as if materializing in the doorway, dropping bundles, and two sleeping bags I noticed. I wonder if he used his creations to narcotize his victims before seduction. I must have stared because he said; "Oh these, something to sit on, or lay down on, sort of like for a picnic." Then he added a small grin.

There lingered that sense of threat and warning after my recent betrayal. How could I explain that if suddenly he wanted me, and I with all my resistance shot to the wind. I asked, "Do you live back there?"

"I have a small studio loft above the shop. I built it in myself, with a shower." He turned his head indicating with a gesture, "There's a half bath in there. The only access is a retractable ladder, and there's only one small dormer window. It looks out over the lake. I find it very cozy and perfect for my needs."

I wanted so badly to ask him to show it to me but decided prudence was a better policy for the time being.

"I was just admiring the Mandarins. They're so beautiful, I had to touch them. I hope you don't mind."

In an instant he had moved to stand beside me. Picking them up, he turned the pair artfully in the light.

"In Asia where they come from, they are considered a sign of felicity in art form. They have been greatly prized from ancient times." His eyes latched on to mine for a moment. . . "These are a little smaller than actual life size, four-fifths scale actually. I think it gives them a delicate and even more desirable presence, don't you think?"

"Definitely, desirable. . .endearing too. They're my favorites, without a doubt. And, I love the cute little curl in his tail-feathers. . ."

"They're yours. They should belong to you."

"Oh no, I couldn't accept, they're too valuable, and I couldn't afford to pay. . ."

"Nonsense, it's more important to me that they go to someone who will value and cherish them."

When he handed them to me I was afraid to touch them. They seemed so unexpectedly delicate and fragile, my hands suddenly became clammy. I rotated them a few degrees to study the small brass nameplate which read simply; "Felicity, by Emile." Beside that I read from a small white sticker, drawing it closer to be sure, then instantly I winced, *$2500.00.*

"Oh my God," I cried. "I can't accept this. It's too valuable." Very quickly, he peeled the price tag off and wadded it up, hidden in his hand.

"I am sorry," I said, my voice hopelessly stunned. "It is just too generous of you, and it is absolutely too valuable. I had no idea they sold for that much," I stammered on; "I couldn't even afford it if I sold my five year old Camaro, which I need badly. . . Do you really sell them for that much? Oh, I am sorry, I mean, of course they are worth every bit of that, even more." Something inside my feeble brain told me to shut up.

"In a Nantucket gallery they bring $4500.00, but of course the gallery operator gets forty percent. Anyway, I can make others, and I don't expect you to pay for them. They're a gift."

I was staring into his eyes, sorry for the pain, "They're just too valuable. . .you don't even know me."

"You sure know how to shatter a guy's ego, you know? I may go into self-destruct, all the way around go, to jail, do not collect $200.00. How can I believe in selling them, when I can't even give them away?"

"I'll never forget this gesture," I said, wiping the tears from my cheeks. He was like a hurt little boy, and I wanted so desperately to grab him, and hold him close. Reeling, I hesitated. In that instant of hesitation, he replaced the pair to their resting spot, saying; "They are here until you are ready for them. But, they're yours. Not for sale."

Then, he went on, as if still trying to sell me on the idea. He was saying, "These are Carolina wood ducks, close cousins to the Mandarin, see how they even look alike. The females are almost identical, yet the two species never inter-breed. Maybe that is why they have kept their unique color distinctions. The Mandarins real home is in China and Japan where they are a familiar sight on ornamental ponds. Of all the duck species, the Mandarin is the most cherished, for the joy and serenity they symbolize. . ."

"I can believe that," I said in a soft small voice.

"In China they were given as wedding presents to symbolize marital fidelity," he said pausing.

"Always in pairs?"

"Always."

"The Carolina wood ducks were hunted almost to extinction. . . at one time."

"Oh no, what a disaster. But why?" I knew the probable why, but I wanted to hear it from him.

He shrugged sadly, as if experiencing some personal loss. "Because they were easy targets, I suppose, and more likely because their plumage suited some inescapable need for decoration."

"How sad. . ."

"They're under federal protection now, and making a comeback."

"I don't understand it, hunting I mean. Like destroying something of value, for no good reason, for a simple thrill of the moment, like killing something of value, like destroying a part of oneself, don't you think?"

Together, we walked the short block down to Willow Point Campground, just across from Library Square amid a shroudy mist, and without meeting a single soul.

He pushed the canoe to the water's edge and started loading it. "Here, you can sit up front," he said. "Are you a good swimmer?"

"Yes." I answered positively, recalling my days in Clear Lake High School as a competition swimmer. Thanks to the swimming program, I had earned my share of medals.

"Here's a life jacket. You can wear it if you want, but we're not likely to get wet, and with you up front I can control the craft better from the rear. You did say you have done this before?"

"I lied," I said, blushing like I was caught and confessing a crime, and I was not, for the moment hidden in the security of a confessional where penance will pay for the sin. That boyish smile of his reduced my guilt to the level of child's play somewhat, but when I took the first step in I knew that I was completely and utterly beyond my element. I very nearly tipped it over, splashing in at that instant, and would have, had not Emile saved me by steadying the craft. I stumbled and struggled so awkwardly until finally settling uneasily onto the front seat. "I didn't know it could be so tricky," I confessed, in an effort to sound amusing. "It feels like it wants to flip over."

"I know," he said, his tone of voice consoling, in an effort to fortify my confidence. "It's sort of like riding a bicycle. When resting still it is difficult to balance because you have no forward motion. Once we're in motion it becomes easier, like second nature."

"Do we have to be so close to the water, I mean won't we get swamped?"

"Don't worry, you're a good swimmer," he chuckled.

"I don't want to swim now. It's too cold."

"Here then," he said, shoving the canoe back to shore. "Step out for a minute." I had forgotten he was calf deep in the water. He held out a hand and once again the awkward process began in reverse.

I stood watching, and it was then that I realized what the sleeping bags were for. With the two sleeping bags, one on top of the other, he fashioned a cushion seat and backrest so I could now sit down on the bottom, facing him.

"Try this," he said. "With your weight on the bottom you'll balance better, and I'll do the paddling."

"Hmm, very comfortable," I said, complimenting him. Then he pushed off and stepped in so smoothly that I hardly felt a shake. In that same instant he was thrusting along with a deep steady rhythm while I relaxed, confident in his world. He shifted from one foot to the other, and then the paddle, two to three strokes on one side and then back to the other. He smiled and gave me a wink, then returned his gaze back to some fixed target, or landmark in the hazy distance.

All at once we were gliding along smoothly with a sensation of moving much greater than I had anticipated. I was keenly aware of the whisper of a trailing wake behind us, ours, the only disturbance of an otherwise glassy water.

"Do I get a serenade?" I teased. Actually it was more like begging; for at that moment a ride with a Venetian boatman poised at the helm had entered my mind. A gondola ride in Venice could in no way be more soothing.

The response caused me to erupt into childish laughter. He sang for me in a mournful, throbbing oscillation: Quack-quack. . . quack, quack-quack. . . quack-quack. . ."

"And just what does that mean?" I chuckled, struggling to hold back a convulsion. "In duck language, that is?"

"It is from an old love song. It means, *My prayer, is to linger with you. . .till the end of each day. . .when my heart kneels to pray.*"

# ELEVEN

To my surprise, I soon learned that beneath that bulky Cardinal sweatshirt and loose jeans Emile was a finely tuned specimen of sinewy strength and masculine energy.

It was after some time of steady stroking when he rested the paddle to shed his threadbare sweatshirt, tossing it casually to the floor of the canoe. The act was accomplished without ceremony. Sweat beads had formed on an almost smooth chest. In that pause he smiled at me casually, big blue eyes, deep in thought and filled with concealed purpose. The craft had merely slowed in its glide to a temporary drift amid placid waters.

Then, just as easily he resumed the steady rhythmic paddling with determined conviction, and the canoe seemed to respond by planing to a predetermined direction .

"I was a little warm," he said plainly.

By now I was wrapped in a cocoon of gentle persuasion, comforted by the gliding motion, watching that ever youthful, yet smooth leathery quality of his skin, and his energy working me like a hypnotic massage. At that moment he appeared as though he could be ageless, and that he might never have to shave.

I must have had a glow on, for I felt a sudden impulse to join in the venture. "I'd like to try it now," I said, "the paddling." His making it look so easy gave me a sense of confidence.

"Okay," he said. "Just turn around and climb in."

I did get turned around, sort of, half kneeling, one leg half over the seat, half facing forward, one foot on the paddle, then the sleeping bags shifted and when I tried to climb over the whole thing became impossibly unsteady. "I think I'll wait till we hit land somewhere," I said.

He chuckled, "We're about half way now. . . There, straight ahead, in that patch of shrouded mist. The fog should lift before long."

I thought briefly how the time had passed without any sensation of measure, as if the suspension was never ending.

"It all looks the same to me, Mount Konocti in the background with a crown of creeping fog like a gigantic cotton night-cap overfull and melting down along the side slopes, "They say, when Konocti is clouded over we'll get rain. Do you believe that?"

"It is an old saying the Indians have, I think. I've never taken count, but the old timers swear by it."

Of all the years living here, until this moment I had never before felt the need to describe this place, I thought, this wonder of a mountain basin with its scenic water. If only I had my diary I could record my impressions.

It seemed like a rare experience, my secret place now, peaceful and quiet where time remained suspended, an escape from the rude intrusion of noise polluters, the annoying bombardment of mega-bass-boom-boxes, no barking dogs and screeching tires. A place devoid of conflict and threat, of peace and quiet.

"It's the musical sound of the wilderness," he said. "Can you hear it?"

"Yes," I agreed. "Like the sound of silence. I had no idea it could be so serene." The soothing rhythm of stroking paddles like soft beating drums blended with the gentle steady hiss of waking water like whispering voices from a background accompaniment.

"Is it always like this, in the morning I mean?"

"This time of year, yes mostly, except for occasional screaming of bass boats in a hurry to get someplace else. In the summer of course, there are always the jet skis and hot boats."

I could feel the vitality of his energy touching me inside in some wholesomely different way.

It had been an unbelievable five to six miles across infinity toward the fog bank, now already thinning in a process of breaking up. The body of water called Clear Lake is somewhat kidney shaped with this being the larger end, and beyond, past Konocti and the narrow isthmus which separates the two main bodies, the smaller end and the Anderson Marsh Wildlife Refuge. Overall it is approximately twenty six miles long. Across from Lakeport and approximately eight miles of water lies sleepy Lucerne along the shore, and to the north, Nice and just a little ways beyond; Rodmans Slough,a popular locale for fishing and duck hunting. On clear days you can see the massive old white mansion resort on the slopes above Lucerne. I felt I was awakening from a deep sleep to discover a vast new world. It seems so ironic that one's world is so small when so much awaits the perceptive eye. The thin layer of dissolving fog was now dividing into pockets of stubborn mist.

For a moment I considered the casual smoke chimney off to the distant orchard flatland where scrap burning was a regular seasonal occurrence, and the only sign of life since departing the shores of Lakeport.

There were dramatic mountain levels and land masses from each shore reaching out to touch each other where that narrow water passage to the small end of the kidney shape hides from view. Some have likened the lake to a tooth with the larger end representing the crown and the smaller legs the roots.

Emile was saying: "If this were summer you might get to witness an osprey gliding overhead, wings spread gracefully while scanning the shallows, circling dogmatically for an unwary fish-meal. They've gone south now, they will return in the spring." He pointed shoreward to a flock of screeching sea gulls working behind the path of coots for a morning meal.

I watched, and he said, "Over there it is. From here Quercus Island is becoming more evident even though it still appears more like part of the main shoreline than a separate island. Yet, when the fog lifts it is still not much. . . three to four acres, depending on the water level. There are a few sheltering willow trees, a rocky outcrop at the center, surrounded by tall tules. It lies only about two hundred yards off the drooping fingertip of Quercus Point."

I had twisted about to support myself on the seat while he described it, then I turned back to face him staring once again at the dramatic Mount Konocti with its gentle slopes and inviting hollows. "I've heard it said that Konocti would make a good ski resort, if only we had enough snow."

"Dreamers," he mused.

I thought of something that Maria had told me in confidence one time. She and other Indians among her tribe thought it would be considered silly, and so it was never repeated. The story goes that some of the local Indians used to believe the spirits of worthy individuals dwelled within great caverns inside Mount Konocti, waiting there in a paradise like existence until their time for rebirth. The myth was not commonly known, she had said.

I had tried to look it up but found no recording of it, and I was saddened to think that so many old folklore beliefs were lost for lack of simple recording.

Geologists claim there is proof that Clear Lake is one of the oldest lakes in the world. Some even claim it is the oldest.

I found myself remembering a poem from my school days. I said to Emile, "Have you heard this? It's called, Clearlake:

"When the Red men first came here
They asked the spirit for a name,
Came the answer from within
"Call the waters Ka-Batin.
Where the mountains touch the sky,
Let the name be Konocti.
Where the straits unite the three,
Call the place Kono Tayee.

Where the nets with fishes swell,
Let the place be called Ka-Bel"
But the white man prove to take,
Called the waters all; Clear Lake.
They should be as they were then,
Now and ever, Ka-ba-tin."

"A local historian named Henry Mauldin recorded the verse, but he credits a man named Rodman for writing it though. There is one version about the legend of Konocti that I recall, perhaps because it is the most romantic and tragic, and of course I am a true romantic at heart.

Anyway, the story tells of an Indian chief named Konocti who had a beautiful daughter named Lupiyoma who loved another younger chief by the name of Ka-bel from a neighboring rival tribe. However, her father, Konocti, disapproved of Ka-bel who also loved Lupiyoma and sought her hand in marriage. The matter was to be settled by trial of single combat between the two chiefs. In the end both were so badly wounded that they both died, and when Lupiyoma found them on the mountain top, she fell into crying over their bodies and she also died. Her tears flowed to form the big water, Ka-batin.

After reading it so many times I found it the most touching. There are other more elaborate ones, but this one remains my favorite.

I said to Emile, "Do you believe that Lupiyoma's tears formed Clear Lake?"

He flashed a jovial grin, "Could be."

"Do you believe there are great caverns inside Mount Konocti where the Indian Spirits dwell?"

"I've heard that one too. Do you want to go there and find out?"

"Will you take me?"

"It is a secret way known only to a few," he said with a mischievous pressing stare.

"Are you being facetious?"

"Aren't we both?"

"I admit it. I am an incurable romantic, but I don't know about you."

"There it is just ahead. I have a narrow path worked through the tules. It's a secret way known only to a few. You may get in, but you may never get out."

"I'm scared."

"Who's jesting now?"

I like this game, I thought. "I suppose you are going to tell me that for a price you could get me released."

"For a price. . . I might pass on the magic words. Okay now, here we are, I'll make a run at it. When we hit ground you can jump out. . ."

"I don't know about this. But I do need the stretch. . . Does it have a bathroom? What's that noise?"

They came in a great rush, waddling, quacking, and leaping into flight. "Is this our welcoming committee?" I shouted above the din of quack-sounds and wing flapping.

"Something like that, or maybe it is the pancakes and graham crackers."

"It seems I've said this before, but I think they know you."

He carried on with the story, raising his voice above the chatter; "Have you heard that Quercus Island is a sacred place where the spirits return periodically on their journey to rebirth? These spirits guard this place against evil because it is hallowed ground to them. . ."

"Are you making all this up, or do you expect me to believe you? If it is so sacred, then how come you can come here?"

"I have the password, *mot de passé*."

"Is that French?"

"I think so. Anyway, it works, most duck hunters don't dare to come near the place."

"Word gets around, huh?"

"Or something. . ."

"And I suppose you had nothing to do with it, right?"

We were still sort of shouting above the noise, having just made our way through the tule entrance when we were greeted by what appeared to be the formal welcoming committee. The quacking and wing flapping had reached a feverish pitch by the time we had touched ground. There were white pekins and buffs, as Emile had called them, Jason I recognized right away as he made his way to the front of the flock to tug anxiously at Emile's pant leg. Mostly they were mallards, drakes of magnificent color who leaped into the air, showing us their aerial acrobatics. The hens were not to be outdone, also flying about with such carefree abandon. Some were diving like daredevils, almost like crashing into the water. Roughhousing adolescents I presumed. They seemed proud and intent on outdoing each other for our benefit, almost crashing into the water at breakneck speed, drawing up at the very last instant to skid along on webbed feet.

"That's quite a reception committee," I shouted to be heard above the cheerful sounding chatter.

Jason, with a few of his friends, was already attacking the unopened bags of food with what seemed to me like excessive vigor.

"Yes, they do seem to know you," I shouted even louder.

That's when he turned to me, his eyes fixed on mine in a pressing gaze. I felt the deep, penetrating shock, engulfing, mesmerizing.

He said, "These are my cousins. . . In another life, I was a duck."

"You're joking," I gulped, but he just smiled intently.

# TWELVE

He had opened the bag and was busy tossing bits of dried bread and pancakes to the flock gathered about his feet. "Now don't fight," he warned in a quacking language intermixed with their own anxious chatter. He knelt down as many more gathered to feed from his hand. "Good morning, Jason," he quacked, or at least I thought I understood his odd blather. "Xanthroppe, what did I tell you about biting?" he said, then turning to wink at me, he added; "She's an old shrew, be careful of her, she nips, mostly the others wing feathers so it disrupts their flying stability. She is the wife of Socrates, and there is Plato close by. And that one with the big flirty eyes, I call Nymph."

"Nymph," Very interesting I said, trying an edge of innocence with my voice.

"Nymph. Come spring she'll be popular with all the young drakes."

"Oh, I see." I mused. I failed once more to tell if he was joking or serious. I tried terribly not to sound condescending. "Do you have names for all of them, and do they know their names?"

"Oh yes. This monster at my feet is Hector, Hector the bully. He can be mean and devious, I should warn you about him. See, he is also very greedy," when he attempted to take a whole piece and run with it. "He can be a terror with the ladies, quack-quack," he said, shaking a warning finger at Hector.

Then Emile crooked his finger, saying; "Come here Minerva. I want you to say hello to Kitty." To my amazement, a proud hen waddled forward with a sophisticated gait. Then he added in a jocular voice; "This is Minerva, matriarch of the clan, or flock, I should say. She is respected for her wisdom. And, this one I call Juno, sometimes wife to Zeus, sometimes to Jupiter, depending on her mood. Together they rule. Cronus is supposed to be the father of Zeus in Greek mythology, but mostly he is just another overgrown mischief-maker. He can be nasty at times too, so keep a wary eye on him. He and Hector sometimes become involved in ill-tempered squabbles. These two beautiful females are goddesses of love. Mars, over there is named after the Roman God of war. However, as ducks make war on no other living species he is relegated to a position of guardian. See how he watches over them and keeps himself detached from these, ever on the lookout for danger."

"Danger from what?"

"They have many predator enemies."

"Which one is Cupid?" I asked, playing along with what I perceived as a game.'"Why right there," he winked again. "He is the Roman counterpart to Eros the Greek God of love. Can't you tell by the carnal way he keeps his eye on you?"

"Not really. You're joking of course. Have you named them all from Greek or Roman mythology.?"

"Not all are named for Gods or Goddesses. Don't you recognize Jason from the park, yesterday? And these of course, how could you forget the three mischievous adolescents, Huey, Dewey, and Louie. If you doubt me, call them by name, and see for yourself. Go ahead, open your bag, and try it."

"Okay, wise guy." I had started to say Jason, but with those big soulful eyes still fixed on me, I said with a mixture of quack; "Eros, you big hunk of gorgeous feathers, come over here." I was stunned, when hardly had I gotten the quack-words off my tongue, before he waddled over anxiously to perch on my foot. After rolling my eyes at Emile, I asked, in quack words, naturally; "Do you really know your name?" He emitted a nibbling sound almost like purring, while taking a piece of pancake gratefully from my hand, all the while sucking gently on my finger, his soulful eyes still fixed on mine. "I'd like to take him to bed with me. Do you think he'd mind?" I said teasingly to Emile.

"I think he would like that. . . I would."

"He won't poop on my foot, will he?"

"I don't think so, no. . .but Hector might. See, that one over beside Hector is Ceres. She's safe. Normally she stays close to Eros. But just now, I think she's a little jealous of you. Those others over there are waiting to meet you. They're safe, but just the same you might want to warn them."

I had no more than lifted my eyes before I was overwhelmed. The flock of perhaps a hundred had split to gather eagerly about my feet, crowding and sometimes pecking at each other or the legs of my jogging pants. "Behave you guys," I warned, "There is plenty for all of you, if you share."

Emile opened his bag again and tossed bits of food around their perimeter, obviously to spread them out and to give all a better chance for an equal share. Then emptying his bag, he said; "Th-th-th-that's all folks." And to me, "Be back in a minute."

"Don't leave me here with this crowd," I pleaded, but he was already at the canoe. Only Jason had followed on his heels.

I remember back when I was a little girl and Mom had taken me to the park to feed the ducks. Everyone did it, I think.

When I had tried to feed them, they crowded around quacking and grabbing greedily at the bits of dried bread. One bit my finger, and only afterwards did I realize that it really hadn't hurt. Yet, it had terrified me, and I had cried elaborately, "Mean old duck." Mother had gathered me in her arms, setting me above them on a picnic table. From up there, I soon realized it was safe, and it soon turned into fun, and safer, much safer.

However, now under Emile's watchful presence the whole act took on a surprisingly new dimension.

For a brief time I wondered about the warning he had given. How could there be danger here, and did his presence among these strange creatures serve as some sort of disciplining effect?

Was he really able to communicate with them? Do they have individual personalities as well as names? And are they really distinctive individuals, instead of masses of squawking feathers, beaks and webbed feet?

I was perplexed also about what he had said when we had landed. Did he believe he had been a duck in another life? With the enigmatic Emile, nothing seemed simple on the surface. Was he teasing, or was he serious? Questions posed, nothing solved, yet. And yet, about that, surely he must be joking.

My bag was almost empty, so I finished as Emile had done, by scattering the last crumbs widely on the ground.

By now he had another surprise treat, a bag of cracked corn which he spread about, and which set them loose on a treasure hunt emitting pleasant chirping sounds. He surely knew their pleasures.

When I stopped to look up I realized the earlier fog had dissipated and the sun had taken command of the skies, warming me to a glow. The time had come to shed the joggers. We were in the inner circle of the tiny island, surrounded by tall tules. I thought of the bathroom and decided to hold it for a while. "Whew, you know I think it is going to warm up. Time for a little sunshine," I said.

My hot pink halter and flouncy satin shorts had been designed to test the male libido, I have been told. These erotic garments are guaranteed to arouse even the most unyielding tendencies. In short, I wanted to test Emile's reaction.

"Ah, sexy," he said, with a stirring grin.

"What, these old rags," I fluttered. "Just something I put on in case it warmed up."

He noticed all right, starting from the top and working down, very boldly, then back up again, pausing considerately twice along the way. I think he liked what he saw, loosely accessible lines, a barely confining top, and wild kinky red hair tied back in a ponytail. I untied the bow and shook it loose while his blues and my dark greens remained locked in the throes of sensual contemplation.

"Would you like to sun bathe?" he managed to get out.

"How did you guess?" I nodded.

"The ground is rather damp. I can lay out a piece of plastic, then the sleeping bags. I do it myself sometimes."

Ah yes, the sleeping bags, I had wondered about the ultimate purpose of these.

He needed no answer. In an instant he was gone, and in another instant he was back. I was to learn that of Emile, the elusive. One minute here, the next minute, gone again.

On the slightly higher ground, beside the rocky outcrop and beneath a giant weeping willow he prepared our nest with a base of tules for padding, then the plastic sheet and the sleeping bags. "How cozy," I said.

"In an hour the sun will begin to creep beyond the tree. This is my favorite spot. I brought along some bread, cheese, and wine. There are some carrot and celery sticks, and pears, if you get hungry," all this he declared matter-of-factly.

Ah yes, wine to ply the merry maiden with, I thought. The spell has definitely returned, stronger than ever. In fact, I wondered if it was working much too fast.

As for the ducks, they were definitely enjoying themselves. Their sounds resembled something akin to utter contentment, scratching and poking about for kernels of corn and scavenging over the last crumbs. For the moment they seemed to have a one track mind, I thought, leading to where the food is.

"The musical sounds of the wilderness,"Emile had called it.

Watching the ducks with keen and suspicious interest, I settled face down with my hands cupped under my chin.

When Emile sat down beside me, I said, "Would you help me? The strap, if you could just unhook it."

"Did you bring any sunscreen?"

"No, I forgot. I had no idea it could be like this, so private, you know?"

"Neither did I. I never use it. But the sun, even this time of year, can be brutal."

"I know. I won't stay exposed like this too long. But if I

doze off, you'll wake me, won't you?"

"I'll keep watch," he promised. It was almost quiet, except for the soothing musical sounds of the ducks chattering about.

"How did you find this place?"

"I thought you wanted to sleep."

"Maybe later. Will you tell me about the ducks?"

"Everyone knows they are out here."

"I didn't."

"I bought the used canoe for a hundred dollars, and I just came out here, and here it was."

I was settling into a dreamlike state very nicely. I felt great. The sun felt great. Even the ground felt good.

"Most of them are mallards, you know." He spoke now in a slow easy voice, smoothly and tranquilizingly. And, I had not yet touched the wine.

I knew they were mostly mallards, yet I said nothing.

". . .Some are pekins, the white ones. . . Some buffs and Indian browns, and a few common blacks and whites. A mixture. The mallards are the oldest ancestors of all domestic ducks. They can be so graceful to watch when flying, sort of clumsy on ground though, but in formation they have no equal. They can climb rapidly, and then dive to land in the water with daring and such carefree abandon.

"They are all dabblers. . . Everyone knows the females are the ones with mottled brown feathers, and the drakes are the ones with the glossy green heads, and striking colors, sort of purplish, with chestnut breasts, and soft gray feathers on their backs. A white ring separates the green head from the body.

". . .After mating season, the drakes lose most of their vivid coloring, and for a time resemble the females. It is a sort of defense mechanism, after the molting process—if you notice, the female has no curly tail like the drakes."

"I like the curly tail," I mumbled. "I think it's cute."

"The female has a loud quack. You can tell the difference because the drakes have a kind of low, hoarse call of a voice."

He was quiet for awhile, and I was drifting off into a semicatatonic state of mind with my physical body approaching buoyancy; floating someplace else.

"Ducklings make a kind of guttural chirping sound, like children. . . babies, sort of lyrical. . . don't you think?"

"Hmmm," I moaned, and he said; "I talk too much. Must be something about you. You're easy to be with. I'm not in the habit of opening up like this. I don't often say much."

"No. Please go ahead, you have a nice voice, sort of hoarse and guttural. I'm kidding. But you do have a gift for story telling, because you believe in what you say. You have me convinced anyway. Like, a sort of obvious vitality in your convictions. . ."

I blinked, and turned my face toward him, opening my eyes for an instant,to see he was staring off to the distance.

". . .During their pairing up season, they go through a very ritualized courtship routine. . . The drakes do a lot of nod-swimming, and the females do a lot of coquette-swimming."

"Then what?"

"Then they get together in communal displays."

"And then?"

"Oh. . . a lot of this, until spring. . ."

"Shucks, why wait till spring?"

"A lot of fore-play. . . I guess. . .and maybe they just want to be sure. . ."

"Who chooses who, whom?"

"Why, the female does the choosing, mostly. But, on occasions she will mate freely with others."

"See there, the female calls the shots, and the males know a good thing. . ."

"Then, you don't think we humans have a much better scenario?"

"Who is being facetious now—? I like to watch their head dipping and coquette-swimming. You get the message right away, and their tails up. What do you call that?"

"That's called *Moby Duck.*"

"Ha, Moby Duck, how cute."

"But it has nothing to do with courtship. It's a feeding technique."

"Nuts, I hoped it was something they were expressing, via underwater smooching signals. . ."

"I don't think so, it's a thought though, however the young are prone to do it more often, so."

"Maybe they know something— something the older ones are missing."

"Most ducks live from eight to twelve years, while mallards may live up to twenty. . ."

I was about to ask why that was, when, from some distant place towards the shore line came the intruding sound of shotgun blasts; blam-blam-blam.

With abrupt suddenness I jerked instinctively alert, and looked into his face. The noise polluters, I thought, the killers, the hunters and the cultists. I felt a hidden fury at the obscene monstrous intrusion. The abominable assault on *MY* paradise. That heinous provoking act of murder. I had read someplace that hunting was supposed to be a sport, yet now it seemed more like killing instinct for fun, on a par with ritualistic cultist sacrifices. No more, no less. Now, at this very moment I realized I was outraged and ashamed at this abrupt and blatant shattering of a rare tranquillity.

"They have been warned not to fly at this time," he said, cringing suddenly as another volley of blam-blam's echoed across the distance. . . "This place is taboo to the hunters," he said, smiling thinly. "The word was spread around."

Yet, watching his face intently, I could recognize the unmistakable signs, he was pained and visibly disturbed.

The ducks were quiet for a moment while Mars, the sentry looked somber and distressed.

Soon, the others were busy, back scratching about, or dozing as though nothing had happened.

# THIRTEEN

*I*n those brief after-moments the flock had settled as if nothing had happened, all relaxed as if nesting, some settled quietly with their heads turned about impossibly, beaks tucked away, and yet, I was still furious and outraged that intruders could wantonly wreck my peace in such an obscene way.

Emile was saying, ". . .Mallards are the oldest ancestors of all domestic ducks, the aristocrats, so to speak. . ." He was trying to be casual for my benefit, I suspected. "They pair up, choose mates in the autumn, but don't actually mate until the spring. See how they have already settled in pairs. It is not uncommon to see two or three drakes paired with one female, and sometimes a single drake will have more than one devoted female, however the latter is less common. Then there are the unruly adolescents, but they too learn the rules fast."

"But, if they don't mate until spring," I said, trying desperately to inject a little levity back into the situation, "That's a lot, I mean a *LOT*, of fore-play.

He was looking at me with a gleeful smile. Then it struck me, I had unwittingly bolted upright, I was exposed, topless, sitting there like a dunce, staring into his eyes. "Oh no, my God," I cried. "I'm naked. How stupid of me." I felt a flush creep across my face, ears burning like hot pokers. "How could I be so dumb. Snap me up, please," I pleaded, quickly turning my back to him.

"I don't know," he said, mockingly. "I kind of like you this way," but I was already working the catch by myself. Then he added, with an edge of disappointment in his voice, "There's no need to be embarrassed. No one will see you here. . ."

"You. . ."

"I won't look— again—if you want, and they won't tell."

"Really," I said, with a hot blush, then turning about to meet his gaze a trifle coquettishly. It was a practiced reaction we girls do sometimes with ultimate designs.

"We can take our bottoms off," he teased. "They won't laugh, oh maybe a quack-laugh or two. . . see, I do it all the time." With that he jumped to his feet, and started to drop his jeans, dark curls of pubic hair popping into view. He wriggled his hips teasingly, saying; "Nooo, you don't want me to do that. . . do you?" his eyes said yes. "Go ahead, I won't look," I chirped, delightfully amused. My brain conferred with my eyes, and one told the other; yes, I will look. "It's not that I am a prude, you understand, but I really think you are trying to corrupt me. . ."

He dropped his jeans and danced around erotically in tight black briefs; "I know. You don't; on the first date. Is that it?"

"Something like that, I suppose," I managed to squeak out, while he moved ever so slowly, wickedly, like a sun worshiper, all the while lowering his briefs a half inch, then back, saying; "Nooo, you don't want me to. . ." My eyes locked on his bulge helplessly. I could never hide an emotion anyway. My facial expression was a dead give-a-way. I said, "No!" But I was tempted to grab his shorts and jerk them down. Then he could have done the same thing to me, and oh, what the hell. That tell-tale flush was on my face again, I felt it, and I knew he recognized it.

"I do it all the time," he said, "alone, of course, see no dividing line." He was teasing all the while, getting into his slow-motion strip with renewed vigor, but I do think he was prepared to go all the way.

Fore-play, I thought, simply fore-play. Was he prepared to wait till spring? What would Minerva think? "I can't tell when you're serious or joking," I said. Then he chuckled a small laugh, big smile, and sat down beside me. I thought, uh-oh, here comes the big move.

"Is it important?"

"Well, sometimes, it is important to know the difference," I said. "Don't you agree?" I had the urge to reach over and touch his hand. I said, "That was cute though, I mean it could have been cute, I mean, Hell I don't know. You took me by surprise, okay. . . Let's do it now," I said boldly, with an added hint of urgency. "Let's lay down together in the sun, nude, soak up the warm rays, side by side. We're all alone, right? And, they won't care, right?"

I'm not sure he heard me, because once again his gaze was fixed far away on Mount Konocti.

He was in a dreamy mood when he spoke again. "Did you know that there once was a species of duck which lived here, in Northern California, with a fifteen foot wingspan. It had a big donkey size head, and a proportionally shorter, but stouter bill. They're extinct now. They have been for a long time."

"Are we being serious, or are you making it up?"

"Supposedly, they were descendants of the diatryma who stood seven foot high. It had a massive, ferocious beak, a nightmare of a looking bird . . . When Kah-bel, the young chief fought Lupiyoma's father Konocti for the right to marry her, it was on that mountain top where they met and died. . .it was the Phororhacos, the duck with a fifteen foot wingspan who carried the young princess on his back, up to where the bodies were. They say the Phororhacos was her devoted pet, and that she often rode, or flew on its back. Until Lupiyoma tamed it, it had been unable to fly."

"You're making this up naturally, but okay, you got me hooked. What happened to the Phororhacos?"

He shrugged impishly, looked me straight in the eye, and said; "Who knows, maybe he was the last of his kind, and he died up there with her of a broken heart."

"You think it was a he now, the gender is clear?"

"It was a he. How else could she have captivated *him?*"

"I just thought of something I once read," I said, ruminating a bit, ". . .Back when I was a little girl, and I got a pet duckling for Easter. . . About Saint Cuthbert's ducks, I think they're called, on the Farne Island, off the coast of Northumberland, in memory of a seventh century saint by that name. Saint Cuthbert had a hermitage there and he decreed that the birds must not be disturbed. The ducks return there each year for nesting because it is quiet and peaceful. No one disturbs them, and they only take their food from the sea, never from the farmers. And yet, humans walk among them, and the ducks have absolutely no fear. . .and there is positively no hunting. . ."

"And the birds know it."

"How?"

"Instincts," he said.

"You've heard of it, Saint Cuthbert's?"

"Did you know that ducks are deathly afraid of hunters, their hunting dogs especially? A wounded duck will dive to the water's bottom, and grasp a reed, or anything it can, until it dies, just to prevent the dogs from getting at it."

He was quiet for awhile, then he added; "They're motivated by powerful instincts and emotions and yet, unlike humans they have no way of considering retribution. Revenge is not part of their character. Trauma or tragedy can stalk a human for years causing a lifetime of anxiety and depression, yet birds, and animals can overcome the results of a vicious attack in moments. When a mother duck loses one of her clutch, to say a large-mouth bass, moments later she will carry on as if unaffected."

"But she has to be affected, doesn't she?"

"I would think so too, but they have such highly tuned instincts for survival. They seem able not to concern themselves with something they have no power to change. If a mother is lost while raising her clutch of young, another mother will take over and raise them along with those of her own. Even an unmated female will raise ducklings that are not her own."

"I have heard that goslings will trail behind the first being they encounter after birth, even accepting a human as parent or mother figure."

"But not mallards, they have learned the hard way to be wary of man. Oh, they will accept food all right but you have to earn their trust. That is why it is so difficult to get close to them. They have so many predators, still they give so much joy, and yet they are always the victims. . ."

His words took on a certain confidential intimacy, as though what he said was meant for just the two of us. I had that innate feeling I was being sworn to secrecy, without going through the rites or formality.

"I know," I said. "I had some ducklings for Easter once. Such cute little feathery things, they were so adorable, like kittens, in a way, or a puppy. . ."

"I wonder sometimes," he said, "if it is right to feed them, if it makes them dependent on handouts, and may eventually rob them of their natural instincts, sort of like the first settlers did with the local Indians. The Indians were doing just fine until they succumbed to a dependency that ultimately changed their over-all diet and character. . ."

"I don't think so, for the ducks, anyway. . ."

"I guess not. I hope not, because I see the handouts as a supplement to their overall dietary needs. . . we do it mostly for our own human gratifications. The Romans and Greeks considered it a worthy pastime to feed the ducks. The scholars wrote that feeding the ducks added harmony to their souls, and the ducks are still surviving."

"Do you suppose they understand when we talk about them. For now, they seem pacified, maybe all ears?"

"Uh-oh, I thought, is this me the psychologist; caught up in a tender little trap of a game? "You don't really talk to them, do you? . . .They're just used to you, and react emotionally, and to hand signals?"

Without moving he said; "Quack-quack, Minerva, come sit on Kitty's lap."

"You're kidding," I said, but then she was already waddling happily towards me. She paused at the edge of the sleeping bag, head tilted, considering me with dark pressing eyes. I smiled, realizing we were both contemplating the other.

"Quack-quack," Emile made a slight motion with his eyes only, "Minerva, on Kitty's lap, she wants to stroke your feathers."

"Oooh, it tickles, her feet are so cool," I moaned. I became keenly aware that my right thigh had been warmed by the sun. The difference was cool and soothing. "She saw you look to my leg."

"Jason, would you, quack-quack, quack, come over and sit by Kitty?"

"Oh, he is a darling, isn't he? And Eros the lover. You can come too Eros," I chuckled. I was so engrossed that I hardly noticed that several others had waddled over to gather around us, emitting gentle quacking sounds. One boldly nibbled at my toes, "Ooooh," I cooed, "that tickles, good tickles though. My feet are so sensitive. I sometimes wonder if all sensations don't originate at the feet." I drew my left knee to my chest, relaxing my legs, and inadvertently opening them slightly. Minerva, still perched on the other suddenly pecked at the head of a drake who had inched closer. She gave him an admonishing quack, then an invective stream that sounded more like a warning. I was soon to understand the reason.

"Ouch," I cried, "he bit me." The drake scooted away, like a raucous rascal, jeering, quack-laughing, racing in vicious circles with Minerva scolding, snapping viciously at his tail-feathers.

"Where?" asked Emile, wide eyed.

"There, look, right there. He left a hickey."

"Want me to kiss it?"

"I think I've been kissed."

"I am sorry. It is my fault. I should have warned you to watch out for Hector."

Minerva was still busy chasing him in ever widening circles, snapping occasional feathers loose and flinging them aside without missing a beat. It sounded like some of the others were enjoying the show, quack-laughing their hearts out.

Minerva was still chasing, quack-quack, quack-quack, her displeasure in no way diminished.

"What's he quacking about?" I asked.

"Oh nothing, he's just boasting."

"Boasting about what?" I demanded, still inspecting my hickey.

"You really don't want to know."

"Oh yes I do."

"No. You don't"

"Tell me," I demanded, with a penetrating stare.

He shrugged, and said, grinning; "He's boasting that the feathers, what we call hair. . ." he was obviously having trouble containing himself while I probed him with my most penetrating stare; ". . .what we call hair, everything is feathers to them. . That you. . ."

"Out with it."

"You know, your feathers are not as red as those on your head."

"So that's it, is it, well let me tell you something, you horny old eider. . ." With that, Hector changed his tone of squawking abruptly. I could understand his outrage. He had been chased a goodly distance away from the flock, like an ornery oaf banished from the kingdom. Minerva was stationed half way between us, guardedly. "I can understand that, he's obviously irate about something."

"Quack-quack, quack-quack-quack, quack-quack-quack-quack. . ."

"Such blather from a mangy feathered critter," I said. I will not be out shouted by a duck. "I even understand some of that," I conceded. "He doesn't like something."

Emile struggles to pull himself together, saying; "He's insulted. You called him an eider."

"He should be insulted. He should be. . .whatever they do to horny, decadent old bullies. Castrated, maybe. Eider, eider, eider, there, take that, blah."

"Quack-quack-quack," raged Hector. "Eiders are dumb domestics, quack, stupid, good only for their down, stupid. I am a MALLARD, not an eider!"

"I think I understood that too," I said to Emile. "But does he always sneak around biting girls' pussy feathers? Human and duck alike?"

"I think it's called a fetish. Seems he likes girls too."

"Well, he can stay away from this girl. Would you look at that? No, don't look." To Hector I shouted, "You horny old dabbling duck, or whatever you are called."

Hector, demanding the last quack-word, turned to stalk away; quack-quack-quack-quack, I'm no *eider*. Eiders are dumb, stupid. I am a MALLARD. Eiders are stupid."

Emile inclined his head to the sun, "Time to go," he said. Then, moving around on his knees facing me, he gripped my feet firmly, applying thumb pressure just below the large joint. . .

"Oooh," I moaned.

"I have a confession to make," he declared with a penetrating stare. "I too have a fetish."

"Yeah?"

"I am a foot fetisher. . . If it is true that great sex starts with the feet. . .and if sex is the only thing one can be six months behind on, and still get caught up on in fifteen minutes. . .then one must not be so anxious to get to the destination. . . that one forgets to enjoy the journey. . .should one?"

He had adjusted to stroking my feet lightly with feathery touches among the fleshy hollows, then he went back to applying a certain elusive pressure. . . "Oooh, oooh, oooh," I sighed, more like a groan, helpless and inexplicably sudden, and jolting, and finally overwhelming me like a flood of erotic emotion.

Am I demented, I thought. There go my panties again. I must truly be kooky; having orgasms that start with my feet.

# FOURTEEN

"*I* want to do it," I said with amusing reassurance.

"Do what?"

"Why paddle, of course. What do you think I meant." I was teasing, and I was well aware that he knew it. "You don't have to fix the bags like a lounge-bed." He was already busy securing the bags and few supplies to the bottom for our return trip.

To myself I was having a fun time, speculating; I wondered just how tricky it might be, and if anyone had ever tried it in a canoe, feet and legs tangled in the cross-brace and center post, heads banging against the seat, and where would the arms go? I bet some of the most daring have tried it, idiots of course, small idiots at that. And, what happens when the damn thing flips over, and both of you get dumped in the cold water? Now that would surely dampen the wickedest of spirits. Still, just to try it once, I though. . .no, no that's crazy, no way. Not worth it. Why beg for trouble, when shit happens all by its self.

He was back with the last armful, knotting the last of it in place.

"Have you ever done it in a canoe?" I just blurted it out.

"Done what?" he said, with a cautious grin.

"Oh, you know, flipped over in the canoe? Will it sink?" I said, trying to sound coy in the process.

"You don't need to worry, it won't sink. Just hold on, but we would have to nurse it back to shore to dump the water out. If we try to climb back in while in deeper water it will just roll around like a soaked log."

"Oh, I didn't know that." I confessed.

"You take the front, and I'll take the rear, that way I can compensate for you by steering."

While he steadied it, I climbed aboard and attempted to center myself by cautiously wiggling my butt in place.

The ducks gathered behind us like a party of saddened relatives, awaiting our departure. Emile had reserved a supply of cracked corn and scraps for the occasion, and yet they still found acquiescent gentle quacks, so that I almost expected them to wave good-by. At a remote distance I noticed Hector half lurking, still half pouting like one of the disgruntled adolescents. "Good-by Minerva. Good-by Jason. Good-by." I waved, thinking how silly I felt talking to ducks by name.

"It'll be a little faster going back," he said. "We'll stay closer to the shoreline this time." All in the same motion, he gave a push and stepped in. Just as quickly we were gliding along smoothly.

"There's a slight wind from the south. That should help us along, and with your help I figure we'll make Lakeport in about two and a half hours."

That was when I took my first strokes. "I can take a hint," I said.

After the indecent incident with Hector nipping at my so called feathers, then in ungallantly boasting about it, Emile had decided it was time to leave. "But why the rush," I had pleaded. "The sun is still out, and I thought you planned to stay overnight, the sleeping bags, you know?" I knew better, but I had the advantage of second-guess strategy. . ."

"Oh those, I always bring them. The tarp too. Sometimes, if the wind comes up, or it rains, I build a temporary shelter. There is no way we could make it back bucking a head-wind, and any kind of cross wind just tosses the canoe around. It would be a futile effort."

I had wanted him to ask me even though I knew I couldn't stay overnight. "I guess you're right," I replied. "I didn't tell Dad when to expect us, and he might have had patrol boats out looking for us. You wouldn't want that."

"Another time," he said pausing. "Next Friday night, or Saturday, maybe?"

"Yes, I think Friday I could leave right after my final class and hurry. . . On Sunday I usually go to church with Dad."

"How did you make it yesterday?"

"I skipped a class."

"Uh-oh."

"Right. I don't dare do it again. Soon anyway."

"Which church do you attend?"

"Saint Mary's. It is only two blocks from my house."

"You're Catholic?"

"How did you guess?"

"Oh, you're Catholic too? Do you know Father Daly?"

"I've listened to his sermons a couple of times. But, I go mostly for the choir singing. I was disappointed to learn that Saint Mary's has no choir. So. . . sometimes I go to the Baptist Church, or the United Christian, or the Mormon Church. They have good choirs. The Lower Lake Methodist Church has the best though."

"Why do you skip around?"

"I just go when the notion strikes me, for the choir."

"Will you be there tomorrow?"

"I'll have to check with my notions."

"Smarty, like the wind, huh? We could have been trapped there for the night."

"Not likely."

"How do you know that?" I said. I was getting the hang of it now. Like two people dancing together in rhythm. Stroking the paddle seemed instinctive, commanding the body, and a free flow of fresh oxygen to the brain stimulated the thinking juices, and the body energies quickened, and in the process; what goes around, comes around. The result was a smoothly gliding craft thrusting over the water, pushing it aside. Pulsing and almost surfing at times. I had completely forgotten about tipping over as though it were a fleeting consideration of the past.

Except for a single white sail tilted in the distant north, we were the only craft on the lake now. On summer weekends these same waters could be a noisy madcap of water skiers, jet boats and jet skis.

I could feel his harmony and his cadence, and I knew he felt mine. We made a good team. I think it may be called Nirvana. I don't think I have ever felt it before.

"Do you want a rest," he shouted so the wind carried his words forward to my ears.

"What, and tip this thing over. Besides, it feels good, and I need the workout."

For a time we paddled steadily and quietly except for the gentle rush of wavelets slapping us along, and the brief visit of squawking sea gulls overhead.

"Is that an osprey, circling over there?" I called back.

"They've gone south already."

"How did you know the wind would not be against us today?"

"I have connections."

"Oh, your feathered friends told you, I suppose."

"Perhaps."

"Really?"

"It's a secret, known only to a few."

"I suppose you could tell me what it will be like next weekend, the weather."

"Not until I read the weather report."

"Smart ass," I said, yet not too loud.

"What?"

"Smart. That's a good connection."

We were skimming along a jutting marshy finger of tules in placid waters while beyond the lake water churned up in choppy wavelets. "I'll bet it could be tricky out there," I called back.

"Right. This is a little longer but in the long run we should make better time."

After some minutes of quiet, I said; "What did you mean back there? When you said, 'In another life I was a duck.'"

"I said that?"

"Yes. You said, 'These are my cousins. In another life I was a duck.' Something like that."

"I must have been joking."

"I don't think you would have said it if you didn't mean it. I'm sure it meant something to you then. . ."

"Have you ever had a *déjà vu* experience?"

"French, isn't it? Means something like; already seen, or something. . ."

"Yeah. Have you?"

"Like what?" I felt as though I was at a distinct disadvantage with his words coming from behind, he could see me, and although I could hear his words carrying forward well enough, I couldn't see his face. I wanted to turn around and watch his expression.

He was saying, ". . .Like suddenly meeting someone for the first time. Someone you are sure you don't know, and yet you are certain you have met them before? Or, like being stranded in a strange place, completely familiar to you when you know you've never left your home town, or state. Consciously, you know you have never been there, and yet your subconscious half tells you differently."

"I get what you mean. But that doesn't have to mean anything."

"How do you know it doesn't?"

"Well, I don't know really, but more than likely, such an experience is the result of an overactive imagination."

"Have you ever had an out of body experience?"

"Like what?"

"Like separating from your physical self in spirit, to look back at your body sleeping?"

"I'm not sure. In a dream, maybe. Have you?"

"I asked you first."

Sounds like the game again, I thought. "Well yes, maybe I have, in a dream perhaps."

"What do you think it meant?"

"I don't know, just a dream. . ."

"But you're sure it was only a dream?"

I stopped paddling for a minute to turn around and face him. My careless shifting of my weight seemed to unbalance the canoe. I was surprised that without my added stroking the craft seemed to lose a measure of its momentum. "Well no, not sure, strange things do happen. But is it supposed to mean something?" When I turned to face forward again, my eyes caught the distant outline of a derelict dredge highlighted by the descending afternoon sun. "Have you ever visited that old dredge?" I asked.

"Would you like to go there?"

"I have never seen it up close. Is it out of the way?"

"Today yes. Another time we can take the time."

"I've heard it has quite a history."

"Yeah."

After a time of quiet paddling he said, "Have you ever known anyone else to have an unexplainable experience?"

"Well, yes now that you mention it. There was this girlfriend, it was the strangest thing. I always wondered about it. She was in the hospital for some minor surgery, and still under the anesthetic when I went to see her. Her parents were there also, and while she was still unconscious, she suddenly started talking and laughing in this strange language. Up till that time she had never left Lakeport, except maybe, to go to Ukiah, or Santa Rosa. . . Anyway she was speaking in this strange dialect that nobody could understand. . . like—?"

"Like what?"

"I was never sure, like in another land, or time. I never heard the language before, nor had the doctor, or her mother and father. But, I would guess it was something like Cockney, maybe, or Welsh. A nurse thought it might have been Gaelic, but I know a few Gaelic terms I learned from my mother, and I couldn't tell. . ."

"And you were there?"

"Yes. I was there."

"Then you know it was no hoax?"

"It was no hoax. I can assure you of that."

"Perhaps she was reliving experiences from another life under the affects of the anesthesia."

"You think that's what it was, don't you?" I wanted so desperately to turn around and watch his reaction this time, but not enough to get us wet and cold. "When you said you were a duck in another life, you meant it, didn't you?"

Simultaneously, we had both stopped paddling for a rest while the wind ceased. Except for gentle ripples, the water had settled to an almost glassy calm. The sun had dropped to the west, a fireball suspended amid reddish skies of 3:30 p.m. autumn cycle. I was all at once overcome, adrift, with the soothing quality of quietude.

"So peaceful, isn't it, out here like this, and all alone, I mean so much like it must have been aeons of time long ago. Before all the change. . . And for just right now, it is all ours."

"Yes. . ." he said, softly, like in a whisper.

"Do you believe in reincarnation?" I asked, managing to turn around and catch his eye response.

"What do you think?"

"It's my turn to ask."

"Is it so unreasonable to you? Reincarnation, another life; another time; in some other body form?"

"You mean like a duck?"

"Like anything."

"I'm not sure. Alone like this, floating, suspended, with time standing still. It is thought provoking."

"I know. . ."

". . .If we are really reincarnated, then why don't we remember past lives. . .and why don't we learn from our past mistakes. . . and do we intermix with other creatures—?"

". . .Maybe we do."

". . .and how come, if we do evolve along with other animal forms, other life forms for that matter. . . how do you equate animal intelligence with human intellect?"

# FIFTEEN

His voice had softened with a soothing ephemeral quality. Again there was that endless peace and musical sound of quiet. We sat together, separate, yet touching, afloat and suspended for a moment in time without measure. The sky glowed aflame with brilliant mottled coloring, and I, I was spellbound, and I knew it. For an instant, I felt myself splitting, no gently separating with the physical transient me, fading, while the spiritual me, that elusive apparition, drifted, levitated to hover and turn back, considering the physical self.

Then I snapped. Was I drunk. Was it the wine, or had Emile cast a spell? . . .No, I had simply been afraid to let the thing happen, and yet I had been so close, so close.

I felt Emile's gaze on me, his eyes canny and shrewd, and to him it must have seemed logical.

All at once, we were moving again, as if by pure physical exertion, so I turned and joined in the rhythm of stroking and thrusting us forward across quiet waters. Waters darkened and black now like a mirror.

That brilliant sky, the shrouded fireball, inching inexorably toward its western sunset, only to be born again the next day with a new life.

I wondered, was my mother, Molly O'Grady-Kreeszowski out there somewhere smiling down at me, a face in the myriad formation of clouds.

I was in a state of paradoxical bewilderment; the brain still stunned and lethargic, and yet the body sprang curiously into action stimulating generous flows of oxygen into the bloodstream, eventually prompting wild curiosities.

Emile's energy was there, almost imperceptibly at first, then like a powerful force, yet salacious and stirring.

When at last I found my senses, I said; ". . .But isn't it absurd to compare human intelligence with that of animals, and birds, for example, reading and reasoning—?"

"Could it be because it is the humans who make the distinction by defining intelligence to suit their own liking?"

"Don't spiritualists, or those who believe in reincarnation believe that humans are the higher order of life, and animals the lower, and that the two cannot intermix?"

"I suppose some might make that distinction, but what do you think another animal or creature might think of a man who becomes lost in the woods and disoriented not far from his home?"

"I get lost in a shopping center parking lot."

"Exactly. And yet, a dog or cat has no trouble finding it's way home from hundreds of miles away. . . in strange places."

"You're saying, that it is the definition of intelligence that counts?"

"Perhaps it is that complacency of definition, say that smug sense of superiority that gets in our way of communication.

"Records show that for centuries man has attempted to communicate with other animal forms, by imitating birds in particular. The Romans and Egyptians, in their times liked to feed ducks and kept them as pets. And I suppose it must have been much in the same way we do today, still some 2000 to 3000 years later we have progressed no further than imitating simple mocking sounds, except for the Indians and a limited few others with advanced ability. The creatures seem more ready to understand us and respond than we do of them.

"Maybe, just maybe, the limitation is our own, and if we humans were tuned in more to listening than childish mimicry, we might learn something. Who then, is the more intelligent, and which standard is the more highly developed? Because we build cars, skyscrapers, and houses are we the brighter ones?

"If only we could really listen to the dolphins and whales, might we not gain some insight to useful scientific advances? Just imagine the intelligence of the whales who migrate over thousands of miles and return; and no benefit of instruments.

"Birds, for example, have evolved a much higher normal body temperature, from 103° to 112° Fahrenheit and so adapted to withstand both extremes of heat and cold, adjusting their pulses voluntarily when desired, to twice that of we humans.

"As for the senses of smell, taste and touch, as well as hearing and sight they have developed far, far beyond our meager ability."

"I don't know about their smell and tastes," I said. "But I can't think of anything in an animal's diet that appeals to my palate."

"Perhaps that is because humans eat mostly for pleasure, cholesterol, sweets, and fatty stuff, whereas animals eat only out of necessity to survive."

"Yuck. I'll take an ice cream cone or pizza any day."

"How about migrations? Humans migrate by the seasons, in cars and airplanes when it suits them."

"If they can afford it."

"Think of trying it the animal way, thousands of miles, year after year like the swallows, ducks, or geese do. And how about the whales and salmon who return year after year to spawn and propagate, all without the aid of navigation."

"Your conclusion then, is that animals are smarter than humans. . ."

"Now you are putting words in my mouth."

"Dad wanted me to be a lawyer, a wife first, of course. What do you think?"

"You could do great on cross-examination. But realistically, I am not claiming that animals are unequivocally smarter, only that there is much we could learn from them, if we were not so busy trying to kill them off. . ."

I was watching the sunset again, like we were in a race to catch it before it plunged out of sight, hot and sizzling beyond the horizon.

"Well then," I said, thoughtfully. "If there really is such a thing as reincarnation, why don't we learn from our mistakes of the past, and why don't we remember that other life?"

"Could be we do, some things anyway. The idea of rebirth is not a new one. Socrates and Plato taught and obviously believed in reincarnation, or transmigration. The old testament contained passages and references to rebirth that have been removed from more recent Bibles.

"Is it so far fetched, unimaginable, to accept that Plato, Socrates, and other scholars may have been onto something that we have missed in our rush for material goods? And how many religious doctrines espoused reincarnation, say even the rebirth of Jesus Christ? At one time Christianity itself was considered a religious cult, and some still do. Even the Knights Templer set themselves apart and believed they were destined for a time of transmigration, depending on their devotion and deeds.

"Socrates was condemned, and forced to take hemlock poison, because his teachings, which were so advanced for his time, caused conflict among the religious leaders of that period, and that was three to four hundred years before the birth of Christ.

"Take the soul, versus the mind, for example. Neither are of physical substance, and yet both exist. If one can accept that the mind is a function of the brain, then why not take that premise one step further by accepting that the body functions as an extension of the soul, and the mind accompanies the soul along its journey to the hereafter like a storage computer, yet frozen from one life form to the other with only a simple key needed to unlock its secrets."

# SIXTEEN

"Plato, Socrates, you're getting in over my head now," I said, trying not to sound complacent. His opening up too, I felt might be contrary to his nature, and I wanted to learn more and keep him going.

"Plato was a student of Socrates. They lived in the third and fourth centuries before Christ. Both were Greek philosophers. Plato was his nickname, meaning broad shouldered. His real name was Aristocles. He was eighty-eight years old, I think, when he died in 347 B.C.

"It was Socrates who taught, but he recorded nothing. It was Plato who wrote later in the literary form, called the Dialogues. In his various dialogues he demonstrates how Socrates taught by asking questions. . ."

"And is that how he taught about reincarnation?" I said, as we both paddled steadily in easy coordinated strokes toward the nearing western shore, chasing that inexorably plunging sunset. It was a race of the mind and body, led by the spirit with natural injections of worthy adrenalin.

"Sort of. . . Reincarnation means coming back into the flesh. Ancient Greeks, as well as primitive peoples had believed in it in various forms. The ancient Babylonians believed that some forms of life, and spirit lived and evolved as long as 36,000 years. . ."

"God, that's a long time, I don't think I could take it, I mean, so many orgasms. . ."

"What? I didn't hear you—?"

"Oh nothing. Just mumbling. Who would want to live that long? I mean, how would they measure 36,000 years. Like shaving every day. And, imagine if you didn't cut your hair, or shave. . ."

"Amusing isn't it? Play with it any way you want, but rebirth was considered an important part of Buddhism and Sikhism, and other doctrines which originated in India. It is also an important dogma of spiritualistic movements related to the law of Karma. . ."

"That's a lot of *ism's.*"

". . .with the higher state reborn into such forms as priests and a lower state such as dogs."

"Or rats?"

"Even a rat."

"Do you believe in Spiritualism?"

"I don't disbelieve in it any more than I believe that Christ arose from the dead, and I don't consider worshiping an idol-figure or symbol on a cross any different than any other figure-worship, such as a totem pole. . ."

"Whoa. . ." I groaned, trying not to sound judgmental, and seem to insinuate an opinion. "You must be a pagan."

"Aren't we all pagans?"

"I for one, never thought of being one. Being a pagan sounds so, so ickish."

"Is there a difference? I mean, when you think about it, have not the modern Christian dogmas changed little from earlier pagan rituals. Take funerals for example, a practice emanating from earlier rites and practices which in modern times have changed only on the surface, while priests and ministers still compete for control of the minds of the masses. . ."

"Religion is a tough controversial subject. I think we strayed from Plato and reincarnation. . ." I said.

"I think you're right. Somehow, discussions about religion always seem to evolve into arguments," he said.

We paddled quietly for awhile, the noise of gears churning wildly in both our heads. "How about getting back to Plato," I said, "Something about Plato fascinates me."

"Back to Plato. . .hmmm, Plato obviously believed, and taught that after the death of the body, the soul migrates into the realms of pure form. . . that the body dies and disintegrates and the soul continues to live forever—the soul exists there, in this realm, contemplating other forms until after some time it is returned to earth in another form."

"And forgets everything from its former life?"

". . .Not necessarily. He or she retains a sort of vague, or dim recollection of that former life. . ."

"And, relearns by questioning?"

"Suppose there is a key to unlocking the past?"

"You mean like when you find yourself someplace you know is strange, a place you have never been before, and yet that place is so familiar. . . and like when you meet some person, a stranger you are certain you never met before, but there is something absolutely familiar about them. . .from another time, or place. . .weird?" I said, excitedly. For a moment I seemed to get a handle on this thing, and then it slipped away, intangible and slippery.

"Plato argued that people fall in love with other people because they recognized some of that same beauty in that ideal that had captivated them before. . ."

"Poor Socrates, he hadn't a chance. . ."

"Why do you say that?"

"He is eternally stuck with Xanthroppe, the shrew."

"I think you got it now," he laughed.

"I know a girl at Stanford who has been married three times, well married the first two times, living with a guy now. . . Each time she gets herself hooked on the same type of creep. . . guys that abuse her, and she can't seem to break the cycle. I hope, for her own sake, she has learned from the other two, and doesn't marry this jerk. If she had any real sense, she would kick him out now."

"Like guys who get hooked on the same type of women, huh?"

"Okay," I agreed. "But, it does seem that we should learn something from our mistakes. . ."

"In one of the Dialogues called the 'Meno', Plato shows how Socrates taught an ignorant slave boy about geometry, simply by asking him questions that unlocked the answers in his own mind. From this example, Plato concluded that an individual is capable of recalling what had already been learned in another life-form."

"Does that have anything to do with the reason birds do not feel conscious pain, and therefor experience no remorse or trauma as we humans might?"

"Could be, once again it's that instinctive intelligence which escapes us. We're so locked in on getting even as an excuse.

"Almost everyday you can read about someone who claims to have lived another life, and all claim to demonstrate irrefutable and convincing evidence that what they claim is absolutely true."

"I watched a demonstration in hypnotism once, and it did seem to me the hypnotist was merely planting suggestions in the subject's head for the mere benefit of sensationalism. . . It was all show."

"Hypnotism might work," said Emile. "I don't know. Maybe we have to figure it out for ourselves, see what does work?"

"I wonder if Plato used hypnotism?"

"I doubt it. I don't think he or Socrates would have thought of it as an ethical method of unlocking the mind. I wasn't there."

"Oh. . . I thought you might have been." I could not resist a chance for a little kidding."

"Sounds like a tempting exercise. Maybe I'll work on it."

"Will you tell me about the trip?"

"We could go together."

"Not me. I'm too pragmatic. . . like to keep my feet on the solid ground, or water."

"Pythagoras taught that souls migrated after death into other body forms, both human and animal. . ."

"Oh, it's Pythagoras now, is it? Well, I think, I would like to become a dolphin, and if you are a duck, then never the twain shall meet. How about flowers, or an eagle maybe?"

". . .He also taught that meat eating was an abominable form of cannibalism."

"Okay, so that leaves out eagles, for me anyway. But, I do like a good old hamburger once in awhile, you know, with everything on it."

"Orpheus taught that man was a guilty polluted being, meat tainted the body, and that the soul, because of it, required purification. . ."

"Orpheus, Aristotle, Pythagoras, I like Plato better. Was he a vegetarian, with broad shoulders, huh?"

"Tall, dark and handsome, too."

"Definitely Plato, and he lived to a ripe old age of—?"

"Eighty-eight, I think."

"I wonder where he is today."

"I like your humor, but don't you think he is way ahead of us, like, somewhere into pure-form by now?"

I sighed a long sigh, resting my paddle while Emile continued to dig away at his regular rhythm. "I guess you must be right, but tell me more about Plato anyway."

"They, Plato and Socrates, taught that the soul had an immortal existence, but for the most part had forgotten its past."

"Shucks, I want to know what happened way back then, in my own past."

"Plato wrote that knowing the father of the universe was a most difficult task and until one knows for certain, how can one proclaim to know."

"Jimmy Swaggart knows. . .and so does Oral Roberts, and Jimmy Bakker. . ."

"Of course they do. They have a direct connection with God, so they claim. . ."

"If all those who claim to, really do have a direct line to God, then God must be awfully busy. I wonder how he finds time for us little guys?"

". . .Do they know more than Plato, Socrates, or any of the early philosophers? Did Jesus ever actually say he was the son of God, or was it others who proclaimed it so in their divine wisdom? Might there be a difference between father of the universe, or what man has claimed as various Gods, or that one God of the Jews predating Jesus Christ, or that of the Christians, or the one the Indians call *Creator*?"

". . .I take it you don't favor the idea of an eternity dependent on the whims of any creator, one God, or any God who sits up there pulling all the strings?"

"Supposedly, Plato-Socratic thought merged with Christian theology to affirm divine transcendence, freedom of will, and immortality of the soul, and that virtue is necessary for happiness. . . but those. . ." He became hesitant momentarily, as if divided, and as though he had gone too far in exposing himself. He needs a little urging I thought. "But those what?"

". . .But those who transgress are sent back to learn their lessons all over again."

"Like sex, do it till you get it right?"

"Or typing, practice, practice, practice."

"Well at least we agree on something," I said. "But, you still haven't answered my other question."

"What. . . oh about pulling strings?"

"Uh-huh. About someone up there pulling the strings?"

"Let's see. Strings, Jesus Christ, and God, huh? I agree that no other living individual has endured, some 1900 years approximately, has endured to affect living man as Jesus Christ has to this day. I doubt that another will, but who can say.

While he collected his thoughts in an ephemeral sense, I wondered about Joseph. Mary was present at the crucifixion, and yet after some twelve years there appears to be no mention of Joseph.

". . .I don't disbelieve that Jesus existed, or may have returned in some other form. I would rather believe that by now he has reached that ultimate state of pure-form. It is those many different manifestations of God that I would dis-pute. The idea of hellfire and damnation, and the doling out of rewards and punishment by self professed individuals who proclaim a direct line to his ear. As for strings, I rather think we are out here on this limb, on our own. . ."

"What of the Bible?"

"A book."

"Just a book?"

"A product for sale. The most successful product of the ages."

For moments I sat quiet and saddened. For all his vitality and convictions, he seemed a lonely complexity, an enigma of which I had only scratched the surface.

"I hope Dad hasn't sent out the forces looking for us."

The lights of Lakeport sparkled like candles and lighting stars as dusk threatened to dispose of the last rays of sunlight with the fireball gone, dipping behind the distant mountain horizon. Death today and rebirth tomorrow at dawn in the eternal Ka-Batin-Guy.

"Me too," he said. "Another twenty to thirty minutes and we're there."

"I really enjoyed this today," I said. "The ducks and all. The canoeing can be a real welcoming workout. I think I have the hang of it finally. You caused me to consider things I had never thought of before, you know that, don't you?"

"What you mean is that I talk too much."

"Not at all. I bet you think I do though."

"I think you just asked all the right questions, and got me started. You're good at it."

"The psychologist, that's me. . ." For a time we sat quietly, paddling together in an easy rhythm, the canoe adding it's own effort in a motion all it's own with very little stroking and it glided quietly and smoothly, like an old horse heading for the barn and some oats.

"Something puzzles me," I said thoughtfully, "In this order of things of the highest and the lowest, what happens to monstrous criminals like Adolph Hitler and Charles Manson, just to name a few? Do they get another chance?"

"Supposedly, the highest order is a spirit realm of eternal meditation. You only know it when you get there. . . In the physical being dolphins and whales are above man, and just a notch below are the. . ."

"Ducks."

"How did you guess?"

"You said you were a duck before, remember?"

"See, it's not so difficult. I think you got it."

That old spell was coming back, and I failed once again to discern if he was serious or kidding. I said, "And the lowest order?"

"Scavengers, like vultures. They have lost their souls as punishment and are doomed to a hell on earth, cleansing the earth of carrion."

"Hitler and Manson?"

"For them there is a special place created for the lowest order. A place of darkness for such as the slug, the snail, and the worm. With never a second chance."

"What about the four hunters. The ones who drowned. Do you think they were murdered?"

"Maybe. Or maybe they are not really dead. Murdered? Just their souls returned to a lower life form with a chance to learn their lessons all over again."

"If it is as ducks, then it serves them right."

"Yeah," he mused. "That would be ironic wouldn't it?"

"Maybe they weren't ready for this step in the chain of life and rebirth."

"Perhaps it was an accident. What do you think?"

". . .Or a spirit messenger with travel instructions. . ."

Just then we reached the shore with several power strokes that skidded the canoe part way onto the beach. It seemed like a long day, and suddenly I felt stiff with fatigue, and the overwhelming desire to pee.

We were no sooner greeted by a group of quacking ducks

when a small brown and white beagle with floppy ears came charging toward us to bark and scatter them frantically into the water and air.

Emile had already tossed out some leftovers. "I always save a little for them," he said, throwing more out into the water. He laughed, saying, "You know what else they like, dogfood, especially in the winter. Dog food has a lot of nutrition and fiber, and all. . ."

He pulled the canoe up and tied it to a tree while I tried to help. A man approached momentarily taking visible pride in his dog's zealous efforts to keep the ducks at bay.

"Hi Pete," said Emile. "Kitty, meet Pete Lomax. Pete this is Kitty. Pete is the manager of the campground, and he allows me to keep my canoe here."

"Hi Mister Lomax," I managed a grateful smile.

"This cute little beagle is Sissy. She's Pete's bodyguard. She likes to play with the ducks, but she wouldn't hurt them, would you Sissy?" He reached down to pat her head. She barked anxiously. Obviously they were on friendly terms.

"Wish you wouldn't feed those damn ducks here though," growled Pete. "They crap all over the place." Then, to me he said; "Hi Kitty, you new here?"

"Oh no," I replied, with a fashioned grin. "I grew up here, hometown girl."

"Funny, I never seen you before. I been here four years now."

"Kitty's been away at college."

"College, humph."

"Stanford University."

"Humph."

"See you, Pete," Emile said, and I added, "Bye."

"Damn ducks, craping all over the place."

"Jolly character you got there," I said.

"Who Pete? He's not as bad as his bark once you get to know him."

"Not as bad as his grouch, you mean." I thought of Dad, not

as bad as his bark either.

Together, we headed up Second Street toward Main and Emile's shop, with bags tucked under our arms and paddles dragging behind.

Already the streets were bustling with foot traffic, children giggling in the park playground, loud cars rolling by, teens going out for pizza and a show. Typical small town Saturday night.

"Do you have plans for tonight?" I asked.

"Are you asking me for a date?" he said smiling sheepishly.

"Well. . ."

"I'm flattered. But no plans yet."

"You can come to my house. Saturday night is our pizza night. Dad usually tosses a gigantic salad and has a beer or two and then falls asleep right after Empty Nest. Sometimes Ned Turner drops by, and Kimberly might be there. . ."

"Sounds interesting, like a party."

"Real swinging Saturday night, better not miss it."

"I'd like that."

We had arrived at the back door to his shop. He opened it and we tossed the things on the floor.

"Come in," he said, invitingly.

I thought of the bathroom. "I really must go. Dad's expecting me."

"Walk you home?"

"Thanks. I think I can find my way." I smiled.

"Sure?"

"Sure. I had a great time. See you later."

"Me too," I said, with a small hand wave. I had turned to leave when he called back. "Next weekend, we can stay overnight. That is, if you want to?"

"Friday. It's a date. Bye."

# SEVENTEEN

*I*n the kitchen Dad was tossing a gigantic salad with an outlandish bombastic flair, straining his deep-throated voice to the opera, *Figaro, Figaro, Figaro,* sounding more Italian than Polish. Crisp juicy lettuce, carrots, chopped celery, kidney beans, diced red tomatoes, a big operation with his own ranch dressing concoction. The smell of zesty garlic bread toasting in the oven sucked me in. I was starved, and prepared to eat the kitchen itself. I mean, from the looks of the mess, you would think Archie Kreeszowski was preparing to feed the whole eighty member Lake County Sheriff's department instead of three or four people.

"Ummm, goood," I sniffed, greeting him with a hug and a kiss on the cheek.

"Have a good time?" he said, between Figaro's.

"Marvelous," I hummed, snatching a chunk of carrot, then a pinto bean, and a leaf of lettuce, then I sidled over to the oven to steal a slice of garlic bread, hot tongue-burning stuff, "ummm, good, ouch. . ." Then after a menacing slap at my hand, I said, "Is Kimberly coming by?"

"She went to pick up the pizza," he said. I snatched another bean and bit of lettuce as he slapped at my hand again.

"Wait till it's ready," he growled. I laughed, then pretended a pout, his growl always preceded his bark.

"I was just about to alert the boat patrol to go looking for you. . ."

"Sorry, Dad." Just in time. The phone rang.

"I'll get it," he said, already reaching for it.

"Think I'll grab a quick shower," I mumbled, choking on a full mouth.

His back was already turned to me, the phone stuck to his ear. The calls were all his anyway, and he had always been very private when it came to company business. In the past he had always shielded Mom and me from his police affairs. If I pried, I might glean a tiny morsel now and then, but only when he was ready, and only after he had mulled it over in his mind thoroughly, finally deeming a somewhat edited version suitable for my tender ears.

My last two years in Southern California as assistant to the eminent criminologist, Carolyn Kosloff had been the turning point in our relationship when he realized I had made a commitment to the family Blue-coat tradition.

In the shower under the endless spray I lathered and shampooed. I like my body and the sensuous feel of steaming suds caressing smoothly, pampering my delicate skin. I like to touch and caress my secret places, and I like to sing. No whole songs committed to memory, but odd bits and pieces of different melodies ripened with the richness of heat streaming watery suds, when suddenly my voice luxuriates with life. I could have been a great opera star, if only I could sing from the shower. Does everyone burst into song from that same private domain? *"I believe for every drop of rain that falls, a flower grows. . . and I believe that somewhere in that great somewhere, somewhere. . . somewhere. . ."* God, I wish I knew the words. The melody is right there drumming away, begging, blending. . . and then a new melody takes over in my hopeless brain; *"And the sea is coming in once more, like the oncoming tide, I rush to your side with one burning desire, and your arms open wide, at least we're face to face, as we kiss in an embrace, I can tell, I can feel, you are loved, you are real, real-l-ly mine, in the rain, like the tide at its ebb. . ."*

I know I have the voice, and the music is booming around in there, maybe I can get words from Emile, and then eat your heart out, whoever you are.

Unwittingly, I had moved to the straining rhythm of my body lathered smooth with Dove soap; the warm shower stream pelting my face and body, fingers and hands gliding ever so slowly, sensuously touching where no hands have touched before; well maybe a few.

I was a disembodied, floating soul until other thoughts trickled into my brain, releasing more reflective thoughts.

Mom, were she still alive, would have been pleased had I married some carpenter or truck driver and brought home many grandchildren for her to dote over and spoil lavishly.

After her death there had been such a vacuum. I missed her so for that first year, and still do. Dad, the unshakable was himself shaken to a solemn and grave shell of his former self. He had tried desperately to shield and cheer that little girl in me, and somehow fill that empty space. As a means of restoring my faith, he had urged me to consider options for my life that somehow go on in spite of the emptiness. "Make a commitment," he used to say, "and give it your best shot. Get involved."

He had tried to get me to consider teaching and even law, and so at his urging I sat in on a few court sessions. At first the drama seemed impressive, even such minor cases like drunken driving posed serious concern about the inner workings of the court system. In one case a young hoodlum had beaten up an old man. What a coward, I concluded, and he looked so damn smug. I wanted to send him up for life, but he had a sleazy lawyer and got off with a slap on the wrist.

Another song worked its way into my head; *"All alone am I. . .with just the lonely beating of my heart."* I turned around, tilting my head to welcome the healing spray that ran through my hair and down my body, fresh, enlivening, and cleansing.

Then one day the court house hallway teamed with lawyers awaiting their turns before the judge, a bunch of Harvard drones, corporate teams, haggling, dealing, corrupting with coiffured hair-dos. Charcoals and pinstripes and navy three-piece suits with their textbook attitudes, like an orgy to see which one would come out on top.In short, a bunch of plastic jerks, schlepps in search of someone's, anyone's blood on which to feed and elevate their elaborate egos.

All of it, a phony stage show with phony emotions, while some poor victim got flushed down the drain, and later, the pinstripes went out together for a beer party.

Maybe that is why I was so shocked to learn that Kimberly had decided to quit the district attorney's office in favor of private practice.

Rena McKenzie is my all time favorite Country Western singer, and the words to *Cassie's Town*, flowed from my lips now. Friends used to say I looked like Rena McKenzie, and I would say; "Yeah, without the boobs." In my shower I sound like Rena McKenzie. I would go any place just to see her perform. Look for me, your look-alike, Rena.

In place of my mom, Kimberly was my role model. I wonder what the outcome would have been, had I studied law as Daddy had wanted. Only Kimberly dressed in her lady's pinstripe, without her Harvard mode seemed to be the exception. Or, perhaps it was that I knew her concerned ethical inner person, when so many lacked her qualities.

I always imagined her as devoted to some crusade, where by contrast she seemed more suited to a career as a model or television spokesperson, with her slender pretty figure, always stylishly dressed. Although her complexion appeared slightly anemic, a little make-up would alter that easily.

I wondered why she never married, and was she still a virgin? And, are men really afraid of beautiful, intelligent women?

"Dammit," I complained, snapping suddenly as a blast of shockingly cold water struck my back like a demon gone mad. I reeled in panic to twist the faucet off. Hot water gone. So much for that quick shower.

There was a knock on the door as Kimberly's voice came flowing through; "Your pizza's ready, Ms. McKenzie."

# EIGHTEEN

*I*n my bedroom and still damp, I studied the wet mop of stringy red hair I called my own. "Not much to do with that," I mused to the mirror. "Dresser mirror on the wall, you never lie, do you?" I loosened the towel wrap, letting it fall to the floor, "You're not too bad kid, not bad at all." I could keep this charade up all night. A little self-praise can do wonders for a girl, besides, the scent of toasty spices beckons.

On the bed behind me Cuddles raised a considerate eyebrow and purred. "Ah, Cuddles you beautiful furry creature, my mentor, and my conscience, what should we girls wear, huh?" I said, turning to stroke her while she rolled onto her back very unlady-like, paws up, gently kneading the air. "What the hell, why not, huh Cuddles, the black lace underwire, to boost these fine specimens up so they can be observed, and how about these black lacy hip huggers with the deep-V. Let the panty line show, just a little suggestion."

In the mirror again, I turned to admire my boldness. Then to Cuddles, I said, "Ah yes, the racy green satin blouse, and the winter white slacks, a little snug around the fanny, don't you think?" She purred appraisingly. "You do agree then, just what a girl needs, approval from one of her peers. . .and, two or three buttons open, like this, four you say, oh Cuddles how daring, *risque*. . . . Oops, oh my, that must have slipped open all by its self, how embarrassing. Good enough for an evening at home with pizza and popcorn. But suppose, someone stops by. A girl should be ready, don't you agree?" Any other night, baggy old joggers would have sufficed.

"Purr-purr."

"Oh, one more thing you say, a splash of *Beautiful* —right in here, in the cleft, another under each earlobe, let it show, just a hint of black lace, how about a dash along the inner thighs?" Purr-purr-purr. "You do agree then. Felines know, and oh, what the hell, a little around the navel, too.

Ready girl? Let's go get some of that pizza and popcorn, the lips and eyes can wait till later."

Just as I had expected, Dad scurried about in his silver and black sweats, his whiffs of white hair, what little was left, mussed and a speck of shredded carrot hung from his chin. I brushed it off. I don't think he noticed but Kimberly did.

"My, don't we look snazzy this evening," she teased. "Are we expecting someone?"

"Just some old things I slipped into," I returned. She always looked great, long shiny hair drawn back neatly in a comb barrette, no make-up, she seldom needed any, a sloppy old shaker knit I had seen many times, and trim fitted faded jeans with those little ribbons at the heels, and red pumps. She could be so casual, and with such little effort. Dammit, she looked great. The warm smile was there too, not a pasted one, but a sincere smile.

At the kitchen table Dad popped another can of beer, pffft, and hissing. When he set it down I stole a sip. He raised a warning eyebrow. He drank straight from the can, naturally. A root beer for Kimberly, in a glass of course, and for me a diet Dr Pepper with a glass, naturally, to be ladylike. On other occasions the bottle or can would do.

Dad had already attacked the salad with his customary gusto. "You like cold pizza," he jibed.

"Just some old things, huh? I hear you went canoeing with Emile, the bird carver today. Have fun?" said Kimberly in a pressing tone.

"Oh, we just paddled around a bit. I wanted to see if I could get the hang of it."

"The hang of what?"

I squinted a few daggers in her direction.

"Why do I detect a budding romance here?"

Dad having already polished one slice of pizza, was busy working on another. But I know him, sly cuss, he doesn't miss much.

I chewed my second bite a proper ten times, along with some salad.

Kimberly was normally a skimpy eater, except when it came to pizza and salad with Dad's dressing concoction, then she could hold her own in any contest.

"What happened to that hot thing you had going a month ago, you know, what's his face from Sacramento, the Attorney General's office?"

"Changing the subject?"

"Same subject. My turn."

"If you insist. One of those on again, off again things, now off again." I thought of asking her if she had gotten any, but knowing even the thought would not get by Dad, I erased it quickly.

"Weren't you two engaged?"

"Sort of."

"Well?"

"I don't think it will stand the test of time."

"Why not? You guys looked great together."

"He patted her butt in public," Dad chimed in. Cuddles stirred, farted, and hopped onto my lap, purring.

"Hey cat, you wanna go outside," Dad scolded, "do that again."

"Better out than in, Mom used to say." I stroked Cuddles. We girls have to stick together. Then to Kimberly, I said, "Well?"

"What is this, a cross-examination? He patted her butt in public, and she told him to get lost."

"Well, are you still engaged, or not?"

"We talked about it."

"Just talk?"

"Well, we pretty much decided that two lawyers in the same family had very little promise. . . Besides, he's there, I'm here, and he is in L A, and I'm here, and he's in D C, and I'm, well perhaps later."

Two slices of pizza left, Dad looked at me, Kimberly looked at me. I looked both of them straight in the eye. "I'm full. I couldn't touch another bite," I lied.

"Me too," added Kimberly.

"Me too," chimed Dad. "Can't let it go to waste, specially with three liars staring at it."

"The great cross examiners," said Kimberly, "I'll finish with salad."

"Daddy, it was a jumbo, loaded, and you ate half of it all by yourself. . ."

Kimberly picked up the wheel cutter and split the larger piece in two. "There," she said with an air of finality, pushing the full piece to me and a half slice to Dad," declaring; "No leftovers in this party." She polished hers off very delicately in three bites.

Kim and I both picked at the salad while Dad clelaned up. He liked to putter around the kitchen at times. It was his domain and he was in charge. No challenges accepted. "You girls go ahead in the living room. I'll finish up here," he ordered.

"What about this big salad?" asked Kimberly.

"I'll work on it during the week," he said. "Turn on the TV will ya? It's almost time for the Golden Girls."

In the living room, Kimberly settled properly into the glider-rocker, I on the couch next to her. I kicked off my pumps and curled my feet beneath me. Cuddles leaped onto my lap and settled in purring like a regiment.

Now that we were in private I suspected Kimberly would re-open the subject of my presumed romance with Emile, so I decided to beat her to the punch. I wondered why he had not showed up. Oh God, I realized I had not told him where I lived, nor had I given him my telephone number. He must surely know it, I concluded. With the remote control, I switched the TV onto the Golden Girl channel.

I could feel the wheels turning in her rumination process with a question soon to follow, so I asked first; "You know, I was shocked to hear that you had forsaken the D A's office for private practice."

"It was a long time coming."

"What happened?"

"In two words, Martin Rosswell."

"That bad, huh? Thinks he's a stud, doesn't he?" That last I said in a conspiratorial voice, two women alone, sharing.

"That, I could handle. A subtle put-down to set him back on his heels. Aside from sex, he didn't need me for that anyway with so many others available. I think he must have considered me as some sort of threat though."

"What then?"

"Maybe it was his swollen ego, or his impudence, or both. Maybe I just figured out how stupid he is. You realize, he always had plans to move up to better things in Sacramento. All he needs is an issue. No telling what he will do about the deaths of those four duck hunters this week. If he could get his name in the papers, or on television, I think he would even prosecute his own mother."

"I watched him in court a couple of times. I thought he was a joke."

"Even back when he was assistant DA he was looking ahead. I remember an amusing incident back when I first joined the office fresh out of college, he wanted to make an impression, me the impressionable young thing, him the world's top stud, wanting to add another notch to his already over-knotched blotter.

This particular day he called me into his office, reared back in his fancy chair with his hands clasped behind his slick hairdo;

wearing a new three piece pin-stripe suit, smug and arrogant. I think he expected me to curtsy and take notes as part of my training."

When she hesitated, I prompted a little, "Come on, what next?"

She allowed a small giggle. "Well, it was the first time I ever met Mister Chester Cowan. He was a scruffy old guy in bib overalls, like he had just come in casually from his farm work. After he let Chester wait out in the hallway, Martin left him standing at his desk like he was rendering judgment. Then he says, 'Seems we have a number of complaints against you Mister Cowan, or is it McCowan. . .'"

"'Cowan?'"

"'. . .serious complaints about poaching, out of season.'

"Martin ordered Chester to sit down, flashing his tough guy look while being magnanimous, making his point. In reality, it was his ego reminding him he doesn't like to look up to people, especially a lowly farmer. Chester Cowan says, 'Don't wanna sit down. Don't plan on staying that long.'

"Humph, grunts Assistant DA Martin Rosswell; 'Game warden has reports you been hunting without a license.'

"Martin stared at Chester with his get tough look again.

"Chester Cowan stared back defiantly, a fiercely independent little man, supposedly overwhelmed by the big fancy office. A thumb tack being pounded into the ground by a mighty sledge hammer.

"'Game warden says he warned you, and filed a report.'

"'Anybody see this poaching?'

"'Well, that is not exactly the point,' Martin growled, coming forward to stare at this little man. 'I want you to know, and I am warning you formally that I intend to prosecute. . .' Well Chester was still standing defiantly when Martin rose to his feet towering over little Chester, his fists strained and planted on his desk when Chester says; 'You tryin to tell me you called me in here to warn me, waste my time, and you got no evidence. You got nothin better ta do with the taxpayer's money. There's dope an rape an stealin out there. . .'

"'Mister Cowan,' said DA Martin Rosswell, 'DON'T YOU DARE, raise your voice in this office. . .'

"Cowan had turned for the door, 'You got any warrant for my arrest?'

"'Nooo, but I can get one.' Martin settled smugly back in his chair, glowering.

"'Well, big shot college boy, go get one, the next time you want to talk at me. I got work to do.'"

Kimberly was smiling now like she was having fun. "That catapulted Martin out of his chair with his fists clenched on his desk, embarrassed and with fire in his eyes, and he says; 'Let me tell you something, you break the law in my jurisdiction, you go to jail, do you understand?'

By this time the little farmer was already at the door," grinned Kimberly. "When he turned to glare back at Rosswell, saying; 'Which bunch of gangsters bought you that fancy pin-stripe suit, Sonny?' Then he slammed the door and left."

In the kitchen the phone buzzed aloud and Dad had it in two rings.

"Cowan did that?" I sniggered. "Dad always said he was a feisty old fart."

"You better believe Martin Rosswell knows it now. That was only the first of their many encounters. Others have been over Chester's refusal to respond to jury summons."

"I heard about that," I said. "But not that first encounter. I bet Martin's tail feathers are still singed."

"Mine too. Here I was sitting there, an associate who was supposed to be impressed, dressed in my own very best navy pin-stripe skirt suit. . ."

"No, you in a pin-striper?"

"I haven't worn a pin-stripe since. I think someday I shall break with courtroom dress code. Court is so drab and boring, not at all like the television versions. Dreary really. Someday I'll wear something in hot pink, or sunshine yellow. A mini-skirt with a diaphanous blouse. . ."

"And a plunging neckline. . ."

". . .bold scarlet pantyhose, the fancy designer kind—"

". . .yeah, and a black bra that pushes your boobs up, like I got on," I demonstrated, "and makes them look like they're double sized. . ." I added.

"Judge Wooden might just wake up, and throw me out of court for non-professionalism, jeopardizing my poor client or some such nonsense."

". . .hip-huggers with a telltale panty-line. . . and. . ."

Dad came into the room with a bowl of popcorn for each of us and flopped himself comfortably in his La-Z-Boy recliner, with his own bigger bowl in his lap, juggling another can of beer. "What are you girls laughing about?" he asked.

"Chester Cowan and Martin Rosswell," I giggled.

"You girls got more problems than a Thanksgiving turkey, you know that?"

"We don't have to figure out what happened to those four hunters."

# NINETEEN

"Don't you want to know who that was on the phone?" Dad said, grinning sheepishly.

"Who?" we chorused.

"It was for you," he said, giving me that look.

"Why didn't you call me?"

"You were having too much fun, gossip and all."

"We don't gossip," I chortled.

"He said to give you a message."

"Who?" I said, looking at Kim. I could see now she was on Dad's side, copying his coy sinister look, ready to spring the trap.

Kimberly said; "Emile, of course."

"He said to tell you he was sorry, but he can't make it. Something about he had to go out of town, sudden like."

"You could have called me."

"I started to but you didn't say anything about expecting a call, or anybody coming by."

Kim was grinning now, her sort of smug-like Cheshire cat grin.

"I just told him to stop by. . .if he wanted, to join us for pizza and salad. . ."

"Sure. Leftover pizza. . ." Kimberly said, giving me the daggers, already digging it in, and twisting.

On Golden Girls Blanche was having a fit again. She didn't want her daughter to get artificially inseminated, the thought of becoming a grandmother loomed totally scary. The whole idea was outrageous and Dorothy started giggling, and Rose started to tell another story about Saint Olaf.

Dad was still laughing. "Almost as funny as Archie Bunker," he cried. "That Blanche is a real character."

The term slut came to mind, a word right out of Dorothy's mouth, right there on TV for kids to see and hear, only kids hardly ever watched Golden Girls to further their education. Only the Geritol age group dug these ladies. Kids had better things to learn about.

Dad said, still laughing, "Boy would I like to take that Blanche out just once, well maybe two. . ."

"Daddy," I snapped. "Aren't you too old for that kind of stuff?"

"Let me tell you something, Little Daughter," when he wanted my undivided attention and insisted on my obedience, he always called me little daughter. From anyone else I would have hated it, and most likely would have dotted both their eyes, yet from Daddy it was somehow endearing.

"Little Daughter," he reiterated. "It's called practice, and all my life I practiced for stuff like that."

"Practice-practice-practice," sniggered Kimberly.

Blanche must have caught the line because she blustered, blushed and cooed coyly, and then came the commercial.

"That Emile doesn't talk much, does he?" Kimberly said. Caution, I thought, she's baiting me again.

Dad said, "I'll tell you one thing; he doesn't take any awards for story telling."

"Oh I wouldn't say that," I returned, smiling glibly, easing Cuddles from my lap. She bounded to the floor, suddenly alert, catlike and a little disturbed. "True, he is a very private person, but I can tell you one thing; he knows a thing or two about feet—"

"*Feet!*" snapped Kimberly, her eyes darting after me inquisitively.

In that same instant I had dashed into Dad's bedroom and

returned with the pair of carved mallard decoys.

The commercial was still on, Leggs Pantyhose, long sensuous legs, silken and filled with vitality and vigor. Dancing legs, and Dad's eyes glued to the TV screen. Cuddles curled up back on the couch, my spot warming her.

I placed the decoys on the floor just around the corner of the coffee table, partially within her sight.

"Watch this," I said. She sprang to life immediately; catlike, the hunter stalking, nose twitching to catch the scent of prey, eyes and ears cannily alert, whiskers twitching, and all in the pouncing posture with her tail flicking ever alert and anxious. Another commercial flashed on. . . She was crouching close to the floor now, intent, then quick subtle animated movements, eager for the kill, a hesitation and then at the precise instant, she pounced on the drake. . .paused, sniffed disappointedly and finally sauntered away toward the kitchen, disconcerted and baffled. . . to her cat food bowl.

"My God," exclaimed Kimberly, "I do believe she thinks they could be real."

"Fools her every time," said Dad. "Fooled me too; that's the reason I bought them. I have to pick them up and examine them to be sure myself sometimes."

Kimberly said, "It's those in the shop that amaze me. Everything is so lifelike, the eyes always looking, pleading. Uncanny." She shook her head, as bewildered as Cuddles. "Really uncanny. . ."

With the commercials ended, Dad was once again glued to the Golden Girls, no doubt fantasizing about Blanche and awaiting her entrance in some revealing silken gown. That unspoken signal meant quiet.

I resumed my place on the couch next to Kimberly as Cuddles wandered back from the kitchen, pausing briefly to sniff the mallards, then pouncing onto my lap, purred, curled up, and purred some more.

Presuming Dad was a lost cause, I said to Kim in a low voice; "I don't believe he can sell enough carvings here in Lakeport to pay the rent. How does he get by?"

"I don't think he does," she whispered; half our attention back on the Golden Girls.

"Dad interrupted, ". . .You looking to set up housekeeping or something?""Dad, do you mind? I just asked Kimberly."

"He won't starve. I can tell you that. I helped his cause a little."

"Yeah, you probably chiseled him down below his cost." I knew better.

Kimberly said, "I want those meadowlarks. I'm in love with them and I stop in his shop just to look at them. He said he would hold them for me. He even offered to let me take them home and pay when I could. . ."

Dad said, "See there, one sale, and he's got a month's pay." The chuckle was for Blanche. She was hysterical again. Rose didn't get it either.

"Be serious you guys," I pleaded.

Dad pressed on with his advantage, "I thought you two don't gossip."

Kimberly came to my rescue. I knew I could count on her. Dad was getting the upper hand and she always sided with the underdog. "As I understand it, his real market is with the galleries, choosy ones that command top dollar. That's probably where he went. He has a Chevy van and he makes a circuit; a gallery in Mendocino, one in Bodega Bay and another in Sausalito, and I think he's in two in Carmel. I think he's in a couple in San Francisco, Ghirardelli Square is one. He wants in one in Old Sacramento, also. That's more than likely where he went. . ."

"He mentioned Nantucket. . ."

"I'm pretty sure he's in some top galleries back east too. I think his work is in demand."

Golden Girls was over. Dad was laughing his head off when he lurched forward in his chair and headed for the kitchen. "You girls want any more popcorn?"

"No thanks," we chorused.

Leaning over to Kimberly, I said, "By 20-20 he'll be snoring like an old bear."

From the kitchen he roared back, "I heard that."

Kim said, "Nothing wrong with his hearing."

I said in an even lower voice; "I want to know more about why you left the DA's office."

Dad came back juggling his bowl of popcorn and another beer.

Empty Nest came on with Dreyfus cocking his soulful eyebrows.

Dad settled back in his La-Z-Boy, popping the beer can and frowning suspiciously; "What are you two conspiring about now?"

# TWENTY

Uh-oh, here comes trouble, I thought; sibling sisters Barbara and Carol of Empty Nest are headed for hilarious problems again. Charlie, the mooching next door neighbor busting in and helping himself in the refrigerator to their milk, drinking straight from the milk carton, Dad the doctor caught in the middle as usual, buzzwords and indignities and catch-phrases. Barbara giving sister Carol the okay to date her ex-boyfriend. I don't believe it. "Is this another re-run?" I said, then I whispered to Kimberly; "What's this about Martin Rosswell?"

"Well, actually it was an accumulation of things," she said. "Like the straw that broke the camel's back. He said, 'Unequivocally. . .'"

"Unequivocally, he said that—?"

"Unequivocally, that I had better get my priorities straight. . .and if I couldn't take the heat, to get out of the kitchen. I'm not a very good cook anyway. You know that. So, nine years shot. So," sigh, "I quit, cold turkey."

"You could have stayed, managed," I said. "Someday he'll trip on his fat ego and fall flat on his conceited face."

"I didn't think so. He had such big ideas."

"Big appetite with a petty brain," I added.

"He can be dangerous, a little bit of knowledge thing, you know. He is always on the lookout for an issue profound enough to propel him onto the steps of the state capitol."

"In front of the camera, no doubt."

"Exactly. But, he wants somebody out in front just in case something backfires; a scapegoat to take the heat. . ."

"How does he get away with it?"

"He's pretty adept at keeping a sacrificial lamb handy for his safety valve. Besides, he has connections, his honor Judge Wooden for one. Don't ask me how. Some secret fraternity for men, maybe."

"Don't you think you could have accomplished more on the inside?"

Uh-oh, Harry the doctor, Harry the father, (Richard Mulligan) and Laverne, (Parke Overall) are into it again. She's going to quit this time for sure. . .

"Do you remember that incident about six months ago. This truck driver rolling downhill during early morning hours on Glasgow Grade to Lower Lake and literally runs over this family?"

"Yes, something about it; two children miraculously unhurt, the parents unhurt, but grandma in the back seat almost died. She was in the hospital for three days in a coma, with twenty three crushed ribs and a concussion."

"She lived, but the trucker clearly fell asleep, or something. The early morning hours are the worst, and he picked up speed rolling downhill and plowed right into the back seat of the family car, a Plymouth, and absolutely demolished it."

"But that was a civil matter wasn't it?"

"Right, but we got drawn into it because the trucker was looking to save his ass by pressing charges of assault and battery. . . and maybe help his own case later on, suing for damages. You see, when the whole wreck finally ground to a stop, grandma was wedged in the back seat, the truck bumper pinning her to the back of the Plymouth front seat. She was out. The trucker got out and staggered toward them, big guy about six feet four. The wife accuses him of falling asleep, or being drunk. The father, a little guy, about five eight tops, clearly stirring with excessive adrenaline looks in to see grandma and says; 'You killed my mother, you bastard.' The trucker says; 'I don't know what happened, I didn't see you.' He is still coming forward when father, all five feet eight inches of him hits the trucker with a devastating right cross," she made a punching motion. "Knocks the trucker to his knees, then forces his way into the back seat, popping the front seat loose and trying to revive grandmother. Mother tends to the crying kids while the trucker staggers around trying to clear his cobwebs. The Highway Patrol arrives and they and the trucker get their heads together. Later, the trucker shows up in a neck brace, saying, 'I don't know what that little shit hit me with,' and he wants us to file charges of assault and battery with intent to kill."

We paused to watch Barbara and Carol conspire over their mutual boyfriend.

"I still don't see how that affects you?"

"Martin hands me the case to prosecute. I find out at the civil trial the insurance companies are supported by a whole herd of pinstripes and the trucker changes his story making himself the hero. He testifies that they cut in front of him, he of course is the professional, and somehow by the grace of *God*, they weren't all killed."

"Yuck, what a creep."

"What a witness, too. That's not all. His macho ego won't let him admit now that the little guy knocked him down for the count. His revised story all of a sudden is that with the help of *God*, he restrains the hysterical father until they can all help grandma."

"And the jury?"

"He had a better lawyer. One guy in baggy jeans and a tattered beige corduroy sports coat with elbow patches walked all over the drones, and the jury buys it."

"He kicked ass," said Dad, sort of getting into it now.

"And Martin Rosswell buys it, also?" I said.

"Right. And he orders me to prosecute. We argue. I tell him the trucker is an unreliable witness and that he brags all over town in the bars about how he got away with it. 'Check it out for yourself,' I tell Martin. He gives it to another prosecutor, and it fades away finally."

"After a lot of wasted taxpayer's money," I added.

". . .and the family got expenses from their own insurance company. That's all."

"That's it?"

"What I heard, but what I would like to have done is prosecute the trucker for perjury."

"I bet Martin liked that."

"Are you kidding, he's the one who buried it."

At commercial time, Dad jumped in. "You recall that incident over the RV'er and Loony Lonny Lawless, the stolen hub-caps?"

"We thought you were asleep, Dad. You were snoring like an old grizzly."

He grinned that wry grin I had come to know all to well, squinting mischievously from the corner of his eyes, that look that tells us he hasn't missed a thing, and I say; "So?" Knowing he will tell me only if and when he wants to.

"You remember Ned telling you how Loony Lonny came in with .22 caliber holes in almost every fleshy part of his body, claiming the RV'er picked him apart on purpose, bleeding like a stuck hog and threw his keys away?"

"No witnesses of course," Kimberly added, candidly.

"The RV'er claims he warned Loony Lonny and Loony Lonny charged him, brandishing the hub-caps, heavy devils, and it was dark and the RV'er thought the last time he used the weapon he had left bird shot in it. He says he was sure it was still loaded with bird shot and he was only trying to scare the thief off, not wanting to hurt him, bird shot not being all that dangerous to humans unless you aim for the face, which he purposely did not. 'Besides, it was self defense, wasn't it?' he says."

"You recall Loony Lonny claimed the guy said; oops," Dad said oops in a gleeful imitation. "Oops, thought those were all bird shot, tough luck, asshole, sorry bout that."

"Who you going to believe," said Kimberly.

"That's right. Who you gonna believe?"

"It's in the DA's hands, right Kim?"

"Sounds like he could have been killed by lead poisoning alone," I added.

"Right," Dad said, pushing out of his chair again. "You girls want anything from the kitchen?"

"No thanks."

To me Kimberly whispered, "I have to go pee."

I said, "Me too. Let's make it a social event. You can go first."

# TWENTY ONE

**20**-20 came on with Barbara Walters and Hugh Downs explaining their program; an interview with Boris Yeltsin, and some very interesting questions. . . and then a look into the life of a teen-age autistic savant, says Barbara Walters.

"That's not the reason you left, is it?" I said, softly again, eyes fixed on Barbara Walters who was presently asking Boris Yeltsin; "Are there still nuclear weapons in Russia under your command?"

Kimberly said, "About a month ago there was another incident, sort of hush-hush now. For me, I suppose, it was the last straw, so to speak. . . Right here in Lakeport, an old man, you probably know the family, 84 years old, helps his 80 year old wife kill herself. . ."

"I know the one," I said. Dad was all ears, I could tell. He'll fall asleep pretty soon.

Hugh Downs was saying something about the search for the real Boris Yeltsin. . .

". . .It was a mercy killing. . .and I suspect it will become one of the top controversies of the future."

"So does Martin Rosswell, I'll bet."

"Well. . . maybe not so much this one right here in Lakeport, unless Martin can help it. I expect that next year we may see some effective legislation on the issue nationwide, no doubt about it. . ."

"Let me guess again, Martin Rosswell wants on the bandwagon early with you as the safety valve."

"It's not that so much, it's the old man, he's 84 and obviously doesn't have long himself. He's somewhat frail, and yet they have managed on their own, but his wife Sarah, has been bedridden for years, crippled with arthritis, osteoporosis, heart, cataracts. You name it. The husband has dutifully cared for her year after year. Finally, she pleads, because they must have talked it over a lot, she begs him that is, when her poor mind is working, to help end it all. Pain killers no longer help. They have had a good life together, children, grandchildren, and great grandchildren were probably the only things that kept the old woman going. Incidentally, all the family is standing by the old man. They agree there was no other way out.

So, with tears in his eyes, he carries her poor body to the garage and sets her up in the reclining seat as comfortably as he can with some soft music and a hose from the exhaust. All she has to do is turn on the ignition key and go off to sleep—"

"I bet he knew all along it would become an issue with himself as the prime example," I said.

"Right, the only reason he stayed behind."

"Right to die. . ."

". . .When an individual's quality of life is no longer worth living, why not?"

"Let me guess the rest; Martin wanted you to prosecute, because it's the law, and his big chance if and when it becomes a big issue, whichever way the wind blows?"

She nodded almost imperceptibly. "He said if I couldn't take the heat, to get the hell out of the kitchen."

"And now you are going to defend the old man?"

"The family has their own lawyers, but I offered to help if I can."

Barbara Walters was saying something about the relationship between Gorbachev and Yeltsin, rumors that they were not on good terms.

Through his interpreter Yeltsin answered, smiling confidently; "That's because in my family I'm the boss—"

I thought about the rift between Nancy Reagan and Raisa Gorbachev; rumors and reports that both made the decisions in their families, both dominant personalities. No wonder the two women locked horns. God, what a tragedy if they had been presidents instead of their husbands.

Barbara Walters says, "Are things moving too fast in Russia?"

Yeltsin says, "The economy in Russia will stabilize in eight months—"

After a grinning pause, Yeltsin said something else when Cuddles stirred, stretching elaborately, and hopped to the floor, sniffed the mallards, and trotted off to the kitchen for her litter box.

Barbara Walters was back on the screen again with her most pressing look; "You have such tremendous courage and confidence."

Boris Yeltsin said, "I strongly believe in what I am doing."

"Have you decided on your master's thesis?" inquired Kim casually.

Cuddles returned with a satisfied swagger, paused briefly to sniff the decoys again, shaking her head dismally, hopped onto my lap purring, and curled into a fur ball.

"I thought I had it all figured out after two years in L A, as assistant to Carolyn Kosloff: Return to Stanford to get my masters in paranormal psychology. . .with a specialty in criminology and my master's thesis would be: *The Self Destructive Need to Defy Authority*, or: *Abnormal/Normal Compulsion to Rebel Against Authority and Absence of Responsibility*. Pretty long title, huh? Maybe formulate it into an acronym."

Kim said, "How about the non-violent psychopathic personality gets what he wants and why?"

"Or should he?" I said with a low chuckle. "Or, How about the super psychopath versus the manipulative super-ego?"

Barbara Walters was asking Yeltsin, "And why should the USA with its own economic problems give aid to Russia?"

Yeltsin hedged, "It's a very difficult question. . ."

Kimberly said, "Or, *The Psychopath Trip With No Sense of Guilt.*"

Yeltsin, "Because it is in their own best interest. . ."

"You know," I said, "I considered something like, CANNABIS, OR MARIJUANA! . . .shorten the title you know, with catchphrases for maximum effect, or some eye popper buzzwords. But after polling some classmates I learned something I should have guessed anyway. It seems everybody is doing something along that same line with excuses to try it. Most already have, or they want to try hallucinogens or LSD. Just once they say. Seriously, can you believe that, just once for research, so they can tell others what it was like from first hand experience, and how to avoid the pitfalls. Some big sacrifice, huh?"

"Sounds like a class of would be martyrs."

"The sad part is, they're serious. Can you believe that?" I said, shaking my head. For a time I sat quietly, gently stroking the soft fur of Cuddles the ever purring furball. At that instant I found myself wondering what she might have been in another life; a duck perhaps, and what form she might appear as in that future reincarnation chain.

Barbara Walters was ready to pop the big hit on Boris Yeltsin; "How are you going to stop scientists from selling nuclear technology to countries like Libya, Iran, and Iraq?"

". . .Then there is the sex disorder category," I went on, mostly for Kimberly's benefit. "A whole range of problems such as appetite and desire. . . and. . ."

Kim said; "And how about; Anomalous Sexual Disorders, hyphen Homosexuality, Old Men and Boys, hyphen and why. Big pretentious titles, but don't expect it to get published."

"Not bad, not bad at all. I should have come to you in the first place." I nudged her, pointing to Dad, "See, it's commercial time and I think we have really lost him."

She allowed a small condoning smile.

Barbara Walters was back with her piercing thoughtful stare of sincerity, her face a little closer, pressing Boris. Here comes the clincher, the sandbag question, I thought. She was dragging it out for impact; "...something— difficult— rumors; that with so much pressure on you... " Again t the pressing stare intensified; "...with so much pressure on you,—you have been drinking heavily." The final touch, a well disguised condescending grin; "Is that true?"

Yeltsin managed his own reaction, a grimace; "What was the question?"

I touched her arm and nodded towards Dad again.

Boris Yeltsin, through his interpreter managed a careful response; "Sports and liquor do not go together..."

"I think we have just about lost him," I tittered, "Daddy and Boris do not go together."

Boris: "I deny all those rumors, people looking for sensational stories..."

Barbara Walters said: "How would you like to be remembered?"

Boris Yeltsin: "...Remembered for the courage to realize I make mistakes...that I am open and honest..."

Hugh Downs: "After this brief message we will meet an amazing teenager with his gifted drawings of a whimsical nature; an autistic savant who grew up in London."

The commercial blinked on and I nudged Kimberly again. She leaned over to look around me, toward Dad sprawled out hopelessly in his La-Z-Boy chair, mouth open, eyes closed, snoring like an old bear.

The savant was a 13 year old black kid named Steven who grew up in London. I watched Steven on TV as he drew pictures of buildings and scenes from memory, totally absorbed, yet unaffected by the capricious nature of his gift. "Amazing isn't it," I muttered. "How he so completely enjoys himself. One look and he turns his back on his subject and sketches the most intricate designs down to the finest detail, and all from memory. . . His delicate and exacting movements shows just how thoroughly he enjoys his gift of talent."

I was somehow aware that Kimberly was also keenly impressed by this young 13 year old. "He could be a study all by himself," I said.

We watched the boy quietly for awhile, then I said; "About my proposed master's thesis. . ." I was half mumbling now, mesmerized by Steven.

Halfheartedly I continued speaking in a low voice to Kim, pausing frequently to consider the story unfolding, saying; "Sadism, Masochism. . . themes that deal with pleasure perceived. . . Sex activities that deal with symbols of sex organs—one title; Object Anomalies such as the Phallic Symbol and Objects. . . including every imaginable range; Pedophilia, (children), Parthenophilia, (virgins), Acrophilia, (tall people), Necrophilia, (dead persons). . . and so on."

Kimberly was watching Steven with intense interest and said; ". . .How about with animals, or midgets. . . One fantasizes it as pleasure and you have another whole range of forces for consideration. . ."

"Did you see that?" I said. "Steven is fascinated with Chrysler automobiles, one glance and he sketches them perfectly, amazing, he is so purely gifted. . ."

". . .Range of forces, and how they start to dominate unfortunate individuals such as that Jones mass suicide in Guinea. . ."

"Or the Freudian theory and his obsession regarding sex."

"He was a prude, wasn't he?" said Kimberly.

"I think so, at least in his personal life, yet he was quite the opposite with his obsessions in professional examinations. Reports say that he never consummated his marriage with his own wife, whatever that means."

"Perhaps that should be a thesis. . ."

"Already done, too many times."

"Oh. . ."

"Some girlfriends at Stanford took a trip last summer to the Orient, Hong Kong, Singapore; in Bangkok they stayed at the Bangkok Hilton. They brought back photos of a shrine within the hotel confines. It was in a secluded wooded area. This shrine had carved wooden penises all around it. It was literally decorated with penises; big ones, some not so big, all bigger than normal though. Some were propped up erect and proudly 4 to 6 feet tall. In this elaborately decorated shrine candles and incense were still burning and even more penises, some type of plea for eternal virility, don't you think? Anyway, in one photo they were riding a penis that was propped up like a cannon ready to shoot, it's head painted all pink with the little hole, 10 to 12 feet long, and they straddled it like riding a horse, laughing their heads off."

"The Thais must have an obsession for larger penises—must be a story there—some kind of ritual, don't you think?"

"Maybe, little squirts running around chanting with a candle in one hand and an enlarged wooden prick in the other," I mouthed the word prick in defense of Dad's sensitive ears.

"I know," said Kim suddenly enlightened; your thesis could be on the MALE ERECTION AND OBSESSIONS WITH IT. Think of all the things you could do in the name of research. Better yet; make it plural, *ERECTIONS.*"

"Yeah, I think you have it, that's it, ERECTIONS-OR OTHERWISE!"

"Kimberly was on a roll now, "Yeah, how about the MYSTIQUE OF THE MALE ERECTION. . ."

"Yeah, as some see it. . ."

". . .Who sees it?"

At that moment I was thinking of Steven and his gift of talent, wondering if Steven had another life form before his present one. Had he learned all his lessons both spiritual and physical? And had he retained all the really important elements attained in that series of birth and rebirth? If so, then surely he had reached the ultimate adjustment in Karma and Nirvana. How and what could we glean from the astute 13 year old boy, so ultimately at peace within himself. I have to wonder if he is aware just how delicate his sense of mental values appear to us, the ones who lay claim to higher sanity. What if I or anyone could reach into the mind of this unique boy who has not a speck of hostility nor animosity toward others and grasp the secrets without disturbing his tender balance? No more wars, no more sickness nor famine, just that last step before pureform. . .

"I think I have it," I said, as the final commercial blinked on, ending 20-20.

"What?" asked Kimberly.

"My thesis, REINCARNATION!"

"Reincarnation?"

"Yeah. . . Dad, you've fallen asleep again, you're snoring."

"No I'm not," he jerked. "I heard every word."

"Daddy, you were asleep. Old machines don't make that much noise!"

"Erections. . . tut-tut, what kinda talk is this from such fine young ladies of refinement.."

"DADD-DY."

"You know what my sin is?"

"Lots of them, calumny topping the list."

"GOSSIP."

"GOSSIP?"

"Yeah, and I can't wait to get out of here, write it all down, tell everybody. . ."

"You wouldn't?"

"Uh-oh," said Kim. "Time for me to go home. Bye."

"You know something else?" he said, grinning smugly.

"What?"

"I don't have to figure on what to write for a master's thesis—"

# TWENTY TWO

Within a six block radius of my house there are at least seven churches. Add a few more blocks to that radius and you have ten churches. In the Lakeport area there are eighteen holy places of worship.

For such a small town, population under five thousand, that seems like a lot of doctrines and deities.

We also have our little share of hellfire and eternal damnation as well, plus a full measure of our own authentic Bible thumpers and door to door canvassers.

My hometown also has its share of barrooms to willingly accommodate the rest of the population, should they seek such additional spirit connections for out of body and mind experiences.

Dad and I attend Saint Mary's Catholic church at 801 North Main Street, a refreshing two block walk on Saturday evening or Sunday morning, whichever the case may dictate, unless of course it happens to be raining.

The last four years we have been somewhat drought stricken, although glancing across eight miles of Clear Lake water one would not think so.

The old church, built in 1916 sits on a lofty hill at the southern corner overlooking the lake from the north end of town. It is a small off-white traditional looking structure of chipping stucco with its reminder of a Spanish bell tower. Hourly electronic carillons now replace the one time bells.

Back in the year 1916 the Parish House was in use as a coach stop, that was just six years after Sheriff Kemp was killed by Louis Augustine, and less than 60 years after the murder of Jeff Warden by Jack Hurt at the fairground racetrack.

I miss going to the old church now that the new one, built in 1987 of light gray stucco, has taken the similar perch on the north corner of that same block, overlooking that same impressive body of water. In my mind's eye, the contemporary design in no way replaces that old one. It has no choir loft, nor has it that time worn feeling of personal cozy atmosphere compared to the old one. Mom loved the old church and used to sing with a choir back then. At other times she would go just to listen. She knew everyone by name. She had an amazing memory for people and their names and dates of incidental happenings.

Dad used to say that he didn't need to go to church because Molly O'Grady Kreeszowski prayed enough for both of them. I know for a fact; he would give anything to have her kneeling in genuflection beside him now. We Catholics don't seem to read our Bibles all that much. Our Priests, or at least Father Daly does that for us, and keeps us well informed. That is, for those who take the time to come and listen to his holy words. I can't recall when I last went to confession. I pray my poor soul is still salvageable, and I know pretty much for certain that Dad has forgotten the ritual. With his acclamation of sins he could spend the rest of his days reciting Hail Mary's, and the stations of the cross. And I shouldn't be far behind I suspect.

No doubt when Father Daly takes the pulpit this day he will be most pleased. The place is packed.

Dad has nodded his recognition to all those he knows, in one capacity or another. All loyal fellow Catholics.

In the row in front of us, halfway down the right side of the right aisle a middle-aged couple paused, and waited while the others inched closer together to make room for them. Before entering, they dipped their knees in genuflection, making their sign of the cross.

They had turned briefly before to exchange glances with Dad, the sheriff. I smiled too, and although they looked familiar I could not remember their names. Molly O'Grady would have, and would have whispered it to me as a gentle reminder.

As they knelt I heard the whispered words; ". . .In the name of the father and of the son. . ." Words from others behind came to me too; "Our father who art in heaven, hallowed be thy name, thy kingdom come, thy will be done, on earth as it is in heaven. . ." Somebody else said, "The Lord be with you. . ."

Church feels good, especially when surrounded by so many warm caring souls. In church as in no other place there is an ambiance of brotherhood; a flood of emotion as if one is already on the road to salvation. . . And when this humble life is done, I wondered; is there another one waiting? Is there another step upward in the spiritual life cycle if you get it right this time? If not, you get a slap on the wrist and back you go.

I felt a sudden tingle of guilt for not attending more often. After all, did I not feel Mother Mary's presence more genuinely right here at home.

That is not to say that we are outright wayward sinners. After all, is not forgiveness divine. . . Dear God, Father almighty, creator of heaven and earth; I pray my thoughts are not considered blasphemous or sacrilegious. I have sinned. Who has not? I do believe in the Holy Trinity, and I do humbly beg your forgiveness, and I promise in the future to do better.

As I wiped a tear from my cheek, I felt really better already. Why does going to church have to feel so like falling into a habit, and at other times a bright revelation with a ray of eternal light at the end of a long tunnel?

We Catholics like to say that praying is like keeping company with God, and that's not bad company once you get your foot in the door.

# TWENTY THREE

Uncle Sid left we Kreeszowskis' with a poetic legacy. He used to joke around a lot, and among other things one particular little verse always seems to rattle around in my head whenever I am in church. When Uncle Sid and his wife visited from Vermont, and he and Dad invariably became overjoyed with beer drinking they would recite the poems from a little book titled; "Accordin to Batiste," by Seth Clement Towle. While a bit tipsy, they used to get this little book out when they argued about the accuracy of their memories regarding some of the lines.

In church I may be singing along from the hymn book or reciting the Psalms, or only half listening to the Priest and the message of the day, and yet in my mind's eye I am watching others while my dominate thoughts are of Batiste and his witty and profound rhymes.

At home Uncle Sid and Dad had often sat bleary eyed, sometimes reciting alternate lines while Mom and Aunt Evelyn scolded them ruefully. I am always guarded about my thoughts when standing side by side by Dad, suspecting he had the uncanny ability to read those private thoughts which rambled around inside my kooky head.

This one is titled; "Church Going" and it goes something like this:

"I spec de beeg queschun in all church today,
Is why sum peple go—whi more sta awae."

Father Daly paused facing the congregation, splendid in his

vestments, hands poised in the customary supplicating gesture motioning all to stand; "We believe in God, the father almighty, creator of heaven and earth. . ." As he continued amid the musical sounds of babies in the far pews, I glanced around, head bowed to steal a peek; children already impatient and uttering small sounds as the words flowed softly, lips moving following the example of their elders.

And once again I thought of Batiste;

De reasons for going— de excuses I've sot,
Here is de ansurs, believe um or not.

And Father Daly said, "Born of the virgin, Mary suffered, was crucified, died and was buried," and I wondered at the purity of little children; do they have a direct line to God?

And through me, Batiste rattled on;

Sum people go jes cause other people do,
And wish dey wus home fore de sermons half thru.

Father Daly was saying; ". . .Resurrection of the body, and life everlasting. Amen."

Amid the sounds of fidgeting children and shuffling shoes plus a few small coughs the Deacon's wife stood to make announcements; "We can use a few more volunteers for the free kitchen project. . ." For the moment I missed the words, I was watching a pious young boy, no different from the others, his small hands still set together in prayer, what message was he seeking? ". . .the ladies guild meets. . ." she was saying while I was studying the posted crucifix, symbol of the Catholic church, Jesus Christ lighted and ascending, and the woman's voice said something about an Italian pasta feed, and finally she spoke of a planned wedding. I studied the displays of fresh flowers and sniffed lightly for the mixture of scents as my Batiste stirred around in my head for word order and pronunciation;

Sum peple go jus to hear the choir sing,
Sum sta home for de very sam ting.
Sum go to church reglar, sum go in a spurt.

That's me I scolded; why do I just go in a spurt?

Sum sta home caus der feelings git hurt.

Again my gaze fell on the different little boy, his hands still poised in prayer, relaxed yet seriously intent, and I wondered if Emile might have been like him in his younger years. I watched the altar boy so neat in his white robe. Would he become a priest someday, or maybe a policeman? Had Emile ever been a choirboy?

The voice of Batiste continued, reclaiming old lines;

Sum peple don't lak long winded pray'r.
Sum go to slepe al de tam dey are dere.

I turned to glance to the rear of the church—to the lighted niche with the statue of our Mother Mary and Baby Jesus, complimented by a vase of fresh flowers.

And now the Deacon stood before us; "To all those who suffer, we pray to the Lord. . ."

While in my head the clatter continued;

Sum go an sit way up in de frunt pue,
Jes to sho peple dat's whot dey shud do.
Probly dat is the feller dat nevur cud sin,
But in a horse trade—jes luk out for him.

The offering basket came my way and I dropped in my pledge envelope, passing it to Dad while he did the same. Then came another basket for two offerings this day. Caught off guard, and embarrassed I dug frantically for another dollar. Must be something special going on that I missed.

Father Daly coughed into his fist to clear his throat. His voice could boom when he wanted it to but this day he had a slight irritation in his throat as he got out a prayer over gifts; "Lord, our God, may the bread and wine you give us. . ." Across the isle from us two boys and a small girl shuffled about impatiently. For them, it was now a time for games and mischief.

And Batiste had found more rhyme for me;

Sum peple set strate wid a sanctimonious grin,
Sum twitch all roun lak dey set on a pin.

Again the two boys could not help themselves as their mother shushed and scolded them. Little sister sniggered triumphantly.

Sum peple go, a goode impresshun to mak,
Udders sta home, dey got auful hedake.

A shuddering thought struck me; I wonder if the children's father was out duck hunting this day?

Father Daly, minus his usual boom was saying; ". . .To be cleansed of sin, and to begin a new life. . . with a rebirth in Christ," he managed a little boom at last so that his words funneled from the pulpit flooding out over the congregation; "We need to touch Jesus and relive God's unconditional love in our hearts—"

Inside me Batiste stormed about to be heard once again with a just reclaimed phrase;

Sum peple go to se al de new hat,
Yu cud gues who dey be, no man go for dat.
Sum peple don't go an use for an xcuse,
De ministers surmon dey h'aint got no use;
He may preche too long or may git under dere nerve,
Dat's damn good xcuse wen no udder wil serve.

I wondered if Batiste had been a Catholic. Obviously he knew the church scene, and I doubt he would have gone in for highfalutin Bible thumping with hell-fire and damnation like the Evangelists and Pentecostals. A simple ceremony with very little staging or dramatics, something with very little ritual would have been more his style. Perhaps Emile was right after all when he claimed that modern church rites have changed so little compared to those older pagan rituals observed beneath the limbs of some sacred oak tree.

Father Daly said, ". . .And gave his only begotten son." I considered the Catholic way; confess, do penance and all is forgiven with the message of; go my child and sin no more.

Batiste knows;

Sum peple go caus dey jes got de habit,
Sum ruther go fishin or shoot sum pore rabbit.

Father Daly ceremoniously held up the round dish with the bread of life and with dedicated purpose folded and broke the wafers into precise pieces.

The organist started playing and singing followed.

"This is my body broken up for you," said Father Daly. "This is my blood, may it bring us pardon for our sins—"

Dad nudged me from my stupor to join those in the aisles, heads partly bent, solemn and humble. And all the while the voice of Batiste reminded me of his presence;

Sum go to church cus dey think it's dere duty,
Sum sta away cus church folks is snooty.
Sum peple fele tired an too lazie to go,
Sum lissen to sermon dat's come on radio.

Back in our pews the priest chanted a prayer in Latin, just to keep in practice he would say. Then we all sang the Lord's Prayer and from behind a woman's beautiful voice resonated into the beam ceiling.

The kids across the aisle were out of control with little sister as the instigating stimulus. I wondered if a few lines from Batiste could gain their attention;

Sum tink dat religion is gone out of style,
An goin to church ain't really wurth while.
But dey is sum peple dat goes fur de good in dere heart,
God bless dem, dey git fewer an set furder apart.

"Turn to your neighbor," said Father Daly. . . and from my side a man touched my shoulder; "Peace be with you, sister." I smiled back, "And to you brother." Then from behind came the same greeting. Some familiar friends hugged.

Batiste was at it again. Go away Batiste, I almost said, I don't want you in my head right now. But Batiste knows where he belongs;

So wid al our excuses what cud any church do,
Or de minister preachin to jes empty pue.
We may foole ourself an de minister too,
But de goode Lord above, I tink he see thru.

Father Daly said, "Let us all offer a final prayer for the unfortunate and untimely death of those four hunters, and their dearly beloved family and friends. . . Forgive them their sins Heavenly Father and receive them as they enter the kingdom of peace and light. . ."

Now I get it; Father Daly and Batiste, they speak the same language, only with a slightly different final message;

So at las wen we knock at de beeg perly gate,
Saint Peter will han us jes bout whot we rate.

The Priest's lasting message, "Go forth. Have a great evening and let there be peace on earth."

The congregation sang and the kids, at last showed visible signs of relief. Dad heaved a great sigh.

Going to church is like going to a great party, I thought. A birthday party with music, and the company's not too bad either.

As for Batiste, Uncle Sid used to muse that we must have a little Acadian blood in our veins. Back in Vermont, one wandering Frenchman stopped by once and must have plied Grandma Kreeszowski with poetry. . .and made her an offer too good to refuse.

# TWENTY FOUR

On the walk home with my arm hooked in Dad's I noticed the flowers in Mrs. Murphy's yard, so well groomed and cared for. I had noticed her and Mr. Murphy at a distance locked in genial conversation with Father Daly and others. I had thought about paying respects then, but they were busy. She would have welcomed Dad and me. Later I will walk over for a visit and in hopes of prying some of her gardening secrets loose. She and Mom had been such good friends and at times together they could affect that distinguished lilting Irish Gaelic in their voices, a gift passed on to Mrs. Murphy by her grandmother from County Cork in Ireland.

"What a beautiful day," said Dad as we approached our own drab gray house hidden mostly by overgrown wild honeysuckle, burgeoning bamboo, nandina, and straggly looking dusty oleanders. The low, once white picket fence with chipped paint and dirty with ages of dust looked about to collapse.

At the gate I said, "Dad," I had to say it twice to get his attention. I didn't think he was listening, with his interest already on some football game or something at the office.

". . .Well, yes Little Girl," he managed, considerately.

"I want to paint the house."

He looked shocked, his mouth gaped wide open as if taken completely by surprise.

"I want to paint it sunshiny yellow, with white trim. . . and I want to plant flowers, lots of flowers. . . and all these old bushes and wild looking vines will have to go. And that ugly looking old dead walnut with the straggly branches should be cut down. It hides the best part of the house. . ."

"Wait,wait,wait," he interrupted. "Just when do you propose to do all this?"

"Right now. The yard anyway. I can start today."

After changing into old clothes I hit the yard like a fury, mowing with one of those old hand things, raking, trimming and weeding. That opened things up at least. Decrepit old rose bushes were severely trimmed back with promises of new life come springtime. So much strangulation had prevented new life and I whispered to them gently urging them out of their fallow state.

Cuddles followed at my heels, purring and begging for attention, jumping at anything which moved. This was her territory and she knew every hollow and hiding place and at last she sensed she had someone to tease and play with. We bandied a lot; I could always talk to Cuddles, and though she was a great listener she had a neat way of making her will obvious to me.

In a protected place I discovered a thriving patch of begonias just waiting for a touch of new life encouragement, and nearby; a patch of pansies with distinctive pixy faces and marigolds. I had to wonder if these were remnants of my mother's days when she had been so busy here. It seemed like a miracle of miracles that they had struggled to hang on to that last strain of life until another pair of hands came along to invite their return.

It must have been half-time when Dad came out to join us finally, guilt stricken no doubt, and with trash bags to gather up the piles of refuse.

"I'll plant now," I said, "so when spring comes we'll have primroses, tulips and daffodils. . .and some iris too. Over here we'll have violets, and look what I found, sweet alyssum."

If it was something Emile had said I don't yet know, but I thought at times I caught Mother's face smiling from the flowers, and I could imagine flowers, fields of them blossoming into smiling faces, then suddenly fading with the changing seasons, only to be reborn once again, and there seemed something of her face in all of them.

I thought also of Lisa, the little girl featured on TV with the deadly tumor in her youthful body; a vivacious and beautiful child so filled with vitality and determination and love. . . who had dragged home a wasting tree to plant, stubbornly convinced it would grow. She died so young, and yet her family cherished the tree as it thrived and grew to become a symbol of Lisa's memory. I wonder, do they see Lisa in that tree awaiting another chance at rebirth? I think I'll watch for Lisa in the flowers too. She could be there in spirit already, she and Molly Kreeszowski, side by side, hand in hand.

# TWENTY FIVE

Monday morning at Stanford U seemed unusually chaotic, or at least in my own mind it seemed more hectic than normal Mondays. At second observation it seemed normal in all respects with sleepy students preparing for another week of dull drudgery.

I could hardly wait though, as if driven by some unknown obsessive force towards my afternoon free period when I could hit the campus library.

Once there and established in the security of what I perceived as my own private study cubicle on the third floor beside an outdoor view window. I need a window looking out into space, preferably over the tops of tree and greenery with people scurrying around below like miniatures. Once wrapped into some semblance of that cocoon I had an hour until my next class.

In a fever I dug from the shelves every book I could find even remotely pertaining to the subject of reincarnation, or transmigration as it was sometimes referred to.

Also, I rooted out anything on today's Catholics. First, I wanted to know the churches position, my church in particular, views regarding the past and future lives in consideration to the eternal souls.

This became difficult, with much effort and time spent and yielding only vague references to the old testament. In the end I derived more questions than I had time to look for answers.

Encyclopedias proved more helpful, but still only on a very general level.

What I did uncover served merely to whet my appetite further. The key I realized was to make that first mark, write the first words, and so I started by jotting down notes. Reincarnation means literally to be born into another body. Karma is an important concept in many eastern religions, especially Hinduism, Buddhism, and Jainism. (In the border I wrote; look up Jainism).

Followers believe that existence is a continuing cycle of death and rebirth. A condition of that person's life is the direct result of his or her Karma, (deeds) in his previous existence.

These individual's actions and deeds determining their future destinies. Still very general, I noted.

The seed had been planted, and now I craved something specific to latch onto. Questions and doubts loomed as challenges. I would like to find something tobelieve in, I wrote, but I need proof.

As my mind filled with doubts it progressed at a rate far greater than I could write, and the search went on at a snail's pace. Settle down, I scolded.

From another text I wrote; Plato himself was a student of Socrates and later of Aristotle, among others.

Plato wrote in the literary form called the Dialogues, recording conversations between two or more persons in the form of dramas.On the immortality of the soul, Plato believed that even though the body dies and disintegrates the soul lives forever and after the death of the body the soul migrates on into the realm of pure-forms. It exists there for a time and contemplates before returning to the physical world in another bodily form.

I wondered if Emile went to college and from where he got the knowledge from which he formed his opinions. He would most likely say; "Why do you have to go to college to have opinions?"

He might also say; "He or she is relearning their lessons before getting another chance. Do your lessons right, okay. What do you want to be this time? Or, you poor soul you screwed up again; bang, back you go." A guy could really wind up in a hole this way. Not a bad system for Adolph Hitler and his boys, right? You want another chance, okay snails, just keep on cleaning up the muck and grime of others. Or, oops no more chances left. Shit happens you know, and you caused your share of it.

In one of the books I found where Plato, in the Meno, portrays Socrates teaching a simple slave boy a lesson in geometry by asking him fundamental questions. . .and concluded that learning consists of recalling what the soul has already experienced while in the realm of pureform or in previous life.

Yeah, I though, Emile told me about this one too, and if it is true, why don't I remember anything from my past existence, and what might I have been in the past? Big question. And where is that Plato book?

Note: Check for the Meno Dialogues in the Plato book, the *Great Books* , I think.

Thinking about what I had just read, I wondered if a person gets a chance to return and correct the bad deeds perpetrated in the past? Then I dug in my bag for my diary.

Dear Diary, I wrote: I don't believe in this stuff, even though it does have some good points. Then my pen skipped and ran dry and I rooted in my bag again until I at last located the last one. Make a mental note to buy ballpoint replacements.

Another book and another viewpoint and the notes continue; with our present limited knowledge there is absolutely no way to prove the existence of reincarnation. Thanks a lot, guy. Take your book back.

Another book: the Karma doctrines must have logic if two thirds of the world believes in it.

The confessions of Saint Augustine 1:6: "Did we not live in another body or some other place before entering thy mother's womb."

Is there a way to remember, I wondered, pen in my teeth, staring blankly out over the treetops into puffs of clouded space. Surely there must be some key, such as hypnotism. The recurring mystery of the familiarity with places when one has not consciously visited those place.

I wrote: And what of the inner senses, are they signals or clues and can they be trusted or are they merely deceptive emotions? In the case of Plato's Meno, was the result simply the logical outcome of Socrates' dominant suggestive power over a weaker impressionable personality? Good title, maybe.

I was flipping through pages now, scanning and looking for something concrete to latch onto when I paused to read about a man's testimony to his past life while under the influence of an induced trance, where he recalls his past sickness, and ultimate death—then rebirth.Then another case of a woman's past life of promiscuity and her present life of dedicated prudence. Pages upon pages of supposedly documented cases.

Note: When did hypnotism or mesmerism become prominent as a means for treatment?

Ah: late eighteenth century. But not until the 1950's did both the British and American Association approve it for medical use; although it had been recorded as not uncommon in the ancient world. I wonder Just how many of these cases are of people fantasizing or of sensation seekers, or just plain misled individuals.

"Oh my God!" I said aloud, then I said in an apologetic whisper to the alerted man across from me; "I'm late for my next class." He lowered the newspaper so our eyes met, warning me that he was visibly aggravated.

"Sorry," I added, defensively as he shuffled the paper crisply so that the front page greeted me.

The San Francisco Times headline spread across the page in big letters read:

**FOUL PLAY SUSPECTED**
**IN DEATH OF 4 HUNTERS**

# TWENTY SIX

*I* was indeed late when I got to class, however not before I had paused before the news rack to scan briefly for other Bay Area newspaper headlines. The result: vague headlines and fewer details.

I had at that moment a frightening hint that this was only the beginning.

As I attempted to sneak into class and secure an obscure seat in the back row I was promptly greeted by the imperious Professor Wooldridge. He stood tall scanning over his half spectacles in baggy trousers and wool tweed jacket with piercing eyes telegraphing an intimidating warning. When he wanted to he could bear down on students with a certain magnetic eloquence. Just now and for my own benefit he favored an autocratic tone; "Why *MS*. Kreeszowski, how considerate of you to grace us with your esteemed presence. We missed your uncommon wit last Friday. . . A busy weekend I trust?"

"Sorry, your honor," I smiled back, sinking meekly into my seat.

For the honor part I got a scathing glare with two cocked eyebrows, a four star admonishment in this class. In return I detected a few sniggers indicating someone else had been his target until my arrival.

The Chronicle headlines had been at least as bold as the San Francisco Times:

**FOUR HUNTERS IN MYSTERY DEATHS**
**ORGANIZED CRIME CONNECTION SUSPECTED**

The headlines giveth while the essence of the stories take back with vague disclaimers and innuendoes that sink the hook so you think you will read something promising. A lot of he saids, she saids, spilling a lot of words that means they really don't know a damn thing, but expect you to continue paying a quarter for some story that isn't there.

Aside from vague inferences that alluded to street corner, or gang warfare and *almost* certain Mafia connections, one thousand words said absolutely nothing which supported either headline, except for the names of the four hunters; Jack and John Hurt, brothers with suspicious underworld connections and their two unfortunate companions; Charles Burrell, estranged from his wife and two children; and Gordon Channing of which little is known at this time. The latter two have no known underworld connections, but there were undertones inferring that the last two had been lured on the hunting trip with promises of better things to come, someone had said.

Since then my mind had been reeling. It was the name of Jack Hurt which rang a nasty bell in my confused brain.

Professor Wooldridge's eyes hinted to a possible forthcoming scolding with severe consequences.

I smiled back weakly in an attempt to prove I hung on his every word of the now elusive lecture, all the while in my mind's eye I reeled through the past for Jack Hurt.

Yes, of course, Jack Hurt: December 31, 1859, murdered Jefferson Warden in an argument at the Lakeport race track by stabbing him in the neck. An old feud? Impossible, I thought, that an incident more than one hundred and thirty years old could have any connection. Still, if my feeble memory serves me at all, Jack Hurt had escaped only to be captured some five years later, was tried and got off because of lack of viable witnesses.

Impossible. Coincidence, pure coincidence, and yet so much for that prayer for Jack Hurt and his pals and their trip to the pearly gate.

After class, in which I was summarily detained by Professor Wooldridge advising me with an intellectual scolding to reconsider the seriousness of my intentions towards his class, and his subsequent dismissal, I rushed back to the library in search of newspapers and something more informative. Headlines and meaningless columns of mere words for a quarter.

I should have guessed though; Lakeport, that dreamy, isolated little town in the mountains by the Big Water Basin had been ushered into the bigger world and grabbing the reins of the limelight bandwagon would be none other than Martin Rosswell, suave, confident and aggressive.

Later, back in my apartment, I sat on the divan in my only Hawaiian mu-mu, legs crossed and eyes glued to the television set.

Weather was the present issue with a very dramatic play about California's five year drought and water needs.

Then there was the President's trip to Japan in an effort to induce the Japanese to play fair and buy more American goods so he can balance the budget and placate the labor unions.

More gang shootings in Oakland and four more rapes scheduled for the already overburdened courts' calendars.

And then there it was; cameras at the Lake County courthouse steps on Forbes Street where I had grown up.

Detective Lt. Ned Turner was speaking for Sheriff Kreeszowski who had declined a camera interview, was saying: "Yes, there is an ongoing investigation. No, we have no reason to suspect foul play at this time. There are no suspects at this time. Thank you."

Then the camera focused on suave District Attorney Martin Rosswell in his three piece pinstripe, beady eyes set seriously, his sandy hair pasted down in a curving wave over his forehead; must take a lot of gel to keep it in place, I thought. Besides it looks phony. A hair-piece could not have looked more unreal.

He was saying: "...The DA's office under my own personal direction is conducting its own investigation. Foul play is a definite consideration at this time as are drug and other criminal connections. From the information I have available it appears we have long reaching ramifications. And, yes I can promise you results... yes the incident did take place on the Pomo Indian Reservation, Native American I should say, and let me assure you that I have the full cooperation of the Native American community... blah-blah-blah..." God he was dragging it out for mileage, like a game for kicks with himself as the winner, continue around go, collect another two hundred dollars. "...And let me assure you my office enjoys an excellent rapport with the news media, blah-blah-blah... I shall personally be pleased to update you at regular intervals... The people have a right to know, blah-blah..."

"Condescending idiot," I snapped, "one half star, no more." Click, off.

# TWENTY SEVEN

Tuesday was to be a day of refocusing, redefining goals, and re-establishment of priorities.

The first of those was to be at classes in their proper order with absolute attention to basics.

It is so easy to fall out of rhythm and lapse back into poor study habits, and so, so difficult to get back in. When in doubt, I always say; call on that old motto: basics, basics, basics.

With my first consideration being applied discipline to my classes and as a result that undivided effort converted lost energy into new energy, with all else temporarily stored away on the back burner.

By afternoon I found myself back at the library in a half-hearted effort to further my notes on reincarnation, after a brief stop at the campus cafeteria for lunch.

After all, I really don't believe in that stuff, some voice in my head kept repeating at odd intervals.

The latest title and subject of my intended master's thesis seemed upgraded to: The Transmigration Mystique, or The Elusive Bird of Death and Rebirth.

Rooting once more among the forest of book shelves I located what I considered to be the most comprehensive book so far; by Jonothan Hilliary Ph.D., and foremost authority on the mind psyche.

A cursory examination showed me quickly that this title of 580 pages would serve nicely as the basic outline contribution for my thesis. It proved to be loaded with thought provoking questions, answers plus testimonies of case histories. It was the most revealing yet and Dr. Hilliary's credentials seemed impeccable:

> Served as Chairperson for the American Philosophical Association for eight years
> Vice President of American Society of Aesthetics President: American Society of Physical Research
> He was a Professor who taught Psychology and Sociology at several prominent universities and had authored a number of academic papers on research plus publishing four books on related subjects.

Some list of credentials, I thought. He must be qualified, and if a guy like this finds the subject worthwhile, then who am I to quibble? Also the contents looked inviting and to boot there were some eight plus pages of references and extensive bibliography.

Thumbing through the pages, I read hungrily, stimulated once more with questions perceived and drawing my own conclusions I began jotting down notes:

To go on living is like being intoxicated with life forever. When sober, is all else a fraud? I wonder what this guy drinks.

Can one return in the next life form simply because he or she wishes to, and if a person or being finds peace in the immortal spirit world why not remain there? Is there a choice?

The mere idea that one can survive from one womb to another seems so improbable. What could be the odds?

Ancient scholars obviously believed it possible; and yet the pragmatic scientific mind seemed in no way willing or ready to accept even the possibility of such theories.

I thought of Emile; a belief in the future life might help if you had learned your lessons, and might you not return better prepared to benefit mankind from those lessons gained?

Why do we believe in God and church doctrines? Because for generations and from early childhood we are conditioned and taught to do so.

Could our minds develop beyond understood limits without the chains of religious doctrines?

Is religion really a form of dominance over the minds of many by the self proclaimed few, for their own selfish personal interests?

Do monks withdraw from society with a sincere purpose to serve humanity in a better way, or are they preparing for the next move up the ladder and into the realm of the ultimate spiritual world?

How many past lives have they lived, and do they have the capacity to recall their past existences plus the lessons needed to endure and to reach their present plateau?

And what of the Jewish Philosophy? Do the strict Orthodox tend to reject the idea of rebirth while some Rabbis accept it as an integral part of Judaism?

The *Nazarene* states: It is not the power to remember but the power to forget that seems important for transmigration of the soul and for the exchange of worldly bodies one must pass through the sea of forgetfulness. But the angel of forgetfulness it so happens forgets to remove from our memory that element of records and recollection of former existence that intertwines themselves into our present existences.

Chewing on my pen and staring through the window at the ever-changing, ever-moving clouds I pondered what I had just read and written at great length. . .

What of the wonders of the known world such as Stonehenge and the pyramids; were these accomplished by obsessed men with the aid of reincarnated souls, retaining additional knowledge acquired from their past lives, and how far back might such souls reach in testimony to their first creation . . . this soul, this dreamy mist with mystical absolute powers far beyond our contemporary understanding, and if it is so, everything takes on a new dimension. And, do these advanced souls have the ability to view we feebler beings and to amuse themselves at our primitive ineptness?'As for these Gods of mythology, were they real after all and are now mere images of our struggling and meager understanding?

The Gods or super souls, did they work at such trivial matters as creating storms, designing monuments, causing rivers and waters to team with life and flow. What might they do for entertainment? Do they copulate, and if so for how long? Just for aeons, or until the next rebirth? Do they enjoy it, and if so, can you tell which reincarnated forms enjoy it most?

In that other spirit world does the soul feel pain, remorse, pity or just plain wholesome joy?

So many questions, I thought still staring out through the window as though somehow disembodied from all those others bent in abject library study, seeking their own answers.

Jonothan Hilliary has all the answers right here among the pages, 580 of them in detail, his answers.

The most enthralling were the stories of individuals' past lives. Charade or truth? Case histories from illiterate itinerant farm workers to college professors. From infants to modern day Methuselahs, all wanting to believe and wanting to convince others they had indeed lived in another time, mostly with a tragic ending, all deserving another chance, and another ride on that merry-go-round of eternal life.

And finally, a who's who in the parade-list of scientists, psychologists and philosophers who have jointed the quest for that fountain of eternity in heaven and on earth with impressive views on immortality. Even Napoleon.

As for my own answers, they must be deeply concealed and masked somewhere within that other self.

Note: What of hypnotism? Carolyn Kosloff had used it in her research of the criminal mind and as a tool to aid in the solving of crimes. I was there and witnessed it. It seemed so simple then, a tool in the hands of an accomplished practitioner with a willing subject.

Emile might be an ideal subject. Already he seemed at ease and in touch with his other self. His emotions were so natural and near to the surface. Kimberly and Dad had said that he never spoke much. It was true, he seemed to be a very private individual and yet completely comfortable with others, and without an ounce of pretense. No doubt about it, we felt good together, we worked, wė jelled. . . I wonder!

Uh-oh, back to basics and notes from Dr. Hilliary: I read rapidly, my mind's eyes devouring lines; more case histories and pages of first hand testimonies, jotting down key words and terms like; Hinduism, Buddhists, and strange cultures, with more research a must for hidden clues among the Taoists, the Egyptians, Persians, early Christians, later Christians and doctrines of Islam.

That the Greek and Roman epoch of the Reincarnation Renaissance all contributed something of a mystery seemed likely. I wondered where the common denominator was.

I paused again briefly before jotting down a quotation from Ben Franklin: When I see nothing annihilated and not a drop of water wasted, I cannot suspect the annihilation of the souls, or believe that God will suffer the waste of millions of minds. . . that now exist and put himself to the continual trouble of making new ones. Thus I believe they must always exist in some shape or another.

A stirring thought I said in my head, should not the creator expect us all to learn such tenets as consideration towards others; selflessness, pick up your own litter, like paper, plastic, oil, and drink cans, instead of wasting natural resources. In theory it doesn't seem too unreasonable. Clean up the mess you make of this earthly paradise before you can aspire to the paradise of the heavens. . . Is the earth to be some testing ground to be discarded before we trash the heavens also?

The Indians of Ka-Batin-Guy believed that each day they were reborn, and each day of that rebirth they vowed to the creator to live a better life, taking nothing from the earth and wasting nothing, with no malice toward any other beings.

Maybe they had the right of it after all, as my dear old grandmother from Ireland used to say.

Even Longfellow's Song of Hiawatha tells us something of the Indian's belief in rebirth:

I am going, oh my people,
On a long and distant journey;

Two lines later Longfellow wrote:

Will have come, and will have vanished,
Ere, I come again to see you. . .

And finally:

Westward, westward, Hiawatha
Sailed into the fiery sunset
Sailed into the purple vapors,
Sailed into the dusk of evening. . .
To the Kingdom of PONEMAH,
To the land of hereafter!

Conclusion: I can accept that Hiawatha's people considered him as something of a God, or at least an immortal spirit due to return someday with significant impact on the whole human race.

Many tribes believed, upon sight of the first white men that these were of an ancient generation who had come to life again and had returned to take back the land that was once their own. With names revered from their history, the natives of Bogota, Peru, and Mexico hailed them as champions of their own era.

No wonder the Spaniards found conquest so simple, regarding those who accepted them as holy spirits and even Gods by repaying them with outrageous betrayal and wholesale slaughter.

Up and down the Americas, natives rushed to meet the first vessels hopefully, while messengers were sent out to proclaim the return of QUETZALCOATL, the feathered serpent.

Note: Recordings of Sanskrit books point to evidence of an ancient highly advanced civilization in Ireland, referred to as,

HIRANYA, the island of the sun. Even the Greeks referred to it as; OGYLIA, the sacred isle.

Accordingly, in Ireland the ideas of Celtic beliefs in reincarnation took seed and sprang to life; it is called the Atlantis Theory, and is widely accepted in scholarly circles. At the time of the great flood migrations of advanced cultures reached Ireland and eventually spread throughout Britain, Spain and over Europe where the doctrines and ideologies eventually became corrupted by jealous Druidic practices. It is written that these highly advanced people predated the Romans, Greeks and even the Egyptians.

I wondered if indeed these were the DANNANS, the *Tuetha dè Dannans*, of which my mother and grandmother had so affectionately spoken of as the mystical little people of, INNIS FAIL, that older name of Ireland.

In the Ireland of the fifth century A.D., and before the coming of Christianity, learning had flourished. Scholars called OLLMANS had been entrusted with guarding the ancient records. At that time there were college courses of 12 years and more in Brethon laws, Philosophy and Druidic secrets. Then came the Dark Ages of Christianity where wave upon wave of new dogmas prevailed in which old records were methodically destroyed, and whatever works of birth and rebirth which had previously existed were eventually forced into secrecy. . .

I paused again, pen in teeth, staring into the distance allowing this last to soak in while considering the wide range of ramifications.

With abrupt suddenness I was jolted from my reverie as a new wave of students erupted into the library, each in search of his or her own elusive truths.

"Oh my God," I murmured. "I'm late again, and am I glad it's not Professor Wooldridge's class." In a desperate effort to regain my composure I thought: Basics, basics, basics, as I scurried off in a rush towards my next class. Anyway, my ballpoint was skipping again. Why do ballpoints always run dry when you need them most. . . and no time to buy a new one.

# TWENTY EIGHT

In the process of refocusing, I had purposely avoided newspapers and even the thought of television news until that afternoon after finishing my last class, when I hurried home to my apartment.

At Raley's I grabbed a Weight Watcher's lasagna and from the deli a nice big green salad, in tribute to Dad's concoction of Saturday night.

From the news stand I purchased anything I suspected might shed light on the deaths of the four duck hunters.

There was no shortage of sensationalism, only vague insinuations lacking any facts. More wasted quarters.

Stories abounded from suspected murder by other jealous hunters with grudges and axes to grind, while others hinted to drug connections ripened with a theme of vengeance.

One story claimed possession of irrefutable evidence of retribution for a rash of home robberies by a supposedly well known local vigilante group in Lake County.

The following day I would read another story supposedly linking these to the rape of two high school girls.

But there were no facts, only spurious hints and mention of District Attorney Martin Rosswell as the defender of the people who vowed to track down any and all evil doers and law-breaking perpetrators and to get to the bottom of the snowballing situation.

## *KA-BATIN-GUY*

My first chuckle came with District Attorney Martin Rosswell, or Mister Rosswell as he demanded of those privileged to work around him. Mister Rosswell was having a field day it appeared. He detested those who presumed to call him by his given name, and so those more daring souls referred to him as simply; Martin, or Martin the warlike, which the name supposedly means. In the process, Martin took hold as a retaliatory measure when referring to the disgruntled DA.

In my own mind he made a great leap in status; a fly-weight weenie, a Vienna weenie, from one half star to two star jerk scratching for the heavy-weight division.

The Channel 3 news did much better in the entertainment field with the weather girl traipsing back and forth before the camera in her now popular tight mini-skirt with lots of leg showing, cackling her giddy giggles, trying to act funny while attempting to relate the news report. News for entertainment in the academy award field, and the nominee is. . .

Next, the repeated flashes of the outrageous beating of Rodney King. It happened last March and still they show it repeatedly. Four Los Angeles police officers beating a helpless black man with their batons. How could anybody beat any living thing that way? And still they show it over and over again, can't they see how they are fomenting more trouble for the sake of sick sensationalism by adding fuel to an already volatile situation. A jury would have to be sick of it, I wonder if Rodney King will be the only one to come out of it a better person. I have to wonder how I would have reacted if I were there, perhaps as one of the officers, and if I might have had the courage to intervene. That's what really scares the hell out of me I guess, what part would I have taken?

And then there they were; the cameras on the front steps of the Lake County Courthouse on Forbes Street; D.A. Martin Rosswell, country club aristocrat and nobility of the bureaucratic establishment in his three piece pinstripe, smug, confident, blah—blah—blah.

And although the cameras were focused on the DA, a surprise shocker stole his act away in the shape of tattered bib overall clad Chester Cowan. The little farmer came from out of nowhere it seemed.

Chester had just been released from enforced jury apprenticeship, I was to learn later, and in which he was not chosen to serve by the way. It seems that some counselors have learned to leave Chester alone. Anyway, he just happened on the scene and without hesitation marched before the cameras to confront the astonished District Attorney.

Chester was indeed a crusty old fart, as Dad had said, and with not a trace of shyness. He didn't mince words with innuendoes either. He came right to the point, accusing Martin Rosswell of being a blundering idiot who should be recalled for being a totally incompetent ass, and he was saying; ". . .Obsessed with his own selfish interest which is out-weighed only by his own ponderous ego. Why, how is Martin Rosswell going to find anything. He can't tell a belly button from a hickey." The pompous DA swelled, flushed bright red, like he might disintegrate at any instant, while Chester went on; "He can't even find a pimple on the point of his nose. . ."

Martin, the warlike, struck back with a sting in his voice; "I have never had a pimple on my nose!"

Chester grinned sheepishly, as if to say, "See." Then added, "You are a pimple, sonny, you are one."

I had long ago learned that Chester had a talent for homespun analogies, and now the media knew it also. They loved it. It was spicy and the kind of action that stirs viewer interest because when a hayseed like Chester speaks, people recognize something of themselves, their heritage I suppose, and they listen, and sometimes they even laugh.

In the background I had noticed a tentative attractive woman dressed in a red dress taking notes. Before Chester's last words, she had surreptitiously found a place close on his elbow. Briefly, I wondered who she might be?

When the courthouse scene had first started I had stepped from the kitchen to the living room to gain a better look and to laugh, with tears streaking down my cheeks, when the smell caught my nostrils.

I burned my goddamn lasagna, but it was worth it. You can always buy another lasagna, but at that moment there was only one glorious Chester. . . and although he was for the time being finished with the bewildered District Attorney, that backbone of the establishment, he was just getting up a good head of wind.

He chose as his next target, that stalwart of the legal system; none other than Judge Wooden, citing numerous instances of ineptness and incompetence and charging him with pandering to criminal interests, and that he was completely out of touch with reality. Judge Wooden should be recalled, and right there on the courthouse steps in front of cameras with a crowd's attention hanging on his every word he started a recall movement.

Of the bureaucratic hierarchy, my dad, Sheriff Kreeszowski, was the only person he had a kind word for. It turned a little embarrassing for me personally as Chester declared the sheriff to be the only one of the political bunch with any common sense, or an ounce of brains to boot.

Of course Dad wasn't there. If he had been he would no doubt have laughed profusely at the unfolding comedy. Nor was Ned Turner. It would have been impossible to contain an outburst of laughter by both of them. But for safety's sake there were a few uniforms standing around in case things got out of hand.

Don't get me wrong, Dad would never miss a good scrap. It's just that he has never been a pretentious sort of guy, and nothing ever, ever shook him. Mr. Steady and Cool. He could go into a dreadful brawl smiling and come out of it still wearing that same wry grin. It was that mystery smile that had soothed so many hot tempers. If you don't know him you don't know how to take him. And, if he got pissed off, even then it was something of a friendly grin that sent an unmistakable message; don't trespass, sucker.

Only a few of us could tell the difference, Mom, Ned Turner, and myself.

On the other hand, Ned was just the opposite, an open book. Ned Turner lie, no way. Although he was a little guy, in a pinch he could kick ass with the best of them.

But that ironic twisted smile belonged to Daddy. It was his style and his trademark.

I think now I recognized something of that same quality in Emile, although he has something of a gentler nature about himself, at least on the surface. Emile and Daddy have another trait in common too, control, total self control. Yet with Emile, beneath that exterior cover, I sense a very complex nature.

As for myself, whenever I am exposed to Chester I feel frivolous and whimsical, traits that are well within my own natural character.

I wonder just where Chester belongs in the ranks of reincarnation and immortality?

# TWENTY NINE

Other news items followed with more coverage of President Bush's visit to Japan along with Lee Iacocca of Chrysler Motors and with other prominent industrial leaders seeking compromises in the trade deficit.

I thought that when Iacocca took over the reins of Chrysler and attempted to reorganize it he was definitely on the right track. I believed in Iacocca back then and agreed with his energetic forward philosophy. The move to nominate him for president didn't surprise me. We could all learn something in the form of cooperation between management and labor. Someplace along the line Lee lost it I think, when that big fat salary went to his head. Lee says that Japan must open its market to American products and import 30,000 automotive units and parts. I disagree Lee; Americans don't make anything anymore, except waste, which they discard so wantonly. We're a nation of computer key punchers and paperwork shufflers. We buy with plastic whether we can afford it or not, and sink further into that bottomless hole of endless debt.

No matter what the issue, I now find myself wondering how Chester would respond.

The following days of news reports would bear me out. Chester had strong folksy opinions on every subject, and Chester had found a platform, or I should say; a platform had spawned Chester Cowan. And, at least for the time being the news media had given voice to the aged folksy pioneer turned latent activist.

"When Lee Iacocca says there has to be a big breakthrough here," Chester was quoted as saying, "... Bush, you and Iacocca, you both read my lips; those insane, unrealistic bonuses have mottled your brains. If you want to cut something, start from the top for once and cut some of those big fat salaries and expense accounts. The Japs won't buy American cars anyway. Why should they? They got a good thing going, and they don't want em and they sure as hell don't need em. In the first place they don't have anyplace to park em or drive em.' The break-through starts right here at home with smug hard-ass union bosses and shop stewards still sitting on their not so hard earned bonuses an benefits an inflated wages. $500.00, $900.00 a unit alone just for health care. I pay my own health care. You guys don't get it, do you? Your union boss leanin back in his plush overstuffed chair, sayin; we ain't givin up nothin. We fought hard for what we got, and we ain't givin up a dime. You guys just don't get it, do you? It's a Goddamned world of competition. You don't wise up and get the act together, nobody has nothin; no benefits, no wages, no damn nothin. Then who you gonna blame?'You got a right to cry about management though. $3 million to $16 million a year they get? Who needs $16 million a year to live on, and who's worth that much in the first place. And, how many dollars a unit does that figure out to; one thousand, two, three thousand dollars. How much more fat is there you guys? We're not gettin no place because everybody wants to sit pat and change nothin. I bet no more'n $500.00 in raw materials goes into each unit, and we're supposed to pay $25,000.00 and hope it holds together till the last payment's made. Hey you guys, Bush, Iacocca, and unions, read my lips; cut the fat about $5000.00 and make em so's we can at least drive em a while before they start to fall apart, then maybe the public will buy em."

Now it seems Chester's spell was upon me too. I almost never miss John Chancellor's commentary, that is, when I can manage to catch it. I almost always agree with John, but on this issue I think something has clouded his vision as well. Perhaps they should all start eating bird seed and try whistling for awhile. He pointed out that in Japan the cars have their steering wheels on the right hand side and that we would have to adjust our manufacturing especially for that market.

The very next day Chester had an opinion on that too. Whether the cameras found Chester or he found them right there on the Lake County Courthouse steps I'm not certain, but Chester was saying; ". . .It don't make no difference where you put the bleep-bleep steering wheels. Put em in the middle if you think it'll help, but the Japs are not going to buy American cars; poor quality control for one thing, they say, and why in Christ sakes should they? They won't even buy our rice, an they need rice, or at least they won't until maybe they figure out how to make Blue Jeans out of it."

And right there behind Chester was that woman again, different red dress, same woman. She must have an obsession with red, I thought, and she likes to hang in there close to Chester a lot.

Each day a headline and news article struck a new note in the never-ending cause of sensationalism; viewer ratings, circulation, and more quarters to feed that everlasting begging machine, always eager to gobble up coins.

I should not have been surprised when those printed toilet paper sheets of the supermarkets, the scandal sheets discovered Chester's uncommon character.

For the tabloids, the issues were made to order. Bev Westerly of the Global Informer championed Chester's cause in the chain of exploitation.

With them hitting the stands on Tuesday, it now seems ironic that it wasn't until Thursday when I caught the connection.

I seldom pay any attention to them anyway, but there it was with Chester Cowan's name in print snapping at my quarters before the market checkstand. Scotts Valley and Lakeport of my hometown grown into the ever larger scheme of things.

Bev Westerly must have sat on Chester's doorstep, and the issue was such a small one concerning market, price and quality of motorcycle helmets and the law concerning the mandatory wearing of said helmets. Chester's stand was predictable; ". . .Every time the government sticks its bureaucratic nose into something that ain't wrong to regulate it, the price doubles, and then an immediate shortage hits the market shelves. Why does the price have to double in the first place? Cause its mandated? Makes a guy wonder if someone in government is in collusion with people in industry." Chester was also quick to point out that: "Next thing you know some big salaried big shot will want to regulate toilet, so's we can all revert to corn-cobs, until we can't afford that too.

So another freedom is lost, and if you don't wanna wear a motorcycle helmet you shouldn't have to. The only thing is; if you get your brains splattered all over the highway, then you better have your own hospitalization plan paid up, an don't expect somebody else to come along to scrape up the mess and pay those outrageous hospital bills for you."

The same tabloid featured an eye-catcher too, and this one in no way smacked of Chester's work. It read:

**KONOCTI SPIRITS TAKE REVENGE FOR VIOLATION OF SACRED ISLAND**

It told in not such accurate terms of the myth and legend of the Indian spirit world seeded deep within the cavernous confines of Mount Konocti.

It also told how the spirits waited for a chance at a good deed which was certain to put them in line for a rebirth trip back into the paradise world of Ka-Batin-Guy.

Four hunters had wantonly violated the sacred grounds of Quercus Island and the spirits had no choice but to respond. Bev Westerly had also authored this one. It seemed she was on a roll. I had to wonder if she had talked to Chief Wilson Johns or even to Maria. Maria, no way. Chief Johns spoke with the simple wisdom of that sensible Indian voice. Or perhaps it came from someone else. Anyway, it was grossly distorted.

By Thursday I couldn't take it any longer and I called Dad after lunch-time. I said, "Dad, what in the world is going on up there?"

"Honey," he said, affectionately. "How are you doing with your classes? Are you learning anything?"

I responded very emphatically, "DADDD!"

"Don't bother yourself with it Little Girl," he said, putting on the Archie Bunker sound. Even though we were miles apart, on the phone I could picture the tufts of gray hair and his wry grin; "Just a bunch of clowns. . . Don't trouble yourself."

"But Chester. . ."

"Chester's a grown man. He can handle himself, he's doin okay."

"It's not Chester I'm worried about."

"Don't you go worryin bout nuthin. It's just a bunch of clowns trying to raise a circus. . . Like Chester says, "What happens here is no more'n a minnow egg in a big mud puddle compared to the overall scheme of things."

I knew before I called that I'd probably get nothing out of him, so I said; "Okay, see you soon. Love ya."

Someone else must have been in the office because he said; "Okay now, cut that out," in his Archie Bunker voice.

For some bewildering reason, I found myself considering everything from Chester Cowan's point of view.

Martin the warlike had recovered and was on the attack again. On the courthouse steps they commanded a daily audience and he was after Chester in a big way, demanding to know where Chester was on that morning of the mysterious deaths of the four duck hunters. Chester responded by saying it was none of his damn business and thereby somewhat implicating himself, where upon Martin declared that Chester was being investigated as a suspect.

Once again Dad was right on, at least about Chester. Chester was saying, staring bluntly at Martin; "Go ahead Sonny, investigate all you want. You won't find no expensive three piece pinstripes in my closet."

Martin, in my mind had advanced to a bona fide three star idiot. . .and yet he seemed even more dangerous now than ever.

By Friday that animal call of the wild beckoned. That emphatic voice in my brain told me I had to get home, Professor Wooldridge or no.

In order to beat the rush hour traffic I had to be across the Golden Gate Bridge northbound by no later than 3:30 p.m. After all, I had a date, an overnight camping engagement with Emile.

On Highway 101 my old Camaro purred like a passionate kitten and my head rattled with the stir of the past week.

These days everything seemed so much more complicated than when I was a kid. Cowboys and Indians, cops and robbers, good guys versus bad guys, all stirred in the same melting pot. The era of simple solutions seemed gone as was the mystique of the John Wayne shoot em ups.

And Monday, well Monday, somehow I'll deal with Professor Wooldridge.

# THIRTY

City traffic be damned. With an early start by mid-afternoon I took the shortcut over the treacherous mountain pass of Hopland Grade and a half hour later cruised north on Main Street, finding a parking space near Emile's shop.

When I opened the front door I was again greeted by haunting melodies and the beautiful sound of *Ebb Tide*. Must be his favorite I thought.

The ever-present bald eagle was still poised lividly above, eyes fiery and threatening. For that moment I froze in front of it until at last I spotted the telltale wires restraining it from flight. The pair of mandarins were still in their place, without a price tag, unmoved and symbolically peaceful and nearby the meadowlarks that Kimberly admired so but could find no funds in her budget to purchase waited. I paused momentarily to study the single preening pintail, then the mallards, and so many others seemingly at ease and unthreatened by the ready eagle poised above with talons bared to strike. Then a peregrine falcon waiting patiently for a sign perhaps, and a nearby flicker curiously watching a mallard hen with her trailing chicks. For an instant I could swear that I almost heard their clucking voices.

At the door to his back shop I paused to watch him sitting positively engrossed and bent over a partially completed wooden decoy he was working on.

When finally he looked up, it was to cast that same spell over me again. I found myself saying, "Hi stranger."

"Hello," he said, surprise in his voice.

"I wasn't sure you would be here," I said.

He waited, tool poised and hesitant while our eyes toyed with each others. There goes my panties again.

"I wasn't sure you would show up. . ."

"I thought about it, especially since you stood me up last Saturday. . ."

"Sorry about that. Something came up," he said. "I called and talked with your dad. . ."

"You don't have to explain," I said, smiling forgivingly. "It wasn't really a fixed date anyway." I moved beside him. "What are you working on now?"

"A pair of nesting woodcocks. . . this one is the male."

"What's this one?"

"He'll be a flicker, settling from flight, rooting for grubs."

"Grubs? Yuck."

"Or something, some tasty insects maybe."

"With ketchup I hope." He had a truly gracious smile when he let it loose. I could tell he didn't mind my wisecracks. "Are we still going camping?"

"If you still want to. . . only take me a few minutes to get things together."

"You're on," I said, allowing a hint of challenge to my words. "But I have to go home first, to tell Dad, take a quick shower and get some things."

"We can meet at the canoe, save some time that way."

"I'll be there in a jiff," I cooed. "Bye."

It was one of those rare bright springlike days in late fall and I needed a stretching walk so I hiked the short block up to the courthouse building towards Dad's office. For a brief instant I half expected to find Chester Cowan and Martin Rosswell locked in verbal combat before the cameras. But I was disappointed. People were milling around and coming and going in that familiar small town manner as though nothing of real importance was happening.

Dorothy said Dad was out in the field, and that I might catch him at home since she knew he planned to stop there for something.

On the way back I caught a glimpse of Kimberly across the street headed in the opposite direction with a three piece suited male, locked in serious conversation, presumably over mutual clients. She was dressed lightly for fall in a fitted medium blue jacket with a white flared skirt spotted with quarter sized polka dots just above the knees, black patent heels and lots of healthy striding legs showing. What a waste, she should be doing a Leggs pantyhose commercial, or be skipping across the cover of Harpers Bazaar. Where were those cameras now? And here I was dressed in my usual, faded jeans and a droopy purple blouse.

When I buzzed home I would hardly have recognized the drab old gray house, if my Camaro had not headed for it like an aging saddle horse seeking his oat bag and the barn.

Even that giant old palm tree, landmark of that corner had sprung into renewed life, and the decrepit walnut tree was gone, stump and all, and in its place a rounded dirt pad of tilled soil awaiting tulip bulbs.

I knew Dad was there by the visible tail end of the county car parked behind the alley garage. I rushed inside full of girlish vitality. He had just gotten up from his roll-top desk to close the lid when I rushed over to grab him with a bear hug and kiss his cheeks. . .

"Hey—hey, cut dat stuff out," he blustered in his Archie Bunker scold. That's how I knew it was okay, his bite's never as great as his bark.

"The house," I shrilled. "It's beautiful, sunshiny yellow and white, just the way I wanted it, and the fence too. . .oh Dad it is beautiful. Mom would love it. But how did you do it?"

He flushed with pride, exhaled on his fingernails and buffed them pompously on his jacket lapel like a magician. "Connections, Little Girl. Connections. . ."

"Connections, with who, your guardian angel?"

"I ain't tellin no trade secrets." The Archie Bunker sound again.

"Tell me, or I'll. . ."

"Well okay. You got me cornered. I guess I gotta fess up."

"Yeah. . .come on. Come clean fella, or I'll dot both you eyes, break dat crooked nose again, an. . ."

"Please officer," he pleaded, hands up in his familiar gesture of supplication.

"I confess. You know the two Clifford brothers—?"

"Yes. The drinking painters who can't punch their way out of a wet paper bag; the ones famous for buying one gallon of paint and five gallons of thinner to do the job. In a pinch they can't pull a sick whore off a piss-pot, I heard."

"Fer shame; such language for a lady of refinement."

"Aw shucks." I said, flashing that little girl look with a pious grin.

"Well yep, that's the ones. In jail again, for drunken brawling, mostly with themselves and anyone else they can find to brawl with. . ."

"I'll bet you have had to put them in jail at least a dozen times over the past years."

"At least. Well nobody will hire them much anymore, and they were serving time in the drink tank so I arranged to get them loose on the work furlough program by hiring them for daytime. When they're sober they can work like hell, and I take them back to their cells at night. They make a little money and it keeps them dried up, at least until their time is up. Maybe they'll wise up someday, who knows," he shrugged.

"What about the thinner and paint?"

"Oh that was a long time ago when everything was oil base paint. Everything is alkyd water base or something now. Good stuff. No lead. Besides I bought the paint and told them how I wanted it done. Work hard as hell when they're sober. Can't drive anymore cause Judge Wooden suspended their licenses over a year ago."

"Well, it's beautiful. Mom's favorite colors, soft sunshine yellow and white."

"Next week it's the roof. What do you think about red?" he said.

"Perfect, just like my hair. And, I think I'll replace those old curtains with some new lacy ones."

"Good idea. Look honey, sorry but I gotta run." With that he closed the roll-top, patted it and I grabbed him for another hug.

"Cut dat stuff out," he chided, and flashed out the door doing his Jackie Gleason shuffle; "And awaaay we gooo!!"

For long moments I stood pleasantly stunned, then collecting my wits, I dashed out the door; "Dad, wait, I want to tell you. . ." I called after him, but he was already gone. Why are men always disappearing. . . "Damn it."

Rooting for a note pad I scratched out a message:

*Dad,*
*Gone camping overnight with Emile.*
*Love ya more than ever.*

# THIRTY ONE

*I* was down at the canoe in a flash, dressed in Stanford Cardinal red and white jogger pants and a sloppy football jersey top. I was still warm with a damp glow because I had hustled all the way. Beneath the sweats I wore a surprise.

In minutes we were skimming over the gentle waters toward Mount Konocti and the obscure Quercus Island with the waning sun on our backs. I felt squeaky clean and vital, stroking easy rhythms with energetic juices coursing through my body. It seemed so easy now, digging the paddle in, feeling muscles tense and quicken, then relax. It was just the medicine I needed after a week of tension and study. It is what I wanted and had eagerly looked forward to. The lake waters were bare and adventure beckoned to me. I sat in front again, poised almost as though thrusting across the water on my own, and yet I could feel Emile's eyes on me and his rhythm matched with my own. But I was working with a fever and he was taking it all in easy stride, a daily event to him, no sweat.

At times I feel so immature and cannot understand why I am so troubled about things over which I have no control, such as global warming, pollution, smoking mothers, smoking, drugs, crime, jobs, the disappearing forests, save the whales, indifference, political corruption and indifference, and yet I know others share similar concerns. I am not alone. Maybe I need a psychologist. Maybe a lot of people need something, and Chester speaks his mind to that troubled concern that plagues so many of us. Emile somehow gentles my own troubled world with his easy manner, and out here alone with him on the water those problems fade into some distant order. Maybe I too should get a simple job and draw that steady paycheck, and not bother with anything, take no chances. YUCK, just another bureaucrat.

Or was the seething dissipated by the ever-approaching twilight hours with the last heat of warming rays of sunset still touching on my back and the painted sky with it's fiery hues of colors and brush stroked clouds. There would be a harvest moon. Emile had promised that. All signs of civilization seemed now vanished with the exception of Lakeport city lights starting to switch on behind us. We had both paused to stare back momentarily and then we were off again, cutting easily across the water, almost planing, like dancing close together, like inexorable energy of two vital beings linked together in a single purpose—one, two, three strokes on one side, then the switch. It had become so easy and natural. An hour and a half had passed I supposed, without need to measure, and still I could feel the surge of elevated epinephrine.

We were going to see family, his family, bearing gifts, full measures of cracked corn, cold pancakes, old bread and graham crackers for dessert. I wondered if they would send out the welcoming committee, and I wondered if Emile liked to dance. "Do you like to dance," I shouted, shattering the musical silence of nature.

"Uh-huh," I felt him nod back.

I wondered about his thoughts, and if he too was troubled by things over which he had no control.

We were part way into the autumn night with twilight and then darkness early on the clock's face. A giant moon was taking shape in the distance with its array of sparkling stars to stir that purity of thought.

I hadn't had a drink and yet I felt bubbly and intoxicated with nature. I squealed, "I think I'm getting a glow on. . . I think. . .I think. . ."

He was quiet while I stared skyward. . . "Can you feel the earth turning?" I called back.

"Why? Are you afraid we might fall off?"

I laughed out loud it seemed like. For some minutes before I realized we were both just sitting there drifting quietly, drinking up that elixir of life, guzzling like a kid in a candy store. Then I said, "That's not the way you play the game."

"What game?" he countered.

I turned halfway around to face him, balancing cautiously, suddenly aware of our precarious relationship with the chilly waters.

A scatter of city lights along the distant shoreline reflected on the water like flickering fireflies, and I knew right then the troubles were left behind, for a time anyway.

Could this be a prescribed therapy for others. I wondered about that too.

"It's called a game of curiosities," I said.

"Oh. I see," he said. "Entrapment."

"Something like that."

I answer your question, and you get to ask me one. . .and if you can't answer, then I get another try," he said. "I think I can handle that."

"That's it," I answered confidently.

"Well, let's see," he said, looking up to study the heavens for long moments; ". . .actually we can perceive the earth turning. It only seems like the sky is moving, like an illusion, compared to drifting clouds, they're moving too. . . but if you stand at the base corner of a tall building and look up, to compare the sky and clouds for example, like using the building to measure with, you can actually feel the earth moving in its rotation. It's an illusion, a deception but it can make you dizzy, and even cause motion sickness. . ."

"Like a feeling that you might fall off if it stops, huh?"

"Something like that—we're so used to it that our bodies take it for granted. A sudden stop and whoopee, we all scramble about looking for something to hold onto; satisfied?"

"Smarty pants," I said, feigning a demure pout. "Not it's your turn."

"Why doesn't the earth shake while it's turning?"

"I don't know. . . dumb question. Let's change the subject." I wanted to ask him if he went to college and where, but I knew his answer might be; why do you think you have to go to college to learn?

"Go ahead try it," he said. "It's your game."

"It's getting darker," I said, a bit more flustered than I wanted. "Shouldn't we start paddling?"

"Try to think about it, or I get to ask another question; like, do people spin like a top at the north and south poles, and do they get dizzy?"

"You only get to ask another one if you answer your own last one. Besides, nobody lives at the poles."

"How do you know that?"

"That's three." I said, and I thought, I'm losing lots of points in my own game.

"Oh. So that's how it works. You get to make up the rules as we go along, cause it's your game, huh?"

"It's a stupid game. Some man must have made it up." I was stroking the paddle once again in frus-tration, digging deeply until we started gliding along smoothly, and I could feel him pick up my rhythm without hesitation; while my brain toyed with an answer.

"Try," he prompted.

I wondered how Marilyn Vos Savant would have responded. "Well," I found myself saying at last; "I think it might be like when there's no bumps in space, and maybe there is no friction either, and we, the earth is spinning smoothly, and that's why we don't feel it—but, if we ever hit something, like an asteroid or whatever, BANG! A big bump. Thank God there is a lot of free space out there."

"With no bumps in our path. . ."

"You know what?"

"What?"

"I think you've played this game before."

I could feel his laugh on my back, and the little boy triumphant look. For an instant I recalled the Plato's Meno, and wondered if he was practicing on me.

"My turn," I called back.

"Your turn."

"Are you ticklish?"

"I'm not talking on that one."

"Okay, how come we don't laugh when we tickle ourselves, but we do when someone else tickles us?"

"Something to do with reflexes, right?"

"Go on."

"A reaction to tickling is a sort of distress signal, a reflex reaction which we can control in ourselves, but not so with others because we are helpless and at their mercy."

"Close enough. Your turn."

"The Dead Sea has no fish. Right?"

"If you say so."

"Why not?"

"Too much salt content. . ."

"Go on."

"Other chemicals too, like calcium chloride, and that's poison. I think some people get dizzy from just bathing in it."

"Close enough. Your turn."

"Why do we dream?" he said.

"That's an easy one," I found myself saying, with renewed confidence, then chewing it around a bit; "When our bodies relax the mind continues to work. While the conscious mind rests the other part continues to function, recounting our everyday happenings. Dreams are vital as a sort of steam valve for the mind, receiving, processing and solving problems, and etcetera, etcetera. . . Some dreams don't seem to make any sense to the individual, but someone trained and skillful can help unlock the subconscious fears and solve our inner mysteries."

"Uh-oh, I forgot that's your field, isn't it?"

"Your turn."

"How come every time you pick up something heavy with both hands your nose itches?"

"I think you got the hang of it now," I said.

# THIRTY TWO

Quercus Island, that vague outline of mystery shrouded in thin mist and the last shadowy rays of twilight, with the strange dark and eerie mountain sloped with its varied ridges and hollows for a backdrop; enigmatic and enduring in myth and legend, consenting only to those who held the key to her mystic secrets.

"Is Quercus a Basque name?" I asked.

"It means oak tree, or oaken," he said.

"I always wondered. I thought it might be Basque."

"It's Latin."

"Oh, and myself a Catholic and not knowin me Latin."

"Fer shame. For punishment you get to recite the stations of the cross and ten Hail Marys. . ."

"And another evening with my Latin dictionary."

Those precious endorphins surged again at an all time high and there Quercus waited, a mere hundred yards before us.

We had discussed the problems of the entire universe at length, and solved nothing, and yet questions I had not considered awaited as if challenging to be unlocked.

Emile had promised a full moon and I was not disappointed. Strange things do happen beneath a full moon and don't be surprised if you witness some unusual animal behavior. "Such as?" I had pleaded but he only grinned that almost familiar wry grin, fending me off.

With an abrupt suddenness the welcoming committee burst into the air, silhouetted by the moonlit background, flying toward us with reckless abandon, streaking past in wild childlike theatrics, quacking their undeniable chatter. Some performing unreckoned aerial acrobatics while others showed off by diving audaciously close only to pull up at the last instant, then plunging into the water beside our canoe. There was a constant quacking gibberish all the while and I found myself quacking back in the language of greeting old friends while still others skidded into the water like daring water skiers skidding on webbed feet.

Just a few yards more and what had been a clearly definable island outline darkened to draw us beneath its folds. The full moon low in the sky our only light now while the dank musty smell of tules and animal life proclaimed itself to our nostrils, and of course the ever present escort of the welcoming committee. Emile had said that wrens and ducks had been popular companions in mythology as sentries for humans. I believed it now.

Expertly he steered the canoe into the almost hidden path of towering tules as a curtain seemed to close behind us.

Fortunately our eyes had long ago adjusted to the forbidding half light of the blazing moon. Even the flickering lights like fireflies of Lucerne and Lakeport were gone now.

Without ceremony we beached at the same spot as before where I immediately leaped to ground, staggering and eager to stretch my legs and aching shoulders, testing for steady earth beneath my feet. Emile was right behind me.

Eagerly they gathered around us; Plato, Socrates, Jason the Indian Buff with his beautiful darker head, all nipping at Emile's pant legs. Xanthroppe the shrew, Juno, Zeus, Aphrodite and Venus and Mars. Eros, the handsome irrestible lover and his jealous Ceres, and right there as if to be hugged, the clan matriarch Minerva. First and most formal greetings must naturally go to Minerva.

Emile was busy already tossing cracked corn about, muttering consolation and salutations.

It seemed I knew them all even in the night light. . .and there with his shrewd eyes studying me was Hector. Hector the bully, Hector the mischief maker. Horny old Hector.

Emile turned to me, saying; "Why don't you finish feeding them while I set up camp over there?"

I looked to him sort of inquisitively and he said the bathroom's in the same place. I thought, yeah, anyplace you can find it.

"Did you bring anything for us to eat?" I asked. "I rushed so that I completely forgot.."

He gleamed a pompous grin, "How about some late harvest Riesling with French bread and vegi-dip, baby carrots, celery stick, and broccoli, and. . ."

"Sounds great. I'm ready."

". . .smoked oysters. . . for passion food."

"I'm ready. I'm ready."

As he got the gear I returned to the pleasure of hosting the party.

I found myself talking to them as if they were my class of children, all except Minerva. In her face and warm eyes I perceived a certain mature intelligence. We seemed to share that feminine link and I decided it would be unwise if she were condescended to.

But Hector was angling around behind me for some sort of diversionary tactic when she scolded him. "Hector," I said, scathingly, "Hector, you horny old duck, you have a one track mind with no brain. If all you want is to sneak around so you can nip ladies on their pussy feathers again. . .I'll, well, you will wish you were an eider. A hen eider with all your feathers plucked. You had better learn your lesson, or snap, back you go. . . You got that?"

Minerva took over then, chasing him about wildly, all the while nipping at his wing and tail feathers, scolding, while he struggled to get away, quacking; "I'm no eider. Eiders are dumb, no eider. . ."

Laughing, I dumped the balance of the bag of corn and added some bread crumbs. Emile had said they don't eat too much at night, but they seemed intent enough just scratching about.

I walked over to where he had spread a plastic ground cover on a bed of matted tules beneath that same giant weeping willow.

The sleeping bags lay ready and separate side by side with a space between, where a camp light glowed over the food and two wine bottles.

For a moment I stood there considering the layout. "Very nice. Romantic really, and inviting," I said with a coy grin. "But what about things like spiders and snakes and scorpions, yucky things like that?"

"Not to worry," he said, reassuringly. "They," he nodded indicating our feathered friends, "They have probably eaten every insect on the island. And as for rattlesnakes, well no self respecting snake would dare come near this place. They'll stand guard anyway."

"I don't know. . ."

"Don't worry," he said.

I had his eyes locked on mine as I glanced to the two sleeping bags, then back to him. I think he got the message, but I mustered a demure frown anyway; "Do these things zip together by any chance?"

He nodded.

"Well," I said coquettishly.

It didn't take another hint. In a jiffy he was busy rearranging the setup.

When he had finished I stripped down ever so delicately to my surprise; a black lace camisole with matching tap pants, those loose fitting inviting things, and I stood there for the moment, then leaped into the sleeping bags, saying; "Hector, you scroungey old eider, eat your heart out." To which he darted around in a fitful tizzy.

Emile was laughing again, and he didn't need a formal invitation. In a flash he stripped to his black jockey shorts and crawled in beside me. Ah-hah, he had come prepared also I noted mentally.

"I'll take some wine now. What did you call it?"

"Late harvest."

"Sounds expensive. Passion food, huh?"

"Guaranteed."

I thought, when this lady's mind is stimulated, watch out fella.

After the first bottle of wine, we lay side by side snuggled cozily inside the zippered bags, counting stars and dippers, tracing the moon's face and comparing imaginary shapes among the drifting ever changing clouds.

"Do you ever wonder why clouds take on different shapes?" he asked in a dreamy voice.

"Are we back in the game," I said.

"Could be."

"Just now I don't," I said with a timorous touch. I know that clouds are composed of ever changing vapors, no doubt unconscious of the shapes they form. . . But, the wine was taking a toll and for the moment I cared least of all about answers and cloud shapes and vapors and. . .

"Okay, my turn again," he said, reprovingly.

"Go ahead," I said. I was drifting towards a sort of fantasy dreamland.

"Why do we think we see stars when there are no stars in the sky?"

"Your turn again," I demurred, while I had some vague or strange notion that stars are really only spots of light, reflections, and something about illusions, but I acquiesced; "Your turn."

He had my hand in his and he pressed it to his lips, saying; "Why do girls like to have their hands kissed?"

"I know that one," I cooed, wide eyed and giddy, then twisting over to my side with my leg across his thighs I teased, "Do it again and I'll tell you."

He did, and I said; "Because it feels gooood, and it makes them, me anyway, tingle. . . and. . ."

"And?"

"And it's sweet."

He examined my hand tenderly, gently kissing each finger, tasting each one in turn, then he stated as if making a formal declaration; "You have artistic hands, slender and shapely. . . You could do anything you want. . . there is magic in your hands and your touch. . ."

"Really!" I tittered, desperately trying to suppress a surge of goose bumps. "Don't stop now, flattery will get you anything, even trouble."

"Your eyes are almost black but in the moonlight they look bronze, almost like golden glows, and I can see myself, and even the moon's reflection in them—"

"That's that expensive wine you plied me with. I'm helpless."

"You're never helpless, vulnerable perhaps, in an adorable sort of way, of course," he added, nodding for effect.

"Vulnerable. Voluptuous you mean." I put his hand on my breast, except for these." He tested it caressingly, then the other, his face a moonlit mask of keen interest, saying; "Girlish. Eternally girlish. I like them, but I'm really a hip and thigh sort of guy, anyway. . ."

"That's the neatest way of saying I don't have any boobs I've ever heard. . . I'm fat, here," I said sliding his hands down along my side and thighs. "See,I'm a plump Irish Polack."

"You're Classic French, Goddess of fertility, generous where it counts most. Ask any Frenchman."

"Oh. But I don't know any Frenchmen."

"The English men like to go to the bars with their buddies and brag about their dutiful women at home. Americans have a fixation on big tits. The Germans like big bossy husky women and the Italians like sultry big busted mamas. The Spaniards like them dark, shapely and alluring. . ."

"And the French?"

"The French like generous hips and thighs, and a keen mind of course. . . No doubt about it, you're definitely Classic French."

"And you know all this because you have made an in-depth study of course. It's okay though. The idea of being Classic French is rather new but I think I can live with that, and don't stop now. Flattery will get you anything, in trouble even, or don't you know that?"

"If I were a sculptor I would want you for my model. You have a very sensual poise that you are unaware of, or perhaps only slightly aware of. At least you have no pretense about it, and that's what makes you extraordinary."

"Extraordinary now, tis it. Boy, do you know how to make a girl feel gooood."

The ducks had been quiet for some time, which was just as well since we were paying no attention to them anyway.

"How do you know so much, unless you are French, I take it?"

"French, Welsh, and hound-dog."

"Ahhh, now the hound-dog part, that explains it."

I liked his smile, even in the pale moonlight I could feel the warmth, and the wine helped. "I thought you were a duck?"

"That was before."

"Be serious. Before that?"

"Before that. . ." He brushed my hand again across his lips sensing the fuzz on my fingertips. "Before that, my mother was a milkmaid, and let's see; yes, my father was a border bandit."

"Is that all?"

"I think maybe along the way, one lonely Indian stopped by for a visit."

"I know a thing or two like that also," I said, amusingly. "My Uncle Sid said one lonesome Frenchman had a thing with Grandma Kreeszowski." I shifted my legs and nudged something strangely familiar, signaling that old reliable hunger of the loins and a stirring of hyper-eager genitals.

"Uh-Oh," I squealed. "How long has it been like this?"

". . .Ummm, a little while. Sometimes it just throbs, and it won't go away."

"Really!" I squealed again, taking a firm hold on it. "I want to see."

"What!"

"I want to see it," I said, grabbing the flashlight.

"Oooh, wait. . ."

"I won't bite it, promise, just a little nibble." In a flash I was squirming beneath the cover emitting merry little sounds. I think the commotion must have awakened the ducks because from beyond I heard the frantic chaos of furious quacking. But no matter, with light in hand I was busy down there exploring amid squeeling sounds."

"Wait," he pleaded.

"It's a beauty," I called back.

He reached down to take the light, and I climbed on, lowering myself joyfully. . . God it was so hard, and like it had a mind all it's own, and it was definitely ready to do it's stuff.

The first one was almost instantaneous. After that it was simply a matter of rhythm and timing. I held on, and somewhere along the way I lost count. I was lost in the clutch of multi-orgasms.

If it is true that pussies and pricks have no consciences, and only minds of their own, I have come to believe it.

That first one had been such a jolt, almost obscene in nature, the kind we girls are not supposed to talk about. I have no idea how long I could have continued, if Emile had not broken into uncontrollable laughter.

Gasping a bit, I came almost to a bucking halt; "And just what are you laughing at?" I demanded.

I studied him intensely for awhile. He was speechless, unable to utter the faintest word, and instead he nodded towards my butt, still slightly geared in motion, I turned to see Hector silhouetted against the moon riding like a bronco cowboy, or an insane creature moving adeptly with the crests and troughs of wild sporadic waves.

"Get off my butt you senile horny, unscrupulous, conniving old eider," I yelled, as I bucked hard; "Get off me you old coot, or. . . or I'll turn you into an ugly old crow," I had no such powers, but maybe he didn't know that, unless I were to wring his scrawny neck.

He let out a disgruntled squawk. I bucked once again, harder, tossing him into the air. He landed in a heap of struggling feathers. The others had gathered around for the show and joined in a heightened pitch.

When he found his wings and feet finally, Hector darted about with Minerva and a couple of aides furiously nipping at him. By then the whole flock had gotten into the act as I shouted; "Hector, you horny old reprobate, you scroungey old eider. . ."

He quacked back; "I'm no eider. I'm a mallard, quack—quack, eiders are dumb. . ."

"Well, you didn't learn much did you? Suppose I send you back to another life to study your lessons again. Maybe next time you'll be a dog, or a rat. . . Hector the rat. . ."

Emile was simply out of control, sniggering from seventh heaven, in uncontrollable spasms. I rolled lamely back by his side, the spell broken, I thought.

By that time I realized the other ducks had gotten caught up in the mood of the evening. Many had paired off while others chased about in some sort of ritualistic selection for an uncompromising mate. Clearly they had found inspiration from our rutting coitus.

To Emile I said, "I think we just shortened their courtship period."

"No doubt," he choked, finding his voice at last.

"I suspect there might be some early clutches of little ducklings this year."

"That wouldn't surprise me," he managed to get out.

At last, finding some humor in the situation I pressed a bit closer, snuggling and squirming, yet somewhat less aggressively.

"I warned you that you could witness some strange happenings," he said.

"Well, they sure don't need much inspiration to entertain themselves, do they?"

"Oh, I'd say they had quite a lot of inspiration."

I pouted a little and pressed closer. Somehow I sensed I had not ceased wriggling during the whole episode.

Unwittingly, I found my free hand tracing down, down— "Uh-oh! I sighed, it's still hard."

"Uh-huh."

"Does it stay that way long?"

"Sometimes all night."

"Hmm, is it true that nice guys really do finish last. . . Are you a nice guy?"

From the corner of my eye I caught a glimpse of Hector, clearly in the mood, astride a more than willing partner. I wondered if it was Minerva.

"Hmmm," I sighed to Emile, holding on with a firm grip; "You want to try that again?"

# THIRTY THREE

By those first faint rays of sunrise we awoke, huddled together, a tangle of body parts plus juices, isolated in the sleeping bag cocoon and charmed by the serenading birds and pleasing sounds of the animal world. While a few of the ducks searched about for remnants of corn and crumbs, for the most part they remained napping with their heads twisted about impossibly in the now familiar dozing duck mode.

I had no complaints, and I wanted to stay right there warm and comfy, but nature has its own demands, even among the eternal animal world.

Emile dug his way out ahead of me while I curled deeper into my shell of security, all the while straining against mother nature's urging. Finally I lost and I too burst out in search of my own private spot, awkwardly stretching the Stanford jersey over my head. Finding the camisole and tap pants would have to wait.

Along the way I shook a threatening finger at Hector lurking nearby with that steady conspiratorial gleam in his mischievous eyes.

When I returned Emile had the bags and equipment rolled and ready to go. The camisole and tap pants folded neatly on top. For a moment he considered me fondly while I tugged the telltale jersey downward daintily.

"There's a pan of fresh water for hands and face if you like. How do you feel?" he asked.

"Can't you tell? My hair's a mess, something must have curled it last night," I grinned, straining my fingers through it desperately.

Soon I was back in my Stanford colors and Emile in his rags. I liked the feral harmony and elements of basic peacefulness. I was in no rush and wondered why he was ahead of me. "I'll take that pan of water now, but I could use a hot bath," I said.

He gestured to the lake. "It may not be hot but there it is," he offered magnanimously.

I faked a shiver, "I'll save it till we get back. . .hopefully that stuff won't sprout growth before then."

"What stuff?"

"You know," I cooed.

"Oh," he allowed in a small voice. I think I detected a hint of blush in his boyish grin. Why are men so immature about some things, such as changing babies' diapers. . .and things.

Somehow he had saved a bag of duck food and they knew it. He opened the bag and began to spread it about to their eager quacking delight. Strange, I thought how their simple sounds can be so distinctive to the alert ear. He was saying something to them in quack language. . .that sounded definitely like a warning.

"What are you telling them?" I asked.

". . .A warning, not to fly over there," he gestured towards the mainland, "it could be dangerous. Hunting season is still on."

"Oh," I said deeply concerned. then. . ."I'm starved."

"I saved a bottle of wine, there in the bag, along with some pears and bananas and some grapes. here are some granola bars too."

"Wine for breakfast?"

"The French, remember, like grape juice."

By nine o'clock we were once again stroking the canoe across glassy water skirting the shoreline toward Long Tule Point, a mere mile and half away, Emile had said.

The welcoming committee had attempted a glorious send-off, and with the exception of an over-eager few who broke into the air, they, for the most part heeded Emile's warning and remained reluctantly grounded.

From the distance we heard the ominous duck calls of alerted hunters straining for their attention.

In less than an hour we were approaching the drooping finger of marshlands and tall tules called Long Tule Point only to find ourselves amongst a scattering of decoys designed to lure unwary prey.

Twenty yards away and a threatening voice rang out to shatter the morning stillness; "Hey you ass-holes, get the hell out of here, unless you want an ass full of buckshot."

"The nerve of those guys," I got out. "Do they think they own the whole damn lake?"

"Tough guys," said Emile calmly, and yet I sensed a touch of tension in his voice.

"What do they think, huh? They buy a goddamn license, and that gives them the right to kill helpless animals. BIG heroes." I was outraged and my voice hopelessly reflected my innermost resentment. Feelings of hostility that until that moment I had been utterly unaware of.

For what seemed like a long time after that neither of us said a word. We just kept on stroking doggedly with our paddles, steadily aware of each other's rhythm.

After a short time all had returned to the musical sound of nature with the steady swish of broken water. "Is this where the four duck hunters were killed?" I asked, then corrected, "I mean accidentally drowned?"

From back at Long Tule Point I heard the ominous duck calls again. The silence broken once more with the sound of deception and betrayal. Was it a very good imitation? I wondered if the ducks could tell the difference? Turning in my seat I looked back in time to see a bunch of them zooming in on the decoys, and then one, two, three shotgun blasts in rapid succession. The flock veered away sharply, just out of range, I prayed. . ."Oh my God," I moaned, shuddering inwardly; what if it had been Jason or Minerva, or event Hector.

"Is this where it happened?" I demanded, a certain harshness creeping into my voice.

"I think right about here is where two of them were found. . . We are about halfway between Long Tule Point and the Rancheria Reservation, the Indians call it Long Point. I believe the other two were found back there someplace, about where the hunters are now."

We were skirting the marshy shore when Emile spotted a place he had been heading for.

"There's a little patch of ground beach ahead where we can get out and stretch our legs, and have another bite to eat," he said.

"I'm not very hungry now, but I could use the stretch and a drink of water."

We grounded and he urged the canoe forward until it was solidly beached, then we both stepped out.

He proffered the bottle.

"No thanks," I had a pout on and I wanted to nurse it awhile for mileage.

"What, no wine," he urged with a musing smile. "Where's your French?"

"Okay," I managed to smile back. "Just a sip."

After I handed it back he took a long drink, swirled it in his mouth for lasting taste like a practiced connoisseur. It seemed only natural drinking after each other. After all we had tasted each other intimately not too long ago.

"Is this one of the places?"

"I don't think so. Over there somewhere," he pointed, "about another hundred yards, and the other two beyond Long Tule Point. . . So the newspapers say."

He shrugged, smiling thoughtfully. After awhile I handed the bottle back; "Well?"

He jerked his head in a gesture; ". . .The papers say they came from the Indian Reservation. Over there. Probably set up blinds around here, maybe over there someplace. . ."

"Well?"

"Well what?"

"How do you think it happened?"

I had not witnessed his cynical laugh before. This first was a brief hint to another side of his enigmatic character. Sometime later I would give it considerable thought, but for the moment I sensed his guard was lowered, his defenses down, and I wanted instinctively to press on. Behind those eyes I sensed a rich reservoir to be tapped, and secrets to be unlocked. And yet there was some hidden glimmer as well, something resembling Dad's eyes that let you understand he wasn't going to tell anything he didn't want you to know.

While I machinated, he recovered quickly with that boyish grin followed by wholesome laughter; "The messenger," he said.

"What messenger?"

"Maybe they just weren't getting it right, and it was time for them to go back and study their lessons some more."

"Be serious," I pleaded. "Then you think they were murdered. . . Indian spirits or some wild thing like that, like that tabloid bull-crap?"

"Hell no. The Indians had nothing to do with it."

"But they were murdered, weren't they, I can feel it." Like a traumatic aura of unyielding forces swirling about. Even the air smacked of strange vibes.

"Who knows," he shrugged, heading for the canoe.

"Wait," I called out. "They were killed and you know something, don't you?" I caught him by the arm jerking him around till our eyes met. Each of us stubbornly measuring the other.

"They drowned," he said, earnestly, "Accidental. That's what your dad the sheriff thinks."

"Nobody knows what my dad thinks," except me, I thought. Sometimes anyway.

"Maybe they had it coming," he said, turning away again, with one foot in the canoe. I caught his arm again, pulled it back, but he twisted away, found his paddle and settled toward his seat.

Was he joking? Did he consider it the ultimate challenge, the final test of manhood rites. One of Dad's greatest fears: the hunter hunting the hunters. The predators getting their own medicine. The quiet dogmatic vigilante acting alone out of a secret purpose.

"Who next then, Emile?" I said, standing there demanding his attention. "The noise makers, the inconsiderate neighbors with their damnable barking dogs, the inconsiderate teens with their incessant mega-boom boxes. And after that, who? The trash throwers and highway litterbugs, the drug dealers and users? Who then, pompous politicians? Who decides, Emile? Do you play God? Can't you see? No one has that right, to play God, decide who lives and who dies. It is not a joke. That's why we have rules, laws and courts. . .otherwise, what. . .anarchy?

He had taken his place in the canoe, paddle in hand, assuming a posture of finality and indifference. An inner signal told me to bite my tongue but I wasn't done yet. I had a good mad going, and I wondered just how red my face might be. ". . .Otherwise, we're back in the dark ages, or worse, back to where it started when Cain slew his brother Abel . . .and how about when Romulus slew his twin brother Remus. What excuse did he have?" I felt my brain reaching for extremes and in the process I hadn't figured how to shut it down. . . "How do you decide then? There are a lot of crude, insensitive self-serving slobs out there," I began to stammer, but I wasn't finished yet; "Who next Emile, you going to kill them all, the ones who drive too fast, or too slow on the freeway, the idiots who drive around frantically flashing you an obscene finger, the con-artists, and every loony. . .who decides? . . .You don't have that right, can't you see? No one individual has the right to play God. . .and suppose you make a mistake. What about that, have you considered that possibility?"

He was easing the canoe away from the shore, and for the moment I thought he was going to leave me standing there alone, until I caught his eyes again, with their pained, hurt little boy look.

Very quickly, and without making a conscious decision I splashed into the water and struggled to my seat, searching for my paddle. For the rest of the trip neither of us spoke a word. Words were on my tongue, yet they were a muddle of thoughts without order, so I chewed my lip all the way.

Physical exertion, I do believe, is unequaled as a means of dissipating stress and hostility. It may even go a long ways towards healing open wounds, and yet time is the only measure of true healing.

We both stroked toward Lakeport with a renewed fury and without another spoken word. I wondered about his thoughts. From behind, he had the advantage of seeing me while I dared not turn to meet his probable prying stare.

It wasn't until we had almost reached the shore of Willowtree Campground that I realized I had seemed to use the incriminating form of *YOU*, instead of the generic, and I had accused him, even blamed him without intending to.

# THIRTY FOUR

At home I took that hot soaking bath, almost sulking away in my own dark mood, when I finally decided the only medicine for escape could be another great expenditure of energy.

In two more hours I had the house cleaned and set in showcase proper order. Dad had been in and out a number of times.

I spent the afternoon alone in the yard and flower garden. Rare November sunshine mixed with the thrill of a new yellow and white paint job triggered a renewed gaiety in my inner mood and very shortly I found myself talking gibberish to the flowers and to Cuddles, who rarely strayed far from my side. All too often she found her own playful interest chasing and stalking some innocent flutter of a leaf, or an unfortunate bug which just happened by.

Dad and I went to Saturday evening mass instead of Sunday because he had some police business on Sunday demanding his undivided attention. Another day of in and out.

In church again I studied the congregation while Batiste unwittingly rattled his innate version about in my head. And all the while I found myself casting about hoping to see Emile there with a forgiving smile.

That evening Dad and I sat quietly alone together after pizza, through Golden Girls, and Empty Nest in which he fell asleep long before 20-20.

I tossed around fitfully all night and in the morning we had breakfast together. After he left I tried to study and when that failed I went to the ever-waiting yard and flowers again.

Even the flowers seemed solemn that morning, or perhaps it was still my mood. As time passed even they with their smiling gaiety and silent laughter offered only moderate consolation, and yet, as it always seems when among the flowers I found myself recalling the occasions Mom and I had played and dug into the dirt together. Steadily I sensed my forlorn mood taking on a certain buoyancy as if her presence was very near. Cuddles must have sensed it also, darting about as she had done as a little kitten in her own inimitable frolicking way.

Then my mood darkened to gloom when I realized my mother wasn't ever coming home again.

I envisioned that last time I had seen her at the San Francisco airport, when Dad had taken us there for her departure.

She would be back soon, she had promised. After all she was only going to New York to visit an ailing aunt.

When Dad had sat me down to explain how it had happened, I don't think I understood the reality of it then.

Sure, she had been struck by a car and had died instantly, he had been told, while returning to my aunt's apartment with an armload of groceries. The driver was not at fault. It had been raining and in her haste she had simply stepped from the curb without looking.

While I stayed with Mrs. Murphy Dad had flown back alone to escort the body home.

I realize now that it was for my sole benefit that he had insisted on a closed casket funeral.

He didn't believe in funerals, said they were old fashioned pagan rituals. But we went anyway. It was expected, I suppose. In church I had sat staring at the cold ornate box while people cried and eulogized, and I was confused because I failed to understand.

In time I was able to come to terms with her passing in a practical sense, although it was to have a strange and unusual effect on me to this very day.

By afternoon I had showered and once again resolved myself to my studies. For that day around the house I wore a pair of lavender jogging shorts, and a white tee with the Stanford logo.

However, as time neared for me to return to school, I found myself at the door of Emile's shop. I drove the Camaro with Cuddles in my lap purring like a contented infant. The sign read, closed; but when I tried the door I found it unlocked.

Among other uncertain reasons, or as an excuse, I had for some time considered an experiment in my mind, and I was eager to try it.

I felt somewhat apprehensive after our intimacy and the final uneasy scene. I rationalized with myself that the experiment was to resolve some more curiosities about human and animal behavioral instincts. Testing the door, I stepped inside as the sweet scent of pine and other wood dust wafted from the back shop to greet me along with the telltale light.

Cuddles, all along had been part of the intended experiment and she snapped alert with immediate alarm just as I had predicted, first bristling, eyes wild with alarm, and claws extended, kneading, tail twitching, testing the air for imminent signs of danger.

The suspended bald eagle, with its claws bared and outstretched wings poised in the air ready to strike, had snatched her attention.

Immediately she broke loose from my grasp leaping to the floor to skulk behind a center display stand, all the while one eye fiercely regarding the descending eagle while the other appeared impossibly crossed, darting about in obvious bewilderment, wary of possible prey. With her hunter instinct subdued, she was momentarily distracted, confused and terrified.

Emile materialized in the back-lighted doorway dressed in tattered jeans and a threadbare tee shirt with a faded wildlife scene on his chest and a raised plastic faceguard. He too, could have passed for a likely demon.

Even from the distance I could smell the scent of wood dust and fresh shavings on his clothes.

"I wanted to see how she would react. . ." I said defensively. Then added, "I think she's terrified of the eagle."

He smiled lightly in agreement, and said; "I have been thinking seriously about getting rid of it. . ."

"Oh no. . . it's. . ."

"It's too bold, and much too harsh among these others. It appears threatening among these gentler creatures. Don't you think?"

I nodded lightly. "I only have a little time. I have to go back to school."

"I know," he said.

"About yesterday. . ."

He dismissed it lightly with a soft smile, removed his face-guard and stepped toward the cowering Cuddles, making a little sucking and whistling sound through puckered lips to attract her attention. He patted his thigh, urging her to him. I knew he had a special way with animals and I shouldn't have doubted he would be any less with Cuddles.

Without an instants hesitation she scampered to him, up his pant leg, and into his arms. He was her white knight in armor, her protector, and she purred in the safety of his protecting cradle.

He petted her and held her to one of the decoys, allowing her to sniff it, saying; "They're only wood and paint. They won't hurt, see." She considered his lips as he spoke, sniffed, tasted his face and purred some more, then sniffed the sculptures as he moved from one to the other, until they came to the eagle. Then she bristled with alarm all over again until he stroked her reassuringly, and finally her confidence returned. She smelled it tentatively until she seemed satisfied and relieved, whereupon he released her, leaping to the floor on her own she went slinking about to continue her own investigation.

"What are you working on," I asked.

"A pair of mallards and some ducklings."

He watched me as I glanced inquiringly to the miniature mandarins. I noticed the price tag was still missing.

"I think she'll be okay now," he said. Then he turned without preamble to the shop and I followed.

At his bench he handed a sanded version of an unfinished duckling to me. Nearby there were seven others in various stages of completion.

I looked around and noticed the retractable ladder to his loft was down.

"Is that where you sleep, up there I mean?" I asked, holding his eyes with intentional purpose.

He nodded. Dazzling him with my most sultry look, I added; "Will you show it to me?"

# THIRTY FIVE

"Just a minute," he said. He went to lock the front door, with Cuddles trailing ever warily at his heels. She was not about to stretch that protective distance between herself and her paladin. The eagle, no doubt still had her number.

Already the experiment had yielded greater dividends than I had expected.

When he returned, he sent me up the ladder first as he followed close behind. I think he was studying my bare legs to their origin, all the way and the thought sent warm shock waves pulsing through me. Nice work lavender and hot joggers, I thought. I wondered why I got so excited by this unassuming man with the sweet scent of wood dust and earthy quality about him.

I stood in the center of the floor of a spacious loft room with it's gentle sloping ceiling and half light from a single dormer window through which there was a sweeping view of the lake over treetops. Mount Konocti loomed gigantic in the distance and now because of the familiar landmarks I knew instinctively where to look for Quercus Island. I squinted briefly, intensely searching for signs of any duck hunters, and was not about to broach the subject.

"What do you think?" he said from behind me. The quiet spell was interrupted by the patter of padded feet coming up the ladder, which at times can resemble a herd of elephants. It seemed Cuddles was not about to let us out of her sight.

"I like it," I said smiling. "It's cozy, and cheerful. . . and very private. . .and neat, very neat."

He nodded gratefully.

"I should have guessed. It's definitely you. Especially the array of wildlife posters. I scanned the room; a stack of books atop a chest of drawers. The chest, no doubt the product of another yard sale. Books about wildlife and mythology.

Cuddles occupied herself with her own investigation, checking out every corner thoroughly.

On a stand there was a small TV and a radiocassette player, a stool and an antique looking wooden rocker, and by the window a sort of weird looking couch.

He saw me looking at the rocker, and said; "I picked it up at a yard sale. I might refinish it someday."

"Is it an antique?"

"I doubt it. Just an old oaken rocker."

I looked around some more and he must have read my mind again. "That's the shower over there. I put it in. The toilet and lavatory are downstairs."

"Can two people fit in it? The shower?"

"Be a tight fit, but worth a try."

I almost asked if he wanted to try right now, but I had had my shower and little time left.

"We can try it someday," he said.

"Sort of inconvenient, isn't it?"

"The shower?"

"The toilet. . .being downstairs."

"Not really," he said matter-of-factly. "I don't mind."

My glance must have unwittingly gravitated to the strange sort of wood-frame looking couch by the window. "No bed?" I said.

Once more he was ahead of me. He moved the couch a little and with another quick move he folded it down, making some clever adjustments and we had a medium sized plush feathered mattress bed. Eider down probably.

"*Vọilà* " he said cheerfully. It's a Futon sofa bed. Very light and when I need to it fits in the back of my van. It doesn't take much space and can be very handy for camping too."

"I see," I said mildly interested, moving to test it.

From beneath the contrivance he withdrew some folded sheets and a single blanket, shook and fluffed the whole affair, and then arranged two pillows properly. All in less than two shakes of Cuddles expressive tail.

Immediately she leapt up on it, testing where to curl up for herself and I shooed her off immediately.

"I think she wants to make this a threesome," I mused.

I started to undress and he helped me. There was not much for either of us to take off and in less than a flash we leaped between the sheets.

There must have been a recipe or formula struggling through my brain, because I started by thinking; to a nominal measure of groping and clutching you add a pinch of eager pawing. Then toss in a full measuring cup of gentle kisses. . .all over of course. . .and to the contents add some more anxious kissing, stir steadily for a proper time, then bring the whole content to a full passionate boil, and *voilà*, we're in business again.

Only the pot didn't get quite to a full boil; for one reason, Emile had his own recipe cooking;

"Pussy get tight,
Dick get fat.
Move it around,
like this and that. . ."

I said, "What was that you said. . .!"

That's when I finally realized he was desperately trying to subdue an encroaching laughter betrayed by minor tremors of indiscriminate proportions.

"What are you laughing about this time," I challenged furtively.

He gestured over my shoulder again, and I paused in mid-motion to hear the steady squeak of the oaken rocker.

This time, I too found the situation amusingly humorous, and this time instead of Hector the bully riding my buttocks like a bucking bronco it was Cuddles sitting upright in the rocking chair, perched alertly, head cocked casually to one side in a bewildered posture of kittenish curiosity, rocking steadily, back and forth.

"Do you think she wants an invitation," Emile asked, still searching for his composure.

"More like she is trying to figure out what is going on. She was spayed years ago."

"Well spayed or not, she's curious as hell." Then he gave a low inviting whistle while patting the bed sheet. "Come here girl."

In two frisky bounds she stood beside us curiously purring to her heart's delight.

"I shall have to write this down in my diary," I said. Everyone should try it once, making love, with their favorite feline nuzzling into the act, breathing into your ears, licking them too, alternately snatching at the covers, then trying to horn in on the act by chewing playfully on one's hair. All this and more during some of those spasmodic kissing interludes. Of course there was more. Emile for one never quite found his composure, although he lived up to that old saying; nice guys really do finish last.

When at last we both lay spent we looked at each other with sheepish grins while it seemed Cuddles was just getting wound up. We agreed it was indeed a healthy recipe.

For a time ephemeral we lay there snuggled side by side with Cuddles curled up between us, purring at a contented pitch. I found myself staring out the window at the clouds beyond. I dreaded the thought of the spell ending, and I started to mutter things softly, inconsequential things, like one does while exposing one's innermost confidential thoughts.

". . .Animals are so strange," I said, sighing thoughtfully. "They don't talk our language, and yet they understand. . .and they communicate in their own unique fashion, like Cuddles, and Minerva. . ."

Emile seemed mentally detached, far away, and yet I had a sense that he might still be listening. So I went on just the same.

". . .I remember once when I was a little girl. Mom and Dad had company, Ned Turner and his wife. We were all sitting around the patio table in our back yard. It was summer time and we, or they, the adults were talking when this towhee fluttered in to join us. Dad was laughing at some joke Ned was telling. He, Dad always says the way to recall a story is simply to remember the punch line, anyway, Ned always remembers the story but forgets the punch line, but Dad laughs anyway. Camaraderie or something, or the buddy system. Ned is so serious that his stories can make you laugh without the finish. Anyway, Ned was sitting there with his legs crossed when this towhee landed on his foot, cocking its head back and forth animatedly like birds do, just like it was listening to every word that was said. When Ned said something, it hopped over to the other knee. It was a perfect stranger to us, and yet it acted as if it knew and understood us. I mean every word we were saying. From time to time it chirped back just like it was engaging in the conversation. Well it was so ironic, I mean it hopped from one to the other of us, and I can still recall the thrill when it settled on my lap. Then it fluttered to the table-top just inches from my face, chirping and staring at me with those friendly eyes in that jerky fashion. . . I remember asking Mom; 'I wonder what it wants?" and she said, "Maybe it's hungry." So when I got up and went to the kitchen it followed me. I had left the screen door open and it flew right into the house where I put some bread crumbs on the counter."

"And when it was satisfied it left," said Emile.

"How did you know that," I said, raising my face to catch his eyes.

"It figures," he said plainly. "Then what happened?"

"I got some bird seed and put it out. It hung around for about two weeks. . .and I never saw it again," I said sadly.

"But it made you happy while it was there?"

"Oh yes. . . Do you think it will ever come back?"

"I'd bet on it," he said reassuringly.

Then I started thinking about school and that it was Sunday afternoon and I had to leave soon in order to get back at a decent hour.

That's when Emile said: "You want to hypnotize me, don't you?"

"WHAT! I said, as I raised on one elbow poised above him, estimating him, impetuously trying to organize my response.

"That could be very dangerous, and, and I'm really not trained. . ."

"But you have thought about it?"

". . .Well, yes. But it's not a good idea. It can be dangerous in the hands of someone unqualified." I was stammering, reaching for excuses, but yes dammit I had considered it, and yes I wanted it more than I had cared to admit.

As Carolyn Kosloff's assistant I had taken notes many times, and I had witnessed her use of hypnotism professionally and effectively as a tool in her criminology practices. And yet, I had never considered attempting it myself. I said, "It can be dangerous. People have been known to lapse into a catatonic state and vegetate there, forever, helpless. . ."

# THIRTY SIX

Looking into my eyes passionately, Emile said, "I'm a very easy subject."

"I bet you are," I countered, with somewhat less than his total confidence.

Disturbing Cuddles, we managed to untangle ourselves and get dressed then he returned the bed to it's former couch position. At the same time I searched my brain secretly for past experiences and reading information.

To anyone involved in Psychology or Psycho-therapy the first name that automatically pops into one's mind is Sigmund Freud of course. He was the father of the science of the mind. I wondered what insights I might glean from the writings of father Freud. He treated numerous patients by using hypnotic techniques he had learned from Charcot. However, I was not Freud nor Jean Martin Charcot, nor was I prepared to *TREAT* anyone.

Now, I was scared. A single individual's well being was poised in my hands. For the reality of that moment I was terrified and I wanted out. Then again, another voice intruded, encouraging me, saying; this could be a once in a lifetime chance to really learn. . . Take the ball and run like hell with it. Look inside this complex individual and see what lurks there.

I realized my hands were suddenly wringing wet, and taut with apprehension. If Sigmund were here to advise me, he might say, "Watch for the Freudian slip;" a simple slip of the tongue or pen, an unintentional act, as a clue which reveals the individual's inner state of mind. Do you have any more advice father Sigmund?

Freud originated the method of free association, and by speaking freely with his patient he claimed to have exposed earlier experiences locked away in the sub-conscious. All too often there had been painful memories held back in the subconscious through defense mechanisms. The act of unlocking these secrets might cause the subject to teeter on the brink of insanity, and even withdraw into a catatonic state.

"I can't do it," I pleaded.

"I've been under before," he said. "Don't worry."

"But this is different. . ."

"How?"

"Because. . . it's totally different than asking someone to recall a subdued incident, where they have suppressed something like. . . like witnessing a crime, or even childhood sexual abuse. . . or. . ."

"Or going under to have a tooth pulled?"

"Yes. Much different."

"I don't think so. But if you don't want to go through with it. . ."

"Yes. . . No. I mean, I do but I want to be prepared. I have to think. This is not something to be taken lightly."

"Okay," he said confidently. He moved the rocker to place it in front of the couch, and sat down with Cuddles curled into a furball beside him. He stroked her lightly and indicated the rocker for me. "There," he said, "I'll sit here and relax, you there. Just relax, and if you get ready—well okay, we'll try it, and if not—well that's okay too."

I wondered if there could be another time later on. No there might not. Anyway, Dad would say, "You gotta make hay while the sun shines." Thanks Dad. Got any suggestions Mom?

Freud wrote that there were symbolic clues to the unconscious memories. He paid particular attention to painful emotions. Free association is the ultimate key to an open and free flow of feelings.

"When I clap my hands and count, you will come out. . . is that understood?" I managed a positive edge to my voice.

He nodded.

I realized more than ever, that to continue, I must first organize my own thoughts, and steady the anxious trembling within myself. In the cause of erudition a mental image began to formulate within my mind. A warning message of another source signaled for me to call the whole thing off. And yet, there was no more ability in me to halt the process already set in motion than there was a means to halt the inexorable process of day into night and back again.

Finally, the trembling gave way to excitement as a seemingly logical order of things followed, almost as if I too were an unwitting tool in the grip of another force. Basics first, I cautioned, back to basics.

The term hypnosis gets its roots from the Greek word *hypnos*, which means to sleep, but with a more active, intense mental concentration. An individual under hypnosis can talk, write, and even walk around to perform certain feats. Usually they are fully aware of what is being done and said. Acts may also involve certain parts of natural behavior while some people may appear to be in a sort of trance. Maybe they found out about self-hypnosis, I thought. Basics, basics, I cautioned.

Such altered states can and do lead to various character changes and phenomena. That voice of caution again. . . The levels of awareness and conscious imagination may become more responsive to suggestions and thereby affect memory and reaction.

There also may be emotional changes such as blushing, increased blood flow, the tension of muscles and loss of pain sensation or heightening of same, paralysis and possible loss of memory and even lapse into an altered state. A shuddering thought.

Even though it was commonly believed in the past that a person could be forcibly hypnotized, we now know that concept to be erroneous. That's comforting, I thought fleetingly. Certain individuals can and do resist suggestions. Freud must have been right. Free flow must have been the safest method.

From the misconception of magic shows there must be an exaggeration, an embellished act, at most with a very willing and simple subject.

While Emile seemed fully relaxed with Cuddles curled beside him I continued rapidly to improvise my own conception of all I had experienced.

Some individuals go under in a mere few seconds, while others cannot be hypnotized at all, or at least with very great difficulty.

There are several methods of testing to determine if the subject is truly under hypnosis. One is the use of shock words and emotion methods. Shock words are used to gauge the degree of the subject's emotional response. The terms may seem crude or vulgar, yet have the ability to trigger vivid mental images and reactions, and if the individual responds in kind, he or she can be assumed to be under the hypnotic influence. On the other hand a comparison of clinical terms such as; vagina, penis and coitus will most likely draw only mild reactions.

Another method was to have the subject raise one arm and hold it there, in which case he or she will hold the position without discomfort or fatigue. Dropping of the arm may signal the individual is either coming out of the spell or may even be faking.

Then there was the obvious choice among professionals. The use of an object to help induce calm and drowsiness along with a soft encouraging voice. In this case a judgment call is an absolute necessity.

Carolyn Kosloff always carried a sapphire pendant on a gold chain for her more difficult subjects.

I had no objects with me, and I had already discounted any such tricky tests. Free-flow was definitely my choice.

All the while I had been keenly aware that Emile was focusing on one particular wall poster beyond my left shoulder.

He was already halfway there, I concluded.

In a soft monotone voice I asked, "Are you ready?"

He smiled easily and nodded with confidence.

I felt overwhelmed with excitement mixed with a sort of sexual intimacy between the two of us, a poignant high I had never experienced before.

The best techniques are simple direct commands, consisting of simple suggestions.

"You will focus on one object of the poster," I said. I had turned briefly to see it. The poster was one of a wildlife scene depicting a flight of ducks in various degrees of flight and descent.

"You are very relaxed. . .breathe deeply. . .deeply . . .deeply. your eyelids will grow heavy, and you will allow them to close. You are relaxed. You are very comfortable. I want you to count backwards from ten. . . nine. . . eight. . . You are descending into a beautiful garden; drifting, drifting. . . back. . . back. . . Back to a happy time. You may have some difficulty in moving your hand. Nod if you can hear me.

He nodded.

I had paused for myself as much as for him, inhaling a deep slow breath.

He twitched, seemingly unable to move the right hand.

"You may relax the hand now."

"Emile, can you tell me where you are?"

". . .Running. . .someone is chasing me."

"Are you in danger?"

He nodded smiling. Almost a small chuckle.

"Where are you?"

". . .Vines and flowers. . . Grapes, for wine."

"Are there others around you?"

". . .Yes. . ."

"What are they doing?"

"Laughing."

"Is this a happy occasion?"

"Yes. . ."

"How old are you?"

". . .Old—?"

"Your age?"

"Age?"

"Who are you with?"

"A girl. . . A boy is chasing us. . .and they are laughing."

"Where is this place? what country?"

"Country?"

"Emile, are there automobiles. . .and airplanes?"

"Just horses and wagons, and peasants, they are called."

"In France?"

"Yes. . . Bordeaux."

"What are you doing?"

"Doing?"

Desperately I fumbled for a clue to the right question, or word, "There is a girl, and a boy, right?"

". . .Yes. They are on the ground playing, and the others are laughing. . ."

". . .And where are you, Emile?"

". . .Inside the girl."

"Oh my God!" I heaved a great sigh. Can this really be true. I thought urgently of the test, but it was too late for that now. And, I must be cautious not to transfer my own emotions to him.

"Emile, I want you to drift forward in time now. . . on your own."

I watched him intently as his face and body revealed a variety of emotional signals, none appearing strained. Finally, when he appeared to lapse into a sudden quiet, sort of peaceful calm, I intruded; "Where are you now?"

"A place. . ."

"Can you tell me about this place?"

". . .A place of soft colors. . . floating. . . drifting. . . like dancing."

"Are there other people?"

"Others. Yes."

"Do you have feet. . . and hands. . . a body?"

"A misty place, no hands. . . no feet. . . no body. A spiritual substance."

Oh my God, what have I done? Basics, basics, basics. Please God, help me.

". . .These others, Emile, can they speak—words?"

"No words. Words are not needed. Exchanging thoughts; touching. . . and dancing. . ."

"Emile, I want you to drift ahead in time now. Stop when you feel like it, and tell me what you are doing."

Once again surrealistic emotions flooded across his face, relating a story all their own. The frowns, twitches, and smiles told of passions, stress and pleasures.

"Emile, can you tell me—?"

"I am on a ship. A big ship made of wood."

"With motors?"

"Sails. . . I am in a shop, working, on wood. The bow figure, I am carving a figure with wings. This morning I worked on a masthead."

"Do you like to work with wood?"

"Oh yes."

"How old are you, what age?"

"Nineteen."

"Where are you going?"

"To Wales."

He seemed to move ahead rapidly as his face grew pinched with concern.

"Emile, is something wrong?"

". . .A storm. . . We are tossing badly. . . a sail is ripped. . . and the mast splintered. . ."

Very quickly I said; "Emile, listen to me. I want you to move ahead in time—to another place, where there is no threat or danger. Can you do that. Move ahead to a happy place, Emile, Emile. . ."

Once more his body settled and the pinched signs of stress faded from his face.

I was pleased with myself. It was going nicely, and I felt in control. When he had settled into a renewed calm, I asked; "Where are you now, Emile?"

". . .Black hills, mountains of big rock, and beyond the marshlands."

"The place?" I guessed. "Wales?"

"Yes," he responded with a curious neutered grin.

"How old are you?"

"Sixteen."

Now I was baffled. "What are you doing?"

"There is a girl. . . A man is coming on horseback. . ."

"Is the girl afraid?"

"No. . ."

"Is she waiting for the man? Is she expecting him?"

"Yes. She is happy."

"Where are you, Emile?"

"Where?. . .I am there waiting for the man. They say he is an outlaw. I am forbidden to see him.

"Who are you, Emile? What is your name?"

"Name. . . I am the girl."

He seemed calm, but I. . . I broke out suddenly in a cold sweat.

Oh God, if only I had more time to explore, and a means to document this. And, should I limit the time he remains under the spell. Might it be more of a risk to leave him under longer. God I need time to think. There may be other times, and then I can be better prepared, and yet, maybe there is no tomorrow. I felt a shameful sense that I just might be losing control of the situation when a mere few minutes ago I had felt so completely confident. How can I ease him back gently without danger?

"Emile. . . I want you to move ahead again. . .to another pleasant time."

Once more he progressed through his range of emotions and when I perceived that he had settled into pleasant surroundings, I said; "Can you tell me where you are now Emile?"

"In America."

"Are you happy?"

"Yes. I work in a shop. It used to be a barn, and then a blacksmith had it. . ."

"What are you doing there?"

"I make carriages."

"Do you enjoy making carriages?"

"Oh yes. Some people say I make the best, because of the carvings. But I think Josiah Graham builds a better carriage. His cost more too."

Now I was really flushed and overflowing with questions, more than I could readily put in order. But I wondered if he could be tiring, plus, how much tension and strain might be working on him. I desperately wanted to press ahead, and yet I was aware that Emile's tone of voice was growing in confidence. I shuddered to suppose he might resist my control altogether. "Emile, I want you to move ahead to another place in time."

Before I had even finished my suggestion he was already flowing ahead to that other time and place and I also sensed he was becoming gradually assertive.

"Can you stop now Emile, where are you?"

With some hesitation, he settled into a sort of ephemeral existence of supernatural suspension.

"What are you doing now?"

"Floating."

"Are you alone?"

"Sometimes. At times we are alone."

"Do you have a body, feet, hands?"

"Only the spirit."

"And you are floating?"

"Floating."

"And this other spirit is sometimes with you?"

"She is always with me."

"Does she talk—?"

"Not in words. We exchange thoughts and we touch. We dance in soft shades of color with music."

"How long?"

"There is no time. We are here, forever, floating like a misty essence. . ."

"Emile, listen to me." For that moment I almost panicked again. I noticed his color fading and his breathing becoming dangerously shallow by the seconds. "Emile," I pleaded. "Emile, don't leave me now."

I was desperate as I pleaded; "Emile, I want you to move ahead in time again."

He failed to respond, and I commanded him; "Emile, you will return to this time. You will come back. You will forget. You will be relaxed and feel refreshed."

When he failed to respond, I clapped my hands loudly; one, two, three.

Oh Jesus, he was not responding. Mother Mary please help me. God please help me.

Again I clapped; one, two, three.

His breathing suddenly became easier as his face filled with emotion, but his eyes remained closed. The lids moved almost imperceptibly. He had not returned.

"Where are you, Emile?"

"I'm flying."

"Are you alone?"

"Nooo. There are others. My family. And, the spirit girl, and others like us. . ."

"What body form are you in?"

"Ducks. . . I tried to warn them, but we are off in a swarm together, playing in flight. Everyone is carefree, diving in acrobatics. It is morning, and others call us to join them."

Maybe he is coming back, I prayed. I thought of the poster. "Emile, can you open your eyes. I want you to open your eyes and focus on the poster. You will be calm and refreshed. I clapped; once, two, three.

"Another family is calling us to join them at the water's edge. I quacked; do not go there. There is danger in that place, but they are hungry, and they like to play games like children;

who can be first, who can dive the fastest and who can perform the best tricks, and they want food. My spirit girl is there, and I must catch her. . . before it is too late."

"Please God no. Not the hunters. . . "Emile, listen to me. Come back to me this instant," I shouted, leaping from the rocker and startling Cuddles for the first time.

". . .That loud noise, and my spirit girl is hurt. Now she is falling, tumbling to the water. Another blast, and my own body strikes with sudden shock. My wing is torn away, and I am falling. . .all is turning black. . . then I hit the water!"

# THIRTY SEVEN

"A monster demon is coming after me," said Emile, his face twisted in fear and torment.

The dogs, I thought. My tremors struck like a sudden seizure. Sweat beaded over my entire body. Cuddles sprang upright in her alarmed posture.

"Emile," I clapped; one, two, three. "Wake up now. Now, dammit."

"The monster dog has hold of my wing and we struggle. The pain is killing me, I break away, to the bottom, the monster follows biting at me. At last, I am free again, in the water's depth where it cannot reach me, but it is still there. I clutch at the roots of a water vine. . . and wait. . . for complete blackness to come. . . and return to the spirit world. . ."

I was on my feet, frantic, and jumped on his lap, straddling him, pleading; "Don't you dare leave me. I love you. . ." I was clutching him, rocking back and forth, begging; "I'll never do this again. Just come back to me. I love you." To myself I prayed to the Virgin Mother with tears streaming down my face for what seemed like an eternity. . . Then I felt him stir. His body quivered in minor-spasms as limbs struggled and jerked innately as though every fiber were fighting instinctively for lifes resumption.

At last, he fought for each urgent breath.

"6-3-6," I urged, with less than steady composure. "Steady. . .breathe deeply and count six, hold for three count, then, exhale completely for a six count. Rest. Relax, then repeat. Finally, I flushed with relief. He was back again, cradled in my arms, forgiving and supple, like a child. He was mine again, part of that maternal instinct I suppose. The warmth returned to his face and as I backed off, the color returned also. I rocked him and clutched furtively, and hugged and rocked him some more. Then I backed off to brush the wetness from my face with the back of my hands. He smiled that little boy mischievous smile, and the thrill between us came flooding over us once more.

"Did you like it?" he said.

"What do you mean?"

"Was it a good act? I've been working on the idea for some time."

"You are trying to tell me you were faking? No way, no way," I said defiantly, leaping to the floor, feet spread apart with hands planted on my hips. My most indignant stance.

"It was just a game," he said, still flashing that mischievous grin. "Now it's your turn."

"You beast," I shouted. Cuddles scampered for the farthest corner while he stood and stretched to strut a few steps.

"Don't be mad," he pleaded.

"Damn you. . . you bastard. How could you do such a thoughtless inconsiderate thing to me, like a prank. . .

"Please don't be angry?"

"You scared the holy stuffings out of me. Damn you," I shouted, enraged. "Damn you. . . and you think it was all a funny stupid game. . .

And all a once I wasn't sure of anything. "Come on Cuddles. It is time to go home," I commanded, with a tone of finality.

I started down the steps with fury still raging within me and she followed dutifully, if not perplexed.

I felt Emile's presence behind me. He had gathered Cuddles in his arms passionately, no doubt stimulating divided loyalties. Divide and conquer was his game too. Well, at least she still believed in him.

As I took her from him he moved between us to unlock the door, his eyes bold and yet forgiving, and pleading all at the same time. With Emile, it was always the eyes; the power to influence, and the warmth too. Within those eyes, I bet he had the power to intimidate as well, although I had never witnessed it as such.

"Will I see you this next weekend?" he asked.

"I don't know," I said, with uncertainty. Then stepping through the doorway to my waiting Camaro, I added; "I don't think I can make it this weekend. I'm too far behind, and I had better stay there to work on my studies. . ."

"I could come down," he said, with that distant faraway smile. "To take a few items to a gallery. We could go gallery hopping and rent a nice seaside cottage in Carmel. Later on, dinner, dancing. What do you say?"

In my head a voice said, you can't. You need time, time to think, to sort things out and to study, basics and commitment. Then I said, relenting a little, "I'll think about it."

He reached inside and came out with a business card. I studied the parchment like surface and duck images in silhouetted flight. . .

"Will you call me when you decide?"

# THIRTY EIGHT

*I* took the mountainous Hopland Grade for a shortcut to Highway 101 southbound. Lord I was brave these days. There was a time in the not too distant past when I would have shuddered at the prospect of driving this treacherous pass. Nowadays, I always seem to be in a hurry.

In less than two hours I should be at the Golden Gate Bridge, and in another hour I would be in my Stanford apartment. By then I would be bushed and with very little energy left for anything, much less studying. I would set the alarm for five a.m. so as to rise early for a fresh start and a couple of good hours with the books. Prepare an especially top grade impression for Professor Wooldridge. The hitch, at five a.m. I just might not be so alert.

Driving the scenic Highway 101 has always been a good time for private thoughts. A time to sort things out, put priorities in proper order.

I popped a tape of Rena McKenzie in the player and sang along with the lyrics to Cassie's Town, my all time favorite. I always liked it when friends say that I look a lot like Rena McKenzie. In my shower I sing Cassie's Town, several times, and sometimes I wail a few lines of Till Love Comes Again. In my shower I sound like her too. In the shower I think everyone must sound like their favorite singer.

For a time the flaming sunset of western mountains hesitated before making its final plunge behind a high crest only to arise once again in another canyon dip before the final sinking disappearance, only to be reborn another day. I wondered if the sun and moon and stars were somehow symbolic in the everlasting chain of reincarnation.

For that brief time the sunset had commanded my attention, and yet my inner thoughts strayed inexplicably back to Emile and our uncommon session.

My subconscious had tossed it about sorting and re-sorting, before handing it back to the ever conscious, relieved of its dreamy state. Back to the logical me. Finally, after many confusing signals, I sensed I had reached conjectures I could deal with.

There was no doubt that Emile was a very complex and challenging individual, and if only I could exclude emotions for a time and forget his beguiling charm he also might fall into some logical order.

That Emile believed he was indeed reincarnated from another time and life forms there was absolutely no doubt in my mind. However, to accept as fact that he had survived as he believed he had, still seemed only remotely acceptable to my other logical self.

And yet the most important consideration was that he believed he was reincarnated, and had even been reborn at various times in his other life, and possibly even in spirit forms. There was a seemingly illogical variation in the time periods related by him, and yet he was able to articulate his most lucid experiences in recall.

Now more than ever there was that inner voice reminding me that he had been a most willing subject. Perhaps it was because he also was eager to unlock the haunting secrets of his own past. I wondered if during a previous hypnosis sequence had he ever gone this far before.

But he was under my influence, of that I am totally convinced, and he was there for me to try again.

The most significant consideration that loomed in my mind now was not that he was actually reincarnated, but that he believed he was. Why, and what incident, if any, had affected him so traumatically? Had the wildlife poster played a part, and he merely became an unwitting candidate for self-hypnosis. And, had any of the wildlife posters had anything to do with the episode? There was so much more to be determined. For example, was Emile capable of self induced trances and unwilling or even unable to separate reality from fantasy in his own mind?

With the karma of Emile still around me, I had entered my own preoccupation and had eased back off the accelerator to an aggravating forty miles per hours. Someone behind me blasted their horn angrily. My rear view mirror revealed a string of cars and trucks gathered snugly bumper to bumper, pressing on me unmercifully.

Looking for the next turn-out I pulled over to let them pass, and got that international high sign for thanks.

Two guys slowed beside me with the passenger window lowered and gave me the finger, shouting; "Asshole Sunday driver!" So damn many fingers, all in one day. I stuck my tongue out, "Blaahhh," just as nasty as I could manage.

There was absolutely no doubt in my mind now, that Emile had been under, and when he had come out of it to give me that story that he was faking, I had been furious. For some time I was still seething and ready to launch a scathing verbal attack at them in retaliation.

But now, after thinking it through, I realize it had been a cover-up, a charade, something Dad might do, to calm me down or to disguise his true emotions, possibly even to shield either himself or me . . . or both. I'll have to work on that one.

I had promised never to do it again. Still, deep down, I knew I had to reach him, at least one more time.

Oh God, I was racing at eighty miles per hour now. Very warily I scanned the highway for any black and whites, back off, don't touch the brakes, a dead giveaway by the tail lights. Dad would never let me forget it if I got a speeding ticket, and Ned might even threaten an unforgiving trip to the woodshed.

By the time I reached Novato I realized I was already looking forward to the coming weekend; a cottage by the sea in Carmel with dancing, candle-light and romance. Two sunshiny days of gallery hopping, and if it rained; well what the hell. A cottage bed can't be all that bad for two days and nights of love-making.

With my faith restored, I looked forward to a week of energetic study and classes. I resolved to call him by Thursday, Friday maybe. Keep him guessing for awhile.

Had I any idea of the shock and surprises the week would bring, I would have done it all differently.

# THIRTY NINE

Monday flew by with all things in proper order just as I had planned. . . until that moment of truth when the evening news flashed on television.

There was scrawny defiant little Chester again, bigger than life, the reluctant spokesman, being led up the steps of the Lake County courthouse on Forbes Street, in handcuffs ushered by uniformed escorts, with busy cameras following close behind, all the while prying for comment.

Chester Cowan had been arrested for questioning and suspicion in connection with the deaths of the four hunters.

One prying reporter demanded to know if it had anything to do with the 130 year old feud. Chester just grinned his old pioneer grin.

Another wanted to know if it were true that he was part Indian, and if the hunters got what was coming to them by violating the sacred burial grounds.

Oddly enough, for once, Chester declined to respond to any of the questions. For one thing, he was being hustled into the courthouse rather quickly.

I caught a glimpse of Kimberly nearby and I wondered if she was representing Chester. Also, as the camera panned the crowd I caught a brief glance of that other beauty in her trademark red dress, thoughtfully jotting notes on a pad. I wondered who she was.

I later learned that Chester flatly refused to state his whereabouts on that fateful morning, and I speculated that he projected himself into the limelight, and thereby drew additional suspicion on himself.

Chester had crossed swords, so to speak, with Martin Rosswell and Judge Wooden on so many occasions in the past. I concluded that he must at least be considered a conspiratorial suspect, and the affair would be Rosswell's. Not Dad's.

The Tuesday morning newspapers had the jump on the story this time. After questioning, Chester had been released with a warning not to leave the area, and he was indeed part of an ongoing investigation. Chester never went anyplace anyway, and was not likely to. If he decided to go, I don't think a warning would have stopped him anyway.

It was Wednesday before I picked up any additional news on Chester. Although he had held his tongue going into the courthouse, probably on Kimberly's advice, he reverted to activist type upon release with caustic opinions on several subjects.

It was purely by chance that I caught his name once again on the front page of that all reliable supermarket scandal sheet, the Word Informer. The article was written by none other than Bev Westerly herself. So much for the identify of the mystery woman in red with her note pad.

The article read: Chester Cowan, released this day after questioning in the Duck Hunter Murder Case, had this to say; "A simple misuse of taxpayer's money by self-indulgent individuals. We all know who they are, dressed in robes and pinstripes. They don't have enough to do with muggers and dope pushers. They got to try and make a case out of some old timer trying to help his poor invalid wife pass onto a better place. These Government bumpkins is over taxed with intellect. They got brain over-load. They got to try and justify them big salaries. They got this machine mentality and computeritus. They wanta know where people go to take a crap in the morning and what brand of toilet paper they used, and tke out a permit for that too.

"I can tell you one thing; it's them gummed up gears of bureaucratic bungling, stubborn robotics, driven idiots like DA Martin Rosswell that's driving us all seasick. Given half a chance that moron could drive a wooden man crazy without half tryin.

"Take that Kevorkian suicide machine. Who needs a Goddam machine to commit suicide anyhow? They can't think without a machine doin it for em. Every body should have the right to decide when they want to leave this world anyway.

"They got lock-jaw-brain on that multi-million dollar orange monster machine to pick up twenty pound bags along the highway. Another lamebrain waste of taxpayer's money, not to mention all them fumes and natural resources. Millions of dollars for a fancy monster contraption to pick up dumb trash bags along the highway after they been placed nice and neat in a row. What are they afraid of; these convicts going to get a hernia lifting 20 pound bags, and throwing them in a dumpster.

These guys is muggers, rapists, murderers and all round hoodlums. They got lots of hostile energy needs workin off anyway.

"And who needs that Kevorkian machine anyhow? We already got cars with polluting exhaust so we don't need to make up some fancy computer or machine to do the job.

"Tell you one thing though, I never knew anyone who didn't want to put it off when their time came near."

So this was Chester's gift to the tabloids.

Chester, I thought, you have really gone too far this time, but not as far as those sleaze-balls who printed it.

# FORTY

On those following days of the week I found myself back in the campus library compiling more notes for my master's thesis. Reincarnation was definitely the major theme with a side slant on hypnosis.

Visions of the coming weekend in Carmel, poised romantic and starry-eyed with music and candlelight dinners loomed as a distinctive rewarding necessity.

In the process I had removed my two seldom used party dresses from the otherwise packed wardrobe of bulky sweaters, jeans, and plain or print blouses, of which most were satin green or lavender and a few see-through whites. I had cleaned my favorite, and only pair of high heels and practiced walking, in eager anticipation.

I decided the dresses were too tight, and in order to splurge Saturday and Sunday I went on a crash diet of carrots, broccoli, celery sticks with sparing measures of light Italian dressing, plus an occasional bowl of vegetable soup with a plain half slice of wholewheat bread. In short, I need a more generous and flattering mirror, and I was headed for a lean, clean, delirious two day interlude of romance and suspense.

I was floating on an all time high of elevated endorphins with a booster shot of adrenalin, all natural, with no sugar added.

Chester was almost completely washed out of my mind. After all, Dad had said not to worry about Chester; he's a big boy and can handle himself. The news and tabloids appeared to support his assumption. So, for those next few days I avoided distractions by dedicating my new flow of energies into demanding studies.

By now I had accumulated piles of notes with more questions than answers and more to come. From my memory I recorded every word and facet of that period during Emile's hypnosis.

All the while there had been a conglomeration of questions pertaining to the reasoning, or lack of same relative to the Scriptures.

About that familiar house or place seemingly locked away in the recesses of one's mind from another life and time; could it be that many buildings, houses and places are already so familiar, or because they are merely figments of other vague forgotten memories instead of testimony in support of reincarnation? It would appear to be quite understandable to confuse the two, especially while under the influence of certain hypnotic suggestions.

I considered a list of different headings; recollections drawn while under hypnosis, here again, could these not be a result of confusing signals , or an assumed familiarity drawn from vivid impressions during impressionable years of youth, such as from books, plays, and movies, or stories implanted in those receptive years of early sub-conscious yearnings?

Fact: Many courts disallow testimony obtained from memory while under hypnosis as being unreliable, there being no way of determining if that testimony is indeed truth, fabrication, or fantasy.

From the scriptures: Matthew 17:12,13—John 1:21—Luke 1:17, and Matthew 4:5,6—Some scholars attempt to point to these passages as evidence that John the Baptist was Elijah, reincarnated.

Quote: when John was asked, "Are you Elijah?" John said, "I am not."

John 9:1,2 has often been cited as proof of reincarnation,

because Jesus healed a blind man. An attempt to indicate the man could not have been blind from birth has often been cited as good opposing reason. And yet, the scriptures declare later that the very same man was indeed blind from birth.

I considered my notes at length, and wondered if I was on the right track. Then, after a brief period of rumination I realized I was hooked on reincarnation as my theme. The premise however, must be broadly stated, allowing for logic from both points of view, pro and con.

I added another note and underlined it; According to Precepts of Reincarnation: when a person dies, that soul, the real self, goes on to a better existence, if, big if, that individual has lived a *proper* life.

Then, the endless cycle of animal and human rebirth can terminate in which the only escape comes after the individual has given up all earthly desires for the physical things that please the senses. . .

Conclusion: The spiritual self must be completely devoid of material desires, which begins with a voyage through time and space where the spirit/soul continues to evolve.

According to the Bible: The soul is the complete person, and if he or she repents for their misdeeds, and changes his or her ways, and if he or she truly believes in reincarnation, God will reward you.

Conclusion: Your reward is because you believe strongly enough in that better life. No matter where you start from, it all comes round to whether you believe or not.

Law of Incarnate: If a man believed himself accountable in the next life, might he not be motivated to make some drastic changes in the present.

Note: The Indians certainly believed in different levels of rebirth. . .and I bet they slept well.

Just why does anyone believe that reincarnation is necessary in the first place? There is the abiding question that has plagued me ever since my first talks with Emile.

I flew through the week as if on wings, high with eager anticipation for the coming Carmel rendezvous, assured of good fortunes.

Even Professor Wooldridge seemed convinced I was seriously back on the right track.

For the whole week long I had planned to keep Emile in suspense, and then call him on Friday. Instead, I acquiesced and called him on Thursday, several times in fact. . . There was no answer.

Friday morning when I called again there was still no answer. No problem I thought, I'll use the library phone later.

It seemed that damn library was eternally destined to serve as my undoing. While sitting at a table, halfheartedly working on my studies, I happened to glance over to a person two tables away, straightening the newspaper so the front page loomed boldly in front of me.

Had I taken the trouble to turn the TV news on Thursday evening, which I was to learn later, I could have caught a first glimpse of the next morning's headline spread:

**WOODCARVER ARRESTED IN DEATH OF 4 HUNTERS**

# FORTY ONE

*I*n a stupor I stared at the newspaper two tables away with a photograph of Emile being escorted up those familiar courthouse steps, handcuffed and compliant, instead of Chester. Somehow it would seem commonplace now with Chester, but Emile. . . This time the photo revealed a media crowd around Emile. I could hardly wait to read the article so I moved adroitly to sit opposite the other unconcerned male to squint and read: Emile Lloyd Osborne was arraigned this day and charged with first degree murder in the case of the mysterious deaths of the four duck hunters in Lake County, California. District Attorney Martin Rosswell revealed to us that Mister Osborne has been under constant surveillance and investigation since the onset, and he, said Mister Rosswell, has irrefutable evidence incriminating Mister Osborne. The District Attorney said that he intends to prosecute the case himself personally because of the serious impact of public concern, and intends to seek the death penalty on the basis of premeditated murder; Emile Osborne moved to the Lakeport area approximately one year ago to open a woodcarving shop. . .

Visions of our romantic weekend suddenly went poof like errant puffs of smoke. My best dinner dress which now fit perfectly, hung worthless in the apartment of my mind, limp and forlorn before my mirror. Emile what have you done to us?

When I phoned Dad at his office, Dorothy informed me that he was out in the field. She could try to raise him by radio, or she would give him a message that I had called. "No, I'll call back,"

I said.

When I phoned home there was no answer. "Professor Wooldridge, drop me if you must," I blurted out. Someone nearby said, "Excuse me?"

"Oh nothing," I said, and thought of my life crumbling about me into ancient bits of dried clay.

I hurried to my apartment and called Dad again. There was no answer at home and he had not yet returned to his office. Dorothy had contacted him by radio and relayed a message that I had called and wanted urgently to speak with him.

Anxiously I paced the apartment floor, finally tossing some things in a bag. I was at the front door when the phone rang.

"Hello, Dad," I barked. "Yes, I was just leaving."

"I want you to stay right where you are," he said, with that fatherly tone of authority in his voice.

"But I have to be there, for Emile."

"Emile is doing okay. He's taking it all very well. He said to tell you he was sorry about the date, and he's using this time to catch up on his reading."

"Dad, what's happening up there? Has everybody gone crazy?"

"Martin Rosswell feels he has enough evidence for a preliminary hearing, that's all. The arraignment was yesterday, and I tried to call you. . ."

"Evidence, what kind of evidence can he have?"

"He thinks he has enough, and apparently Judge Wooden agreed to go along with him."

"This is crazy, Dad. . . Emile couldn't hurt a soul. He's too gentle. Anyway, what kind of evidence can there be?"

"We'll just have to wait until Tuesday to find out. For once, Martin Rosswell is tight-lipped. He may present his whole case, or. . ."

"Yes. Or what?"

". . .or he may hold back, offer just enough to get an indictment. Either way, we have to wait and see. . . The ball's in his court right now."

"This whole thing is absolutely insane. Emile couldn't hurt a fly. . . First, it was a conspiracy with the Indians and their mythical spirits of Mount Konocti. . ."

"The Indians had nothing to do with it. I told you that before." His voice sounded reassuring. "They are the ones who found the hunter's bodies. They have cooperated fully and every alibi has been checked out thoroughly. All the rest is media wash. Those four hunters had no idea they were trespassing on Indian Reservation land, an unfortunate coincidence that only fueled speculation. Stories, that's all. It is simply not in their nature to be hostile unless provoked. And there is no sign of any confrontation, not even a hint. Anyway, the most they would likely have done is to tell the hunters to leave cause they were trespassing, unless of course they were offended or aroused. But nobody in their right mind would butt heads with a group of 300 pound Indians who have been offended, even drunken idiots with shotguns in their hands."

I thought that sounded strange; Dad taking up for the Indians and I recalled brief stories of a past altercation between an Indian named Steve Raymond and a would be shotgun wielder. I said, "Then there's the arrest of Chester and that 130 year old feud story, and that Chester is part Indian."

"Ha, ha," he chuckled. "Well, if Chester's part Indian the records sure don't bear it out. Chester's stuck his own neck in the proverbial noose, and he's done it before. He thinks he's having one hell of a good time, even though he keeps stepping into one bucket of dung after another. He's got Rosswell and Wooden riled and Rosswell's taking a desperate shot in the dark, with scatter shot at that."

". . .So that's it. It's Rosswell all the way. Kimberly says he can be dangerous, and I tend to believe her, especially now that Emile's involved. She also says that Rosswell is a case of a little bit of knowledge being dangerous. . ."In my mind I just advanced Martin Rosswell to a 5 star idiot. I'm going to run out of stars if this keeps on.

"He's the DA and he just thinks he's doing his job."

"Sniffing around like a bird dog with his nose up his butt, that's what he's doing. . ."

"Now Little Girl. I never raised you to talk like that. Sometimes it pays to play your cards close to your chest, till you see the other hands laid down." His voice was so calm and comforting. I could almost picture him across the line, grinning sheepishly.

"I just packed some things. I was at the door when you rang. I'm coming home right away. . ."

His voice shifted to firm and authoritative, which he seldom did unless he meant business. I would have to think twice before crossing my dad.

"Now listen to me," he said. "I want you to stay right where you are. Do you hear me? Good. You let me deal with Martin Rosswell till this thing is either settled, or blows over."

"Deal with Martin? How? I want to help. I can testify."

"That's what he wants. You're too close and you are too emotionally involved. He wants an excuse to call you as a witness."

"I want to testify. . . I can help."

"You can help by staying right where you're at."

"But. . ."

"No buts. Stay where you are. Work on your studies. You can't be doing too great lately. . . and let me deal with Rosswell."

"Will you call me if anything—?"

"I'll call you, and I want you to call me every day, or whenever you feel like it. I told Dorothy to put you through whenever."

"I'm going to feel like it a lot."

"Good. Don't forget to go to church."

# FORTY TWO

After an uneasy weekend of vacillating decisions in which I agonized through Monday, I found myself striking northbound across the Golden Gate despite Dad's warnings ringing in my ears. I believed my presence was a necessity to Emile's well-being.

Bright and early bucking a steady stream of frantic traffic I crossed the Golden Gate into the land of the BMW, Sausalito, Mill Valley, and Marin, a bumper to bumper battle through a string of affluent cities, all bastions of the upper middle-class immersed deeply in their yuppie period. . . realm of the status symbols with marinas filled with tall stems of expensive sailing crafts, many of which have never left their slips.

Land of the BMW, home of modern medical technology and research. Ranging hillsides covered with expensive condos and town houses hinting of hidden mansions somewhere else among groves of seclusion. And the ever presence of shopping centers dotted continuously along the highway. Where do the support working class dwell, I always wondered.

Land of the BMW, where once I counted while driving this track; nine Mercedes and thirteen BMWs before spotting a single other brand of automobile; where competition was always at a peak to outshine thy neighbor. Land where Volvo's waning grip struggled for a place in the top choices by the weary grit of its teeth; where Lexus was coming on strong to fill that void of individual pretense in the American dream. Where the only Cadillacs still driven are by old Jews, still loyal to their own creed of that same dream.

Thirty miles of jam cluttered highway where Mercedes and BMW owned the road, and not a Buick in sight. The absence of that one time bulwark of GMC lends a grim testimony to the once dominant American auto industry.

I wondered if it was like that on the east coast and in Detroit where they fought hard to get what they got and were not about to give up a dime or an inch. Where overpaid executives were not about to chance changing the status quo. They want to keep what they got too, fading positions started years ago and they are too smug to realize it. I wonder if Chester plans to write a book about that, one nobody would dare to read?

This also was the realm of the plastic credit cards, just numbers, letters, and symbols in a checking account that is rarely ever balanced, due to monthly lease payments up to their nostrils.

I had at one time yearned for a place in that exclusive status club of the BMW.

Now, every time I pass through this corridor amid derisive scowls I am grateful for the rattling of my old Camaro with its bumper sticker that reads; “Don’t laugh, I’m paid for.”

Monday spilled itself over into Tuesday, as Mom used to say. By 10:30 a.m. I found myself sitting in the Lake County courtroom where I had often sat before to observe and learn about the law and courtroom procedures.

Finding a seat had not been easy. The courtroom was packed as was the hallway, with an array of hapless individuals, and too many lawyers in yesterday’s wrinkled suits. Even with the ventilation system going full bore the place was stuffy with an atmosphere of orgy bound contestants clawing and bemoaning to each other, strangling the whole third floor to see who would end up on top of the mass of burned out bodies.

I wondered just where I fit into the woeful melange and how these others perceived me, or if anyone at all considered my presence.

Then, there was that ever present stink of rancid smoke filled waxy hair and clothing punctuated by hoarse cackle-laughs, dropouts and doping mothers, wasting the lives of their next born for the thrill of a cheap trip. Not so cheap after all.

I considered these as characters in a modern setting compared to a Shakespearean tragedy.

His honor, I learned, was busy in his chambers conferring with opposing attorneys on the present case. This I learned by eavesdropping on a nearby conversation. So, for the time being, the courtroom took on the aura of a social gathering, and the highlight of the occupants present existence.

There were three guys sitting in the first row of the jurors' box, dressed in state orange jump suits with two court bailiffs posted strategically nearby. One of the three, a white guy, a Charles Manson look-alike with shifty eyes like dark pools staring nowhere. The two deputies, big tough looking guys with guns and heavy hardware belts, kept a wary eye on the crowd, especially the three toughs in state orange and chains.

At the opposite end of that same front row seats sat two females, one a chubby young Indian girl, stoic and half asleep and worn out looking. Probably in for clobbering her man after he got drunk and beat her up.

The dirty blond next to her slouched down in her seat, feet cocked up boldly, perched up on the divider rail. She was busy cutting up, a smart-ass chick with all the smart-ass answers. She knows it all, just ask her. The deputy had to tell her to sit up and put her feet down again, "What, me? I ain't doing nuthin," she whined, putting her hands up in that common supplicating gesture followed by the familiar hoarse giggle and whiskey cackle. She took her schooling on a barstool in those same threadbare dirty jeans. A young barstool bimbo with a crotch full of trapped yeast infection; that if suddenly unleashed would throw the ventilation system into overload and clear the courtroom in a rush. Some soap and a hot bath could do a lot of good, I thought

Then there was the nearest guy in convict orange, a tall dude with a diamond in his nose and a ponytail, slouching in his seat. He bared his teeth a lot, like snarling and yakking with the third guy, all the while making signals to the female sitting in front of me. She was the one bragging about their connections. She got his message and left for something. They had this private little fraternity going. Herself and the three guys maybe.

The third acted smug and was trying to get something going with the dirty blonde at the other end, past the sleeping Indian girl. He raised his hands to show off his shackles, just like they were a badge of accomplishment, symbols of meritorious service, telling the dirty blonde this was his sixth time, telling how he was gonna be out cause his lawyer was striking a plea bargain. "We gonna get it on later, huh?"

Tough ass white guys, almost as tough looking as the big black dude, wild knotty braids and droopy eyelids sitting between them, scanning the room from the corner of his eyes, sinister and sneering, except to his colleagues the two white guys.

The whole thing was a waiting courtroom drama like a bad play with bad actors, unfit for the cameras, showing off their social status. Drop-outs and losers, tough guys and wasting bimbos, all jiving the system, and jiving themselves instead.

I had been jotting down notes of my impressions, and as I paused to read them, I scratched them out.

I had to get out of there, Emile's hearing had been set for the afternoon, and God I felt depressed, and sad. . .

When at last I caught up with Dad after lunch back at the courtroom hallway, that same hallway had been flushed out. There was to be only one principal this afternoon.

I felt sure Dad wasn't surprised to see me. I guess he knew I could hold back only so long. Maria and B.B. were there as were Ned Turner and Kimberly.

Maria and B.B. were gathered nearby with a familiar looking plainclothes and the two morning bailiffs. I guessed Maria and

B.B. must have the two p.m. shift with this afternoon's bailiff duty. The plainclothes was a guy I knew but couldn't put a handle on his name. Maybe he had something to do with the case?

Dad, Kimberly and Ned had their heads poised together separately.

B.B. was one of those arguing about talk over an upcoming boxing match between Holmes, the challenger and the heavyweight champion, Holyfield.

The plainclothes got into it too, saying, "Holmes doesn't have a prayer. Holyfield's the smartest fighter in the ring today, and he's not going to sign on anybody unless he knows he can beat them." B.B. saying, "Holmes may be over forty but he survived over sixty fights, and he was the longest reigning heavyweight champ. . ."

Maria quietly winked at me. She's taking the whole thing in like she was one of the guys joking around. God she looks good, and happy. I wonder what her secret is?

The bailiff way saying, "It's all fixed, just like the Foreman/Holyfield fight. It's the big money that pulls the strings. Foreman had him in the last rounds and held back. He even thanked Holyfield after the fight for giving him a chance at that big purse. Those in the clique take care of each other."

The plainclothes said, "Maybe so, but Holmes don't like nobody; and Holyfield don't like him back. Holyfield and Foreman respected each other."

B.B. says, "Bullshit, that's all pre-fight hype. . ."

The deputy bailiff says, "You got it right there buddy. It's the money that controls the purse strings and the action too. Mark my word, if they ever do fight, Holmes is clued in; if Holyfield gets hurt or too tired, back off, or no more big money gates. Holmes knows he better back off too, because it is already arranged, and they all got a good thing cooking. Holyfield is the *in* guy right now, and the money's on him. It's just like the

Foreman fight, they put on a helluva good show though. But, they got it all set up to stretch it out, bilk the public for those monster gates. Holmes is part of it. He won't screw up the whole scenario, cause then, there's the Foreman/Holmes gate to count on afterwards. . ."

"Then there's Tommy Morrison coming up," said the plainclothes. "All those black guys need another white guy to beat up on. You see?"

"Bullshit," interrupted B.B., sounding riled by the affair. "You trying to say it's all a fix?"

"Either way," said the plainclothes. "My money is on Holyfield. I haven't lost with him yet."

Maria smiled and winked again. I winked back with an equally savvy grin. I hoped we could have a chance for a few words together later.

# FORTY THREE

Once again the hallway started to buzz with activity after the lunch break purge, which had emptied suddenly like a flushing action.

Martin Rosswell stepped from the elevator dressed in his dapper presentable pinstripe, confident and superior, with an equally impressive stack of files tucked under one arm and an attache case in the other. He looked his usual smug self with his pasted wave curved down over his forehead.

Kimberly moved over to exchange a few private words with him, while Dad and Ned urged B.B. and the plainclothes aside for their own privy talks.

For a brief moment I was left alone. Then Maria and I exchanged acknowledging glances before seeking a private corner of our own. Everybody knows we girls can conjure up better gossip than the guys on any given occasion.

"Martin looks like he has a good mean on this morning," I said.

"He works hard at it," she grinned.

"Do the Pomo have a name for him?" I asked.

She gave a low chuckle, "You mean something like, man who speaks without thinking."

"Yeah. Or, I thought it might be something like, man with thorn in his butt, he looks more antagonistic than usual."

She leaned closer, dropping her voice in a slightly conspiratorial tone, "Rumor has it he's worried; he leased one of those new 325i BMW convertibles and likes to drive it around town showing off. Rumor also has it that he's counting on a big raise to help with the payments, and afraid he might lose it if things don't go as planned."

"Ah-hah, so that's it. . ."

"How about the Pomo saying for Dad?"

"B.B.?"

"Big man with bees in his breeches."

"How about Ned?"

"Sour stomach."

"And how about me, what do they call me?"

"Girl with hair on fire, or flaming hair, or. . ."

"Come on."

"Girl with pouting mouth."

"Really, you must sit around the campfire making up names for people, sounds like a fun game."

She chuckled back at me, beaming that gregarious smile. "We do. It is."

"Do you have a name for Emile?"

She nodded. "Strange one who feeds the birds."

"Do your people think Emile had anything to do with the four hunters?"

She shrugged lightly.

"Not saying, huh?"

Just then Judge Wooden appeared in the hallway from his chamber door, allowing a condescending nod to Maria, he glanced past me to the others as if I didn't exist and painfully limped past Kimberly and Martin who had just parted unfriendly like.

"What do call his honor?"

She chuckled again, "Lame humping rabbit, and man who wants to screw but can't."

"Really? how do you come by that one?"

"Word around is; he screwed for a half hour on Sunday and then played church softball in the afternoon and threw his back out. Too much for one day, and his sciatica is killing him."

"Ah-hah, so that's why he looks so cross."

"Looks like I better grab B.B. and head for the courtroom. We have the bailiff duty this afternoon. Let's do this again some time."

"I'd like that. I'd like to join in on one of those name game sessions too. Sounds like fun."

"Takes a special invitation," she winked. "But I think I can arrange it. Things might be a little more inhibited than usual with a white person present."

"Unless, that person got into it too, huh?"

As Maria and B.B. left, Kimberly, Ned, and Dad came back to me, steering us to an even more isolated corner of the hall so we could talk in hushed tones.

Kimberly said, "Martin plans to call Ned first, naturally, then Pete Lomax. . ."

"Pete Lomax?" I whispered, and got a look from Dad that said, "LISTEN."

". . .Chester Cowan and last is Emile himself."

"Chester! But what does Chester have to do with it?"

Uh-oh, another look from Dad.

Kimberly glanced to Ned, yielding the floor.

Ned said, "I'll have to give testimony pertaining to the investigation. . . Pete Lomax witnessed Chester and Emile heading off in the canoe a number of times. Emile, in particular going in the direction of Quercus Island the morning in question. And, Emile's background. . ."

"Background?"

"It seems," Ned went on at Dad's nod, "It seems our boy, Emile Lloyd Osborne has some questionable history on his back. . . he's been around, carving his ducks and things, and everywhere he was at before he came here a year ago, there have been some mysterious deaths of duck hunters. That's his real name though. . ."

"That's purely coincidental, circumstantial, isn't it?" I managed, looking inquiringly to Dad, then to Ned and Kimberly, each in turn.

Ned shrugged, "The DA thinks there's more."

"Emile's connection with Chester and that 130 year old feud?"

"That too. We traced them both back quite away. There appears to be no obvious, or related connection that I can find," said Ned. "As for Chester it's a little different. He goes way back. Lots of connections with some of the old pioneer names of Scotts Valley, especially on the Jones side and the Wardens."

Dad said, "And Chester doesn't help things any by being so damn stubborn and refusing to answer questions."

Kimberly said, "It would seem to point to a feud connection, but there just isn't one."

Ned went on; "As far as we can ascertain, Chester wasn't anywhere near Emile that morning. They meet, feed the ducks and sea gulls together sometimes, probably where they met in the first place, or Emile's shop. Chester won't even answer to that, and if Chester doesn't want to answer, then Emile won't say either. Confounds the whole situation. They go canoeing together occasionally, and Emile visits Chester's place, but that's it."

"That's all Martin has?"

"We don't know how much he has. Only what he got through us. But we do know he is an avid duck hunter. "

I raised an eyebrow at that. They were considering me with a sort of silent scrutiny. I felt I was being tested. Things didn't look to good for Emile, with his own background, Wooden with sciatica, most likely bitter as hell at the moment, and Martin Rosswell the duck hunter with an ax to grind and brand new BMW with heavy payments hanging over his head.

Dad said, almost nonchalantly, "It seems everywhere your friend Emile has been they are experiencing a drastic decline in duck hunting; an understandable reluctance for hunters to frequent that particular location."

"How about the hunters, any connections?" I said, inquisitively.

"These guys are no mystery," Ned said. "Jack and John

Hurt were brothers all right. A pair of petty characters with a rap sheet as long as my arm. By the way that's not their real names. They change aliases about as often as a farmer changes overalls. But it's all small time punk stuff, urination in public view, on the highway; a pair of exhibitionists, petty theft. They once got arrested for running an elderly couple off the road for driving too slow; speeding, unsafe vehicular operation, open containers in the vehicle, flashing the high sign and threatening other drivers, brandishing a weapon. Real low lifes. You name it, they did it. Beat up an old man and robbed him of $13 once, and too damn dumb not to brag about it. I don't know how but Jack has, had a wife, who's more than glad to be rid of him. He beat her up a few times too. . ."

I thought of the barstool bimbo with dirty blonde hair and the jerk in state orange earlier putting on a show for each other. Could be them all over again.

"A pair of real winners," Dad sniggered.

Ned went on, "Gordon Channing and Charles Burrell are another story though. No records. On the surface a pair of decent guys. Gordon had a wife and two kids. They split up a month ago and the wife knows nothing about his connections with the Hurt boys."

Dad said, "Looks like they got themselves caught up with a pair of unsavory characters. . ."

"Kimberly added, glancing at her watch; "Their worst crime is the company they kept."

"How long have you known all this? I asked pointedly.

They exchanged perfunctory glances. Dad said, "Ongoing investigation."

"When I was going with Emile?"

"You're a grown girl," Dad said, matter-of-factly. It was just like him, to put the ball back in my court. "And you didn't ask for my permission."

"But you knew something, even then?"

"Look, it's not settled yet. Let's wait till all the clues are in before we draw any conclusions," Dad warned.

Kimberly said, "Remember this is only a preliminary hearing to determine if there is enough evidence to warrant a trial. And I am defending Emile because I believe he is innocent and that he had nothing to do with it. . . and the lack of evidence supports it."

Dad raised a cautious eyebrow. I wish I knew what he thought, or suspected.

Ned added, "Chester will be a hostile witness subpoenaed by the District Attorney's office. . ."

"Yeah," I said, "With Martin Rosswell just laying to get him on the stand."

Dad said, "As I said before; Rosswell is resorting to the shotgun effect, he's gonna spray a lot of bird shot around hoping to hit something."

"I can help," I said, pleading more than I cared to show. "I know Emile better than anyone. He's a very gentle and considerate individual, perhaps even a bit fragile. . . I want to testify on his behalf."

Kim was looking deep into my eyes while Ned and Dad considered my at length. "and. . ." I added, "Emile couldn't hurt a soul. . .he hates shotguns. . ." OH DARN, I thought.

Kim said with candid consideration, "What do you think Rosswell could do with a statement like that?"

Oh my God I thought, but it was true. He had not said it in so many words, and yet I knew. I just knew.

While Ned and Kimberly exchanged glances, Dad came to my rescue. "You see why I don't want you to be around here now, don't you? And why Rosswell would like to get you on the stand? But don't worry about that now. You're here, and this is only a preliminary hearing with the judge and no jury. Only the principals are allowed in the courtroom at this time anyway."

Kim added a little wisdom that finally sank in also, "You're too close and too emotionally involved for you to be objective. It would be much better if you stayed clear for awhile. I don't think you could help his chances, and I feel you could be used to hurt him."

"I suppose you are right," I nodded and conceded, thoughtfully.

Dad and Kimberly excused themselves and headed for the courtroom, leaving Ned and I alone together.

From his pocket, Ned took a roll of Rolaids, nervously extracted three, popped them in his mouth, crunched and swallowed, with a pinched look on his face.

"Ned," I said.

"Yeah?"

"If you could be reincarnated, what would you come back as?"

"A goddamn alligator," he said without a moment's hesitation.

"An alligator?"

". . .Or something that don't get heartburn and ulcers. Did you know an alligator can eat any god damn thing it wants to? They got cast iron stomachs."

# FORTY FOUR

From the courtroom door Kimberly beckoned to Ned Turner.

With the exception of Pete Lomax waiting nervously for his turn to testify, the hallway traffic had dwindled to a few secretaries and clerks.

When I nodded to him he seemed determined to ignore me, so I walked over to peer through the porthole sized observation window to the courtroom.

Martin Rosswell and Kimberly were standing before, and addressing Judge Wooden who already seemed well shrouded in one of his familiar brooding moods.

Martin, as he was affectionately called among his peers favored a compulsion for strolling about thoughtfully while addressing the court with his thumbs tucked alternately in his vest pockets, portraying a strident Machiavellian air as though the weight of the entire world depended on his every word, then turning away from the witness, or victim, before his fatal stroke, real cagey.

Ned waited on the stand while being sworn in. He often complained that with so much time required in the courtroom; how was any law officer expected to get much time on the streets where he was most needed.

Kimberly sat down patiently. I remembered how she looked in the hallway, and hoped my envy had not betrayed me. She always looked great, like she had just stepped from the cover of some prestigious fashion magazine, with a tunic length peach jacket and short ruffled skirt that swished boldly when she walked, bone high heels and beige sheer hose with a cute butterfly at the ankle, a white diaphanous blouse with ruffles at the neck, open a little, and yet not too much. Her long lustrous blond hair was drawn back strikingly with a ribbon barrette.

I was to learn later that it was the sight of her that had shaken Judge Wooden out of his complacent reverie of austere public posture with that autocratic tone in his voice; "Well counselor, are you expecting a party?"

"Why Your Honor?" she asked, demurely.

"You seem to be dressed for one, either coming or going—?"

Judge Wooden had been known to send female coun-selors in search of more conservative dress, citing the lack of consideration for their clients well-being and their own professionalism.

Kimberly had responded, saying; "Actually your honor, this is my client's wishes that I dress in a fashion of gaiety more suitable to the occasion."

"Humph."

Emile, from what I could see of him looked great too, dressed in gray slacks, a light olive turtleneck, and matching darker olive sport coat. He was clean-shaven and neater than I would have expected with his blond hair brushed back casually, handsome and rugged though, unpretentious and thoroughly unaffected by the whole affair. Once, he turned his face to me and flashed a distant disarming smile, winked and turned back to the court.

At that time, how was I to know it was the last time I was to see him?

I returned to the hall bench and waited for awhile.

What I can relate is bits pieced together from what I learned from Ned and, mostly Kimberly later on.

Martin Rosswell started by questioning Ned about the circumstances surrounding the reporting of and subsequent recovery of the four hunter's bodies. He then pressed on in dogged fashion about specific dates and locations of similar reports on so called accidental deaths of other hunters, fourteen in all.

From his notes, Ned verified that Emile Lloyd Osborne's presence had indeed been witnessed in the general vicinity of the said hunter drownings at the time in question, and yes; the deaths of the other fourteen hunters seemed linked by similar mysterious events, and all within the recent two year period.

When Kimberly had cross-examined Ned by asking him if there was any other evidence linking her client to any of the accidental drownings, he testified there was none, and had the four bodies shown any signs of struggle, the answer was none that could be determined. Then there was no forensic evidence to indicate there was any kind of struggle as well. Again the answer was none. . . Then the official autopsy finding was that the four hunters died by accidental drowning? The answer was, "Yes, that is correct."

And did the autopsy show that these men had consumed fair amounts of alcohol."

"Affirmative," Ned responded frankly.

When Ned stepped down from the witness box to take his customary place at the prosecutor's table Pete Lomax was summoned as the prosecutor's second witness. I was left alone in the hallway.

Martin Rosswell started his questioning by asking if Mister Lomax was acquainted with the accused, Mister Osborne.

"Yes," said Pete Lomax. "I let him keep his canoe at the Willow Point Campground. The guy who had it before stayed there and when he moved, Emile," he pointed, "Mister Osborne bought it for a hundred dollars. I asked him not to feed those damn ducks. . . they crap all over the place. . . and feeding them just encourages them to hang around more."

"And, did he stop feeding them, like you asked?" said Rosswell casually.

"After awhile he did. Yes."

"And you allowed him to keep the canoe there, without charge."

"Yeah, he seemed like a nice honest fella. Gave me a carved decoy duck."

"He gave it to you?"

"Yes sir."

Martin Rosswell turned away thoughtfully, slicking his wave down, getting ready for the big strike, then turned back to face Lomax, relenting out of generosity; "Now MISTER Lomax," he said, when ever he said MISTER he made it sound condescending like an adult getting ready to scold an unfortunate child. "Mister Lomax, can you please tell the court how many times MISTER Osborne there," he pointed dramatically with an accusing finger; "Emile, as you call him, took the canoe in the direction of Long Tule Point?"

"Exactly?"

"Approximately will do," said the district attorney.

"Oh, three, four—four times a week since he bought it, I'd say."

"Pretty regular wouldn't you say?"

"Yes, pretty regular."

"And what time of day did he take this canoe over to Long Tule Point—?"

"Your honor I have to object," said Kimberly, calmly. "The witness's knowledge of just where Mister Osborne went with the canoe has to be conjecture and clearly the result of opinion or hearsay."

"Sustained."

". . .Well, Mister Lomax, do you know for a fact where he went in his canoe?"

"Well. . . no. . ."

"But you do know from personal observation in what general direction he took the canoe. Is that correct?"

"Well yes, but I do know he went to Quercus Island and Long Tule Point."

"Objection your honor. Unless the witness has actually seen Mister Osborne there or. . ."

"Sustained."

"Let me rephrase the question for the benefit of my learned colleague," said the District Attorney, smugly.

"Mister Osborne went in the direction of Long Tule Point and Quercus Island, is that correct?"

"Yes."

"And you watched him?"

"Until he was out of sight."

"And, he always went in that same direction? Is that not correct?"

"Well yes, most of the time. Sometimes he went south along the shoreline, but he always ended up in the direction of Quercus Island eventually."

"Did that seem suspicious to you?"

"What?"

". . .That he always ended up in the same location; the very vicinity in which the bodies of the four hunters were found?"

"I have to object your honor, calls for an opinion. . ."

"Sustained."

"Sure did look suspicious, that's why I watched him, to figure what he was doing out there all the time."

The Judge considered another warning, while Rosswell grinned, jumping into his next question quickly.

"Did Mister Osborne always depart that same time of day?'

"Not always. Mostly he left early in the morning, around five thirty or six o'clock. . . Sometimes in the evenings, and he'd stay overnight. When he left in the mornings, he usually came back that same night."

"Mister Lomax, have you ever been to Quercus Island or Long Tule Point?"

"Nope. No need to. Haven't lost anything there."

"Did Mister Osborne always go alone?"

"At first, mostly he did, yes. But then sometimes later Chester Cowan would go along. . . and lately a young woman went along. Twice I think. Stayed overnight the last time," he said, casting a calculating glance to the judge.

Judge Wooden lifted his face from his cupped hand in a frown, cocking a wary eyebrow judiciously.

"This court is more than familiar with Mister Cowan," reminded Martin Rosswell. "Now Mister Lomax when did Mister Cowan go out in the canoe with the accused, Mister Osborne?"

"Oh, about mid-summer, July, they started going out together. Some of the time, anyway."

"This took place before the death of the four hunters, when they started. . ."

"Oh yeah, long before that. Regular too."

"But the young woman only started going after that? After the death of the four hunters. Is that correct?"

"Yes. Two weekends past the last."

"I see." Rosswell turned away slightly, smoothed his wave around, like recoiling in preparation for his final stroke of genius. "Now Mister Lomax, in your own words can you tell the court what you witnessed on the morning the bodies of the four duck hunters were discovered?"

"Sure can. I remember that morning because it was earlier than usual, about four o'clock, and I woke up with Sissy barking, and I looked at the clock. Sissy's my beagle dog, and I got up and took her out for a walk."

"What kind of morning was it?"

"Foggy, thick as cake frosting, stirring about kinda eerie like. Enough to give a person the creeps. I thought that was strange when I saw Emile there," he pointed, "Mister Osborne shoving off in his canoe on an eerie morning like that."

"Did Mister Osborne see you?"

"I don't think so."

"How was he dressed?"

"Shorts, cut-offs, and old sweat shirt with the sleeves cut off too. Most of the time his usual."

"Did you think that was suspicious?"

"Sure did, cold and dank as it was. Sure give me and Sissy the shivers."

"Did you watch where he headed?"

"Sure did, until he disappeared into that fog-bank, in a straight line for Long Tule Point. Sure thought it was strange him going out on that kind of morning too."

"And still you were able to tell which direction he was headed?"

"Sure. No doubt about it. Long Tule Point, like he was in a canoe race."

"Where the bodies of the four duck hunters were discovered later that same morning?"

"Objection, Your Honor."

"Sustained."

"Was the accused alone when he departed, and do you know when he returned?"

"He was alone all right, unless he picked up somebody else along he way."

"Your Honor, I must strenuously object to the witness's attempt to incriminate my client with incautious insinuations. I believe the court and the defense has shown generous restraint in the latitude allowed the prosecution, however I find I can no longer. . ."

Judge Wooden raised a placating hand, thoughtfully; "Your objection is well taken Counselor Lambertis. The witness will confine his answers to the questions put before him."

"Thank you, Your Honor."

"Did you witness the return of Mister Osborne, that same day," asked District Attorney Rosswell.

"No. But I saw his canoe there the next morning. That's when I knew he was back."

"Thank you Mister Lomax," said Rosswell, turning abruptly to Kimberly in a manner of smug composure; "Your turn Counselor."

"Does the defense have questions of this witness, *MS* Lambertis?" asked Judge Wooden.

"Only a few, Your Honor."

"Now Mister Lomax, you have testified that you have never been to Long Tule Point or to Quercus Island. Is that correct?"

"Right."

"Have you ever had occasion to visit the Pomo Indian Rancheria Reservation at Long Point?"

"Why would I want to go there?"

"I take it that is a no answer?"

"Right," he nodded.

"And that you have actually never witnessed the alleged location Mister Osborne goes to when he departs in his canoe. Is that right?"

"No, but I know he goes in that direction."

"From your vantage point at the Willowtree Campground, Mister Lomax, is Quercus Island visible to the naked eye?"

"Well, no, not exactly. . ."

"And the same holds true for Quercus Point and Long Tule Point, as well as Long Point, is that correct?"

"Well, kinda, but I know where they're at."

"And yet, Mister Lomax, is it not true that you have never personally witnessed where Mister Osborne goes once he is beyond your sight?"

"Well, yeah. . ."

"Now Mister Lomax, has Emile, the accused ever given you or anyone of your direct knowledge reason to believe he has committed acts of hostility towards any living being?"

". . .Your Honor, the question calls for an opinion."

". . .or to your recollection." To Judge Wooden she said; "Since this is a preliminary and not a formal trial, and since the defense has allowed the prosecution the greatest latitude, Your Honor. . ."

"I'll allow it," he said hesitantly.

"Mister Lomax, has Mister Osborne ever, in your presence shown any hint of hostility towards your person, or for that matter anyone else?"

"Not exactly."

"No exactly, or none?"

"None."

"None. None at all?"

He nodded.

"Has he ever given you or anyone of your direct knowledge cause to suspect him of acts of aggressiveness which took place between himself and the four duck hunters, or anyone else?"

"No."

"In other words, to your first hand knowledge, Mister Osborne has always been the perfect gentleman?"

"I guess so."

"Would you say, Mister Lomax, that a gift, such as an expensive piece of art, such as a hand-carved decoy was an act of friendship and good-will."

"I guess so. . . But what do I need a duck decoy for anyway?"

"The defense is finished with this witness for now, Your Honor."

The court recorder rested and flexed her hands with a temporary sigh of relief, while Emile seemed to be watching Maria and B.B. making funny faces to each other.

Judge Wooden looked to the prosecution while Ned Turner seemed bored with the whole affair. No doubt wishing he was someplace else. "You may call your next witness Mister Rosswell."

"The prosecution calls Mister Chester Cowan, and I would like to remind the court that Mister Cowan is under subpoena and must be considered a hostile witness with added complicity in the case himself."

"Need I be reminded that the court is well acquainted with the shenanigans of Mister Cowan," frowned the judge.

# FORTY FIVE

When Pete Lomax came out through the courtroom doors to leave, that's when I wanted to be in the courtroom in the worst way. Had she been there, I think I would have defied even Mother Theresa and the Pope himself for a ticket, but not my Dad.

As I watched through the small door window while B.B. led Chester to the witness stand, I realized all at once why two bailiffs were needed. If Chester or Emile for example had to be led away, there would still be the other deputy standing by in case of further complications. There was no doubt in my mind that Chester would be led away to the think tank before this session was over.

Watching the court dramatics through a peek-hole, and yet unable to hear more than a passing word at a time was sheer agony. At times I labored up, then down the deserted hallway in an effort to burn off unwanted nervous energy.

When at last I paused before the large view window to stare out across the lake waters toward Quercus Island and Mount Konocti I watched the gathering of dark storm clouds. It was a magnificent view however gloomy, perhaps even a portent, or warning of the creator's displeasure, and all at once I felt hunger. No, not just hunger, but a pure craving, for a big fat pizza, a fat juicy cheeseburger, a bowl of rich spicy Italian minestrone with a crispy salad on the side. . . or why not all, two of each even.

Disheartened, I flopped down on the same bench with the realization that my only option was to sit and wait for word on the inner-sanctum process.

All at once it seemed as though we of modern civilization have not progressed very far since the dark ages. Whimsical pagan rites were still in progress, frozen minds and bodies still locked away in another time. Instead of gathering in a grove beneath a so called sacred oak tree, we use brick and concrete reinforced with tons of steel, structures of pretentious magnitude for courts and temples so a few can struggle to control the minds of the many. Free-thinkers are not allowed here; witch hunts and fear are still the order of our time.

After being sworn in, Chester who was dressed in his usual tattered bib overalls and faded blue worker's shirt took the stand facing the District Attorney.

Martin Rosswell was saying to Chester on the witness stand, "Are you acquainted with the accused," he pointed, "Mister Osborne?"

"We're friends," replied Chester, easily.

"Close friends?" Rosswell was trying to sound like the nice guy, condescending.

"Friends."

"Would you mind telling the court how you came to be friends?"

"We met at the park."

"Met at the park. . . hmmm. . . I see."

"Feeding the ducks and sea gulls," added Chester.

"Feeding the ducks and sea gulls. . ." snickered the District Attorney.

"Yup. You ought to try it onced in awhile. Good for what ails you."

"And this. . . friendship developed while you were feeding the ducks and sea gulls—?"

"Crackers."

"Crackers?"

"Yup. The sea gulls like to snatch them out of the air. You just give them a flick of the wrist and sail them way out there. They sail quite aways cause they're flat. . ."

"The crackers I take it, are flat?"

"Yup. That's why the sea gulls like them. Acrobatic crafty boogers, the sea gulls and like to play games, like an outfielder chasing a fly ball. Why if the Giants and the A's outfielders was to watch them, say Canseco or Ricky Henderson was to pay attention, they could learn a thing or two from the sea gulls. The ducks too."

Martin the warlike had his victim loosening up now, talking freely, but not necessarily answering the questions though.

"Now about this friendship Mister Cowan; I'm curious about what friends do. You know with the big difference in you ages. Interests have got to be different, besides feedin ducks and sea gulls." Martin thought he was trying to drop himself to Chester's level by speaking country like.

"We visit."

"Mister Osborne comes out to your place in Scotts Valley to visit?"

"And I visit him in his shop, on Main Street. You want the address?"

"No, I have the address, but can you tell the court what it is that you do together? Your place, and his shop."

"Visit. We talk. Tell stories. Laugh. Sometimes I watch him carve. That boy has pure talent; a delight to watch him work with his hands. Pure talent. You should try it sometimes. Good for what ails you."

"This is at his shop?"

"Yep."

"What about when he's at your place?"

"He does some carving on those big beams I got. We walk, simple things, like going for a canoe ride."

"A canoe ride out to your place?"

"Hell no. No water for canoes out to my place—at his place, down by the park is where the canoe's at."

"Ah-hah, and where do you go, when canoeing, that is?"

"Any damn place we want to. You oughta try it. . ."

"Yes, I know. Good for what ails me."

"Now you're gettin it sonny."

"Your Honor, would you please instruct the witness to address the court in a proper manner?"

Judge Wooden shook his head and rubbed his chin in an effort to shake off his malaise.

Kimberly came to her feet; "Your Honor, I fail to see any point to this line of questioning. It also seems clear that the prosecution is attempting to bait the witness.

"Do you have a point to make Mister Rosswell?"

"Yes indeed, Your Honor." He turned abruptly to face Chester, ready to strike; "Have you, Mister Cowan and Mister Osborne, visited Long Tule Point and Quercus Island?"

"Yup."

"When?"

"Lots of times."

"When out canoeing, is that correct?"

"Yup."

"How many times?"

"Lots."

"Once hundred, fifty, twenty five, five?"

"Never counted."

"Your Honor. . ."

"The witness will answer to the best of his ability," said Wooden.

"Not a hundred," Chester conceded.

"Fifty then?"

"More like ten, twenty times."

"Ah, then where else did you go, when you were together in the canoe?"

"Along the shoreline sometimes. Other times straight out. Whatever we feel like. Depends on how the notion strikes us."

"Your Honor, this line of questioning seems to be dragging on pointlessly."

"Your point is well taken Counselor."

Martin turned away momentarily, slicked the wave over his forehead and then jerked about abruptly to confront Chester; "Mister Cowan, where were you on the morning the four duck hunters were murdered?"

"Well sonny, you really don't learn very fast now do you? You asked me that before. I wasn't where those four hunters were found drowned, I can tell you that." Chester hesitated as if waiting for something to sink in, glaring at the District Attorney who was by then inches from his own face. Both remained locked in a daring stare-down, until Martin broke away to pace the floor thoughtfully.

"You were with Mister Osborne that morning, were you not?"

"As I understand it, he went canoeing all by hisself that morning."

"We already know that he departed by himself, but, did you not meet," he pointed an accusing finger to Emile, "at a trysting place with the preconceived intentions of committing the foul act of murder against the four duck hunters. Isn't that the truth?"

"Your Honor," protested Kimberly. "The prosecutor is obviously on a fishing expedition. His whole line of questioning is clearly preposterous."

"Mister Prosecutor," interrupted Judge Wooden. . ."

"I have only one more question, Your Honor, if it pleases the court?"

Judge Wooden shifted his body cautiously, his face pinched. His sciatica killing him no doubt. He nodded consent.

"Mister Cowan, where were you at on the morning of the deaths of the four hunters?"

"I told you where I wasn't. I don't have to tell you where I was at. If you want me there, YOU got to prove I was there. I'm no fancy lawyer, but it seems to me that's the way the law is supposed to work."

"Your Honor, will the court please instruct the witness to

answer this one question?"

"Mister Cowan, I must warn you to answer the question as it is put to you, is that understood?"

"Your Honor, I told you I wasn't there, and my word should be good enough for this court."

"I must warn you," said Wooden, "that you are trying the limited patience of this court; and that you are hovering dangerously on the brink of contempt."

"You gonna send me to jail again, Judge?"

"If necessary, yes."

Rosswell recovered and intervened, his approach once more smooth as silk; "If you will answer this one question to the court's satisfaction?"

"I can't figure out why *this court*, is so all fired up about my whereabouts on any morning, when the court has so many other important things to deal with?"

"*That*, Mister Cowan, is exactly the point," said Martin Rosswell.

"Just answer the question," ordered the Judge.

"I told you, Sonny, where I wasn't and I figure that should be good enough for the court. You can figure out the rest with that fancy degree you got."

Judge Wooden warned, "Mister Cowan, you have one more chance to answer the question put to you, before I hold you in contempt."

"Well. . . I tell you this Judge. I just can't understand why the government just spent twenty million dollars on a fancy new jail building to hold some old guy like me cause he don't want to tell you where he goes to take a crap in the mor-ning, and what brand of toilet paper he uses."

Wooden looked visibly as if he had been struck by a baseball bat. Kimberly and Emile could hardly contain themselves and even the normally stoic Ned Turner cracked a wide grin, as did the court recorder who all at once seemed suspended in midsentence. For a brief moment Rosswell tettered there like a giant tree ready to topple. Maria and B.B. gleamed knowingly to each other.

Wooden exploded, his gavel shattering violently into pieces. I mean he aa-sploded. Once when I was a little girl and I had to go to the bath room, I waited a little too long, as children often do when over occupied—and I recall telling Mom, embarrassed and crying; "I couldn't help it Mommy." I was utterly devastated; "I'm sorry Mommy, I just aa-sploded."

Well, first Wooden sucked in, his face a tortured mask of violent blue; imploded is a better term, and then he aa-sploded, hopelessly and helplessly. All his saved up composure aa-sploded in one violent burst.

Only Martin Rosswell seemed momentarily recovered, poised once more for the final stroke, the *coupe de gracè:* "Mister Cowan, we are all well aware that you would have us return to the good old days of the *outhouse*."

"Well Sonny, that outhouse wasn't all that bad . . . For one thing, it didn't take seven and a half gallons of water to flush down two ounces of pee, like your so called modern toilet. And another thing, that's seven and a half gallons of water that will never see purity again. Of course, you can call that advancing civilization if you want."

I guess that must have been when all the others had blown whatever cool they had left, all except Martin Rosswell who looked stricken and wobbly again, and recovering Judge Wooden who commenced striking his bench with the remains of his gavel handle, shattering it till pieces went flying wildly about the courtroom.

Chester wasn't finished yet though, "You two guys remind me of another fella I heard about once. He had this enormous bowel movement every morning at six o'clock, but couldn't drag hisself out of bed till seven."

Judge Wooden was shouting, ". . .I order this man remanded to the custody of the court bailiff, pointing to B.B. he added; "Deputy, remove this. . . this specimen from my courtroom for contempt of court. Mister Cowan is to be confined to the county jail until I decide on his disposition." Then for a moment he seemed at least partially recovered, "A nice long stay might clear away the cobwebs."

"For me, or you, judge?" said Chester, with a parting dig as B.B. led him away.

"Get him out of here. . ." then rooting about somewhat confused, he added; "WHERE'S MY DAMN GAVEL?"

# FORTY SIX

Chester was the highlight of the day for me as I watched from the porthole. It made the whole trip worthwhile. Even marching off to the lion's den he appeared bigger than life and the system. Chester had triumphed, although I don't think he saw it as a contest. Chester was simply Chester.

As for Emile's testimony, he took the stand voluntarily and in his own defense. I am still not certain even Martin Rosswell himself fully understands to this day just what he had hoped to accomplish. However there was one certainty to me from my vantage point; although Judge Wooden recovered his composure very quickly, a solemn air had gripped the courtroom. The judge had had a rough day, and he was still suffering from an even more painful weekend; and his only wish was to get the whole mess over with, quickly.

For Martin Rosswell, perhaps the shock of dealing with a Chester Cowan was indeed a lesson in futility, however that lesson only served to set him back on his heels temporarily. In minutes he was once again restored to Martin the warlike, Martin the people's advocate; adroit and suspicious and all the while challenging with an intimidating aggressiveness.

The district attorney began his interrogation by stating dates and places where similar occurrences had been reported and testified to previously by Ned Turner. Emile's complicity, or lack of same had also been determined and testified to by Ned, suspiciously, or coincidentally corresponding to the same incidents.

Emile was just as candid and open with the district attorney as he had been under Kimberly's questioning. And still, with each of Martin's charges came the judgmental pointing of an intimidating finger, and the implicating gesture, and to each charge, Emile properly responded with a frankly stated; "Yes, I was or, I believe I was at that location approximately one those dates," either visiting for an art show or, attending a carving show. No, I had no knowledge of the deaths of any duck hunters. Coincidence is the only reason I can see to explain my presence at any location in relation to such incidents. And, only since there has been so much news coverage, had I become aware of any incidents involving the deaths of four duck hunters, and I know only what I have read or heard, or have seen on television, which I seldom watch." . . . No, he had had no intention of meeting Chester Cowan on that day. No they had not met anyplace that day, nor had they bothered even to discuss the four hunters, ever. And certainly they had not discussed or known of the reported one hundred thirty year old feud, if ever there was one, and finally, no, absolutely they had had no contact with the four duck hunters, previous or otherwise, that he could remember.

The shocker came with swift, unexpectedness suddenness, after the court occupants had once again been lulled into monotony.

Perhaps once again Martin was overcome with in-furiating futility, when unexpectedly he turned away in his trademark mode, slicking his wave and recoiled to face Emile, feet wide, hands firmly planted on hips, eyes glaring and his most indignant stance, his face just inches from Emile's, he said: "Do you, Mister Osborne, expect this court to accept that the death of those four duck hunters was a simple matter of coincidence, and that no relevance exists in the murder of eighteen known duck hunters when you, Mister Osborne are placed unequivocally at the scene of each incident?"

Martin Rosswell thumped his chest in triumph, contrived and fearfully daunting, as though he intended to shout; me macho-man, look, me great hunter, me kill ducks. Then he declared, still glaring intensely in to Emile's face; "I too am a duck hunter!"

"Then you could be next," said Emile, in that grinning smile so similar to Dad's.

This time Martin Rosswell aa-sploded, well first he sucked in gravely, then swelled like a bloated demon with fire in his throat, hovering there on the brink of disintegration, struggling for words. I actually expected to see fire and steam belch from his throat. "Your Honor," he finally man-aged to get out. "This witness is clearly attempting to threaten this court of law, and my own person, the people's representative."

"Your Honor," Kimberly pleaded, bouncing to her feet immediately. "What is clear here is the prosecutor's attempt to intimidate my client not only with his manner, but with his whole unwarranted line of questioning. . ."

Judge Wooden said to Emile; "Young man, do you realize just how close you have come to compromising your case, not to mention incurring my wrath and a charge of contempt?"

"Your Honor," snarled Rosswell, "I believe I have clearly exposed the underlying hostility of the witness, moreover I believe the court must realize a legitimate cause exists in the justification for arraignment of Mister Osborne on a charge of premeditated murder in the first degree. . . The prosecution pleads further cause in the re-examination of the witness, Mister Chester Cowan."

Judge Wooden said, "Mister Rosswell, will you contain yourself?"

Kimberly was still on her feet and moved beside Rosswell, still pleading for the judge's attention; "Your Honor, this whole episode is irrational, the prosecution's whole case is completely incongruous . . .absurd from the onset. . ."

Wooden seemed distracted momentarily, Kimberly glared at Rosswell. Only Emile looked pathetic and the least threatening of all, while Wooden at last finding himself and in the absence of his broken gavel, smashed his fist down repeatedly on his bench. . . "Order. Order," he shouted. " I will have order in MY court, or I'll find the lot of you in contempt."

Martin stood glaring at Emile, his eyes on fire, hands on hips, powerfully indignant and challenging while Emile sat unmoved and unimpressed, smiling back. One could sense the heavy intensity throbbing between the two.

At last Kimberly said calmly, "Your Honor, if I may remind the court; Mister Osborne has patiently withstood the bullying assault of the prosecution, answering all his questions with frankness and honesty to the best of his ability, throughout, I might add, Mister Rosswell's repeated insane effrontery."

*"INSANE!"* shouted Rosswell.

Down came the fists again, repeatedly until at last quiet was restored. Then turning to Emile, he charged sternly; "Mister Osborne, do you comprehend the gravity of your statement? Do I understand correctly that you threaten a member of this court?"

"A threat? My God No, Your Honor. . . If I seemed to threaten, I apologize to Mister Rosswell, and to the court. My response was instantaneous and unintentionally ill-spoken. But to myself it seemed only a logical conclusion to advance Mister Rosswell's own hypothesis; and if all those men who died were indeed duck hunters, and there is some connection as he contends. . . then it seems only logical that he too could be next, or even Your Honor could be next. I could be next merely by my affiliation with the creatures, but if only duck hunters are the victims. . . If I gave the impression of a threat, I apologize, Your Honor."

"Humph," grunted Wooden, who seemed to be chewing it around in his jaws. . . Then to the attorneys he said, with a tone of finality, "Do either of you have any further questions?" The sleeping judge was clearly awake and alert now.

"None, Your Honor," said Kimberly.

"If the court pleases, Your Honor, and if the court will once again direct the witness to answer one final question about his presence on that morning. . ."

"Mister Rosswell!"

"Your Honor, I must strenuously object. The prosecution has asked the same question many times over, to the great indulgence of the court and the defense."

"Your suggestion is well taken," said Wooden. "Now, have either of you any other business?"

"No, Your Honor," they chorused.

"Have you prepared closing statements?"

"Yes," they agreed.

The District Attorney in his closing argument contended that he had indeed shown probable cause supporting a conspiracy between the accused and possibly other persons, namely Chester Cowan. He had not offered all his evidence, having not deemed it necessary at this time, and that an indictment was in order. Further, the accused should be held without bail considering the obvious revelation that his nature was definitely hostile and unpredictable.

All the while Emile sat alert and politely attentive, and yet seemed the least menacing individual I have ever witnessed. I wondered how Judge Wooden perceived him.

Kimberly's closing argument was equally as brief, and more to the point, both realizing that Judge Wooden's patience had been over-strained.

She offered for consideration, "Not only has the prosecution failed to establish that there was a motive; nor was there a weapon. And through Detective Ned Turner's unimpeachable testimony that there were no signs of a struggle, no conflict of any kind, and her client could not even be placed near the scene by way witness's testimony or his own candid responses. Furthermore, the autopsy clearly demonstrated that the four hunters had consumed fair amounts of alcohol and two bodies had signs of drug content as well. The prosecution has not even demonstrated that murder or conflict of any nature had contributed to the unfortunate deaths, which I realize I need not remind the court was concluded as death by accidental drowning by the coroner's office.

Of all the flaws, Your Honor, in the prosecution's argument, Mister Rosswell seems to have blatantly omitted one very important consideration; I don't see how we can expect a jury to believe that one man acting alone could have subdued four healthy armed men by himself, without leaving a single clue, or trace of struggle, nor that my client, or anyone for that matter, had the desire or motivation to commit such an act.

My opponent's case clearly lacks the barest elements of even circumstantial evidence, and furthermore. . ."

About this time, Wooden lapsed back into his inconiderate malaise, another trademark of his station.

". . .And furthermore, Your Honor, my client seems obviously to be the victim of media sensationalism and personal ambitions. Your Honor, I move that the case against my client, Mister Emile Lloyd Osborne be dismissed."

With that, Judge Wooden seemed to heave a great sigh of relief, pondering his next action with serious intent. "I shall take your motions into consideration, until after my deliberations. Until then the accused will be remanded to the custody of the court."

"In the matter of bail, Your Honor?" pleaded Rosswell.

"Will it be a brief consideration, Your Honor?" asked Kimberly.

"You will be the first to know, counselor."

"Court adjourned;" then came the incessant searching, "*WHO*, took my gavel?"

# FORTY SEVEN

Outside the courtroom I met with Ned and Kimberly, then after a few brief words Ned excused himself, saying he had to get back to work.

Kimberly and I headed for the outside stairs, both in dire need of fresh air and exercise.

I don't know if she noticed Martin Rosswell or not, but I caught a glimpse of him alone in the elevator alcove, with his back turned to us and his briefcase open. He looked pinched-faced and worried, and had a bottle of Super Maalox antacid open. He downed a large gulp, made a nasty face and shook his head insufferably.

I wondered about his future and wondered how I might in the future as a practicing clinical psychologist treat someone with a history of stomach conditions after they had run the gamut of various ulcer drugs like Zantac and Tagamet and could no longer tolerate the medications, and yet suffered further mental and physical complications.

I realized then as I should have before; if I was ever to become a practicing physician I would need an extra measure of compassion and understanding. Martin Rosswell was only one of the many stress driven individuals of our time. . . and all at once I felt sorry for him.

Outside, dark rain clouds threatened overhead, so that it seemed more like night than four o'clock in the afternoon.

Without realizing it Kim and I headed for the Park View Cafe at a brisk pace while she filled me in on the blank spots of the past hearing.

At the corner of Main and Second Streets I realized the wind was working up into a furious blow off the lake. "If this breaks we'll have snow in the mountains by Thanksgiving," I said.

"Won't the skiers love that?" countered Kimberly. Then, "Thanks for the offer, I am starved, but I must get back to my office."

"I know," I said. "Guess I'll see you later." She turned to run, and I called after her; "That was a great summation."

I had no more than turned away from Kimberly, with a half block to go when the sky broke open with a hellish blast of heavy rain and wind. Winter was late but it had arrived with an undeniable opinion.

I found the Park View Cafe almost empty which was a rarity. On any given fair day it was always packed, the upper deck and the sidewalk patio tables alike, all gay Parisian style, especially in summer time.

At the door I tried to shake myself dry in defiance of the howling wind, stringy red hair and all. My blazer was soaked and a chill warned me I needed something hot to drink. Glancing around I settled in a booth by a front window, a cozy spot to watch the driving storm vent its fury.

Near the center of the dining room I noticed a table that was occupied by two men and a woman, strangers, their heads locked together in surreptitious conversation, enjoying an occasional private laugh.

In a far corner sat a familiar figure bent over a writing tablet. She paused momentarily to touch a light to another cigarette, drew a deep breath and dusted it in the ashtray thoughtfully with a halo of gray smoke stirring around her head, then inhaled another sip from her coffee cup. After a moment's consideration I remembered her as the woman in the red dress at Chester's elbow.

"Looking for your Dad?" asked Louise.

"Oh hi. I don't really expect him until later," I replied.

"We don't see him around here much lately either. He probably goes down to the Candlelite, or The, or the Cottage Shop, or maybe he goes home. We are even more crowded at mealtime with all these news people in at the same time. It takes a reservation then, but we'll probably wonder what to do with ourselves when it comes to an end," she said.

"Can I get a salad and an order of sourdough French. . .and oh yeah, how about a cup of herbal tea, hot. Better bring a pot, and some lemon."

"Gotcha. Anything else?"

"That'll do for now. Can't stay too long."

"See that one over there," she gestured with her head. . . "Look familiar?"

"Yeah, kinda."

She bent closer to whisper, "Bev Westerly."

"Really?"

"Kind of cute, isn't she?"

"Yes. She looks good on television too." I wondered how anyone could be cute with a cigarette and smoke coming out of her face, but I added; "She writes for one of those scandal sheets, doesn't she?" I thought she must be here for some other big occasion, the old shrew, most likely Emile's hanging.

"I got a cute story for you if you don't mind company. I can take a break before the dinner crowd strikes, if this storm lets us have one. What a monster we got blowing up out there, huh?"

"Good. I'm all ears. Bring two pots of tea."

Not only did she bring a pot of tea, she had her own salad and two cups of minestrone plus a big basket of hot bread which we shared.

When she sat down, she leaned over to talk in hushed tones while we buttered the bread lavishly and ate, the hot juices striking bottom where it was most appreciated. She wore one of those clever grins on her face which aided the story's other embellishments; "See those three over there," she indicated with her head and eyes.

I nodded, trying not to stare.

"Well. . .they have been in here quite a lot ever since this duck hunter thing started. They sit a lot, talk, drink coffee and smoke a lot too. But, don't let that sweet appearance of Bev Westerly fool you. On the surface she looks a lot like Olivia de Haviland. . .like in the movie GONE WITH THE WIND, sweet, naive, vulnerable, but beneath it all she's more like the part in that movie that was on late TV the other night, you know; DARK MIRROR, where she plays twin sisters, with this doctor, I think his name was Lew Ayres."

"The psychologist."

"That's the one, came out in 1946. Anyway, the one sister is the sweet, nice little thing, the usual Olivia de Haviland, while the other one is sinister and conniving; well that's her. Sweet until she opens her mouth, then the fangs come out, and she's a viper with a venomous tongue.

Well, anyway these three were talking, they talk a lot, heavy thinkers too, and she's at the next table taking it all in. The place is packed, lawyers mostly and reporters. The chatter is deafening. Can't hear to take an order. But she's taking it all in while they're talking about some guy, a real bad dude and the things he did to other people, and how they're going to get rid of him. Maybe even find a way to kill him off. They're getting into the plot pretty heavy when she decides to confront them, threatening exposure. By then the crowd had left and we're pretty much alone, and I'm cleaning the plates and stuff off their table.

Anyway, she confronts them. Lays her card down and introduces herself. She heard the whole thing and has the name of the guy they plan to dispose of. . ."

"You must be kidding," I said.

"I'm standing there shocked too, because I know something she doesn't. Anyway, after she leaves, we're all trying to contain ourselves, because they say to me; "'Do you think we ought to tell her?'"

"Tell her what," I blurted out anxiously, all caught up in the mystery by now.

"They're writers. . ."

"Nooo!"

"That's what they told me. They write movies for television, or something, and they're going to knock off this *character*, they have been working on."

"You're kidding."

"Honest truth," she said, crossing herself. She, Bev Westerly left just before you arrived but hurried back in because the rain drove her back in here, then settled in her favorite corner and started writing. What do you suppose she is writing about?"

"One guess."

"And that's what they're laughing about so smugly over there."

"Or maybe they are working on another character to destroy."

"I'm anxious to read about how it turns out, aren't you?"

"Me too. . . Sells papers," I chuckled.

# FORTY EIGHT

Later that night I found myself turning onto Hendricks Road from Scotts Valley Road, and then up the long, forbidding drive to Chester's mansion. I had the eerie feeling of trespassing in a place where I might not be welcome. I had an indescribable feeling that I was intruding, but I knew Chester was locked away in jail at Judge Wooden's order, and was not likely to be home for at least a few days.

The night was black at times, except when the full moon escaped from its shroud of drifting clouds, an ever changing sensation of darkness, then partial light, then the foreboding gloom of long blackness and hope for light again. A peek-a-boo moon playing games with a curiosity of its own, leaving behind a sense of an old-time monster, thriller movie. I was scared and I didn't know why. But I kept on going just the same.

While the rain had not let up in Lakeport until well after six o'clock it was dry at Chester's place, as ultimately it is apt to do, with a monsoon in one place and a mere few miles away, not a drop. And yet, the same omnipotent threat hovered overhead.

As soon as the rain had allowed, I had fled the comfort of the Park View Cafe and Louise's company. A light crowd of customers had been filing in, a promising number for a rainy night anyway.

In the process of conversation, I had recovered my appetite and had chomped down a juicy cheeseburger with fries, a piece of homemade pear pie, plus uncountable cups of herbal tea. I thought I would never stop peeing.

At the courthouse I had discovered everything locked up, and at my next stop I found Dad busy at his office working late again.

There was good news. Emile had been released. Judge Wooden had had quite enough of the whole affair and wanted a quick solution. He had reconvened an hour later, delivering a very short deposition. And, he had wisely avoided any media coverage by doing so. Everyone had predicted it would wait until the next day, and suddenly it was all over almost before it had begun.

I was ecstatic. I hugged and kissed Dad, then rushed down to Emile's shop. I tried the front, and then the rear door. He was gone, as was his van.

At home I had waited anxiously for a phone call which never came, and finally unable to take the suspense any longer I rushed back down to the park. The canoe was still in its place. I guess I had supposed he might want to be alone, and I would have gladly disappeared with him to his island retreat.

Back at his shop I found the van was still missing, and I casually recognized his utility trailer still in its place.

When I shot back up to the jail, I learned he had been gone for some time since his release and had not returned. Why should he?

I had one last hope, realizing he and Chester had become good friends, and that he just might be out at Chester's place. It seemed logical at the time.

Pulling into a clearing beneath a giant oak tree at Chester's, I parked, and waited in darkness for another appearance by the moon to give me light. And then I realized there was no other vehicle in sight.

As I stepped tentatively into the night with headlights still on and door open for added dome-light support, the moon drifted into a space of open sky. I turned the lights off and closed the door, all the while wanting to call out. The house with its towering dark outline appeared dismal with an aura of foreboding presence, a massive structure highlighted by flickering shafts of moonlight and eerie shadows. It was a lonely scary place on a night such as this, with hills of untouched wilderness beyond. I had that added intuition that humans had no rights to this place, and yet, here I was, like it or not.

For some unexplainable reason I felt scared and jittery approaching familiar steps I had once been welcomed to. I remembered the giant bearskin rug on the floor inside by the fireplace and the story of young Chester killing it, and then without warning the moon deserted me once again. I prayed for a flashlight, for any light, and that's when my eyes caught a flicker of light from around the side of the house.

Somehow I felt myself inexorably drawn to that light and the vaguely familiar sound emanating from it.

Warily I turned the corner, stalking as Cuddles might have, hiding from view, in search of a commanding vantage point.

Then, for long moments, I stared at the sight, half hidden from behind a bush, wary and circumspect. . .

Dad had told me stories about these hills, still wild and untouched by humans. In my feeble brain demons and monsters flashed by at a maddening pace . . . and I recalled a time Dad had told me about one of Chester's distant relatives on his mother's side, a cousin of the pioneer Jones clan. Cougar Jones he had come to be called, because he had killed a full grown female cougar after tracking it back to its den, where he had discovered two young cubs. It had destroyed the occupants of his hen house. In the process he had taken the two cubs and had raised them to adulthood. He would bring the cubs into Lakeport and all the kids thought it was a big show to watch them rip and tear the upholstery from the inside of his old forty one four door Chevy. He would park across from the old courthouse facing Main Street, now a museum, and leave the cubs alone in the Chevy. The kids would tease and laugh at them until Cougar Jones returned and threatened to turn the cats loose. Then they would scatter to a relatively safer distance to continue the game. The cubs always put on a thoroughly ripping show, tearing the head liner and seats to shreds. The whole inside shebang was a holy mess, much to the bystanders delight. The old Chevy had, in its heyday become a major attraction in Lakeport. Whenever it was parked in the usual location, the word had gotten around quickly; and people had left home to witness the show.

But in time the two cougars grew to enormous size, very quickly in fact, in less than one full summer, as the story goes. A big part of the show was Cougar Jones returning to the seemingly ferocious cats and with a scolding he quickly calmed them into passivity.

Dad said that stories abounded about the condition of Cougar's house and his eventual ability to control the brutes all by himself. Dad said also, the old Chevy had a front door that failed to lock properly, and one day the cats got loose in town, racing among frightened people, causing holy chaos, and eventually chasing the ducks unmercifully around the park, leaping in the air, and causing one hell of a squawking commotion.

That incident signaled the end of Cougar Jones and his pets. They were captured with his help and sent off to the San Diego Zoo, where I heard Cougar Jones used to go visit them occasionally.

I had visions of wild cougars gnawing away on human flesh. An inner voice urged me to race back to my own car, get away, go for help, and yet something vaguely familiar about the animal sounds drew me closer. As I crept closer a flash of light half exposed the telltale roof flasher of a county patrol car.

With renewed concern I inched toward the passenger side of the sheriff's patrol car. I could tell plainly that the driver's side door was open wide, and the reason for the lighted dome light that had caught my attention originally. The mixed sounds were clearly of animal and human, plus the constant beeping of the police radio.

By now I had horrible visions flashing through me of a giant, wild grizzly gnawing away at some unfortunate deputy's head. A thorough awareness of nausea threatened to overwhelm me. I was terrified.

If only I could reach the car, jump in and slam the doors, and radio for help. . .or maybe grab the fallen deputy's weapon, and scare the beast away, or per chance if the Shur-Lock might be open, I could stick the shotgun in the monster's mouth like Chester had done, or maybe just frighten the animal away. It seemed logical, and with renewed courage I sneaked closer, ever wary for a change of plan, and possible escape. . .

When I got to the passenger trunk side, the mixture of animal and human sound suddenly seemed less threatening. There were the whining and purring cries, and familiar shuffling of eager bodies, gasping more for ecstacy than from horror. I peeked around the corner, and cried; "OH, damn you guys. . . you scared the living shit out of me," then collapsing beside the fender of the patrol car, I gasped for relieving breaths of air. . .

"KITTY!"

"B.B.!"

"KITTY?"

"Maria?"

"Kitty. . ."

The sight wasn't a bit funny to me, and I doubt if it was for them either. The scene was a semi-nude, groping, humping affair entwined on a spread out ground blanket, with weapons and belts tossed haplessly aside in a fit of necessity. . .

"Damn you guys," I gasped. "You scared the holy stiffings out of me. . . I was afraid some wild animal. . ."

"Kitty. . ."

"Kitty. . ."

"Don't you Kitty me," I said, indignantly.

"Kitty, what are YOU doing here?"

"Me. Never mind what I'm doing here. You guys are supposed to be on duty." That voice in my head struggled to find words for a way out of the mess. "Can't you guys do this on your own time."

B.B., by this time had jumped up in disarray, stumbling about for his clothes, his tee-shirt rolled up under his armpits like a spare tire, boots still on and pants a tangle about his ankles, his dick with a frustrated posture all its own, still engorged, and yet obviously unspent. B.B. was a scared pathetic looking sight.

Maria was not in much better condition, scrambling about on all fours for her uniform, embarrassed, her black lace bra open and tangled about in her armpits, one leg of her pantyhose still intact, while the other leg trailed behind snagging on leaves and grass with her shiny bronze body glistening beneath the flashes of moonlight. She too, was otherwise naked.

I said, in a not so pleasant scolding tone of voice; "You guys scared the holy stuffings out of me, you know that don't you?" and I stormed away.

From behind I heard their bewildered voices call after me. . ."Kitty, wait. . . Kitty wait, we can explain. . ."

# FORTY NINE

The first half of duck season closed on November 16th, and the second half opened on November 30th.

At 162 Main Street where Emile's shop had been there is now an art gallery and custom frame shop. The store had been empty less than two weeks. During that two week period I had returned home just once. It was the weekend following Emile's release and subsequent disappearance.

When I had looked into the sterile emptiness of the front window over the FOR RENT sign there seemed not a single clue that he had ever been there. The front had been locked, and so I walked around back to test the rear door. The second hint that he was gone forever were the empty spaces where he had kept his van and utility box trailer.

Upon trying the back door with a good shove it gave way, and I stepped expectantly into the emptiness. It also was thoroughly cleaned out and sterile. The ladder to his loft had been left down, and so I climbed it, once again to stand in the nearly depleted surrounding. I looked out through the small dormer window to Quercus Island where we had made love with such reckless abandon, and I thought about Jason and Minerva and Hector, and all the others. Who could forget Hector. I wondered if Hector and Chester had some affinity with a common spiritual being. I considered the spot where I then stood; where the Futon bed had been spread so accommodatingly, and where we had also succumbed to love-making with special attention given to Cuddle's presence. With my fingers I tentatively touched the strands of hair she had pawed at and chewed on while we laughed and groped at played and kissing and so on.

The wildlife posters were also gone, and I thought of the hypnotic sequence; had that been a charade, a mere game, or had there been even a spark of reality in that also. I suppose I shall never know. The only sign he had ever existed was the old oaken rocker and dresser he had picked up at a garage sale. Apparently, he hadn't enough room to take them with him.

After a time I hurried down the short block to Willow Point only to find the canoe was also gone. I wondered if Pete Lomax knew where he went, if not Sissy might.

Emile had come into my life and had stirred emotions and curiosities I was not aware existed, and now he was gone, as though he had never existed.

In the two weeks that passed I had almost constantly agonized over the past chain of events, sorting and trying to place them in some sort of order with logical conclusions.

Strangely, Dad had not uttered another word about those events, and yet, somehow I keep thinking I somehow held the key to his mind, and I drew some conclusions of how he might have reasoned about the whole affair. He was not one to rationalize or accept excuses, and I feel certain he had come to some practical set of solutions.

For one thing, he always feared reactions that might lead to vigilante recourse, and if I were to speculate; I fear that consideration must have weighed heavily on his mind about how he treated specific situations. To my dad, upholding the law had its responsibilities. . . and he was the law.

And I know of all his concerns, he hated to think there might be someone out there seeking the thrill of the ultimate hunt. A man alone hunting the hunter, the human animal. This ultimate hunter who might take to hunting the human animal who was well armed when he was not, and was well versed in the hunting skills and weaponry. This ultimate hunter might strike his prey at random, leaving behind no pattern nor obvious motive.

Emile had seemed to represent a pattern, and I cringed to think that I alone might be the only person to understand his motive. Perhaps Chester understood it more than I, but Chester is another complicated story in his own right. Someday, I thought, I would approach Chester, when I felt ready, and perhaps Chester knew of Emile's whereabouts.

I can appreciate that Dad must have figured in his own mind that one man alone, with the element of surprise on his side could have surprised at least two other men, flipping the boat over, causing one man to plunge over the opposite side while he caught the other from behind, forcing the one under with his jaw pinched open so that he gagged and was forced to swallow his tongue in the fateful first gulp. The act would have to be timed precisely with quickness and daring, and of course the second victim would have little time to recover before he too suffered the same fate. After all, they were all well chosen and heavy with bulky clothes and equipment.

In the case of the four hunters, the second pair were reported some distance from the first and thereby allowing the hunter, or messenger as Emile had put it, ample time to regroup before they too met with a similar fate. One or two victims for prey, in this scenario, would seem to be the norm while four must represent the ultimate challenge.

It was far fetched to my own logical way of thinking. And yet, I shuddered at the thought. As for a man's way of thinking, such as my Dad, a warrior male may draw on another set of conclusions.

I still felt Emile was incapable of such hostile action. He was capable of such tenderness and understanding, and in court he had shown the least promise of hostility of all the men present. I wondered if that was what Judge Wooden saw, and if it was that sensitivity which caused him to act swiftly and decisively.

But what if Dad had drawn similar conclusions, and had one of his little talks with Emile, and for one reason or another advised Emile to leave town, now that seemed logical too.

As for Chester, I learned that four days after the hearing in which he was jailed for contempt, he had been released.

Emile had disappeared but Chester was still an item. The woman in red was getting mileage out of Chester, and Chester willingly enjoyed one last hurrah before his self imposed exile.

For one, he was featured on the front page of PEOPLE'S magazine with an article, among some few other odd quotes. Once Chester had found an audience he had never lacked for opinions.

As it turns out, Chester while in jail treated himself to rare glimpses of interview shows. One featured cults that supposedly espoused theories on immortality. They claimed there is no need for death; and with their guidance the body can even get younger looking with them, simply by unlocking the secret DNA. After all, had not METHUSELAH lived for 969 years before spending the rest of his life with God? Live forever, with their secret, they claimed, by conscious choice of a positive mental attitude. I had seen the show also, and the bunch selling this idea didn't look like they had beat the aging process, and yet, they were boldly featured on television selling an age old idea. The message, give money for their secret research; and they promise no less than the fountain of youth for that chosen class who can pay the most. The first step is to eliminate sugar from one's diet. Sugar is an addiction that poisons the body and betrays the spirit. . . Secondly, send more money for research and join us for our tour of seminars, at thirty dollars a head.

Chester says, "It's all just another sham. Another old con game with a different cover, and new suckers as the targets. Pay me, they say, just like Jerry Falwell, Jimmy Swaggart, and Jim Bakker, old sham artists peddling snake oil; climb on my bandwagon and join my elite country club sect for favors and eternal life, spiritual or physical imagery. . .as always the hidden message is send money, buy my product. . . Garbage. Same old pitch. Suckers."

Another article quoted Chester on the issue of a proposed increase of trash dump fees; ". . .Not just here in Lakeport, it's a universal problem lacking common sense in the way we think. And, mostly its those damn bureaucrats again. The system stinks. No wonder there's trash and litter all over the place. It costs too much to go to the dumps, so just dump it on the road when nobody's looking. And another thing, how is a person supposed to have personal pride when the system penalizes people with higher taxes for fixing their places up with flowers and keeping it neat, while the guy next door lives like a slob, keeps his place looking like a junk yard, and he gets off cheaper with less taxes. . . The whole she-bang is bass-akwards.

You Government people want to take a step in the right direction; charge the slobs more, and give the guys who take personal pride in their surroundings a break, and make it easier for people to use the dumps instead of harder."

And that was Chester's last hurrah. I heard from a very reliable source that Chester Cowan will never be called for jury duty again, and that his name has been dropped from the lists.

What a pity, I thought; when Chester stepped from the dung bucket back into seclusion.

It was the first weekend following the second half opening of duck season that I found myself home again. Christmas spirit was in the air, and things had quieted down in remote backwater Lakeport which had for the winter at least, reverted to its former personality of a sleepy little town. There was talk of another traffic light and the possible coming of natural gas. With a dusting of snow on the nearby mountain tops, there was talk of snow machines for Mount Konocti and a ski resort. For the Ka-Batin-Guy, as far as the news was concerned, we became all but forgotten in the overall scheme of things.

Friday was a free day, and with no Professor Wooldridge to satisfy, I rushed home to decorate and spend some few hours as the sun might allow, in Molly Kreeszowski's flower garden.

I planned to do some sewing for Dad too, but not on Sunday. Mom used to remind me of an old Irish saying; "If you sew on Sunday, you chew it out on Monday with your teeth, stitch by stitch." She always affected the accent for my benefit when it came to her favorite sayings.

While on my knees amidst the winter flowers, dressed in a dirty old sweat suit I momentarily considered Cuddles nearby darting about and leaping into the air. She could find so much joy in a simple flower petal, or an odd twig. If cats truly have nine lives, then Cuddles will live forever and will remain eternally kittenish and young at heart.

Sometimes I think of Emile and the things we talked about. I don't know if I have come completely to terms with reincarnation as a scientifically acceptable doctrine yet. But whenever I look into the beautiful faces of flowers I can't help but think of Molly O'Grady Kreeszowski. There seems always to be a touch or sense of her there, and I find myself unwittingly talking with her, or is it them?

I know she died. I was told so, and I have accepted it as fact. But, since I did not see her cold and waxen in a fancy casket, and when I did last see her she was vital and happy, I still have a feeling she exists somewhere that way. Perhaps still back in New York, and just maybe she will show up here some day, as though returning home from a visit away.

I think Dad intended it that way when he had insisted on a closed casket ceremony. That was one of his many gifts to me. . . There should be no funerals at all, I think, only celebrations of rebirth instead of mourning the dead. Mom believed in Irish traditions and another one she would have approved of would be the gathering of friends and relatives to recall the happy times, after a loved one's passing.

Maybe there is something to be learned in the way some black people do it in New Orleans; with a parade, making it an occasion of celebration, where you say so long for now, until the time of rebirth.

# FIFTY

Late that same afternoon I found myself inside at the dining room table again, diary open, jotting down notes from thoughts that had pursued me around the flower patches.

In my mind's eye I considered Emile's faraway smile and whimsical nature. I wondered what that romantic weekend in Carmel might have been like.

For some time a little rhyme had been busy playing around in my head. It was one of the many Dad had teased me with when I was a little girl, and without warning it composed itself into sudden and unexpected order. I had always wanted to write the silly thing down, and so with ballpoint in hand I chose a fresh page and wrote:

> This old lady from Riggles,
> Who had a case of the wiggles,
> Alone on her sack,
> She laid on her back,
> Till she fell on the floor with the giggles.

Dad used to tell it to me when I was a little girl, and then tickle me. I always suspected it had a different order and he had cleaned it up a bit for my benefit. He always said the trick to remembering a story or limerick was to think of the punch line or finish, and you can always reconstruct the rest, but I wanted his exact words for the record.

I was ready for that hot shower now, so I left the pen and diary open there on the table, ready and waiting for my next inspiration.

In my shower I am Rena McKenzie, Rena on my lips and on my tongue, and I sing for Rena. I like my boobs, especially since Emile convinced me they are special, eternally girlish he had said. I feel good in my shower with a steady stream of water caressing and massaging my skin. I know I sound like Rena McKenzie and I would go anyplace to see her perform, and all the while I chanted away to the words of my all time favorite;

Don't want your arms
about me—any-more.
There's some-one new,
right here in town. . .
who gives me lov-in,
and takes me a-round.

In my shower I am beguiling, I am beautiful as I sway and dance to undulating rhythms, and I am irrestible because I am sensuous, and I can sing . . . I CAN SING. . .

I am one of those fortunate women who is comfortable with her own body. I can explore my private places that set me atingle because I am the goddess of erotica, swimming in a watery world of sensual bliss that gives me that twitch of excitement between my legs.

When I shampoo my hair I close my eyes and feel the sudsy effervescent sensation trickling over me. . .

He's com-mig to see me,
in Cassie's town. . .

Who needs a man anyway, I thought.

Suddenly there came another intruding sound from the front door by way of the hall chime, a persistent buzz to shatter my private reverie. It had the urgent sound of someone who refused to give up. I blinked, to listen more alertly and suds rushed in to sting my eyes.

Quickly I toweled off and slipped into my short terry robe, the suds still clinging to stringy strands of hair. I was a mess.

Wrapping the towel around my head turban style, and leaving a trail of wet footprints behind, I hurried to the front door just in case it might be important.

Through the lace curtain and etched glass I perceived the shape of a uniformed figure, someone quite unconcerned with my obvious vulnerability.

When I opened the door B.B. stood there, tall and boyishly handsome in his cop's uniform. I said, "B.B., what do you want?"

"I saw your car in the driveway, and I knew you were here. . ." he said nervously, peeking around me.

"I was showering, do you mind?"

"Is the chief here? I've been looking all over for him."

"B.B. you know he is never here this time of day."

"I thought he might be. . ." He looked around me again, then gave me his big helpless, boyish grin and sparkling white teeth smile. I clutched my robe a little tighter, suddenly aware I was slightly exposed, and still dripping wet. My toes twitched into curled knots uncontrollably.

"What is it you want, B.B—?"

"Well, I need to know what your dad wants me to do."

"Yes," I said tugging the terry tighter.

". . .It's these kids, teens, young punks who've been cutting class pretty regular. They're trying to play tough guys by confronting old ladies near the school. They blocked this one's way, and asked her in sort of threatening tones, if she had any money on her. She told them to get to school where they belonged, and then reported it. It's not the first time these same kids pulled these stunts. They're going around wearing black Raiders jackets and trying to act like gang toughs. . ."

"So, what do you want from me?"

"It's your Dad. I want to know if he wants me to bring them in. Scare their little asses a bit. I have a good idea who they are. . .or maybe he wants me to shake up the parents. . .or. . ."

"If he comes I'll tell him."

He stood there waiting, and I said; "Is there anything else? I have to get back and rinse my hair."

". . .Well, there's this other thing happened to me at the Oak Knoll Shopping Center. . . Some other teenagers, trying hard to adopt the gang mentality. They were heating up the parking lot, disturbing a lot of people and making a lot of noises, so I sent them home to think about it, mostly repeaters. Guess we'll have to have a heart to heart talk with their parents too."

"I heard the sirens earlier."

"That was something else. Up at Dick Knightly's house, you know, the city administrator. The city has a big dog barking problem. Well Dick Knightly's little pooch stands out there in his yard and barks like hell after Dick and his wife go off to work each day. Antagonizes the hell out of a big Rottweiler next door and the two of them start barking up a storm. Neighbors complain, but can't get nothing done. Well this Rottweiler is a bit of a vicious thing and he finally breaks through the fence and mauls Knightly's pooch. Dick happens to be home for lunch, and he races out with a broom and the Rottweiler attacks him, punctures the femoral artery in his left leg and Dickie almost bleeds to death before they get him to the emergency ward. . . Now the city powers that be want to do something, new ordinances and such because one of their own is directly affected. Before they didn't want to be bothered.

Then this other thing is; some kids, maybe part of one of the other groups, loaded their Super Soakers with mom's household ammonia and went around squirting barking dogs in the face. Who knows what they will be shooting at next."

"I wondered about the siren. Is Dick all right?" I said.

"Still up at the hospital. He's a little pale. Scared the holy hell out of him."

"That's it?"

"Well. . .after the rowdy teams left the shopping center parking lot, I noticed this nice looking lady; about forty and she's watching me all the time, with the kids. She has this shopping cart full of dog food, see. So like a good public servant I say, 'Can I help you lady?' And all the while she's giving me that hot come on look, and says in her sweet voice, batting her long eyelashes; 'Oh officer, would you help me please?' Like she needs some immediate attention."

"Sooo?"

"So what?"

"The eyelashes were phony?"

"Yeah, maybe, but she's got this big bag of dog food, weighs maybe fifty pounds, and she weighs 105 tops. The bag weighs half as much as she does, see, and I say 'Sure ma'am,' and she says; 'Could you help me load this in the trunk please.' All the time rolling those eyes, like I was some kind of uniformed grocery clerk.

"Then she says, "Oh officer, I don't know how I'll manage when I get home,' with the sexy eyes again, 'could you please follow me there?'

"'I think that could be arranged, ma'am,' I say," said B.B.

"Well, her house is only a few blocks away and I carry the bag inside while she holds the door open."

"'Put it down here,' she says. Like I'm supposed to do this every day. 'You can open it,' she says, forgetting to say please. Then she takes out one of those skinny brown cigarettes and touches a light to it. She's hard faced now, and walks over to a back window, staring out. I remember the place now, cause we get reports about barking there too. She says, staring at these two dogs; 'Aren't they beautiful? My prize Rottweilers. The bitch is in heat.' I could see they were humping, and she's puffing frantically on her weed, real excited like. Weed smells like burning garbage.

"I'm standing there feeling stupid, and she says; 'Aren't they just beautiful. Most important things in my life, Rottweilers. . .' I step over beside her to get a better look and she says again;

Most important things in my life, they're so beautiful.' She's standing there, shaking her head like it only happens once in a lifetime, her arms folded, and her face pinched tight, and she's all wrapped up in these two Rottweilers' humping their butt's off. All the while they're puffing and grunting, and the male's barking like he is ready for his last gasp, with his stubby tail bobbing away. She gives me that big stupid look, takes another long drag on her weed, then exhales, shaking her head, like the most important thing in her whole life is still those Rottweilers and that stinking cigarette."

I know I looked impatient, my hair felt sticky, and B.B. could drag out a short story into a long one worse than anyone I ever met, "Does this thing have an end to it?" I said, with a touch of urgency in my voice.

"I wonder, see," he went on; "No husband, no kids, and no signs of a man around. Maybe they left when she kept saying how those Rottweilers was the most important thing in her whole life. It was like she put up a barricade; don't touch me, and I feel so stupid standing there like a grocery clerk in a dumb uniform. . ."

"Well?" I said.

"Well what?" he countered, looking at me with that blank boyish grin.

"Did you screw her or not?"

"Hell no! I'm not that hard up. She gets her kicks from watching them dogs go at it. . . Damn barking must sound like music to her. . ."

"B.B., I'm disappointed in you."

". . .Got the hell out of there before she asked me to clean up after them. She's still standing there watching them, arms folded and shaking her head, puffing away and muttering; 'Most beautiful things. . . most important things in my life, those Rottweilers.'"

"And that's it?" I asked.

"People got Rottweiler mania. Everybody walks their Rottweilers around, saying; 'Look at me, I got a Rottweiler; oh you only got one, how sad, I got two and I'm getting another one.' I know these people got six of them, all barkers. One sounds like a cannon going off. Six sounds like a war. People have gone Rottweiler crazy, like saying; don't mess with me sucker, I got a Rottweiler. Chief says he's getting so many barking complaints, it'd drive a wooden man crazy. . ."

"You got a point here, B.B.? My hair is. . ."

". . .But what gets me is, suppose somebody is robbing her, the one with the dog food bag, or somebody's breaking in her house, and I show up to save her skinny ass; she gonna say 'No thanks.' Rottweilers most important thing in her life. She don't even say thank you officer when I carry in the bag. . . I say, let the Rottweilers do it. . ."

"Do what?"

"Save her ass."

"I'll tell Dad you stopped by."

"Never mind," he said. "I'll check on the radio, see if maybe they located him yet."

When I started to close the door he just stood there with that goofy look all over his face. . . B.B. tall and handsome in his cop's uniform, twenty five years old, going on fourteen."

"Is there something else, B.B.?"

". . .Well, about that night, with me and Maria. I want to explain. . ."

"That's past history B.B. It's done, and I don't want to hear or talk about it."

"Well, there's this. . ."

"B.B., it's getting cold here, and I have to go rinse my hair. If you have something else, spit it out."

I've got these two tickets to Luther Burbank Center in Santa Rosa, and I thought you might like to. . .you know?"

"B.B.," I flushed, "Are you to asking me for a date?"

"We could go down there about four. It's for tomorrow night and we could go to this place I know for dinner, and dancing after, or to a show. I know this high class place, you'd like. . ."

And then what, I thought, it would be too late to drive sixty miles home that same night and we would have to stay at a motel. He got this devilish grin on his face with him looking down to my legs where the terry robe had worked itself partially open. He smiled broadly, smug-like, maybe thinking he had it made.

"B.B., I really am flattered. . ."

"Then it's a date?"

"I'll have to think about it."

"How long?"

"I'll let you know," I said, then added; "I'm flattered you asked me."

He turned to go and when he reached the gate, I called to him; "What's the show?"

He looked back, as if I should know.

"Who's performing?" I said.

"It's live. Rena McKenzie is performing live. We got second row seats. . ."

Back in the shower I was singing away, full volume to the sound of Rena McKenzie's TILL MY NEW LOVE COMES ALONG.

My hair was still full of rinse when the door chime sounded again. I dried quickly a second time, and slipped into my short robe with my hair a dripping stringy mess and headed for the door. Beyond the door, a uniformed figure turned and started down the walk. Damn B.B., I thought, then opening the door, I said; "Yes," in a snapping voice.

"UPS ma'am. I have a package for Ms. Kitty Kreeszowski, if that's you."

"For me? I'm not expecting anything."

"Are you Kitty Kreeszowski?"

"Yes. Where is it from, and who?"

"No name, ma'am, but the address is 308 Vallejo Avenue in Suisun City."

"I don't know anybody down by the delta. . ."

"It's for you though. If you will sign here please?"

Inside I tore open the cardboard box and extracted two miniature mandarin duck carvings.

As I brushed the wrappings aside and settled them on the table to consider their beauty, Cuddles hopped on a chair, standing on hind legs with her front paws on the table to contemplate them in her own way.

For a moment I thought of Kimberly when she had told me how Emile had given her the choice of his shop for his down payment on her fee. The meadowlarks had been her favorites and Emile had given her others as well. She had joked about the incident, and seemed well pleased with her bargain.

Dear Diary, I wrote: Today I received a package from Emile with the pair of mandarin carvings I had cherished so much and had fallen in love with the first time I visited his shop. . . Oops. . .

Damn ballpoint pens, why do they always seem to run dry when you need them the most?

I rooted around in my bag and when I could find no replacement I went to Dad's rolltop desk, opened it and continued my search. I had one in my hand when I caught a glimpse of police reports placed there for his review. It was the one on top that captured my attention. It read:

TWO DUCK HUNTERS FOUND.

CAUSE OF DEATH; ACCIDENTAL DROWNING.

TIME; OPENING DAY, SECOND HALF OF DUCK SEASON

LOCATION; SUISUN MARSH WILEFOWL RESERVE,

THREE AND ONE HALF MILES FROM SUISUN CITY.

## ABOUT THE AUTHOR

Robert Clifton-Wallace lived his early school years in New Orleans Louisiana and has traveled widely throughout the world. He has tried his pen at screenplays and presently lives in Lakeport, California with his wife Rena where he busies himself on the release of his next novel.

### novels

*The Preacher Bird*
*A Journey for Conor*
*Ka-Batin-Guy*
*Mons Graupius*
*The Wall*
*The Pelagic Legacy*
*Calgacus*
*Kitty's Diary*